Will he

Tall, Dark
and Italian

Three exciting, hot and intense romances from
three fabulous Mills & Boon authors!

Tall, Dark
and Italian

ANNE MATHER

CAROL MARINELLI

CATHERINE SPENCER

DID YOU PURCHASE THIS BOOK WITHOUT A COVER?

If you did, you should be aware it is **stolen property** as it was reported
unsold and destroyed by a retailer. Neither the author nor the publisher
has received any payment for this book.

All the characters in this book have no existence outside the imagination of
the author, and have no relation whatsoever to anyone bearing the same name
or names. They are not even distantly inspired by any individual known or
unknown to the author, and all the incidents are pure invention.

All Rights Reserved including the right of reproduction in whole or in
part in any form. This edition is published by arrangement with Harlequin
Enterprises II B.V./S.à.r.l. The text of this publication or any part thereof may
not be reproduced or transmitted in any form or by any means, electronic or
mechanical, including photocopying, recording, storage in an information
retrieval system, or otherwise, without the written permission of the publisher.

This book is sold subject to the condition that it shall not, by way of trade or
otherwise, be lent, resold, hired out or otherwise circulated without the prior
consent of the publisher in any form of binding or cover other than that in
which it is published and without a similar condition including this condition
being imposed on the subsequent purchaser.

® and ™ are trademarks owned and used by the trademark owner and/or its
licensee. Trademarks marked with ® are registered with the United Kingdom
Patent Office and/or the Office for Harmonisation in the Internal Market and
in other countries.

First published in Great Britain 2010
Harlequin Mills & Boon Limited,
Eton House, 18-24 Paradise Road, Richmond, Surrey TW9 1SR

TALL, DARK AND ITALIAN
© by Harlequin Enterprises II B.V./S.à.r.l 2010

In the Italian's Bed, The Sicilian's Bought Bride and *The Moretti Marriage*
were first published in Great Britain by Harlequin Mills & Boon Limited in
separate, single volumes.

In the Italian's Bed © Anne Mather 2004
The Sicilian's Bought Bride © Carol Marinelli 2004
The Moretti Marriage © Spencer Books Limited 2004

ISBN: 978 0 263 88115 8

05-1110

Printed and bound in Spain
by Litografia Rosés S.A., Barcelona

IN THE
ITALIAN'S BED

BY
ANNE MATHER

New York Times bestselling author **Anne Mather** has written since she was seven, but it was only when her first child was born that she fulfilled her dream of becoming a writer. Her first book, *Caroline*, appeared in 1966. It met with immediate success and since then Anne has written more than one hundred and forty novels, reaching a readership which spans the world.

Born and raised in the north of England, Anne still makes her home there, with her husband, two children and, now, grandchildren. Asked if she finds writing a lonely occupation, she replies that her characters always keep her company. In fact, she is so busy sorting out their lives that she often doesn't have time for her own! An avid reader herself, she devours everything from sagas and romances to mainstream fiction and suspense. Anne had also written a number of mainstream novels, with *Dangerous Temptation*, her most recent title, published by MIRA Books.

CHAPTER ONE

THE man was standing outside the Medici Gallery as Tess drove past. She only caught a brief glimpse of him, concentrating as she was on keeping Ashley's car on the right side of the road. She saw him look after her as she turned into the parking lot behind the smart row of boutiques and cafés that faced the flower-fringed promenade of Porto San Michele. And wondered if she wasn't being paranoid in imagining there had been a definite air of hostility in his gaze.

She shook off the thought impatiently. She was imagining things. He wasn't waiting for her. Besides, she wasn't late. Well, only a few minutes anyway. She doubted Ashley's timekeeping was any better than hers.

There were few cars in the parking lot at this hour of the morning. Tess had discovered that Italian shops rarely opened before ten and were definitely disposed towards a leisurely schedule. Her neighbours on the parade—Ashley's neighbours, actually—seldom kept to strict opening hours. But they were charming and helpful, and Tess had been grateful for their advice in the three days since she'd been standing in for Ashley.

She hoped she was mistaken about the man, she thought as she let herself into the gallery through the back entrance. She hurried along the connecting passage that led to the showroom at the front and deactivated the alarm. Perhaps he was a friend of Ashley's. Perhaps he didn't know she was away. She glanced towards the windows and saw his shadow on the blind. Whatever, she was evidently going to have to deal with him.

Deciding he could wait a few more minutes, Tess turned

back into the passageway and entered the small office on the right. This was where Ashley did her paperwork and kept all her records. It was also where she took her breaks and Tess looked longingly at the empty coffee-pot, wishing she had time to fill it.

But Ashley's boss wouldn't be pleased if her tardiness turned a would-be patron away and, after examining her reflection in the small mirror by the door, she pulled a face and went to open the gallery.

The door was glass and, unlike the windows, inset with an iron grille. Taking the precaution of opening all the blinds before she tackled the door, Tess had time to assess her visitor.

He was taller than the average Italian, she saw at once, with dark arresting features. Not handsome, she acknowledged, but she doubted a woman would find that a disadvantage. His features had a dangerous appeal that was purely sexual, a sophisticated savagery that sent a shiver of awareness down her spine.

Oh, yes, she thought, he was exactly the kind of man Ashley would be attracted to, and she guessed his visit to the gallery was of a more personal nature than a commercial one. When she pulled the door wide and secured it in its open position, he arched a faintly mocking brow in recognition of her actions. It made Tess want to close the door again, just to show him how confident she was.

But, instead, she forced a slight smile and said, *'Buongiorno. Posso aiutare?'* in her best schoolgirl Italian.

The man's mouth twitched as if she had said the wrong thing, but he didn't contradict her. Nor did he immediately respond. Pushing his hands into the pockets of his jacket, he swung round and surveyed the contents of the gallery, and Tess wondered if she was wrong about his association with Ashley and that he expected her to give him a guided tour.

Who on earth was he? she wondered, intensely aware of the ambivalence of his gaze. She was sure he wasn't a tourist and it seemed far too early in the day for him to be a serious collector. Besides, the paintings they were exhibiting were hardly a collector's choice.

Realising she was probably completely wrong, she nevertheless suspected he hadn't come here to look at the paintings. Despite his apparent interest, the harsh patrician lines of his profile displayed a contempt for them—or for her. This man would not take rejection easily, she mused, wondering where that thought had come from. But if Ashley was involved, she didn't envy her at all.

Tess hesitated. She wasn't sure whether to leave him to his own devices or ask again if she could help. His elegant charcoal suit—which had to be worth a year's salary to her—made her wish she were wearing something other than an ankle-length cotton skirt and combat boots. The spaghetti straps of her cropped top left her arms bare and she felt horribly exposed suddenly. In her place Ashley would have been wearing heels and a smart outfit. A linen suit, perhaps, with a skirt that barely reached her knees.

Then he turned to face her and she prevented herself from backing up only by a supreme effort of will. Deep-set eyes—golden eyes, she saw incredulously—surveyed her with a studied negligence. She realised he was younger than she'd thought at first and she was again aware of his primitive magnetism. An innate sensual arrogance that left her feeling strangely weak.

'Miss Daniels?' he said smoothly, with barely a trace of an accent. 'It is most—how shall I put it?—enlightening to meet you at last.' He paused. 'I must say, you are not what I expected.' His regard was definitely contemptuous now. 'But still, you will tell me where I might find my son.'

Was that a threat? Tess was taken aback at his tone, but at the same time she realised he had made a mistake. It must be Ashley he wanted, not her. Yet what on earth could Ashley possibly know about his son? She was in England looking after her mother.

'I'm afraid you've made a mistake, *signore*,' she began, only to have him interrupt her.

'No, Miss Daniels, it is you who have made a mistake,' he snapped harshly. 'I know you know where Marco is. My—my *investigatore* saw you getting on a plane together.'

Tess blinked. 'No, you're wrong—'

'Why? Because you are here?' He snapped his long fingers impatiently. 'You bought tickets to Milano but you must have changed planes at Genova. When the plane landed at Malpensa, you and Marco were not on board. *Di consequenza*, I had no choice but to come here. Be thankful I have found you.'

'But, I'm not—'

'*Prego?*'

'I mean—' Tess knew she sounded crazy '—I'm not Miss Daniels. Well, I am.' Oh, God, if only she could get her words straight. 'But I'm not Miss *Ashley* Daniels. She's my sister.'

The man's eyes conveyed his disbelief. 'Is that the best you can do?'

'It's the truth.' Tess was indignant now. 'My name is Tess. Teresa, actually. But no one calls me that.'

His eyes, those strange predator's eyes, swept over her, rejecting her contention out of hand. 'It's the truth,' she said again, unknowingly defensive. Then, on a wave of inspiration, 'I can prove it. I have my passport with me. Is that good enough for you?'

The man's eyes narrowed. 'Let me see it.'

Tess's eyes widened at the command but there was something about him that made her hurry into the office to collect her bag. The passport was zipped into the side pocket of the backpack and she brought it out triumphantly. But when she turned to go back into the showroom she found he was behind her and with a gesture of defiance she thrust it into his hand.

He was successfully blocking her exit now, she realised, aware of a stirring sense of panic. What did she know about this man, after all? Only that he apparently knew her sister—or rather knew of her—and what he knew seemed hardly flattering.

Or true?

'Look,' she said as he continued to flick through the mostly empty pages of her passport, 'I don't know who you are or what you want but I don't think you have any right to come in here and accuse me—accuse Ashley—of—of—'

'Kidnapping my son?' he suggested scornfully, tossing the passport down onto the desk, and Tess's heart skipped a beat at the ridiculous accusation. '*Attenzione*, Miss Daniels,' he added, sweeping back the thick swathe of dark hair that had invaded his forehead as he studied the pages, 'just because you are not your sister changes nothing. Marco is still missing. He left with your sister. Therefore, you must have some idea where they are.'

'No!' Tess hardly knew what she was saying. 'I mean—I do know where Ashley is. She's at her mother's house in England. Her mother is ill. Ashley is looking after her.'

His expression didn't alter. 'And that is why you are here taking her place?'

'Yes. I'm a schoolteacher. I was on holiday. That's how I was able to help her out.'

'You are lying, Miss Daniels. Why are you not caring for your mother? I have just read in your passport that you live in England. So tell me why you are not taking care of your mother in your sister's place?'

'She's not *my* mother,' Tess exclaimed hotly. 'My father married again after my mother died.' She took a deep breath. 'Now, I think that answers your question. I'm sorry your son is missing but it's nothing to do with us.'

'You are wrong.' He didn't accept her explanation but at least he stepped back into the passageway to give her some room. When Tess escaped into the comparative safety of the showroom, he followed her. 'Whatever you say, Miss Daniels, your sister is not caring for her sick mother,' he insisted. 'She and Marco are still in Italy. He does not have his passport with him, *capisce*?'

Tess pressed nervous hands to her bare midriff, feeling the quivering beat of her heart palpating between her ribs. 'You said—she'd kidnapped him,' she reminded him tensely. 'That's a ridiculous accusation. If—and it's a big if—Ashley and your son are together, then surely that's their affair, not yours?'

'*Non credo*. I do not think so.' He was contemptuous. 'My son is sixteen years of age, Miss Daniels. He belongs in school, with young people of his own age, not chasing around the country after your sister.'

Tess swallowed convulsively. Sixteen! She couldn't believe it. Ashley wouldn't—couldn't—be involved with a boy of sixteen! The whole idea was laughable. Involved with *him*, perhaps. That Tess could believe. But not with his teenage son.

Besides, she told herself again, clinging to what she knew and not what he suspected, Ashley was in England. Dammit, she'd spoken to her just a couple of nights ago. That was why Tess was spending part of her Easter break filling in for her. Ashley couldn't leave the gallery unattended and she'd promised it would only be for a few days.

'If you've not met my sister, how can you be sure that she's involved?' she asked unwillingly, realising she couldn't dismiss his claim out of hand. Ashley might not have been in England when she'd phoned her. She could have used her mobile. How could she be sure?

The man gave her an impatient look now. 'I may have met her once, but that was some months ago and I have met many people since then. In any case, the person who has been watching her would not make a mistake. I have been out of the country, regrettably, but my assistant contacted your sister just a week ago. She swore then that she would speak to Marco, that she would tell him there was no future in their—association. She is what? Twenty-four? Twenty-five? Much too old for a boy of sixteen.'

Tess pressed her lips together. 'She's twenty-eight, actually,' she said, as if that made any difference, and watched his scowl deepen as he absorbed her words. She didn't know what to say; she hardly knew what to think. But if it was true, she agreed with him. Could Ashley have told her an outright lie?

She could, she reflected ruefully. And she had to admit that when Ashley had asked her to help her out while she took care of her mother, it had seemed a little out of character. Ashley's mother, Andrea, had never been a particularly strong woman and since their father had died of a heart attack just over a year ago, she'd suffered from a series of minor complaints. Tess had suspected that that was why Ashley had taken this job in Italy. Looking after a fretful parent who was halfway to being a hypochondriac had never seemed her style.

All the same, this situation was no less incredible. Surely even Ashley would draw the line at getting involved with a boy of sixteen? There was only one way to find out and that was to ring Ashley's mother. But Tess was loath to do it. If Ashley was there, it would look as if she didn't trust her.

'I don't know what to say,' she murmured now, her fingers threading anxiously through the wisps of pale blonde hair at her nape. She'd had her hair cut before she came away and she wasn't totally convinced the gamine style suited her. She'd hoped it would give her some maturity, but she had the feeling it hadn't succeeded. He was looking at her as if she were no older than one of her own pupils. Oh, Lord, what was she going to do?

'You could tell me where they are,' the man declared tersely. 'I realise you must feel some loyalty towards your sister, but you must also see that this situation cannot be allowed to continue.'

'I don't know where they are,' Tess insisted. 'Honestly, I don't.' And then, realising what she'd said, she added hastily, 'As far as I know, Ashley's in England, as I said.'

'*Bene,* then you can ring her,' he said, voicing the thought

Tess had had a few minutes before. 'If she is with her mother, I will offer you my sincerest apologies for troubling you.'

'And if she's not?'

Tess looked up at him, unable to disguise her apprehension, and for a moment she thought he was going to relent. But then, with a tightening of his lips, he corrected her. 'You are confident she will be there,' he said, and she had the fanciful thought that this man would take no prisoners. She just hoped Ashley had taken that into consideration before she'd taken off with his son.

If she'd taken off with his son, she amended sharply. She only had his word for that. And that of his *investigatore*— his investigator, she assumed. But she was becoming far too willing to accept what this man said as if it was the truth.

'If—if she is there, who shall I say is asking for her?' she inquired abruptly, realising she had been staring at him for far too long. He probably thought she was a flake in her long skirt and combat boots, she reflected ruefully. After all this, it wouldn't do for him to think that Ashley's sister might be interested in him.

He hesitated a moment, evidently considering her question. Then, he said briefly, 'Just tell her it is Castelli. The name will mean something to her, I am sure.'

Tess guessed it would, though what she didn't dare to speculate. Oh, please, she begged, let Ashley be staying with her mother. Apart from anything else, Tess was going to look such a gullible fool if she wasn't.

'All right,' she declared briskly. 'I'll ring her. If you'd like to give me a number where I can reach you, I'll let you know what she says.'

'If she says anything,' murmured Castelli wryly, and then his dark brows drew together. 'But perhaps you would ring her now, Miss Daniels? I will wait while you make the call.'

Tess caught her breath. He was certainly determined to have his way. But she'd been chivvied long enough. 'I can't ring her now,' she said, not allowing him to intimidate her.

'I'll ring her later. And now, if you'll excuse me, I've got work to do.'

His scepticism was evident. 'You have?' He glanced round the gallery. 'You are not exactly overrun with customers, Miss Daniels.'

Tess stiffened her spine. 'Look, I've said I'll ring Ashley and I will. Isn't that enough for you?' The underlying words were almost audible. *But not until you have gone!*

His faint smile was sardonic. 'You are afraid to make the call, Miss Daniels,' he said impatiently. 'Be careful, or I shall begin to think you have been lying to me all along.'

Tess's anger was hot and unexpected. 'Oh, please,' she exclaimed fiercely. 'I don't have to listen to this. It's not my fault if your son's been foolish enough to get involved with an older woman. You're his father. Don't you have some responsibility here?'

For a moment, his stillness terrified her. He was like a predator, she thought unsteadily, and she waited in a panic for him to spring. But suddenly his lips twitched into a smile that was blatantly sensual. A look, almost of admiration, crossed his dark face and he appraised her small indignant figure with a rueful gaze.

'*Dio mio,*' he said, and her heart quickened instinctively. 'The little cat has claws.'

His analogy was startling. It was so close to what she had been thinking about him. Though he was no domesticated feline, she acknowledged urgently. Those strange tawny eyes belonged to a different beast entirely.

And, despite her determination not to let him have his way, she found herself stammering an apology. 'I'm—I'm sorry,' she said. 'I shouldn't have spoken as I did. It—it's nothing to do with me.'

'*No, mi scusi, signorina,*' he said. 'You are right. This is not your problem. Regrettably, my son has always been a little—what is it you say?—headstrong? I should not have allowed my anger with him to spill over onto you.'

Tess quivered. His eyes were softer now, gentler, a mesmerising deepening of colour that turned them almost opaque. They were locked on hers and the breath seemed to leave her body. Oh, God, she shivered, the impact on her senses leaving her feeling absurdly vulnerable. What was wrong with her? She was behaving as if a man had never looked at her before.

'It doesn't matter,' she managed at last, but he wouldn't let it go.

'It does matter,' he said. 'I am an unfeeling moron, and I should not have called your honesty into question. If you will give me your sister's number, I will make the call myself.'

Tess stifled a groan. Dear Lord, just as she was beginning to think the worst was over, he sprang this on her. Having reduced her to mush with his eyes, he was now moving in for the kill. He hadn't given up. He'd only changed his tactics. And she couldn't be absolutely sure that this hadn't been his intention all along.

She moved her head in a helpless gesture. How could she give him the number? How could she allow him to speak to Ashley's mother if Ashley wasn't there? Andrea would have a fit if he told her that her daughter was missing. And if he added that he suspected she was with his sixteen-year-old son, heaven knew how Ashley's mother would react.

Concentrating her gaze on the pearl-grey silk knot of his tie, Tess strove for a reason not to give the number to him. But it was hard enough to find excuses for her reaction to a stranger without the added burden of her own guilt. 'I—don't think that would be a very good idea,' she said, wishing desperately that someone else would come into the gallery. But no one did, and she continued unevenly, 'Ashley's mother isn't well. I wouldn't want to upset her.'

Castelli heaved a sigh. '*Signorina*—'

'Please: call me Tess.'

He expelled a breath. 'Tess, then,' he agreed, though she hardly recognised her name on his tongue. His faint accent gave it a foreign sibilance that was strange and melodic.

'Why would my call upset her? I have no intention of intimidating anyone.'

But he did, thought Tess grimly, almost without his being aware of it. It was in his genes, an aristocratic arrogance that was dominant in his blood. Who was he? she wondered again. What was his background? And what did his wife think of the situation? Was she as opposed to the liaison as he was?

Of course she must be, Tess told herself severely, averting eyes that had strayed almost irresistibly back to his face. But if Marco was like his father, she could understand Ashley's attraction. If she had been attracted to his son, she amended. She must not jump to conclusions here.

'I—Mrs Daniels doesn't know you,' she said firmly, answering his question. 'And—and if by chance Ashley is out and she answers the phone, she's bound to be concerned.'

'Why?' Once again those disturbing eyes invaded her space. 'Come, Tess, why not be honest? You are afraid that your sister is not at her mother's house. Am I not correct?'

Tess's defensive gaze betrayed her. 'All right,' she said unwillingly. 'I admit, there is a possibility—a small possibility—that Ashley isn't in England, after all. But—' she put up a hand when he would have interrupted her and continued '—that doesn't mean she's with—with Marco. With your son.' The boy's name came far too easily. 'She might just have decided she needed a break and, as it's the Easter holidays, I was available.'

'You do not believe that,' he told her softly, running a questing hand down the silken length of his tie. The gesture was unconsciously sensual, though she doubted he was aware of it. Sensuality was part of his persona. Like his lean, intriguing face and the powerful body beneath his sleek Armani suit. 'I also think you are far too understanding. I hope your sister realises what a loyal little friend she has in you.'

It was the 'little' that did it. Tess had spent her life insisting that people not judge her by her size. 'All right,' she said again, anger giving her a confidence she hadn't been able to summon earlier. 'I'll phone her. Now. But if she is there—'

'I will find some suitable means of recompense,' he finished softly. 'And if your sister is like you, then I can understand why Marco found her so—appealing.'

'Don't patronise me!' Tess was incensed by his condescension. 'As it happens, Ashley's nothing like me. She's tall and more—more—' How could she say curvaceous to him? 'Um—she's dark and I'm fair.'

'So…' His tone was almost indulgent now. 'Once again, I have offended you, *cara*. Forgive me. I suppose, being the younger sister—'

'I'm not the younger sister,' Tess broke in hotly, wondering why she'd ever thought that cutting her hair would make a difference. 'I told you, my father married again after my mother died.'

'Non posso crederci! I can't believe it.' He shook his head. 'But you told me your sister was twenty-eight, *no*?'

'And I'm thirty-two,' said Tess shortly, struggling to hold on to her patience. She paused, and then in a more civil tone she added, 'Don't bother to tell me I don't look it. I've spent the last ten years trying to convince people that I'm older than the kids I teach.'

Castelli's mouth tilted at the corners and she was struck anew by his disturbing appeal. 'Most women would envy you, Tess. My own mother spends a small fortune on retaining her youth.'

'But I am not most women,' she retorted, realising she was only putting off the inevitable. 'And now, I suppose, I'd better make that call.'

CHAPTER TWO

RAFE DI CASTELLI paced tensely about the gallery. All his
instincts were urging him to join her in the small office, to
be present while she made the call. To make sure she actually called her sister, he conceded tersely. Despite her apparent innocence, he had no reason to trust Tess Daniels
any more than her sister.

But courtesy—and an underlying belief that she wouldn't
lie to him—kept him out of earshot. He didn't want to know
how she phrased her question; he didn't want to hear her
distress if he was right. And he was right, he told himself
grimly. Verdicci had been adamant. Two people had got
aboard the plane to Milano, and one of them had been his
son.

It seemed to take for ever. He was fairly sure her Italian
wasn't fluent and it might have been easier if he had placed
the call for her. But any suggestion of involvement on his
part would have seemed like interference. Besides, impatient
as he was, he was prepared to give her the time to marshal
her thoughts.

She emerged from the office a few moments later and he
saw at once that she was upset. Her hair was rumpled, as if
she'd been running agitated fingers through it as she spoke,
and her winter-pale cheeks were bright with colour.

She looked delectable, he thought ruefully, despising the
impulse that would put such a thought in his mind at this
time. Was this how she looked when she left her bed? he
wondered. All pale tangled hair and face flushed from sleep?

It was a curiously disturbing picture, and one that he
chose to ignore. Engaging though she was, she could mean

nothing to him. He was amused by her naïvety, but that was all.

'She's not there,' she burst out abruptly as he paused, expectantly, looking at her. 'Andrea—that's Ashley's mother—she hasn't seen her.'

Rafe felt a mixture of resignation and relief. Resignation that his information had been correct, and relief that there was not some unknown woman involved.

'You knew that, of course,' she went on, regarding him half resentfully. Green eyes, fringed by surprisingly dark lashes, surveyed him without liking. 'So—you were right and I was wrong. What do we do now?'

'We?' Her use of the personal pronoun caused an automatic arching of his brows and she had the grace to look embarrassed at her presumption.

'I mean, I—that is, me,' she fumbled. 'What am I going to do now? I can't stay here indefinitely. I'm due back at school in ten days' time.'

'As is Marco,' he observed drily, feeling a little of her frustration himself. 'May I ask, what did your sister tell you when she handed the keys of the gallery to you? Did she give you any idea when she would return?'

Tess sighed. 'I haven't seen Ashley,' she muttered, lifting both hands to cup her neck, and his eyes were unwillingly drawn to the widening gap of skin at her midriff. Such soft skin it looked, creamy and flawless. Such a contrast to the ugly boots she wore on her feet.

Dragging his thoughts out of the gutter, Rafe tried to absorb what she was saying. 'You have not seen her,' he echoed blankly. 'I do not understand.'

'Ashley phoned me,' she explained. 'She said her mother was ill and was there any chance that I could come here and look after the gallery for a few days while she went to England. She said she wanted to leave immediately. That she was worried about her mother and she'd leave the keys with the caretaker of her apartment.'

'So you crossed in transit?'

'In a manner of speaking. But Ashley's mother and I live in different parts of the country.'

'Ah.' He nodded. 'So your sister had every reason to believe that she would not be found out in her deception.'

'I suppose so.' Clearly she didn't want to admit it, but Rafe could see the acknowledgement in her face. She shook her head. 'I can't believe she'd think she'd get away with it. I could have phoned Andrea. I could have found out she wasn't ill for myself.'

'But you did not?'

'No.' Tess shrugged her slim shoulders and her hands dropped to her sides. 'Ashley knows I was unlikely to do that, in any case. Andrea and I have never been particularly close.'

'Yet you must have been very young when your mother died,' he probed, and then could have kicked himself for his insensitivity. But it was too late now and he was forced to explain himself. 'I assumed this woman—your father's second wife—would have cared for you, too.'

Tess shook her head. 'Andrea has always been a—a delicate woman,' she said. 'Having two young children to look after would have been too much for her. I went to live with my mother's sister. She'd never married and she was a teacher, too.'

Poor Tess. Rafe made no comment, but it sounded to him as if Andrea Daniels was as unfeeling and as selfish as her daughter. 'It seems we have both been deceived,' he said, softening his tone deliberately. 'It is a pity your sister does not carry a mobile. Marco's is switched off.'

'But she does,' exclaimed Tess excitedly, animation giving her porcelain-pale features a startling allure. Her smile appeared and Rafe had to warn himself of the dangers of responding to her femininity. 'Why didn't I think of it before? She gave me the number when she moved to Porto San Michele.'

Rafe expelled a harsh breath. 'You have the number with you?'

'Of course.' She swung about and headed back into the
office where she'd left her bag. She emerged a few seconds
later, clutching a scrap of paper. 'Here it is. Do you want
to ring her, or shall I?'

Rafe realised suddenly that, almost without his volition,
they had become co-conspirators. She was now as anxious
to know where her sister had gone as he was. But once again
he reminded himself not to get involved with her, however
innocently. She was still his enemy's sister. In any conflict
of wills, she would choose Ashley every time.

'If you wish that I should make the call, then I will,' he
told her politely, but he could hear the formal stiffness in
his tone. 'Even so, perhaps it would be wiser for you to
phone her. If she hears my voice...'

'Oh. Oh, yes.'

He didn't elaborate but Tess understood at once what he
was saying. The animation died out of her face and she
averted her eyes. It was as if she'd just remembered that
she owed him no favours either. That however justified he
felt, she had only his word that Ashley was to blame for his
son's disappearance.

With an offhand little gesture, she returned to the office,
only to emerge again a few minutes later, her expression
revealing she had had no luck. 'Ashley's phone is switched
off, too,' she said, and Rafe could see she was losing faith
in her sister. She heaved a sigh. 'It looks as if you were
right all along. What are you going to do now?'

Rafe wished he had an answer. There was hardly any
point in saying what he'd like to do. 'Continue searching,
presumo,' he replied at last, choosing the least aggressive
option. 'There are many holiday resorts between here and
Genova. It is possible that your sister hired an automobile
at the airport. They could be anywhere. It will not be an
easy task.'

'Mmm.' Tess was thoughtful. A pink tongue circled her
lower lip and Rafe realised she didn't know how provocative that was. 'Will you let me know if you find them?' she

asked 'I mean—find Ashley.' Becoming colour scored her cheeks. 'You know what I mean.'

Rafe knew what she meant all right. What he didn't know at that moment was whether he wanted to see her again. She was far too young for him, far too vulnerable. Despite her being the older, he'd stake his life that Ashley was far more worldly than she was.

The notion annoyed him however. What in the name of all the saints was he thinking? She wasn't asking to see him again. She was asking if he'd keep her informed about her sister. *Va bene*, he could get his assistant to do that with a phone call. Providing he found out where her sister had gone...

'*Sì,*' he said abruptly, buttoning his jacket in an unconsciously defensive gesture and heading for the door. He turned in the doorway, however, to bid her farewell and was surprised by a strangely disappointed look on her face. With her slim hands clasped at her waist, she looked lost and lonely, and before he could stop himself he added, 'Perhaps you could do the same?'

Her green eyes widened. 'I don't know where to reach you,' she said, as he'd known she would. *Maledizione*, he hadn't intended to give her his phone number. How easily he'd fallen into the trap.

He would have to give her his card, he decided, reaching into his jacket pocket. That way Giulio could handle it and he needn't be involved. To give her his mobile number would have been kinder, obviously, but why should he put himself out for the sister of the woman who had seduced his son?

He took a few paces back into the gallery and handed the card to her. Her fingers brushed his knuckles as she took it and he couldn't deny the sudden frisson of desire that seared his flesh. He wanted her, he thought incredulously. Combat boots and all, she attracted him. Or maybe he was feeling his age and seducing her would give him some compensation for what her sister had done to Marco. What other reason could he have for the feelings she inspired?

Whatever, he dismissed the idea impatiently. He was obviously having some kind of midlife crisis because girls like Tess had never appealed to him before. He liked his women young—well, reasonably so, but far more sophisticated. They wore designer dresses and heels, and they'd never dream of going out without make-up on their faces.

Vigneto di Castelli, his card read, and he watched Tess's expression as she looked at it. 'You have a vineyard,' she murmured. 'How exciting! I've never met anyone who actually owned a vineyard before.'

Nor had her sister, thought Rafe drily. He was too cynical to believe that Marco's background hadn't figured in Ashley's plans. He still had no idea what her ultimate intentions were, of course, but he suspected that a pay-off would be part of it. He'd encountered the ploy before with his daughter. But fortunately Maria had been eighteen, not sixteen at the time.

'It is a small operation, *signorina*,' he said now deprecatingly. 'Many families in Italy have taken to growing grapes with the increase in wine drinking in recent years.'

'All the same…' Her lips curved beguilingly, and Rafe felt the familiar pull of awareness inside him. Time to go, he thought grimly, before he invited her to visit the villa. He could just imagine his mother's horror if he returned home with someone like Tess in tow.

'*Ci vediamo, signorina,*' he said politely as he retraced his steps to the door but she wouldn't let him have the last word.

'My name's Tess,' she reminded him, following him out onto the esplanade and watching as he strode away towards his car.

And, although he didn't answer her, he knew that was how he would think of her. Somehow the name suited her personality. It was as capricious and feminine as she was.

*   *   *

As he'd half expected, his mother was waiting for him when he returned to the Villa Castelli.

A tall, elegant woman in her mid-sixties, she'd moved back into the villa six years ago when he'd divorced his wife. Rafe's father had died almost twenty years before and he was sure that looking after Maria and Marco had given the old lady a new lease of life. Of course, she'd never forgiven him for divorcing Gina. In the Castelli family marriages were made to last and her strict religious beliefs rebelled against such secular freedom. Nevertheless, she had proved a tower of strength on many occasions and it was only recently that she had decided that the time had come to move back into the small farmhouse she'd occupied on the estate since Raphael's father's death.

Rafe knew her decision had been partly influenced by his son's behaviour. Although Maria had had her own period of rebellion, she had been fairly easy to control in comparison to her brother. Marco was self-willed and headstrong—much as he had been at the same age, Rafe acknowledged honestly—but without the sense of responsibility his father had instilled in him.

'You've seen her?'

His mother's first words reminded Rafe that, as far as Lucia di Castelli was concerned, Ashley Daniels was still running the Medici Gallery. His main reason for visiting the gallery had been to find out if Ashley knew where Marco was hiding. Instead of which he'd met her sister and discovered he was not too old to make a fool of himself, too.

'She's not at the gallery,' he said with contrived carelessness, strolling onto the loggia where his mother was waiting enjoying a mid-morning *cappuccino*. It was very warm on the loggia and Rafe loosened his tie and pulled it a couple of inches away from his collar before approaching a glass-topped table and helping himself to one of the thin, honey-soaked *biscotti* Lucia loved. 'Verdicci appears to have been correct. They have gone away together.' He glanced round as a uniformed maid came to ask if there was anything he required. 'Just coffee, Sophia,' he replied pleasantly. 'Black.' Then to his mother. 'Her sister is looking after the gallery while she's away.'

'Her sister?'

His mother was sceptical, and Rafe guessed she'd jumped to the same conclusion he had. 'Her sister,' he confirmed, flinging himself into a cane-backed chair and staring broodingly out across the gardens below the terrace. 'Believe me, she is nothing like this woman Marco has got himself involved with.'

'How do you know this?' Lucia's dark eyes narrowed. 'I thought you said you wouldn't recognise the woman if you saw her.'

'I wouldn't.' Rafe realised he had been far too definite. 'But Tess is a schoolteacher. And, believe me, she's as much in the dark as we are. Ashley had given her some story about going home to care for her sick mother.'

'*Tess!*' Lucia scoffed. 'What kind of a name is that?'

'It's Teresa,' replied Rafe evenly, thanking the maid who had delivered his coffee. He turned back to his mother in some irritation. 'We won't get anywhere by picking fault with one of the few people who might be able to help us.'

'How can this woman help us? You said yourself she doesn't know where her sister is.'

'Ashley may get in touch with her. If she wants Teresa to go on believing the story she's given her, she may feel the need to embellish it in some way.'

Lucia's mouth drew into a thin line. 'It sounds to me as if this—this sister of the Daniels woman has made quite an impression on you, Raphael,' she declared tersely. 'Why do you believe her? What proof do you have that she's telling you the truth?'

None at all! 'Believe me, she was as shocked as we were,' he responded stiffly. 'You can't blame her for what her sister's done.'

'And has she contacted her mother?' Lucia was scathing.

'Forgive me, I know I'm old-fashioned, but don't English girls keep in touch with their own parents these days?'

'Of course they do,' retorted Rafe testily. 'But Ashley's mother isn't her mother. Their father married twice. Teresa is the older sister.'

'*Che sorpresa!*' What a surprise! Lucia was sardonic. 'People get married and divorced at the drop of a hat these days.' She crossed herself before continuing. 'Thank Jesu for the Holy Catholic church. At least most good Catholics take their vows seriously.'

Rafe knew that was directed at him but he chose not to rise to it. It wasn't worth it. He contented himself with saying drily, 'I understand Teresa's mother is dead.' Then, refusing to feel defensive, added, 'In any case, as you'll have guessed, Ashley wasn't at her mother's home. It seems she has told her sister a pack of lies.'

Lucia shook her head. 'It sounds very suspicious to me.'

Rafe controlled his temper with an effort. 'Well, I cannot help that,' he said grimly.

'But you must admit it is strange that this woman—this Teresa—doesn't know where her sister is.' She arched an aristocratic eyebrow. 'Why on earth would she want to keep her whereabouts a secret from her?'

'Because she knew her sister wouldn't approve any more than we do?' suggested Rafe tightly. 'I don't know, Mama. But I believe her and I think you should do the same.'

Lucia sniffed and Rafe thought how ridiculous this was, having to explain himself to his mother. Sometimes she behaved as if he were no older than Marco. He supposed it came of giving her free rein with the household after Gina walked out.

'So what happens now?' she inquired at last when it became obvious that Rafe was going to say no more. 'Do I take it that unless the woman gets in touch with her sister, the information Verdicci gave you is our only lead?'

'I will also speak to Maria,' said Rafe. 'She and Marco share most things and she may know where he's gone. It's a long shot and for the present we only know they disembarked in Genova. I suspect the Daniels woman guessed we might check the airlines and buying tickets to Milano was meant to throw us off the scent.'

'And knowing they might be in Genova helps us how?'

'Well, obviously she didn't know we were watching her. She has no reason to believe that we might question whether they completed their journey. Ergo, she will expect us to make inquiries in Milano. Inquiries which, as we now know, would have gained us nothing.'

'Very well.' Lucia accepted his reasoning. 'But Genova is a big city. How do you propose to find them there?'

'I'm hoping Ashley will have hired an automobile,' replied Rafe, finishing his coffee and getting to his feet again. He paced somewhat restlessly across the terrazzo tiles, staring out at the distant vineyard, hazy in the morning sunshine. 'Verdicci is checking the rental agencies at the airport. If she has used her own name, we will find them, never fear.'

'And if she hasn't?'

'Car rental agencies need identification. If my guess is correct, she will have used her passport to confirm her identity. Either that or her work permit. In each case, she will have had to use her own name. She may even have had to give an address—a local address, I mean. Somewhere she plans to stay. Where *they* plan to stay.'

Lucia's lips crumpled. 'Oh, this is so terrible! Every time I close my eyes, all I can see is Marco and that woman, together. It's—appalling! Disgusting!'

'Don't exaggerate, Mama.' Rafe could see she was building up to another hysterical outburst. His lips twisted. 'For all I know, Marco may be more experienced than we thought. He must have something to have attracted the interest of a woman of her age.'

'Don't be offensive!' Lucia gazed at him with horrified eyes. 'How can you even say such things? Marco is just a child—'

'He's nearly seventeen, Mama.' Rafe was impatient now. 'He's not a child. He's a young man.' He paused. 'With a young man's needs and—desires.'

Lucia's spine stiffened and she pushed herself rigidly to her feet. 'Very well,' she said coldly. 'I can see you are not prepared to discuss this sensibly so I might as well go. I should have expected this of you, of course. You've never taken a strong enough hand with that boy and now we're all suffering the consequences.'

Rafe blew out a breath. 'You're not suffering anything, Mama. Except perhaps from a little jealousy. I know you've always thought the sun shone out of Marco's—well, you've always favoured him over Maria. Perhaps you ought to wonder if you are in any way responsible for his apparent rebellion against parental authority.'

Lucia's jaw dropped. 'You can't blame me?'

'I'm not blaming anyone,' retorted Rafe wearily. 'You are. All I'm doing is defending myself.'

'As you did when Gina decided she'd had enough of your indifference?' declared his mother tersely, making for the door. 'You've always neglected your family, Raphael. First your wife and now your son. With you, your work must always come first.'

'Gina slept with my estate manager,' said Rafe through his teeth, but Lucia was not deterred.

'She was lonely, Raphael. She needed love and you didn't give it to her. What did you expect?'

Trust? Loyalty? Rafe didn't attempt to dispute her words, however. This was an old argument and one he had no intention of rekindling. Gina hadn't wanted love, she'd wanted sex. Her affair with Guido Marchetta might have been the reason he'd divorced her, but it hadn't been the first. He had never told his mother that and now was not the time to do so.

'Look,' he said, his tone neutral. 'Let's not get into blaming ourselves. Marco's somewhere out there and I'm going to find him.'

Lucia shrugged. 'If you can,' she said scornfully, determined to have the last word, and Rafe let her enjoy her small victory.

CHAPTER THREE

As Tess had half expected, Ashley's mother rang the gallery just after the man, Castelli, had left.

Tess didn't blame her. She wouldn't have been satisfied with the terse explanation she had given her. But once Tess had ascertained that Ashley wasn't there, all she'd wanted to do was get off the phone. It had been bad enough having to relay the news to Castelli. Discussing Ashley's whereabouts with her mother while he'd listened in just hadn't been possible.

Even so, when the phone pealed in the small office she paused a moment to pray that it might be her sister instead. The gallery was still empty and she had no excuse for not answering it. And it could be anyone, she reminded herself, not looking forward to explaining the situation to Andrea.

'Teresa?' Clearly Ashley's mother had no difficulty in distinguishing between their voices. 'What's going on? What are you doing at the gallery? Where's Ashley?'

Tess sighed. When she'd spoken to Andrea earlier, she hadn't mentioned the gallery. But it was only natural that Andrea would ring here when she got no reply from Tess's flat. And this was where her daughter was supposed to be, after all.

'Um—she's taking a holiday,' Tess managed at last, deciding that the best liars were those who stuck most closely to the truth. 'It's good to hear from you, Andrea. How are you?'

'Never mind how I am, Teresa.' There was no affection in the older woman's voice. 'Five minutes ago you rang here asking to speak to Ashley. You must have known how upsetting that would be for me. As far as I knew, she was still in Porto San Michele.'

'You've heard from her?'

Tess couldn't keep the excitement out of her voice and her stepmother detected it. 'Of course, I've heard from her,' she said shortly. And then, more suspiciously, 'Why shouldn't I? She still cares about me, you know.'

'Well, of course she does—'

'Just because you encouraged her to leave home and live alone, as you do, doesn't mean Ashley doesn't have a conscience,' continued Andrea preposterously. 'I know you've always been jealous of our relationship, Teresa, but if this is some ploy to try and get me to think badly of—'

'It's not.'

Tess couldn't even begin to unravel what Andrea was talking about. She hadn't encouraged Ashley to leave home and work in Italy. She had certainly never been jealous of her relationship with her mother. Envious, perhaps, because her own mother wasn't there to share her hopes and fears; her development. But Aunt Kate had been a wonderful substitute. And what she'd lacked in experience, she'd more than made up for in love.

'Then why ring me?' demanded Andrea accusingly. 'Worrying me unnecessarily, making me wonder if something terrible had happened to her.'

'It's not like that.'

'Then what is it like? You ask me if I've heard from her as if she's gone missing. Don't you have her mobile phone number? Why don't you ring her on that?'

Tess hesitated. 'Her phone's not working,' she admitted. 'And—well, I just wondered if Ashley had gone to England after all. As you'll have guessed, I'm looking after the gallery while she's away.' She paused, seeking inspiration, and then added unwillingly, 'I—I had a customer of hers asking about—a painting.' *Liar!* 'I—I just thought it was worth seeing if she was staying with you.'

Andrea snorted disbelievingly, and Tess felt a growing

sense of injustice at the impossible position Ashley had put her in. Not only had she left her to deal with her boyfriend's irate father, but she must have known Tess might ring her mother when she believed that that was where Ashley was.

All the same, it wasn't in Tess's nature to upset anyone unnecessarily, and, taking a deep breath, she said, 'I'm sure she'll be in touch with me again in a few days.' She'll have to, Tess added to herself. Ashley knew she was due back at school in ten days as well. 'But—um—if you hear from her in the meantime, could you ask her to ring me? The—er—the customer I was telling you about, he is pretty eager to speak to Ashley himself.'

Andrea was silent for so long that Tess began to hope that she'd pacified the woman. But just as she was about to excuse herself on the pretext that someone had come into the gallery Ashley's mother spoke again.

'And you have absolutely no idea where Ashley is?' she asked again urgently, a worrying tremor in her voice. 'If you do know anything, Teresa, I demand that you tell me. Do you think I should come out there? If Ashley's missing, the police ought to be informed.'

'Ashley's not missing.' Tess hurried to reassure her, cursing her sister anew for getting her into this mess. 'Honestly, Andrea, there's no need for you to concern yourself. Ashley's taken a break, that's all. She's probably turned off her phone so she isn't bothered with nuisance calls.'

'I hope you're not suggesting that if I ring my daughter she'd regard it as a nuisance call!' exclaimed Andrea at once, but at least the disturbing tremor had left her voice.

'Of course not,' protested Tess, determining to find out exactly what Ashley had been telling her mother about their relationship. Andrea hadn't always treated her kindly, but she hadn't regarded Tess as an enemy before.

'Oh, well…' There was resignation in the woman's voice now. 'I suppose I have to take your word for it. But, remember, I expect you to keep me informed if there are any developments. And if you hear from Ashley, you can tell her that I expect her to ring me at once.'

'Okay.'

Somehow, Tess found the right words to end the conversation, and with a feeling of immense relief she put the handset down. But her sense of indignation didn't end when she severed the connection. She was beginning to feel distinctly put upon and she wished she'd never agreed to come here in the first place.

An image of Castelli flashed before her eyes, but she refused to acknowledge it. She had no intention of allowing her interview with the Italian to influence her mood. Besides which, he was just someone else who regarded her as unworthy of his respect.

She scowled. This was not the way Ashley had sold this trip to her. Her sister had asked her to babysit the gallery, true, but she'd also sweetened the request with promises of long sunny days and evenings spent exploring the bars and *ristorantes* of the popular resort. Not that Tess cared much for bars, but the idea of eating in real Italian restaurants had been appealing. And, like anyone else who held down a job, she'd looked forward to spending some time on the beach.

Now it was all spoilt. After spending the first couple of evenings tidying Ashley's apartment and making sense of her bookkeeping, she was confronted by this situation. It was typical of Ashley, she thought flatly. Typical of her sister to trample over everyone's feelings if it made her happy. And there was no doubt that Ashley had known how Tess would have reacted if she'd told her what she'd intended. That was why she'd made sure she'd been long gone before Tess had arrived.

It was so frustrating; so disappointing. She should have guessed there was more to it than Ashley had told her. She should have rung Andrea before she'd left England. It was her own fault for not expressing any interest in her stepmother's health. But for now she was helpless. Until Ashley chose to contact her, there was nothing she could do.

She had planned on treating herself to an evening meal at the local *pizzeria* before returning to the apartment, but she changed her mind. After spending an uneasy day jumping every time someone came into the gallery, she was in no mood for company. She would buy herself some salad greens, she thought, toss them in a lemon vinaigrette, and grate some parmesan for flavour.

She was about to lock up when a man appeared in the doorway. He had his back to the light and for a ridiculous moment she thought Castelli had come back. Her heart skipped a beat and hot colour surged into her throat. But then the man moved and she realised her mistake.

It was Silvio Palmieri, she saw at once, the young man who ran the sports shop next door. Though perhaps calling the establishment he managed a sports shop was understating the obvious, Tess mused. With its windows full of endorsements from famous sports personalities and the exclusive designer gear it sold, it was definitely not just a sports shop.

Still, she acknowledged she had been foolish to mistake the younger man for Castelli. Silvio was dark, it was true, but that was where the resemblance ended. He didn't move with the instinctive grace of a predator or regard her with tawny-eyed suspicion. Silvio was just a rather pleasant man who had taken it upon himself to look out for her.

'*Ciao,*' he said. Then he noticed her expression. '*Mi scusi*, I startle you, *no*?'

'Oh—I was miles away,' murmured Tess, gathering her composure. 'You surprised me, that's all.'

Silvio frowned. 'You have not had bad news?' he asked, with surprising perception. 'Ashley's mama—she has not had a relapse, *spero*?'

'Not as far as I know,' said Tess drily, not at all sure how Andrea must be feeling at this moment. 'Um—have you had a good day?'

Silvio shrugged. 'What do you say? So-so? *Sì*, it has been a so-so day. How about you?'

Tess felt an almost irresistible urge to laugh, but she doubted Silvio would appreciate her hysterics. She couldn't involve him in her problems. Ashley wouldn't like it and Castelli definitely wouldn't approve.

'It's been—interesting,' she said, moving to drop the blinds on the windows. 'But I'm not sorry it's over.' And that was the truth.

'I saw Raphael di Castelli come into the gallery earlier,' Silvio ventured, his brows raised in inquiry, and Tess wondered if she was being absurdly suspicious in thinking that that was the real reason he had come. 'He is quite a well-known person in San Michele. In the season, many people work at the villa. Picking the grapes, *capisce*?'

Tess stared at him. 'You know him?' she asked, absorbing the fact that his name was *Raphael di* Castelli. She moistened her lips. 'Does he have a large vineyard, then?'

'I think so.' Silvio was regarding her curiously now. 'And, no, I do not know him. Well, not personally, you understand?'

Tess hesitated. Ashley's interest in Marco was beginning to make sense. 'And Ashley?' she asked, trying to sound casual. 'I believe she knows his son?'

'Ah, Marco.' Silvio nodded. '*Sì*. Marco is—how do you say?—the artist, *no*?'

'Marco's a painter?'

'He would like to be.' Silvio spread a hand towards the paintings lining the walls of the gallery. 'He would like the exhibition, I think.'

Tess caught her breath. Castelli hadn't mentioned that his son wanted to be a painter. But perhaps it explained how Ashley had come to know Marco, however.

Now she looked around. 'Are any of these his paintings?' she asked cautiously and Silvio laughed.

'*A mala pena.*' Hardly. 'But he is ambitious, *no*?'

'I see.' Tess nodded. 'Does his father approve?'

'I think not,' said Silvio, sobering. 'Di Castellis do not

waste their time with such pursuits. Besides, Marco is still at school.'

'Ah.' Tess thought that explained a lot. 'Well, thank you for your insight. It was certainly—um—interesting.'

'And Marco's father?' prompted Silvio. 'You didn't say what he wanted.'

'Oh.' Tess had no intention of discussing the reasons for Castelli's visit with him. 'He—er—he was looking for Ashley.' She crossed her fingers. 'He didn't say why.'

'Mmm.'

Silvio didn't sound convinced, but Tess decided she had said enough. 'Now, I've got to go,' she said. 'I want to go to the supermarket before I go home.'

'Or you could have dinner with me,' Silvio suggested at once. 'There is a favourite *trattoria* of mine just a short way from here.'

'Oh, I don't think—'

'You are not going to turn me down?'

Silvio pulled a petulant face, but Tess had had enough. 'I am sure there are plenty of women only too eager to dine with you, Silvio,' she said firmly. 'I'm sorry, but it's been a long day and I'm tired. I wouldn't be very good company tonight.'

'But Ashley, she said you would be glad to go out with me,' he protested. 'She tell me you are not—attached, *no*?'

'Did she?' Tess wondered what else Ashley had told these people about her. 'Well, she was wrong, Silvio. I do have a boyfriend.' Boy*friends*, anyway, she justified herself. There was no need to tell him there was no special man in her life.

Silvio shrugged. 'But he is not here,' he pointed out blandly, and she sighed.

'Even so…'

'Another evening, perhaps,' he declared, evidently un-deterred by her answer. Then to her relief he walked towards the door. *'A domani, cara. Arrivederci.'*

'Arrivederci,' she answered. 'Goodnight.'

Tess waited only until he'd stepped out of the gallery before shutting and locking the door behind him. Then, leaning back against it, she blew out a relieved breath. What a day, she thought. First Castelli, and then Silvio. She would be glad to get back to the apartment. At least there she could be reasonably sure she wouldn't be disturbed. Unless Ashley had some other secret she hadn't bothered to share with her sister, that was.

She slept badly, having only picked at the salad she'd prepared for herself. She kept thinking she could hear a phone ringing, but it was only the wind chimes hanging on the balcony outside the bedroom window.

In the event, she dropped into a fitful slumber just before dawn and when she woke again it was daylight and the sun was filtering through the blinds.

After putting on a pot of coffee, she went and took a shower in the tiny bathroom. The water was never hot, but for once she appreciated its lukewarm spray. She even turned the tap to cold before stepping out and wrapping herself in one of the skimpy towels Ashley had provided.

After pouring herself a delicious mug of black coffee, she stepped out onto the tiny balcony. The world looked a little less hostile this morning, she thought. But that was ridiculous, really. It was people who were hostile, not the world in general. And if anyone was to blame for her present situation, it was Ashley.

Her sister's apartment was on the top floor of a villa in the Via San Giovanni. The road was one of several that climbed the hill above the harbour, and, although the building was rather unprepossessing on the outside, at least its halls and stairways were clean and didn't smell of the onions and garlic that so many old buildings did.

Ashley's apartment was fairly spartan, but it was comfortable enough. She had added rugs and throws and pretty curtains at the narrow windows, and Tess had been pleasantly surprised to find it had a separate bedroom and bathroom as well as a living-room-cum-kitchen with modern appliances.

Now as she leaned on the balcony rail she amended the feelings of betrayal she had had the night before. Okay, Ashley had lied to her—had lied to all of them—but from Tess's point of view nothing had really changed. She was still filling in at the gallery and she had only herself to blame if she didn't enjoy the novelty of a break in such beautiful surroundings.

But it was hard not to wonder what Ashley was doing. Getting involved with a teenager seemed crazy, even by her sister's standards. Yet Ashley had always been a law unto herself. Tess could remember her father grumbling about his younger daughter's antics on one of his infrequent visits to Derbyshire to see her. He and his new family had still lived in London, but Tess had moved away when she'd become a teacher. It had been easier not to have to make excuses for not visiting her family as often as her father would have liked.

Realising her mug was empty now and that she was just wasting time, Tess turned back into the bedroom. Shedding the towel onto the rail in the bathroom, she walked naked into the bedroom again to find something suitable to wear.

Ignoring the suspicion that Raphael di Castelli's visit the previous day was influencing her, she chose a cream chemise dress that was spotted with sprigs of lavender. It was long, as her skirt had been, but she chose canvas loafers instead of the boots she'd worn the day before.

Her hair had dried in the sunshine and she surveyed its wisps and curls with a resigned eye. Some women might appreciate its youthful ingenuousness, but she didn't. She should have left it long, she thought gloomily. At least then she could have swept it up on top of her head.

Shrugging off these thoughts, she rinsed her coffee mug, left it on the drainer, and exited the apartment. Three flights of stone stairs led down to the ground floor and she emerged into the warm air with a growing feeling of well-being. She wasn't going to let Ashley—or Castelli—spoil her holiday, she decided. She had a good mind to shut the gallery early and spend the latter half of the afternoon on the beach.

Ashley's little Renault was parked a few metres down from the apartment building and it took some patience to extricate it from between a badly parked Fiat and a bulky van. It didn't help that she had to keep control of the vehicle by using the handbrake, the steep slope of the road making any kind of manoeuvre an act of faith.

She managed to regain her composure driving down to the gallery. Tumbling blossoms on sun-baked walls, red-and-ochre-tiled roofs dropping away towards the waterfront, buildings that seemed to be crammed so closely together, there didn't seem to be room for anything between. But there were gardens lush with greenery, fruit trees espaliered against crumbling brickwork. And the sensual fragrance of lilies and roses and jasmine, mingling with the aromas from the bakery on the corner.

The phone was ringing when she let herself into the gallery. Ashley, she thought eagerly, hurriedly turning off the alarm as she went to answer it. 'Hello?'

'Teresa?' Her spirits dropped. She should have known. It was Ashley's mother again. 'Teresa, where have you been? I've been trying the apartment but you weren't there.'

'I expect I was on my way down here,' said Tess, adopting a pleasant tone even though she felt like screaming. Then, with sudden optimism, 'Have you heard from Ashley?'

'No.' The clipped word conveyed it all, both distress and impatience. 'Have you?'

'If I had I'd have let you know,' said Tess flatly, and heard Andrea inhale a sharp breath.

'As would I, Teresa,' she said. 'And there is no need for you to take that tone with me. If you don't know where your sister is, I consider that's your mistake, not mine.'

Tess bit back the indignant retort that sprang to her lips. It was no use falling out with Ashley's mother. She was upset, and who could blame her? Her daughter had gone missing and she was over a thousand miles away.

'I suppose I assumed she'd keep in touch,' she said at last, deciding she didn't deserve to shoulder all the blame. 'And I did speak to her a few days ago.'

Andrea snorted. 'You didn't tell me that yesterday.'

Tess sighed. 'I forgot.'

'Or you kept it from me, just to worry me,' Ashley's mother said accusingly. 'Didn't you ask her where she was?'

No. Why should she? But Tess kept that question to herself.

'I never thought of it,' she said, which was true enough. 'Anyway, she'll be in touch again, I know, when she finds the time.'

'Well, I think it's a very unsatisfactory state of affairs,' declared Andrea tersely. 'And if it wasn't for this customer of Ashley's wanting to speak to her, I'd have heard nothing about it.'

Nor would she, thought Tess ruefully. But that was another story.

There was an awkward silence then, and before Tess could think of anything to fill it Ashley's mother spoke again. 'You know,' she said, 'I'm getting the distinct impression that you know more about this than you're letting on. And if Ashley was forced to ask you to stand in for her, she must have been desperate.'

Gee, thanks!

Tess refused to respond to that and Andrea continued doggedly, 'Well, all I can do is leave it with you for the present. But if you haven't heard from her by the end of the week, I intend to come out to Italy and see what's going on for myself.'

Tess stifled an inward groan. 'That's your decision, of course.'

'Yes, it is.' Andrea had obviously expected an argument and Tess's answer had left her with little more to say. 'All right, then. So, the minute you hear from Ashley, you'll ring me? You promise?'

'Of course.'

Somehow Tess got off the phone without telling the other woman exactly what she really thought of Ashley's behaviour. And then, after hanging up, she spent several minutes staring gloomily into space. She no longer felt like closing the gallery early and spending the rest of the day on the beach. This so-called holiday had suddenly become a trial of innocence and she was the accused.

It wasn't fair, she thought bitterly. It wasn't her fault Ashley had disappeared; it wasn't her fault that she had taken Castelli's son with her. So why was she beginning to feel that it was?

CHAPTER FOUR

SOMEHOW Tess got through the rest of the day. For once, she had several would-be customers in the gallery, and she spent some time talking to a couple from Manchester, England, who were visiting Italy for the first time.

Nevertheless, she was enormously relieved when it was time to close up. She returned to the apartment and another lonely evening feeling as if she were the only person in Porto San Michele who wasn't having any fun.

The next morning she felt marginally brighter. She'd slept reasonably well and, refusing to consider what would happen if Ashley didn't turn up, she dressed in pink cotton shorts and a sleeveless top that exposed her belly button. Why should she care what anyone thought of her appearance? she thought, slipping her feet into sandals that strapped around her ankle. This was her holiday and she meant to enjoy it.

With this in mind, she decided to give the car a miss this morning. A walk down to the gallery would enable her to pick up a warm, custard-filled pastry at the bakery, and the exercise would do her good. Italian food was delicious, but it was also very rich.

It was another beautiful morning. Outside the sun was shining, which couldn't help but make her feel optimistic. Whatever else Ashley had done, she had introduced her to this almost untouched corner of Tuscany, and she had to remember that.

Several people called a greeting as she made her way down the steep slope into town. She didn't always understand what they said, but she usually managed an adequate response. Her Italian was improving in leaps and bounds, and before all this business with Ashley had erupted she'd been happily planning a return to the country, maybe taking in Florence and Venice next time.

The pastry she'd bought at the small *pasticceria* was oozing custard onto her fingers as she let herself into the gallery. The alarm started its usual whine and she hurried to deactivate it before opening up the office and setting her backpack down on the desk. Then, before she had time to fill the coffee-pot, the telephone rang again.

Dammit, she thought, she couldn't get through the door before someone wanted to speak to her. Depositing the sticky pastry onto the notepad beside the phone, she picked up the receiver. 'Medici Galleria,' she said, expecting the worst.

'Miss Daniels?'

Tess swallowed. She would have recognised his distinctive voice anywhere. 'Signor di Castelli,' she said politely. 'What can I do for you?' Her heart skipped a beat. 'Have you heard from your son?'

'Ah, no.' His sigh was audible. 'I gather you have not heard from your sister either.'

'No.' Tess's excitement subsided. 'Nor has her mother.'

'I see.' He paused. 'You have heard from her?'

'Oh, yes. I've heard from Andrea.'

Tess couldn't keep the bitterness out of her voice and Castelli picked up on it. 'You sound depressed, *cara*,' he murmured sympathetically. 'Ashley's mother—she blames you, *sì*?'

'How did you know?' said Tess ruefully. 'Yes, she blames me. I should have asked Ashley where she was going when I spoke to her before I left England.'

'But you thought she was going to visit with her mama, *no*?'

'Andrea doesn't see it that way. In any case, I couldn't tell her what Ashley had told me.'

'*Povero* Tess,' he said gently. 'This has not been easy for you.'

'No.' Tess felt a momentary twinge of self-pity. 'So—' she tried to be practical '—was that the only reason you rang? To ask whether I'd heard from Ashley?'

'Among other things,' he said, rather enigmatically. Then, without explaining what he meant, *'Ci vediamo, cara,'* and he rang off.

Tess replaced the receiver with a feeling of defeat. So much for his sympathy, she thought gloomily. For a moment there, she'd thought he was going to offer some other alternative to her dilemma, but like Andrea he had no easy solutions. And, unlike Andrea, he had more important things to concern him than her situation, even if the two things were linked.

The pastry had oozed all over the notepad and she regarded it resignedly. So much for her breakfast, she thought, pouring water into the coffee maker and switching it on. Pretty soon the sound of the water filtering through the grains filled the small office, and the delicious smell of coffee was a temporary antidote to her depression.

Realising she still hadn't opened up the gallery, she went through into the studio and unlocked the door. Sunlight streamed into the gallery, causing her to wince at its brilliance, but everything looked brighter in the healing warmth of the sun.

Already the parade outside was quite busy. Cars and tourist buses surged past, looking for parking spaces along the popular esplanade. There were tourists and local fishermen leaning on the seawall across the street, and beyond the beach several yachts could be seen tacking across the bay.

They were heading for the small marina south of town and Tess envied them. There was something so exciting about being able to do whatever you liked on such a lovely day. With worrying about her sister, she'd almost forgotten what it was like to feel carefree, and her plan to loaf on the beach seemed far out of her reach today.

She stood for several minutes at the door of the gallery, watching the activities outside, trying not to feel too let-down. She didn't want to think of what she'd do if Ashley hadn't turned up by Friday. The prospect of her stepmother flying out here to join the search didn't bear thinking about.

There was a windsurfer out on the water. He had seemed fairly competent at first, but now she revised her opinion. He was probably a holiday-maker, she decided, trying his hand at sailing the narrow surfboard across the bay. And when an errant breeze caught the craft, he wobbled violently before overbalancing and tumbling head-first into the water.

To her relief, his head bobbed up almost instantly beside the capsized craft, but he couldn't seem to pull it upright again. She'd seen the experts do it, vaulting onto the board and pulling up the sail, but this poor man could only drift helplessly towards shallower water.

Tess couldn't suppress a giggle. Everyone on the beach and leaning on the seawall was enjoying his predicament. It wasn't kind to laugh, but she couldn't help herself. It was such a relief after the pressures she'd endured.

'You seem happier, *signorina*,' mused a low voice, and Tess turned her head to find Raphael di Castelli propped against the wall beside the door. His dark-complexioned features seemed absurdly familiar to her and she chided herself for the flicker of awareness that accompanied the thought.

'Signor di Castelli,' she said, knowing she sounded stiff and unwelcoming, but she hadn't expected to see him again so soon. 'You didn't say you were coming to the gallery today.'

'It was a sudden impulse,' he said, straightening away from the wall, and she was instantly intimidated by his compelling appearance. He was dressed less formally this morning, though his black trousers and matching silk jacket were no less exclusive in design. Still, he wasn't wearing a tie, she noticed, even if the dark curls of hair nestling in the open neckline of his black shirt provided a disturbing focus. 'And who told you my name was *di* Castelli? Have you spoken to Ashley, after all?'

'No, I haven't.' Tess was defensive now, backing into the

gallery behind her, allowing him to fill the doorway as he followed her inside. Married men shouldn't be so attractive, she thought, wishing she could be more objective. She didn't want to prove that she was no better than her sister, wanting something—or someone—she could never have. 'Besides,' she added, striving for indifference, 'that is your name, isn't it?' She paused and then went on defiantly, 'I'm told you're quite a celebrity around here.'

His eyes narrowed. It was obvious he didn't like the idea that she had been discussing him with someone else. 'Is that what your informant told you?' he asked. 'I think he is mistaken. Or perhaps you misunderstood.'

'I don't think so.' Tess moved hurriedly to open the blinds, anything to dispel the pull of attraction that being alone in a darkened room with him engendered. She moistened her lips. 'Did you forget something?'

Castelli arched a mocking brow. It seemed obvious that, unlike her, he had had plenty of experience with the opposite sex. And, just because he was married, he couldn't help amusing himself at her expense. He must know from her attitude that she didn't want him there, yet he seemed to get some satisfaction from her unease.

'As a matter of fact, I was on my way to Viareggio when I saw you standing in the doorway,' he declared at last, tracking her with his eyes as she moved around the room. 'You looked—*triste*.' Sad.

Tess caught her breath. 'You don't need to feel sorry for me, Signor di Castelli,' she said sharply, resenting his implication. 'I was just wasting time, actually. While I waited for my coffee to heat.'

Castelli regarded her indulgently. 'If you say so, *cara*,' he said. 'But I know what I saw in your face.'

Tess stiffened. 'Actually, I was watching a windsurfer,' she said. 'He made me laugh. Perhaps you mistook my expression for your own.'

'Do not be so defensive, *cara*. It is natural that you should feel this—excursion—has not been as you planned.'

'You got that right,' said Tess, heading towards the office. 'Now, if you'll excuse me…'

If she'd hoped he would take the hint and go, she was wrong. As she was standing staring down at the unappetising remains of her breakfast a shadow fell across the desk.

'Come with me,' he said, startling her more by his words than by his appearance in the office. She looked up to see he had his hands bracing his weight at either side of the door.

His jacket had parted and she noticed his flat stomach and the way his belt was slung low over his hips. Taut muscles caused the buttons of his shirt to gape; tawny eyes, narrowed in sensual appraisal, caused heat to spread unchecked through every pore.

Realising she was gazing at him like some infatuated teenager, Tess dragged her eyes back to the congealing pastry on the desk. 'I can't,' she said, without even giving herself time to consider the invitation. He must have known she'd refuse or he'd never have offered, she assured herself. 'I'm sorry. But it was kind of you to ask.'

'Why?'

'Why—what?' she countered, prevaricating.

'Why can you not come with me?' he explained, enunciating each word as if she were an infant. 'It is a beautiful day, *no*?'

'No. That is, yes—' Tess knew she must seem stupid, but it wasn't her fault. He had no right to put her in such a position. 'It is a beautiful day, but I can't leave the gallery.'

Castelli's mouth flattened. 'Because Ashley asked you to be here?' he queried sardonically. '*Sì*, I can see you would feel it necessary to be loyal to her.'

Tess stiffened. 'There's no need to be sarcastic.' She paused. 'In any case, I have to be here in case she rings.'

Castelli straightened away from the door. 'You think she will ring?'

Tess shrugged. 'Maybe.'

'And maybe not,' said Castelli flatly. 'I have the feeling

your sister will not get in touch with you until she is ready to return.'

Tess had had the same feeling. She didn't want to admit it but it would be counter-productive for Ashley to contact her, particularly if she'd taken pains to keep her whereabouts a secret.

'Whatever,' she said now, glancing round for the box of tissues Ashley kept on the filing cabinet. Pulling a couple out, she started to tackle the curdling pastry. 'I promised to look after the gallery. That's all there is to it.'

Castelli shook his head, and then moving forward he took the sticky tissues from her hand. 'Let me,' he said, glancing sideways at her as he gathered the crumbling remains of the pastry together, and her nerves spiked at the automatic association her senses made of his words.

She wanted to protest, to tell him she was perfectly capable of cleaning up her own mess, but she didn't. Instead, she stood silently by while he tore several damaged pages from the notepad, wiped down the desk and dumped the lot into Ashley's waste bin.

'The domestic will empty it,' he said, when Tess looked at it a little anxiously. Then, indicating his hands, 'You have a bathroom, *sì*?'

Tess moved aside, pointing to the door that led into the small washroom, and presently she heard the sound of him rinsing his hands. He came back, drying his hands on a paper towel that he also dropped into the waste bin. Then, he propped his hips against the desk, folded his arms and said, 'Are you not going to offer me a cup of coffee for my trouble?'

Tess had forgotten all about the coffee simmering on the hob, but now she took a spare mug from the top of the filing cabinet and filled it carefully. Her hands weren't entirely steady, but she managed not to spill any, offering the mug to him as she said tightly, 'I don't have any milk or sugar.'

'Why spoil a good cup of coffee?' he countered smoothly, though she guessed he regretted his words when he tasted the bitter brew. 'Mmm.' He managed a polite smile, but he put his cup down rather quickly, she noticed. 'It has a— distinctive flavour, *no*?'

'It's stewed,' said Tess shortly, tempted to remind him that she hadn't asked him to join her in the first place. 'I'm sure you're used to much better.'

Castelli's mouth twitched. 'I am sure I am, too,' he said without modesty. 'If you will come out with me today I will prove it.'

She shook her head. 'I've told you, I can't.'

His strange, predator's eyes flared with impatience. 'Because you do not trust me, perhaps?'

'Trust has nothing to do with it,' she said, though he was right, she did know very little about him. Stepping back from the situation, she could see he might have a point.

'What, then?' He moved to the door and glanced into the gallery. 'You have no customers. I doubt anyone will be too disappointed if you close. It is hardly an active concern. That is why Scottolino is thinking of moving his interest to *Firenze*—ah, Florence.'

Recognising the name she'd seen on the top of invoices Ashley had typed, Tess realised he was talking about the gallery's owner. 'Mr Scottolino is moving out of San Michele?' she asked in surprise. 'Does Ashley know that, do you think?'

'I doubt it.' Castelli was dismissive. 'Augustin is not the kind of man to keep his employees appraised of his plans. Particularly when it will mean that your sister will be out of a job.'

Tess's lips pursed. 'And your enquiries—as you so politely put it—won't have flattered her reputation, no?'

Her sarcasm was obvious and Castelli spread his hands, palms upward. 'You do me an injustice, Tess. I am not your enemy.'

You're not my friend either, thought Tess dourly, but his use of her name caused another unwanted frisson of excitement to feather her spine. She'd expected him to have forgotten it, she realised. It was Ashley he was interested in, Ashley who was his focus. Yet when he said her name in that low attractive voice that was as smooth and dark as molasses, her brain scrambled helplessly and she could have melted on the floor at his feet.

Fortunately, he didn't know that, but she did and it annoyed her. In consequence, her tone was sharper than it might have been when she said, 'You didn't tell me how your son met Ashley. Considering the opinion you apparently have of the relationship, it seems an unlikely event.'

Castelli was silent for so long that she thought he wasn't going to answer her. *He doesn't want to tell me that Marco has ambitions to be a painter,* she thought smugly, feeling as if she'd got the upper hand for once.

But she was wrong.

'They met last September,' he conceded at last. 'At the *vendemmia,* the grape harvest. There is always a celebration when the grapes are ready to press. Someone must have invited your sister to the gathering. For one evening of the year we keep open house.'

Tess frowned. 'Then you must have met her, too.'

'As I told you, I am informed I did.' He shrugged. 'There were many people. I do not remember.'

Tess absorbed this. 'I assumed they'd met at the gallery. I understand Marco is interested in art.'

'Now where did you hear that?' Castelli's eyes were once again focussed on her. 'It seems you, too, have been making the enquiries, *cara.*' His lips curled. 'My son's—interest in painting came after meeting your sister. It was an excuse to visit the gallery, nothing more.'

'You sound very sure.'

Castelli shrugged. 'Marco has never shown any aptitude for art before. He is a science student. He has always been more interested in the reality of life as opposed to the ideal.'

'Ah, but wasn't it Jean Cocteau who called art ''science in the flesh'',' Tess pointed out triumphantly. 'And surely you can't deny that Leonardo da Vinci was a scientist, as well as being one of the most influential painters of all time?'

Castelli pulled a wry face. 'You are determined to win this argument, are you not?' he remarked ruefully. 'And when it comes to quotations from the classics, you obviously have the advantage. But, please, do not tell me that Marco's infatuation for your sister is, as Ruskin said, "the expression of one soul talking to another", because I do not believe it.'

Tess was taken aback by his knowledge, but not really surprised. Raphael di Castelli struck her as being a very intelligent man and, contrary to his declaration, she doubted she had any advantage over him. But she understood his feelings, understood that it must be a source of frustration to him that Ashley had caused such a rift between him and his son.

'I can't imagine what Ashley thinks she's doing,' she murmured now, half wistfully. 'Her mother thinks I should report her disappearance to the police.'

'La polizia?' He seemed taken aback. 'But this is not a criminal matter.'

'No.' Tess didn't know why but suddenly she wanted to reassure him. 'I've managed to persuade her that there's no need to involve the police at present.'

'Grazie.'

He was obviously relieved and, taking advantage of his momentary weakness, she said, 'I gather your investigator hasn't turned up any clues.'

'No.' He was resigned. 'He is still in Genova, checking the automobile rental agencies, as I believe I told you. So far, he has had no luck in tracing their whereabouts.'

Tess sighed. 'I'm sorry.' And she was. As much for him, she realised with some confusion, as for herself.

His expression softened. 'You are not getting a very favourable picture of my country, are you, Tess? Or perhaps I should say, of my family. Despite his youth I accept Marco is also to blame.'

She managed a smile. 'Thank you for saying that.'

'My pleasure.' His voice stroked her senses. Then, with gentle insistence, 'You are not at all like your sister, are you, little one?'

Despite his reference to her size, the sudden intimacy of his words couldn't be ignored and she seized on the first thing she could think of in response. 'You're sure they're in Genoa, *signore*?' she asked hurriedly. 'Is it a big city?'

'It is a very big city,' he said drily, 'and at this point I am not sure of anything.' A trace of weariness entered his voice. 'That is why I am going to Viareggio. Marco may have confided his plans to his sister.'

'To his sister? I didn't know he had a sister.'

And why should she? she thought foolishly. It wasn't as if Castelli had confided his family connections to her. But somehow she'd got it into her head that Marco was an only child. Or perhaps, she'd only hoped he was. If Castelli had more children, he was even further out of reach.

He was regarding her with mild speculation now and she wondered what was going on behind his polite façade. What was he thinking? That she'd been presumptuous to say what she had? Or that she had no right to question his private affairs?

'My daughter married at the end of last year,' he replied at last, apparently deciding she deserved an answer. 'Maria—that is her name—she and Carlo, her husband, own a small *albergo* in a village not far from the city.' He paused. 'If you come with me, you can meet her for yourself.'

Tess sucked in a breath. She hadn't expected him to repeat his invitation and now that he had she was unsettled again. She knew she should still say no. Closing the gallery would be irresponsible and reckless. How would his daughter feel if her father turned up with a strange woman? Pretty peeved, Tess was sure.

No, she couldn't do it. Even if the idea of taking off for the day was almost irresistible, she had to keep her head.

Italian men had a reputation for liking women and Castelli was a married man besides. She'd be mad to put herself into his hands.

'I'm sorry,' she said at last, feeling real regret as she voiced the words. 'I don't think your wife would approve.'

'My wife?' He gazed at her strangely. 'What does my wife have to do with my asking you to accompany me on this trip?'

'Well…' Tess's face felt as if it were burning. Put like that it did sound as if she was attributing motives to him he clearly didn't have. 'I just thought—that is, I'm sure the rest of your family will think it odd if you turn up with—with a strange woman.'

His mouth flattened. 'Ah, a beautiful woman, *cosi intendi*?' he remarked softly, and Tess felt as if she couldn't get enough air. A faint smile lightened his expression. 'You think my wife and my daughter would not approve of my friendship with the attractive sister of my son's *innamorata, no*?'

Tess had never felt more embarrassed in her life. 'We're hardly—friends, *signore*. I just meant—'

'I know what you meant, Tess,' he assured her smugly, and she felt as if she wanted to scream with frustration. 'Relax, *cara*. There is no conflict of interest. There is only my daughter. My wife and I live separate lives.'

Tess wasn't convinced. 'But she still lives in your house, yes?'

'She lives in my house, *no*,' he teased her mockingly. '*Sono divorziato*, Tess. We are divorced. Gina makes her home in New York.'

CHAPTER FIVE

SHE didn't look as if she believed him and Rafe acknowledged that divorce was still not a common thing in his country. Indeed, hadn't his own mother been horrified that he should consider such a thing? Catholics did not get divorced, she'd told him severely. Marriage vows were meant to last.

But Rafe couldn't believe that anyone should be condemned to spend their lives with someone who flouted their vows so freely. Who, he suspected, had only married him to escape the rigorous dictates of her elderly father.

'I'm sorry,' Tess said now, cupping the back of her neck with her hands and drawing his eyes to the rounded breasts pressing against her sleeveless top. 'It's really none of my business.'

'No.' He conceded the point because he realised he was behaving totally out of character for him. *Dio mio*, he was too old to be—what?—flirting with a girl who was almost young enough to be his daughter. Well, perhaps that was an exaggeration, he conceded. But he was forty-three. More than old enough to have more sense.

'Anyway,' she continued, evidently taking his response at face value, 'I mustn't keep you.' She forced a polite smile. 'Will you let me know if—if your daughter does know where they are?'

And Rafe felt his resolve faltering. Dammit, what was wrong with inviting her to go to Viareggio with him? It wasn't as if he had any ulterior motive for doing so. She was Ashley's sister. She deserved to know what was going on.

Yeah, right.

'I had thought you might like to question Maria yourself,' he said, ignoring his conscience. 'Can I not persuade you to change your mind?'

Her hands dropped to her sides then and the colour that had ebbed and flowed from her cheeks all the time she had been speaking to him deepened again. 'Oh—really,' she said, making a distracted gesture towards her outfit. 'I couldn't go out dressed like this.'

'Why not?' She looked perfectly fine to him, bare legs and all. *And when had he noticed them?* 'This is not a formal visit, *cara*. You must have considered that what you are wearing was good enough to come to work, *no*?'

Tess lifted her shoulders, once again attracting his attention, this time to the gap of creamy flesh that widened between her top and her shorts. 'I don't know,' she murmured uncertainly, but he could tell she was weakening. 'How long would I be away from the gallery.'

'Um—two hours.' *Or three!* Rafe was not altogether truthful. 'Does it matter? Which is more important, pleasing your sister's employer or finding Ashley?'

'Well—finding Ashley, of course.'

Rafe inclined his head. 'Then shall we go?' he said, knowing he was giving her no option, and with a nervous little shrug she obediently picked up her bag.

He'd parked the Ferrari in a no-waiting zone and he noticed how her eyes widened at his audacity. Or perhaps she was just impressed with the automobile, though he doubted it. He didn't know why, but he had the feeling that possessions didn't matter much to Tess Daniels. Which was a novelty.

'I suppose it would be worth more than a parking attendant's job to tow your car,' she remarked as she folded her legs into the front passenger seat and Rafe felt a momentary spurt of indignation. He didn't need her to remind him that the authorities often turned a blind eye to his indiscretions. But he doubted that any defence he made would enhance his reputation in her eyes, so he chose not to comment on it.

'Are you comfortable?' he asked instead, getting behind the wheel, and he was gratified to see that she looked embarrassed now.

'How could I not be?' she remarked at last as he started the powerful engine. 'This is a Ferrari, isn't it? I saw the horse on the bonnet.'

Rafe winced. 'It's a stallion,' he said drily, and then wished he'd kept his mouth shut when she said,

'Oh, yes. An Italian stallion. I'd forgotten.'

Rafe glanced in his mirror and then took his chance to pull out into the stream of traffic. But her mocking words still rankled and, ignoring the safer path, he said, with a definite edge to his voice, 'I hope that was not meant as a criticism.'

Her lips parted then, and she turned her head to look at him, wisps of white-blonde hair blowing about her face. 'I don't know what you mean,' she said, lifting a hand to tuck several strands behind her ear. And, although he was fairly sure she knew exactly what he'd meant, he chose not to argue with her.

'*Non importa.* It does not matter,' he declared, but he was intensely aware of her beside him. Aware of her bare arms only inches from his sleeve, aware of the way her shorts rode up her thighs, exposing a smooth length of slim leg. He took a breath. 'Do you know Viareggio, *signorina*?'

She hesitated and he wondered if she intended to pursue what he had said earlier. But eventually all she said was, 'I've never been to Italy before so all I know is Porto San Michele, I'm afraid. And my name is Tess. I know you haven't forgotten it. Or have I offended you and that's why you've suddenly become so—so formal?'

They were leaving the small town behind them now, the hilly environs above the harbour giving way to a coast road that wound its way south. But it wasn't of the elegant little seaport of Viareggio that Rafe was thinking. He was wondering how to answer her without compromising his fear that he was getting in too deep.

'You have not offended me,' he told her neutrally. 'I do not offend that easily. But perhaps you are right. We do not know one another very well.'

The look she cast his way now was wary. 'So why did you invite me to come with you?' she asked, and Rafe's fingers tightened on the wheel.

Good question, he thought drily. But...

'You know why I invited you to come with me,' he said firmly. 'So you could talk to Maria yourself.'

'Mmm.' She didn't sound convinced. 'You think my presence will encourage her to talk? If she knows anything, that is?'

'I do not know.' He didn't like the feeling of being on the spot. 'But as this is your first visit to Italy, perhaps you will enjoy seeing a little more of my country.'

Tess gave him an undisguisedly disbelieving stare. 'But you didn't know it was my first visit to Italy until I said so,' she pointed out mildly, and Rafe expelled an impatient breath.

'No,' he conceded flatly. 'You win. I wanted your company.' His lips twisted. 'So sue me.'

Tess's jaw dropped. 'You wanted *my* company?' she echoed. 'Why?'

Were it anyone else, he might have been tempted to wonder if she was fishing for compliments. But not with Tess. There was such a look of perplexity on her face that he couldn't hide the humour that was surely evident in his eyes.

'I don't know any more about Ashley's whereabouts than I've already told you,' she continued, misinterpreting his expression. 'I want to find her just as much as you do. And if you think—'

'I believe you, *cara*,' he interrupted her gently. 'I know you have not been lying to me.' And then, because he wanted to wipe the suspicious look off her face, he added, 'Why should I not enjoy being with a younger woman? Just because I am over forty does not mean I am—what is it you say?—over the hill, *no*?'

Her eyes widened for a moment. Then she shook her head. 'I think you're teasing me, *signore*. It's kind of you, but I wish you wouldn't. I know my own limitations better than anyone.'

His eyes narrowed. 'And they are?'

Her colour deepened. With her face free of any obvious make-up and her hair blowing wildly about her head, she looked little more than a teenager, and he marvelled anew that she was older than her sister. From Verdicci's description, he knew Ashley Daniels was far more sophisticated— and comparably more worldly. She knew what she wanted and went after it, no matter who got hurt in the process. Including her own sister, he acknowledged as Tess moved a little uneasily in her seat.

'They're too many to mention,' she said at last, shifting her attention to the view. 'Oh, is that a monastery over there?'

Rafe decided to let her divert him, taking his eyes briefly from the twisting road ahead of them. A green rolling landscape, dotted with pine and olive groves, rose steadily inland. There were isolated farms, some of them with their own vineyards, and small villages visible among the trees. Some farmers grew vines between the olive trees, providing a much-needed boost to their economy in years when the grape harvest was poor.

Each village sported its own spire or *campanile,* and, hearing the distant sound of bells, Rafe guessed that was what Tess had heard, too. 'I think it is a church,' he said, returning his attention to the road. 'There are few monasteries surviving in this area. There are ruins, *naturalmente*, if you are interested. But I fear the thought of the noble priests does not inspire any enthusiasm in me.'

Tess frowned. 'Because you are divorced?' she asked innocently, and he smiled.

'No.' He cast a fleeting glance her way, once again

amused by her refreshing candour. 'I do not think I can blame them for that.'

'Then why—?'

'I was taught by the Jesuits,' he said. 'Who as you may know are not known for their *misericordia*—their mercy, *no*?' He paused reminiscently. 'It is a long time ago, but I have not forgotten.'

Tess seemed interested. 'You went to school here, in Tuscany?'

'No.' Rafe shook his head. 'I went to school in Rome.' He grimaced. 'My mother's greatest wish was that I should enter the priesthood.'

Her lips parted. 'The priesthood?'

'Unlikely, is it not? Is that what you are thinking? That this man who has been married and divorced should have been considered worthy of such an office?'

'No.' She spread her hands. 'I was surprised, that's all. I've never met a would-be priest before.'

'And I was never a would-be priest,' he assured her drily. 'That was my mother's dream, not mine. Fortunately my father was of a more practical persuasion. While he indulged her to the extent of allowing her to choose my source of education, I was his only son. It was necessary that I should inherit the vineyard, that I was able to take over from him when his health began to fail.'

'Is your father still alive?'

'No.' He spoke regretfully. 'He died almost twenty years ago.'

'He must have been very young.'

'He was fifty,' acknowledged Rafe ruefully. 'But he had always been a heavy smoker, *cara*. He knew the risks he was taking, but he could not shake the habit.'

Tess nodded. 'My father's dead, too,' she said, confirming something he had already suspected. 'He died of a heart attack last year.'

'Ah.' Rafe was silent for a moment and then he said, 'Do you miss him?'

'Not as much as I would have done if we'd lived together,' she admitted honestly. 'As I believe I told you before, I was brought up by my aunt when my mother died. Then, after college when I started teaching, I moved to another part of the country. Dad and I used to see each other from time to time, but it was never the same.'

'I get the feeling that your stepmother has a lot to answer for,' said Rafe drily. 'I suspect she is more like her daughter than you thought.'

'Oh, Andrea's all right.' Tess was instantly defensive of her family and he had to admire her for it. 'She only ever wanted one child. She hadn't bargained for two.'

'But she must have known your father was a single parent before she married him,' Rafe pointed out reasonably as Tess made a play of examining an insect that had landed on her bare leg.

'Is this a mosquito?' she asked, deliberately creating a diversion, and Rafe had stretched across and flicked it away before he gave himself time to think.

It wasn't until his hand was safely back on the steering wheel and his fingertips were registering the soft brush of her flesh that he realised what he had done. This wasn't his daughter, he reminded himself. She wasn't even his cousin. Tess was a virtual stranger and he was treating her like a friend. Or more than a friend, he conceded, his skin burning where he had touched her. And he wanted to touch her again, he thought, in places that were hot and wet and definitely forbidden.

As if she sensed his guilty attraction, Tess turned away from him now, pressing against the door beside her, keeping her eyes on the view. But only after they'd exchanged one searing look of raw intimacy that left Rafe at least stunned by the strength of his own response.

They were silent then, each of them occupied with their own thoughts, pretending an interest in their surroundings that Rafe was sure neither of them really felt. Or perhaps he was only imagining it, he thought irritably. Whatever, he was much too old to play these childish games.

Only there was nothing childish about the way he was feeling and, realising he had to normalise the situation, he was relieved when a cluster of villas strung out along the coastline came into view. 'This is Viali,' he said, trying to recover his earlier optimism. 'It is really just an extension of Viareggio these days. The port has expanded so much. But Viali is pretty. It has its own personality. And, although it cannot boast the art nouveau architecture for which Viareggio is famous, many people prefer it to the larger resort.'

'Is this where your daughter lives?' asked Tess, apparently prepared to meet him halfway, and he agreed that it was.

'Their *albergo* is situated just outside Viali on the way to Viareggio. They will not have too many guests at this time of the year. Maria should have plenty of time to speak with us.'

The Villa Puccini looked chic and elegant dreaming in the noonday sun. Lush vegetation provided a colourful backdrop to the warm cream walls of the villa, and the blue waters of a kidney-shaped swimming pool vied with the vast expanse of the Gulf of Genoa that lapped at the sandy shore below the gardens. Glancing at Tess's face, Rafe suspected it was far more attractive than she had expected, and he felt his own spirits lifting at more than the prospect of seeing his daughter again.

'Is this it?' Tess asked as he drove between the stone gateposts that marked the entrance to the drive, and Rafe blew out a breath. 'Do you like it?' he asked, slowing to avoid a group of holiday-makers who were heading into town. 'Carlo's family is heavily involved in the leisure industry. This is one of their smaller properties and the first one Carlo has managed alone.'

'One of the smaller properties,' echoed Tess disbelievingly. 'It's much larger than I expected. I thought an *albergo* was something like a bed-and-breakfast back home.'

Rafe gave her a brief smile. 'I think you are thinking of a French *auberge*, Tess,' he said, his use of her name coming far too easily. 'An *albergo* is a hotel. Sometimes large, sometimes small. The Villa Puccini falls some way between the two.'

Tess shook her head as they rounded a flowering trellis and a cluster of orange-tiled buildings came into view. It was obvious that the villa had been added to over the years. Some extensions were taller than others. But the overall effect was charming, set as it was beside the breathtaking beauty of the bay.

'It looks very impressive to me,' she said doubtfully, and he saw her give another anxious glance towards her bare legs.

'It is a holiday hotel,' he assured her gently. 'And you look exactly like one of the visitors.' He switched off the engine of the Ferrari and unfastened his seat belt. 'I intend to get rid of this jacket as soon as I am out of the car.'

She didn't look entirely convinced and, now they were here, Rafe had to admit to feeling a little apprehensive himself. It was the first time he had brought a young woman to his daughter's home, and, no matter how often he assured himself that his motives were innocent, the fact remained there had been no need for him to bring Tess along.

She unfastened her own seat belt now, and before he could forestall her she had pushed open her door and got out of the car. With the sunlight blazing down on her bare head and the flush of heat in her cheeks, she looked absurdly young and beautiful. As he shed his jacket and hooked it over his shoulder, he had to accept that Maria would be suspicious. It was not that she hadn't been urging him to find someone else for the past six years. It was just that this gamine slip of an English girl was unlikely to have been what she meant.

But, before he could marshal any arguments in his own

defence, he heard his daughter calling to him. She was coming from the direction of the gardens, a flat basket containing long stems of white and yellow blossoms draped across her arm. Maria's hair, which was as dark as his own but much longer, was confined in a single braid, and her chemise dress of simple white organza complemented the warm tan of her bare arms.

She looked as elegant as her surroundings, he thought, with a rueful sigh. A product of his mother's policy that a woman should always look her best, whatever the circumstances. Even if she'd been gardening, which was highly unlikely in Maria's case. His daughter might enjoy arranging flowers, but she left the planting and the picking of them to someone else.

The contrast between her and Tess was marked. And it was obvious that neither of them appreciated the comparison. As she drew nearer he saw Maria's dark brows arch in polite inquiry, but Rafe could tell from her expression that, however pleased she might be to see him, she didn't care for him bringing a strange woman here without forewarning.

'Papa,' she greeted him warmly as he stepped forward to meet her, reaching up and bestowing light air kisses beside each of his cheeks in turn. But then, with a lightening turn of mood, she began reprovingly, *'Avresti dovuto dirmelo che—'*

'Inglese, Maria, per favore,' he interrupted her smoothly, turning to beckon Tess to join them. His eyes met hers briefly, and then he turned back to his daughter. 'Tess, this is my daughter, Maria. Maria, this is Tess Daniels. You may recall, her sister is at present looking after the Galleria Medici in San Michele.'

There was a moment when he thought Maria looked almost guilty. She obviously recognised the name, though she tried to hide her reaction from him. *'Buongiorno, signorina,'* she said, forgetting in her confusion that he had asked her to speak English. And then, rescuing herself, *'Scusi, Papa.*

Non ricordo. How do you do, Miss Daniels? Are you enjoying your holiday?'

'Tess is not on holiday,' Rafe asserted, before Tess could explain herself. After Maria's telling little response to his question, the last thing he wanted was for Tess to warn her of why they were here. 'She is standing in at the gallery while her sister is away,' he continued smoothly. He put a cautioning hand on Tess's shoulder, trying to ignore how aware of her he was. 'I hope you don't mind, *cara.* I invited her to come see a little more of the area.'

Maria's lips definitely tightened. 'You should have told us you were coming, Papa,' she declared, offering Tess a limp hand. She regarded the other woman warily now as she added, 'Is this your first visit to Italy, Miss Daniels?'

'I'm afraid so.' Tess was not without perception and Rafe knew she must be blaming him for bringing her here. 'And, please, call me Tess.' She glanced about her, her gaze flicking over Rafe's as she did so. And over his hand on her shoulder. 'This is a beautiful spot. Your father didn't tell me how delightful it would be.'

Maria softened, but she was watching them closely and Rafe was reluctantly obliged to remove his hand. '*Sì,* it is beautiful,' she agreed, with a momentary air of satisfaction. Then she looked at her father again. 'Are you staying for lunch, Papa, or is this just a brief visit?'

Rafe shrugged. 'We are not in any hurry, *cara,*' he said. 'But we are both hot and thirsty and a cool soda would be welcome. We can decide about lunch later, *no*?'

Maria looked as if she would have preferred some kind of explanation as to why they were here before she offered them any refreshment. He doubted she had bought his story about giving Tess a guided tour of the area. But courtesy demanded that she play the generous hostess and a thin smile appeared as she said, '*Ma certo*, Papa. Please, come with me. We can have drinks on the patio.'

CHAPTER SIX

CASTELLI'S daughter led them along a path between a clump
of oak and cypress trees. There was the scent of pine and
the unmistakable tang of the sea. And when they emerged
onto a private sun terrace, Tess could see a handful of guests
basking on the beach below the hotel. There were striped
chairs and tilted awnings, pedalos lying dormant in the
noonday heat. Some children were paddling in the shallows,
searching for shells, while their parents stretched out on
towels on the sand.

She hadn't been exaggerating when she'd told Maria it
was a beautiful place. The small town of Viali occupied a
curving headland and the cliffs that rose above it were thick
with pine and spruce. The beach was deep, stretching out
some distance towards the water, with gently rising dunes
studded with flowering cactus and prickly pear.

The terrace Maria took them to was separated from the
public areas by a trellis totally covered with flowering vines.
A teak table and chairs were set beneath a pale green um-
brella, and as they approached a girl of perhaps eighteen,
dressed in the uniform of a maid, bustled out to see if there
was anything she could get them.

Maria ordered refreshments, consulting her father before
adding a bottle of Chianti to her request. Then, after handing
the basket of flowers to the girl, she gestured to Tess to take
a seat.

It was all very polite, very civilised, but Tess knew that
Castelli's daughter had not been pleased to see her. Oh,
she'd hid it well, due no doubt to her father's influence, but
Maria obviously considered Tess's presence an intrusion.

And it was, thought Tess unhappily. She should never

have agreed to come with him. It wasn't as if this trip was going to achieve anything except highlight the immense gulf between his—and Marco's—lifestyle and that of herself and Ashley.

Unless that was what he had intended to do, she reflected, resting her elbows on the table and cupping her chin in her hands. Though what influence he thought she might have on her sister, she couldn't imagine. The whole situation just got more and more bizarre and this had to be the last time she let him make her decisions for her.

He had seated himself beside her now, dropping his jacket over the back of his chair and rolling back the sleeves of his shirt over his forearms. A lean brown-skinned arm, liberally sprinkled with dark hair, rested on the table only inches from her elbow and she quickly withdrew back into her chair.

She hadn't forgotten the brush of his fingers against her thigh or the disturbing weight of the hand that had rested so briefly on her shoulder moments before. It was stupid to think it, she knew, but there'd been something almost possessive about the way he'd gripped her bones. He'd probably only done it to stop her from blurting out why they were really here, but that hadn't prevented the unsettling feeling it had given her in her stomach.

Had Maria noticed? She had certainly observed Castelli's hand resting on her shoulder and she was bound to be speculating about the kind of relationship they had. *No relationship*, Tess tried to communicate silently. This visit was far more innocent than it appeared. Maria didn't have to worry that her father was having a midlife crisis over her.

The maid returned wheeling a trolley. From within its chilled cabinet she took a jug of freshly squeezed orange juice, another of what looked like lemonade, and a squat jug of fresh cream. Riding on top of the trolley was a pot of coffee and some hand-painted cups and saucers, as well as a dish of almond biscuits and the bottle of wine Castelli had requested.

There were glasses, too, and a cut-glass vase containing a newly picked red rose still not fully in bloom. The girl placed everything on the table along with a handful of scarlet napkins, taking the trouble to set everything out so that her mistress could have no complaint, Tess was sure.

'*Grazie.*'

It was Castelli who thanked her, his infrequent smile causing her to blush with obvious pleasure. But then, he had that ability, thought Tess ruefully, to make any woman feel as if she was important. She had to remember that, too. It wouldn't do for her to think that his interest in her was anything more than self-serving.

Yet there had been that moment in the car when they'd talked more easily. He'd told her a little about his childhood and she'd explained how she'd felt when her father had died. He was easy to talk to and for a little while she'd forgotten what she was doing there and where they were going. However when his questions had become too personal she'd made the mistake of using the insect that had settled on her leg as a distraction, and suddenly she'd been painfully aware of how naïve she was.

The way he'd looked at her then had been far from impersonal. There'd been that stillness in his gaze that she'd seen once before and a frankly sensual curve to his mouth. He'd looked at her as if he was assessing what kind of partner she'd make in bed, she thought uneasily. It had been a devastating assault on her senses that had left her feeling confused and shivery and distinctly weak.

Of course moments later she'd been sure she'd imagined it. He hadn't repeated the look. In fact, he'd spent the rest of the journey in virtual silence. It hadn't helped that she hadn't been able to think of anything to say either. All she'd done was withdraw into her corner as if having a man stare at her had scared her to death.

But it was foolish to be thinking about such things here with his daughter regarding her with obvious suspicion and Castelli himself near enough to touch. Oh, God, she thought, this was getting far too complicated. She didn't want any kind of involvement, with him or anyone else.

'So, Papa,' said Maria, when the maid had departed again. 'How did you get to know Miss—er—Tess?'

'Teresa,' Castelli corrected her shortly, and Tess could only imagine the warning look he cast his daughter and which caused Maria's face to darken with colour. 'We met at the Medici Gallery, *naturalmente*. I was looking for her sister and she was not there.'

'No?' Was that a slightly uncertain note she could hear in the younger girl's voice now? Tess wondered. Whatever, Maria evidently tried to appear only casually interested. 'I did not know you were acquainted with the gallery, Papa.'

'I am not.' Castelli was sharp and to the point. 'But your brother is, *capisce?*'

Maria's jaw dropped. 'Marco?' she echoed, and Tess wondered if she was only imagining the consternation in the girl's voice now. '*Ma perché? Prego*—but why?'

'You do not know, *cara?*' There was no mistaking the censure in Castelli's tone. 'Do not lie to me, Maria. You knew of Marco's sudden interest in painting. I have heard him discussing his aspirations with you.'

'Well, yes.' Maria lifted her shoulders defensively. 'But why should I associate his interest in painting with the Medici Gallery?'

Castelli's eyes narrowed. 'You tell me.'

Maria cast a malevolent look at Tess, clearly resenting her observance of this embarrassing scene. If she could, Tess would have left the table then, just as unhappy with the situation as Maria. But she was a stranger here. She didn't even know where the restrooms were. And she was supposed to be monitoring the girl's reactions too. Did she know where her brother was or didn't she?

'I do not know what you are talking about, Papa,' Maria said at last, reaching for the jug of fruit juice and pouring some rather jerkily into an ice-filled glass. Her hand was shaking, however, and she spilled some of the orange juice onto the table. She only just managed to stifle her irritation as she snatched at a napkin to mop it up. Then, turning to Tess, she arched her brows. 'Juice or coffee?

'Juice is fine,' said Tess, not wanting to risk the chance of getting hot coffee spilled over her, deliberately or otherwise. 'Thanks.'

'Papa?'

Castelli shifted in his seat and, although she was supposed to be concentrating on their exchange, Tess flinched at the bump of his thigh against her hip. Despite her determination not to get involved with him, she couldn't help her instinctive reaction to the contact. His thigh was hard and warm and masculine, and she felt the heat his body generated spread across her abdomen and down into the moistening cleft between her legs.

She doubted he'd noticed what had happened. After all, what had happened? Just a careless brush of his leg against hers. If she was absurdly sensitive, that was her problem. Castelli was totally focussed on his daughter. She might as well not have been there.

He made an eloquent gesture now, as if having to decide what he wanted to drink was an annoying distraction. 'Chianti,' he said after a moment, nodding towards the bottle of wine the maid had left uncorked in the middle of the table. 'But you will not divert me, Maria. Marco is missing. If I find out you know where he is, I shall not forgive you.'

Maria gasped. 'What do you mean, Papa? Marco is missing? Has he run away?'

'Do not be melodramatic, Maria. I suspect you know perfectly well what is going on. But in case you have any doubts, let me enlighten you, *cara*. Your brother has gone away with Ashley Daniels, Tess's sister.'

Tess wasn't sure what Maria's reaction meant then. She was shocked, certainly, but whether that shock was the result of Marco's behaviour or because her father had found her out, it was impossible to judge.

'But—that cannot be,' she said at last, her voice a little

unsteady. 'You are saying that Marco has some interest in the woman who runs the Medici Gallery? That is ludicrous. She is far too old for him.'

Tess decided not to take offence at Maria's words. After all, she was right. Ashley was too old for Marco. They were all agreed on that. Of course, hearing the scorn in Maria's voice did make her feel ancient. But what of it? It didn't matter what Maria thought of her.

'You knew he was seeing her, *no*?'

Castelli was relentless, and Maria sighed. 'I knew he visited the gallery,' she admitted. 'But he visited a lot of galleries, Papa. He told me he was interested in art. Why should I suspect his visits to this woman's gallery meant anything more than the rest?'

'Because he told you?' suggested her father grimly. '*Vene*, Maria, I am not a fool. Marco tells you everything. If he was interested in this woman, he could not have kept it a secret from you.'

Maria looked tearful now. 'You have to believe me, Papa. Do you think I would have encouraged him to do something like this?'

'I am not saying you encouraged him,' retorted Castelli. 'I believe you are far too sensible for that. But I do think he mentioned his interest in this woman to you. To—what shall we say?—to brag about it, *force*? Did he tell you the kind of relationship they had?'

Maria sniffed. 'I do not believe it.'

'What do you not believe? That Marco could be infatuated with an older woman? Or that he would hide his true feelings from you?'

'That he could be so—so stupid!' exclaimed Maria, looking at Tess as if she were in some way to blame for this fiasco. '*Bene*, Papa, I knew that he admired this woman. But she is old. I assumed she would have more sense than to take his advances seriously.'

'*Basta!*' Castelli threw himself back in his chair, his frustration evident, and Tess shifted uncertainly as he cast an impatient glance in her direction. 'At last we have the truth. You knew of Marco's affair and you chose not to tell me.'

Maria stifled a sob. 'There was no affair, Papa. *Solo*— just a silly infatuation. If Marco has gone away, you have no reason to believe he has taken this woman with him.'

Castelli shook his head. 'We know they went together, Maria. They boarded a plane to Milano several days ago—'

'*A plane!*'

'But when the plane landed in Milano, they were not on board,' he continued. 'We suspect they disembarked at Genova. I am still hoping you can tell us why.'

Maria's lips parted. 'Me, Papa?'

Castelli nodded. 'If you have any information, any information at all, I advise you give it to me now.'

'But I do not.' Groping for one of the napkins, Maria broke down completely. With tears streaming down her cheeks, she exclaimed, 'I have told you all I know, Papa. I am as unhappy with the situation as you are.'

'*Veramente?*'

Her father did not sound sympathetic and Tess wished again that she'd passed on this trip. This was a family matter and her involvement was an intrusion. All right, she wanted to know where Ashley was, but it wasn't the matter of life and death it seemed to the Castellis.

With Rafe di Castelli seething beside her, she felt as if she couldn't get enough air and, picking up her glass, she gently eased away from the table. Crossing to the low wall that marked the boundary of the patio, she took a sip of the fruit juice, wishing she possessed the sense of well-being that had seemed so attainable before she'd left England. Now she was on edge, embarrassed, conscious that she was in some small part responsible. If she hadn't agreed to stand in for her, Ashley could never have planned this escapade.

The sound of footsteps caused her to turn in time to see another man come out of the building behind them. Not as tall as Castelli and obviously much younger, the man went straight to Maria's side and pulled her up into his arms.

'*Amatissima,*' he exclaimed, gathering her close and gazing accusingly at her father. '*Che c'e, cara. Si sente male?*'

'There is nothing wrong with her, Carlo,' declared Castelli in English, rising impatiently to his feet to face the other man. 'She is upset because her brother has disappeared and she might have been able to stop him.'

Carlo. Tess remembered the name. This obviously was Maria's husband. But his father-in-law's words had brought a frown to his fair handsome features and, despite his concern, he drew back to regard his wife's tear-stained face.

'*E vero?*'

He asked her if it was true and Maria nodded unhappily. But before she could say anything in her own defence her father intervened.

'Let me introduce you to my companion, Carlo,' he said, indicating Tess. 'Her grasp of our language is not so great. That is why we are speaking in English. Tess, this is my son-in-law, Carlo Sholti. Carlo, this is Tess Daniels. Her sister is the woman Marco has become infatuated with.'

Tess remained by the low wall, offering the young man a polite smile in greeting. She had the feeling Carlo was as curious about her presence as his wife had been earlier. But, at this point in time, Tess considered that as immaterial as her participation in this trip.

'Marco has disappeared,' put in Maria, regaining her husband's attention. 'Papa says he has gone with that woman who runs the gallery in San Michele. He thinks I should have told him they were friendly. But I had no idea Marco would do something like this.'

Carlo pressed Maria back into her chair and then turned to face Castelli. 'What is this woman's sister doing here?' he demanded, in English this time. 'Does she not know where they have gone?'

'Obviously not,' said Castelli curtly, as if he resented the implication of complicity. 'And I invited Tess to accompany me. Do you have a problem with that, Carlo, or is this the usual way you treat unexpected guests?'

Now it was Carlo's turn to look embarrassed. '*Perdone, signorina,*' he said stiffly. 'I did not mean to be rude.'

'It doesn't matter,' mumbled Tess, wishing she could just leave them to it. 'I'm sorry we've upset your wife. We're just trying to find out where my sister and your brother-in-law have gone.'

'Neatly put,' remarked Castelli drily, and meeting his eyes Tess was again reminded of how disturbingly attractive he was. Even here, with his daughter and his son-in-law watching their every move, she was supremely conscious of his maleness. And the dark colours he wore accentuated it; gave him an energy and a feline power that couldn't help but stir her blood.

'No problem,' she said at last, when it became obvious everyone was waiting for her answer. She moistened her lips. 'I think we should be going now. I—well, I've got to get back to the gallery.'

She'd half expected an argument; half hoped for one, she acknowledged uneasily, not looking forward to the journey back to San Michele. Castelli, sociable, Castelli friendly, she could handle. But Castelli impatient, Castelli angry, even, was something else.

'I think you are right, *cara.*' He chose to agree with her and she wondered if he used the endearment deliberately. He must know his daughter would resent the apparent familiarity between them. He swallowed the wine in his glass and set it carelessly back on the table. 'Much as we would have liked to join you for lunch, Maria, I agree with Tess. We should be getting back.'

'But, Papa—'

'Not now, Maria.' He was polite, but firm. 'If you think of anything else, I am just at the other end of the phone, *no*?'

'You will let us know, as soon as you have any news?'

That was Carlo, and Castelli's lips flattened against his teeth. 'If I can return the request,' he said. 'Maria may remember something she has presently forgotten.'

Both Carlo and Maria came to see them off. Maria had dried her eyes now and looked more resentful than upset. She looked on sulkily as Castelli swung open Tess's door and waited for her to seat herself before closing it again. Once again, Tess was intensely conscious of her bare legs and of how provocative her appearance must seem to the younger woman.

But she couldn't do anything about it. She just hoped Maria didn't think she had designs on her father. However attracted she might be to him, she thought she was sensible enough to know he was far beyond her reach.

As they drove away Castelli seemed absorbed in his thoughts, and Tess was glad to relax after the tensions of the last hour. Nevertheless, she found herself replaying all that had been said and she wondered if Maria was doing the same.

'Do you think I was cruel?' he asked abruptly, and Tess marvelled that he should have guessed her thoughts so exactly. 'I can see you are troubled,' he went on wryly. 'I was not very sympathetic, was I?'

Tess hesitated a moment, then she said, 'No,' in a noncommittal voice. His relationship with his daughter was nothing to do with her and she wished he wouldn't behave as if it were.

'And how would you have handled it?' he inquired, his fingers flexing on the wheel. He had very masculine hands, broad yet long-fingered. She had a momentary image of those hands brown against her white body. Of how the blunt tips of his fingers would feel caressing her quivering flesh.

Dear God!

She was still fighting to dispel those feelings when he looked at her again and she realised he was waiting for her reply. 'Um—I don't know,' she muttered. 'It's nothing to do with me.' She tried to think positively to prevent the inevitable rejoinder. 'I—er—I think she was genuinely shocked about what had happened.'

'Oh, so do I,' he concurred drily. 'I am sure Maria is

upset because Marco did not confide his plans to her. But she is also jealous of your sister.' His tawny eyes swept over her appraisingly. 'She finds it hard to accept that her brother might have needs she cannot satisfy.'

Tess felt the insidious warmth spreading up from her throat and struggled to divert the conversation. She couldn't discuss his son's sexual needs with him! 'The—er—the *albergo* was very nice,' she said, smoothing her damp palms over the hem of her shorts. Then, realising he had noticed what she was doing, she tucked her hot hands between her knees. And because the adjective she'd used was so insipid, she added, 'It must be wonderful to live in such a lovely spot.'

'I am glad you liked it,' he said at last, and she wondered if the delay was a deliberate attempt to disconcert her. If so, it had worked. 'It is a pity you did not get the chance to see more.'

'I don't think your daughter would agree with you,' murmured Tess, almost without thinking, and Castelli's brows drew together as he absorbed her words. 'I mean, I don't think she was in the mood for visitors,' she added hastily. 'She hasn't been married very long. And she does seem very young.'

'Maria is nineteen,' he told her evenly. 'And I know exactly what you meant. You think my daughter did not approve of my bringing you with me.' He shifted in his seat. 'But like my son, I too have my own life to lead.'

Tess had no answer for that. Turning her head, she stared out blankly at the fields of waving poppies that stretched inland in a colourful swath. She saw a village clinging to the hillside, and tried to be objective. But how was she supposed to deal with him? The experiences she'd had in England, infrequent as they'd been, had not prepared her for his magnetism.

Pursing her lips, she decided not to let him faze her. She was a grown woman, for heaven's sake. Not some impressionable girl who was overawed because a man had paid some attention to her. 'I expect there are many women in your life, *signore*,' she said, with amazing nonchalance. 'Someone of your experience must be very much in demand.'

The breath he expelled then conveyed a mixture of admiration and humour. 'You think?' he murmured faintly. 'And call me Rafe, if you will. Not *signore*.' He paused. 'And now you have surprised me, *cara*. I am not sure whether that was a compliment or not.'

Call him *Rafe!* Tess swallowed. She could just imagine how Maria would feel about that. 'I was merely stating the obvious,' she said, managing to avoid calling him anything. 'If Maria objected to your companion today, it was not because she'd never seen you with a woman before.'

'No?'

'No.' Now she'd started, she had to finish, and Tess inhaled a deep breath. 'I'm just different from the usual women you have dealings with. Maria was resentful because—well, because of who I am.'

'Ashley's sister,' he said mildly and she sighed.

'That's the least of it and you know it.' She paused. 'I don't fit the image of the kind of woman you obviously prefer.'

He glanced her way then, and Tess was intensely conscious of the intimacy of his gaze. 'And that image would be?' he said, causing her no small measure of uneasiness. 'Come, Tess, you cannot say something like that without elaborating. So tell me. What kind of woman do you think I like?'

She bent her head in confusion. As usual, he was determined to have the last word. 'Someone more sophisticated; someone more elegant,' she muttered at last, lifting her hands and cupping the back of her neck almost defensively. Then, exasperated, 'How do I know? I'm just guessing that your companions don't usually wear shorts.'

The car slowed then and for a moment she thought he was stopping so that he could continue the argument more forcefully. But, instead, he pulled onto a gravelled headland overlooking the beach below. There was a van parked there, too, the kind that supplied snacks and sandwiches to weary travellers, and, after turning off the engine, he said, 'I think it is time for lunch, *no*?'

CHAPTER SEVEN

RAFE could see she was surprised by his choice of venue. It made him wish he had asked his housekeeper for a packed lunch that they could have eaten in more salubrious surroundings than this. But then, he hadn't known he was going to ask Tess to join him when he'd left the villa that morning, he reflected drily. That impulse, like the impulse he had now to comb his fingers through the silky tangle of her hair, was not something he should consider repeating.

Now, however, she looked at him out of the corners of those limpid green eyes of hers and he realised she had misread his intentions. 'Do you usually patronise sandwich bars, *signore*?' she asked tightly. 'Or do you gauge your eating habits according to the sophistication of your companion?'

Rafe pulled a wry face. 'You are offended because I have not taken you to an expensive restaurant?' he queried innocently, and saw the familiar colour darken her cheeks.

'You know that's not what I meant,' she declared hotly, pushing her back against her seat. 'But if you're only stopping because of me, don't bother. I rarely eat lunch anyway. I can wait until we get back to San Michele.'

'Well, I cannot,' he retorted, pushing open his door and getting out of the car. 'And contrary to popular supposition, plenty of good food can be found at roadside kiosks, *no*?'

'I can't see you eating a burger, *signore*,' said Tess, pushing open her own door and joining him. The brilliant noonday sun immediately burned on her uncovered head and shoulders, and she caught her breath. 'Goodness, it's hot!'

Rafe studied her bare arms with some concern. 'Perhaps

you should stay in the car,' he said, resisting the desire to smooth his fingers over her soft skin. 'It is cooler there.'

'What? And miss the chance to see what the chef has on offer?' she asked lightly, and his pulse quickened at the unexpected humour in her face.

'Okay.' He saw her looking at the curving line of the shoreline that fell away below the promontory. 'Let us get something to eat and drink and find somewhere more private to enjoy it, *no*?'

Tess caught her breath. 'You mean, go down to the beach?' she asked, viewing the precipitate descent with some concern. 'Isn't it too steep?'

'Do not tell me you are afraid of heights, *cara*.' He teased her mercilessly. 'Where is your sense of adventure?'

Tess shook her head. 'I don't think I have one, *signore*,' she murmured unhappily. 'But—if you can do it—'

'An old man like me, you mean?' he queried wryly, and she turned to give him an impatient look.

'You're not old, *signore*,' she protested, and he sighed at her continued use of the formal means of address.

'Then why do you persist in calling me *signore*?' he countered, his eyes intent on her flushed face. 'You know my name, Tess. Use it.'

'I—I don't think I should call you Rafe,' she exclaimed, and he had the impression that she found it difficult to drag her gaze away from his.

'Why not?'

He couldn't prevent himself from pursuing it and this time she succeeded in breaking the connection. 'Because— well, just because,' she mumbled lamely. Then, in an effort to divert him, she added, 'Oughtn't we to choose a sandwich or something? The owner will think we've just stopped here for the view.'

'Works for me,' murmured Rafe before he could stop himself, and she cast one astonished look in his direction before moving away towards the van.

Rafe was pleased to see that the man who ran the booth

was offering cheese-filled *panini* and steaming slices of pizza as well as the more common *tramezzini* or sandwiches. There were ready-made salads, too, in foil-wrapped containers, and spicy *bruschetta*, spread with olive or tomato paste.

It was obvious Tess didn't know what to choose, so he took it upon himself to place two orders for pizza and salad, and a slice each of *tiramisu* for dessert. Sealed cups of black coffee completed the meal and he was aware that Tess looked at him rather doubtfully as he carried his purchases back to the car.

'I—how do you propose to carry all that?' she asked, and he remembered that she still thought he intended to scale the cliff to reach the beach.

'You will see,' he said, opening the boot of the Ferrari and putting the bags and containers inside. He smiled to himself at the thought of what his mother would think of him—as she would put it—abusing the automobile in this way. Tess hadn't been far wrong. He wasn't in the habit of eating the food from roadside kiosks. But that was not to say he wasn't going to enjoy it this time.

Tess was frowning now, and circling the car, he swung open her door. 'Get in, *per favore*.'

Tess hesitated. 'I thought you said—'

'Just get in,' he urged her softly, and, although he could see the uncertainty in her face, she was too polite to refuse.

He watched as she swung her legs inside, assuring himself he was only waiting to close the door when in his heart of hearts he knew he had a more personal reason. He enjoyed watching her, enjoyed disconcerting her. However much he might regret his impetuosity tomorrow, for today he intended to live each minute as it came.

A moment later, he slid in beside her, instantly aware of the feminine aroma of her heated skin. It was a disturbing scent, unfamiliar and definitely sensual. It aroused him as nothing had that he could remember, and the urge to touch her was almost overwhelming.

But he controlled himself, consigning the insistent pull of attraction to the back of his mind. All right, he sensed she was aware of him, too, but she'd probably run a mile if he acted on it. Apart from anything else, they hardly knew one another. So why did he feel as if he'd known her for half his life?

Casting her a brief half-smile, he started the car and drove away from the headland. But not far. Just a few yards further on, a winding track almost overhung with wild bramble and juniper dipped away from the coastal road. Anyone who didn't know it was there would never have noticed it, particularly at this time of the year when the blossom was out.

He was aware that Tess had turned to stare at him now and he guessed what she was thinking before she spoke. 'You never had any intention of climbing down the cliff, did you?' she exclaimed, but her tone was more relieved than accusing. Then as the car swung round a hairpin bend she groped for the edge of her seat. 'Is this road going somewhere or are we likely to get stuck halfway down?'

'Relax, *cara*,' he said, taking a hand from the wheel to briefly touch her knee. 'I know what I am doing.'

But did he? he wondered as he withdrew from that strangely intimate connection. Once again, he had acted on impulse and now her gaze was decidedly uncertain as it darted away from his.

'I hope so,' she mumbled almost under her breath, but he heard her and chided himself for causing more tension between them. He'd intended this to be a light-hearted interlude before he returned her to Porto San Michele, but he was in danger of creating problems that might be far harder to deal with than Marco's boyish infatuation for her sister.

The track narrowed as it neared the bottom of the cliffs and he winced as the untamed bushes scraped along the sides of the car. A mistake in more ways than one, he thought ruefully, but that didn't stop him from feeling an ungovernable sense of anticipation at spending a little longer in Tess's company.

As he'd hoped, the shallow plateau above the beach was deserted. There was just room enough to turn the car and his satisfaction at their seclusion was only equalled by his relief that his memory of the place hadn't been faulty.

And it was just as beautiful as he remembered. The untouched stretch of beach was enclosed on either side by a rocky promontory, and the sand was as pure and untouched as when the cove was formed. At the shoreline, waves broke into rivulets of foam, and beyond the dazzling brilliance of the sea the sky rose, a cloudless arc of blue above. They could have been alone on some desert island were it not for the sails of a yacht heading far out towards the horizon.

Tess thrust open her door as soon as he stopped the car. Getting out, she walked to the edge of the turning area and lifted both hands to protect the top of her head. He wondered what she was thinking as she stared out to sea. He hoped she wasn't regretting coming with him. For the first time in more years than he cared to calculate, he was enjoying himself and he didn't want anything to spoil it.

But he had been sitting there too long watching her, and when she glanced back over her shoulder he saw the doubt in her eyes. He at once opened his door and, pushing his feet out onto the sun-baked earth, he crossed the space that divided them.

'I suppose you knew this was here,' she said as he joined her. Then, turning back to the view, she added somewhat wistfully, 'It is a marvellous place.'

'You like it?' He was pleased. 'Thankfully, it has not yet been discovered by the tourists.'

'Down that track?' A smile was in her voice. 'I dread to think what you've done to your car.'

'It is only a car,' he assured her mildly. 'If it needs a paint job, then so be it.'

Tess shook her head. 'You say that so casually. Most people have to take care of their possessions.'

Rafe sighed, realising he had been careless. 'Perhaps I measure my possessions differently, *cara*,' he said softly.

'People are more important to me than—what shall I say?—pretty toys, *no*?'

She shrugged and as she did so he noticed how the sun had already tinged the skin of her upper arms with a rosy glow. She would burn easily, he thought, the knowledge increasing the sense of protection he already felt towards her. He wanted to—

But, no. He was already getting ahead of himself and, turning back to the car, he collected the bags containing their lunch from the boot. 'Come,' he said, stepping into the tangle of reeds and grasses that bordered the plateau. 'We can have lunch in the shade of the cliffs, yes?'

'Okay.'

He saw her give another glance back towards the car before she followed him down onto the sand. Then, kicking off her shoes, she seemed to relax, and by the time he had spread his jacket for them to sit on she was right behind him.

'I know,' he said as she dropped her shoes beside her. 'This will not do my jacket any good either. But in this instance, it can be cleaned.'

'If you say so.'

Apparently deciding she had no choice than to trust him, she seated herself at the edge of the jacket, drawing up her knees and wrapping her arms about them. Rafe dropped down beside her, trying not to stare at the smooth flesh disappearing into the cuffs of her shorts. Imagining what lay beneath the pink cotton was not only unforgivable, it was stupid, and he distracted himself by opening the bags and containers and setting them out between them.

'What would you like to eat?' he asked, when Tess seemed to be more interested in the tiny shells that dotted the sand at her feet than the food. 'Salad? Pizza?'

'What? Oh—' He was suddenly sure she was only pretending not to have noticed what he'd been doing. 'Um—salad sounds good.'

He met her wary gaze with a deliberately neutral stare. 'Only salad?'

She shifted a little awkwardly. 'Well—maybe a slice of pizza, too,' she agreed, accepting the salad container from his hand. 'Thanks. This looks good.'

'I hope so.' He helped himself to a slice of the pizza and bit into it with feigned enthusiasm. The tomato juice oozed onto his chin and he grabbed a napkin to wipe it away. 'Hmm. *Molto bene.*'

'I'm sure you're only saying that,' she murmured, forking a curl of radicchio into her mouth. 'But it was kind of you to do this. I appreciate it.'

'I did not do it out of kindness.' Rafe was stung by the implication that there could be no other reason for him to want her company. He swallowed another mouthful of pizza, licking the melted cheese from his lips before continuing tersely, 'It is I who should thank you for accompanying me to Viali.'

Tess hesitated. 'I don't know why,' she said at last. 'It would have been easier for everyone if I hadn't been there.'

'I think we covered that some miles back.' Rafe was impatient. 'Can we not forget the reasons why we started out on this expedition and concentrate on the here and now? Are you not enjoying yourself, is that what all this is about?'

Tess cast a brief glance his way. 'All what?' she queried tensely and he blew out a weary breath.

'You know,' he told her flatly. 'Ever since we left the *albergo*, you have been as—as jumpy as a cat. What did I do? What have I said to upset you?'

'Nothing.'

The answer came far too quickly and Rafe thrust his pizza aside and got abruptly to his feet. 'If you would care to finish your salad in the car, we can leave immediately.'

'No.' That answer came quickly, too, but this time it was accompanied by an embarrassed glance at his face. 'Please, I didn't mean to annoy you. It's just—well, I'm sure there are places you'd much rather be than here.'

'And if there are not?'

Her tongue appeared between her teeth and he felt the sudden tightness in his loins as she wet her lips. 'You're sure you're not just saying that?'

'No.' He hunkered down beside her, one hand moving of its own accord to cup her cheek. He tilted her face to his. 'Believe me, *cara*, at this moment there is no place I would rather be than here.' His eyes darkened as they rested on her mouth. But only for a second. He was on dangerous ground, he realised, aware of what he really wanted to do. Withdrawing his hand abruptly, he got to his feet again, looking down at her. '*Bene,*' he said tensely. 'Enjoy the rest of your meal. I will not be long.'

Her eyes widened. 'Where are you going?'

Rafe stifled a groan. He wondered how she would react if he told her the truth. That he was desperate to put some space between them before he did something unforgivable. He didn't just want to stroke her cheek or make casual conversation as they'd done in the car. He wanted to put his tongue where hers had been a few moments ago, to cover her mouth with his and find a partial release of his frustration in a kiss.

'I thought I might take a walk,' he offered at last. 'I need to stretch my legs.' *And cool my libido.*

Tess's eyes moved from his constrained features to the undulating water and he glimpsed the wistful look that crossed her face. But, 'Okay,' was all she said and it was left to Rafe to feel a heel for behaving so callowly. He'd brought her here, *per amor di Dio*. It wasn't her fault that he couldn't control his rampant desires.

'*Io*—come with me. If you wish,' he said, before he could stop himself, and she sprang eagerly to her feet.

'You don't mind?' she asked, dropping the carton containing the remains of her salad onto the sand. He gave a faint smile of acquiescence. It seemed the decision had been made and he would have to live with it. It wasn't as if he wanted to leave her alone.

Tess left her shoes with the rest of their belongings, practically skipping across the sand to dip her toes in the cooler waters of the gulf. She shivered dramatically, laughing as the incoming tide swirled about her ankles. She was like a child, he thought ruefully. As natural and uninhibited as his own children had been before adolescence, and their mother's desertion, had had such an impact on all their lives.

'Oh, this is heavenly,' Tess said, linking her fingers together and stretching her arms above her head in obvious delight. 'Thank you so much for bringing me.'

'I am happy you are enjoying yourself,' he said politely, forcing himself not to linger. He was quite sure she was unaware of the effect she had on him but it was far too easy to imagine his hands circling that deliciously bare midriff as he tumbled her onto the sand.

Unknowingly, he had quickened his step and by the time he realised it and glanced over his shoulder Tess was some distance behind him. She was following much more slowly, splashing through the shallows, her delight in her surroundings apparently dissipated by his indifference. Once again he felt the familiar pangs of guilt. It wasn't fair of him to spoil the day for her.

Despite his reluctance, he waited for her to catch up with him, but now she wouldn't meet his gaze. She halted beside him, her eyes seemingly glued to the yacht that was now disappearing over the horizon. She had obviously sensed his ambivalence and misread the reasons for it.

'What is wrong?' he asked, as if he genuinely didn't know. 'It is very hot, is it not? Have you had enough?'

'Have you?'

Her retort caught him unawares and he didn't have an answer for her. 'It is—getting late,' he said lamely, although it was barely three o'clock. 'I would not want you to get burned.'

She lifted first one arm and then the other, looking at them as if she hadn't considered them before. But she didn't look convinced. Despite the fact that the skin of her shoulders looked slightly sore, she gave a careless shrug. 'Perhaps you're right,' she said without conviction. 'If it's what you want.'

Rafe stiffened. 'What I want does not signify.'

'Oh, I think it does.' He caught a glimpse of indignant green eyes, quickly averted. 'I should have realised before. When you said you were going for a walk. You didn't really want me to come with you, did you?'

'*Io*—' Rafe was nonplussed. He hadn't realised he had been so transparent. 'That is not true.'

'I don't believe you, *signore*.' She used the term deliberately, he was sure, and it infuriated him. 'All this—buying the food, bringing me down here—was just a way of appeasing your conscience.'

Rafe's jaw dropped. 'Appeasing my conscience?' he echoed, stung by the accusation. 'Why should I feel the need to appease my conscience? I have not done anything wrong.'

Yet.

'You feel as if you have,' said Tess doggedly, and for a moment he wondered if she'd read what he was thinking. He hoped not. And, to his relief, she seemed to confirm it. 'You think you've upset both your daughter and me,' she continued. 'So you decided to pacify one of us with a peace-offering. In this case, an hour of your precious time, right?'

'Wrong.' He was annoyed by the objectivity of her reasoning. Not least, because it was so far removed from the truth. 'When I invited you to have lunch with me, it was because I wanted to. Not for any other reason.'

'So why do you want to cut the afternoon short?' she asked impulsively. 'Am I keeping you from some important previous engagement?'

'No.' His breath gushed out in a rush. 'I am sorry if I have given you that impression.'

'Well, what else can I think when you seem determined to avoid me?' she countered, looking up at him now with a wary, uncertain gaze. 'You seem to—to blow hot and cold in equal measures. I—well, I don't know how you really feel.'

Rafe's good sense deserted him. 'I was not trying to avoid you,' he said huskily. 'If it seemed that I was—and I am admitting nothing, you understand?—perhaps it was because I find you far too—appealing, *no*?'

He'd shocked her now. He could see it in the face that she turned up to him. But, what the hell, he'd shocked himself, and that was far more disturbing.

'You don't mean that,' she said, and he knew that this was his last opportunity to escape the consequences of his outburst. He had only to tell her he was teasing and he might be able to get out of this unscathed.

But he didn't do it.

'I do mean it,' he said, the words coming even though his brain was trying desperately to silence him. 'You are— enchanting. And beautiful. And I would not be a man if I did not find you desirable, *mi amore*.'

Her lips parted then, and, although he sensed she was as uncertain of the good sense of what they were doing as he was, she didn't move away. Instead, she came a little nearer, her toes brushing the front of his loafers, those clear green eyes keenly searching his face. Almost involuntarily, it seemed, she lifted her hand and stroked the roughening skin of his jawline, and Rafe could no longer control the instinctive hardening between his legs.

'So—do you want to kiss me?' she breathed barely audibly, and the quicksands of passion moved beneath his feet.

'Tess—' he said hoarsely, and even then he thought he might have found the will to resist her. Yet when her hand dropped to the open neckline of his shirt and he felt those tentative fingers against his bare skin, he totally lost it. The groan he uttered was purely anguished, and his hands found her shoulders to haul her into his arms.

Her lips were already parted, inviting the hungry invasion of his tongue. He didn't disappoint her. One hand moved to grip her nape, angling her face towards him as his mouth

fastened greedily over hers. His kiss both enticed and seduced, drawing a response from her that sent his head spinning. He felt his own gnawing hunger controlling his actions
as his senses whirled out of control.

Her arms wound around him, her palms spreading against
the damp curve of his spine. She must have been able to
feel the heavy weight of his erection throbbing against her
stomach but she didn't recoil from him. When his hand
cupped her buttocks, bringing her into intimate contact with
his arousal, she arched against him, letting him feel how
responsive she also was to his touch.

A sexy little moan emerged from lips that were already
wet and swollen from his kisses and his conscience resurfaced. *Dio mio*, he thought, if he didn't stop this soon he
would go all the way. He was in real danger of acting out
the images that had been taunting him all morning, and
while he couldn't deny he wanted her, she was simply not
for him.

She was too young, for one thing, and she probably saw
this as just a pleasant adjunct to her holiday. She'd had a
tough time of it so far, what with Ashley's disappearance
and her stepmother breathing down her neck. Not to mention his own less-than-subtle hints about what he thought of
her family. He wasn't conceited, but he could quite see that
having him lusting after her might offer some compensation.
Particularly if, as seemed likely, she had little experience
with older men.

His own feelings were less straightforward. And however
tempting making love with her might be, he still had enough
sense to step back from the ultimate betrayal. He could do
without any more complications in his life, he thought cyn-
ically. From his point of view, it would be a recipe for
disaster.

Which was why, when he lifted his mouth from hers, he
didn't succumb to the urge to slide his hands beneath the
hem of her tank top and let his thumbs caress the undersides
of her breasts. He wanted to. *Dio*, he wanted to feel her pert

nipples taut against his palms and to take those firm mounds of flesh into his hands. Instead, stifling a groan, he gripped her forearms and put her gently away from him, feeling every kind of a heel for having led her on in the first place.

Her confusion was obvious and he couldn't blame her. He hadn't been able to hide his body's reaction to her and in her book there was probably only one conclusion to this affair. But when he met her troubled gaze with eyes that were deliberately regretful, she soon got the message. She took a stumbling backward step before turning and hurrying away along the beach.

'*Cara!*' He couldn't use her name, that would be too familiar. '*Cara,*' he called again. 'I am sorry. I do not know what came over me.'

She muttered something then, but she was too far away for him to hear it. But he could imagine it wouldn't be complimentary and who could blame her? He had behaved abominably and she deserved so much better. She was bound to think he had as little respect for her as he had for her sister.

CHAPTER EIGHT

THE wind chimes woke her.

Tess had thought that she wouldn't sleep, but surprisingly enough she'd fallen into a deep slumber as soon as her head touched the pillow. Perhaps it had been the heat or the tiring quality of the journey, she mused, rolling onto her back and staring up at the dust motes dancing in the rays of sun seeping through the blinds into the bedroom. Or more likely it had been the stress, she thought bitterly, as the remembrance of the previous day's events hit her. Oh, God, she had behaved so stupidly. And that after the embarrassment she'd suffered at Maria Sholti's hands.

Pushing herself up into a sitting position, Tess rested her elbows on her knees and pushed frustrated hands into her hair. The whole outing had been a mistake, from start to finish. Castelli should never have taken her with him, and, just because he had, she shouldn't have run away with the idea that he was attracted to her.

How had that happened? All right, he'd given her some pretty smouldering looks, but he was an Italian, for God's sake. Italians were supposed to be the most romantic race in the world, weren't they? She'd obviously read more into it than he could possibly have meant. She should have been on her guard. After that scene at the Sholtis' hotel, she should have been wary of any uncharacteristic behaviour on his part. A man who could treat his daughter so coldly was surely not to be trusted.

Yet what had happened on the beach hadn't been entirely her fault, she consoled herself. She'd provoked him, yes, and he'd responded. It had been as simple—and as complicated—as that. She should have let him take his walk alone.

She should never have tagged along. If she'd stayed and finished her salad she wouldn't be berating herself now.

And she wouldn't be facing the ignominy of further humiliation when she saw him again.

If she saw him again, she amended, though she really had little expectation that she wouldn't. Ashley was still missing; Marco was still missing. And until that particular problem was solved, she was going to have to live with it. And with him.

She threw back the sheet and slid her legs off the bed. Sitting here brooding about it wasn't going to achieve anything. The gallery wouldn't open itself, and, despite her anger with Ashley, she had promised to look after the place in her absence.

All the same, as she stood in the shower she couldn't help reliving the agony of the ride home. Although Castelli had attempted to restore their earlier camaraderie, he had been fighting a losing battle where she was concerned. Her own responses had been monosyllabic, she remembered, cringing at the way she'd blocked his every overture. She'd let him see exactly how hurt she'd been, and he must have been so relieved when they'd reached San Michele and he'd been able to drop her at the gallery. She'd probably convinced him she was no better than Ashley, after all. He no doubt considered he had had a lucky escape.

With thoughts like these for company, Tess didn't spend long in the shower. Towelling herself dry, she contented herself with running a comb through her hair before dressing in a lemon chemise top and a green and blue Indian cotton skirt. Canvas boots completed her outfit and, after viewing herself without enthusiasm in the mirror of the carved armoire where Ashley kept her clothes, Tess left the apartment.

The morning passed, thankfully without incident. The only visitor she had who wasn't a would-be customer was Silvio and he seemed to find nothing amiss with her appearance.

'*Cara,*' he exclaimed, his use of the familiar endearment reminding her painfully of Castelli, 'how are you today? You are feeling better, *spero*?'

'Better?' Tess frowned. 'I'm afraid I don't understand.'

'*Mas, ieri,*' said Silvio, wide eyed. 'Yesterday. You close the gallery early, *no*? *Naturalmente*, I think you are not well.'

'Oh.' Tess felt her face heat. 'Um—yes. I did close early. You're right. But—' she couldn't tell an outright lie '—it wasn't because I was ill.'

'No?' Silvio gave her an inquiring look and she knew she had to elaborate.

'No.' She paused. 'I—it was such a lovely day, I decided to—to take a little time off.'

'Ah.' Silvio regarded her with narrowed eyes. 'And you enjoyed this—this time off?'

No.

'Very much,' she said, deciding one white lie was in order. And then, to distract him, 'Isn't it hot today? I've got the fan going but it just seems to be moving the air around.'

'It is warm air,' he pointed out drily, and she wondered if he was entirely satisfied with her reply. 'So, do you have any plans for lunch?'

'Lunch?' Tess had the feeling she would never want to eat lunch again. 'Oh—no.' Then, realising what was coming next, 'I'm too busy to think about lunch. Taking time off is all very well, but it just means the work piles up in your absence.'

Silvio glanced about him at the empty gallery. 'It does not seem so busy to me.'

'Oh, it's paperwork,' said Tess, realising she was having to lie again. 'Honestly, you'd be surprised at the number of enquiries Ashley gets about this or that artist. And then there are the bills…'

'In other words you do not wish to have lunch with me,' remarked Silvio flatly. 'You do not have to—if you will forgive the pun—draw me a picture, Tess. It is obvious some other man has—what do you say?—beaten me to it, *no*? Who is he, eh? Do I know him?'

'No!' Tess spoke impulsively and then, realising her words could easily be misconstrued, she hastily amended her answer. 'That is, there is no other man, Silvio. Um— not here, anyway,' she added, her face burning with embarrassment. 'I just can't keep taking time off, that's all. It wouldn't be fair to—to Signor Scottolino.'

Silvio shrugged. 'As you say.'

'I'm sorry.'

'*Sì. Anch'io, cara.*' Me, too. He gave her a small, strangely knowing smile. 'Do not work too hard, *ragazza*. All work and no play is not good, *no*? *Ciao!*'

Tess breathed a sigh of relief as he disappeared through the open doorway and, deciding she'd earned a strong cup of black coffee, she went to put water into the pot. But she couldn't help wondering if Silvio's visit had been as innocent as he'd pretended. Could he possibly have seen her leaving with Castelli the day before?

Of course he could, but if he had there was nothing she could do about it now. And, besides, she had a perfectly legitimate excuse for the outing if she was asked. But she wouldn't be. Silvio had said his piece and no one else was interested. Except Maria and her husband, she amended. And they knew nothing about what had happened after she and Castelli had left the *albergo*.

Thank goodness!

By midday Tess was feeling a little more relaxed. Her fears that Castelli might decide to pay her another unexpected visit had not been realised, and, with her stomach reminding her that she'd not had any breakfast that morning, she decided to slip out to the bakery to buy a sandwich for her lunch.

She'd only closed the gallery for a few minutes. The bakery wasn't far. But when she came hurrying back along the parade of shops she saw a woman trying the door with obvious impatience. With the blinds pulled up, it appeared that the gallery was open, and Tess thought it was just her luck that a customer had arrived in the short time she'd been away.

'*Mi scusi,*' she called, reaching the woman just as she was turning away. The woman turned back and Tess saw she was older than she'd thought. '*Eccomi, signora. Posso aiutare?*' Can I help you?

Dark brows arched aristocratically over equally dark eyes. The woman was tall and exquisitely dressed in a taupe silk suit and high heels. Because of her height, she towered over Tess, her whole manner one of undisguised condescension.

Yet for all that, there was something familiar about her. Tess knew she'd never seen the woman before but the annoying sense of familiarity remained. Tess had barely registered the fact that she reminded her of Maria Castelli when the woman spoke, and her words gave substance to the thought.

'Miss Daniels, *e*?' she inquired coldly, looking down her long nose at Tess in a manner intended to intimidate. 'Ah, *sì*. You recognise the name. Let us go inside, Miss Daniels. I desire to speak to you.'

'All right.' Tess was too taken aback by this turn of events to offer any resistance and she unlocked the door and allowed the older woman to precede her into the gallery. Then, gathering herself, she said, a little less submissively, 'Do we know one another, *signora*?'

The woman didn't immediately proffer a reply. Instead, she stood in the centre of the floor surveying the paintings that lined the walls with evident dislike. They were not all good paintings, Tess acknowledged, but some of them weren't at all bad. They didn't deserve the contempt with which they were being regarded. Her visitor was acting as if they were little better than trash.

Or perhaps she'd got it wrong, she mused suddenly. Perhaps it was she whom the woman considered to be trash. That would fit if she was some relation of Maria Castelli— or rather Maria *Sholti*. And despite the relief she'd felt at

Castelli's non-appearance, now she felt a growing sense of resentment that he should have sent this woman in his place.

The woman swung round at last. 'I know *of* you, Miss Daniels,' she said, and Tess had to remind herself of what she'd asked moments before. 'My son has spoken of you to me. I am Lucia di Castelli.' She said the name arrogantly. 'The boy your sister has corrupted is my grandson.'

Tess caught her breath. So this was Castelli's mother. She should have guessed. The similarity wasn't totally confined to his daughter.

But Castelli wasn't going to help her now and, holding up her head, she said stiffly, 'We don't know that Ashley has done anything of the kind.'

'Oh, I think we do, *signorina*.' Lucia was scornful. 'I cannot think of any other reason why a woman approaching thirty should encourage the attentions of an impressionable child, can you?'

'Marco's hardly a child,' protested Tess indignantly. 'In England, boys of sixteen can be quite—mature.'

'And there you have it, Miss Daniels.' Lucia's lips curled. 'As you say, in England things are very different indeed. Young single women think nothing of having a child—children—with several different partners. Marriage is considered an outdated institution and the church's teachings are ignored. That is not how things are done in Italy, Miss Daniels. Here we respect our institutions, we respect our elders. And we expect visitors to our country to do the same.'

Tess licked her dry lips. 'You paint a very unattractive picture of my country, *signora*,' she said, keeping her voice calm with a definite effort. 'But I can assure you that we are not a totally godless society. As with everything, the truth lies somewhere in between.'

Lucia snorted. 'You would say that, *naturalmente*.'

'Yes, I would.' Tess gained a little confidence from the fact that the woman didn't immediately contradict her. 'We are not heathens, *signora*. And how honest is it for a woman to marry one man and have an affair with another? Is that considered acceptable in Italy?'

A faint trace of colour entered Lucia's cheeks at her words. 'You have been speaking to Rafe, have you not?' she demanded harshly, shocking Tess by the vehemence of her tone. 'Of course you have. That is why he is so—so *sensibile* to your feelings. He sees in you a justification for his own actions.'

'No!' Tess was horrified. She'd spoken impulsively, never thinking that Castelli's mother might associate her words with her son's divorce. 'I mean, yes, I've spoken to your son, *signora*. You know that. He thought I might know where Ashley was.'

'But you do not?'

'No.' Tess was polite, but firm.

'Did my son tell you that he has spoken with his daughter, also?' Lucia continued. 'Maria is married and lives in Viali, some distance from here.'

The query seemed innocent enough at face value, but Tess was wary. Was it possible that Lucia di Castelli knew she had accompanied her son the day before? Had he told her? Had Maria? And if not, how was she supposed to answer that?

'He—I—yes, I knew,' she mumbled at last, unwilling to venture further. Besides, why shouldn't Castelli have mentioned that she'd gone to Viali with him? With certain abstentions in his narrative, of course.

She took a deep breath and then was relieved when a young couple came into the gallery. They were obviously holiday-makers and she doubted they intended to buy anything. But her visitor didn't know that.

'Was there a reason for your visit, *signora*?' she asked, indicating the newcomers. 'Because if not, I have customers. If you hoped I might have any more information than I've given your son, then I'm afraid I must disappoint you.'

Lucia's lips tightened. 'I think you know more than you

are saying, Miss Daniels. Unlike my son, I am not beguiled by a sympathetic manner and a pretty face!'

Tess was taken aback by her rudeness and she glanced awkwardly about her wondering if their exchange could be heard by anyone else. But to her relief the young couple had moved to the farthest side of the gallery and she thought it was unlikely that they'd noticed anything amiss.

'I think you'd better go, *signora*,' she said in a low voice, refusing to humour her any longer. 'I'm working and I'm sure you have better things to do than stand here wasting my time. I'm sorry about your grandson, I really am. But there's nothing I can do about it. Ashley didn't confide in me before she took off.'

Lucia's nostrils flared, and for a moment Tess expected another rebuke. But then, amazingly, the woman's haughty arrogance crumbled, and with a gesture of defeat she pulled a handkerchief out of her purse.

Tess didn't know which was worse, having Castelli's mother berating her as an accomplice or breaking down in front of her. Tears were streaming down the woman's face now and she was obviously distressed. Any moment Tess's customers were going to notice and, despite herself, she couldn't allow that to happen.

With a feeling of resignation, she took Lucia by the arm and led her back into the office. Then, after seating her at Ashley's desk, she indicated the small bathroom. 'You can rest here,' she said. 'Come out when you're feeling better. No one will disturb you. I'll see to that.'

As she'd suspected, the young couple had no intention of buying anything, and she had to acknowledge that Signor Scottolino had a point. Since she'd been looking after the gallery, she'd sold a grand total of three paintings, which was clearly not enough profit to pay the bills.

It was another fifteen minutes before she remembered her sandwich. She'd put it down as she was talking to Signora di Castelli and now she saw it wilting in the noonday heat. She would have liked to have gone into the office and made herself some fresh coffee. Signora di Castelli might even like one. Although, remembering her son's reaction when he'd tried the filtered brew, she couldn't guarantee it.

However, she'd told the woman she wouldn't be disturbed and she kept her promises. It was obviously going to take a little time for Lucia to compose herself again. Until then, Tess contented herself with straightening the pictures, picking up a leaf that had blown through the open doorway, and adjusting the blinds to limit the sunlight.

After half an hour had gone by, however, she was beginning to get anxious. All sorts of thoughts ran through her head, not least the worry that Lucia might do something desperate in her grief. Which was silly, she knew. The situation was not that serious. They might not know exactly where Marco was, but if he was with Ashley, he could hardly come to any harm.

Or could he? Tess supposed it depended what your interpretation of harm was. As far as Lucia was concerned, Ashley was little better than a baby-snatcher. The fact that Marco sounded like a precocious teenager seemed to mean nothing to her.

At the end of forty-five minutes, Tess was desperate. All right, she'd promised not to disturb the woman, but that was ages ago now. Squaring her shoulders, she picked up her sandwich and went to the half-open door of the office. 'Signora di Castelli,' she said, pushing it wider. 'Are you feeling better?'

She needn't have bothered with the softly-softly approach. The office was empty. While she'd been fretting in the gallery, Lucia must have let herself out of the back exit. So much for Tess worrying about her. She had evidently dried her eyes and made herself scarce.

Tess didn't know whether she felt relieved or resentful. She was glad the woman had gone, of course, but she might have asked her permission to use the back door. As it was, it was standing ajar and Tess went to close it. It would have been all the same if she'd had valuable paintings on the premises. With the alarm turned off, a thief could have had a field-day.

A check of her bag assured her that there'd been no intruders in her absence. Her passport was still there and the several hundred Euros she'd brought for the trip. She frowned suddenly. She could have sworn her passport had been in the side pocket of her backpack as it had been when Castelli had asked to see it. But now it resided in the main compartment alongside her wallet-purse.

She shrugged. She must have made a mistake when she'd put it away. She hadn't needed it for the last couple of days so she couldn't be absolutely sure which compartment she'd put it in. Castelli had got her so flustered, she might have put it anywhere. In any case, so long as she had it, that was the important thing.

She spent a couple of minutes emptying the coffee-pot and refilling the reservoir. Then, after putting several spoonfuls of ready-ground coffee into the filter, she sat down at the desk to have her sandwich.

It wasn't very appetising. Having waited for almost an hour, it was definitely dry. Thankfully it was cheese. She was afraid any meat would have proved inedible. Even so, if she hadn't been so hungry, she might have put it into the bin.

As she drank her coffee she idly opened the drawers of the desk. She was not really looking for anything, but she was still conscious of the doubts she'd had before. Once again, she was fairly sure nothing was missing, and as she'd riffled through the drawers herself days ago, looking for any clues to Ashley's whereabouts, she wasn't really surprised when she found nothing useful now.

The niggling doubts remained, though, and she wondered if Lucia di Castelli had searched the office before she'd left. It would explain the discrepancy about her passport. And perhaps explain the reason why she'd left without saying goodbye. Though, remembering Castelli's mother, Tess doubted whether she'd care if she offended her. Until her emotions had got the better of her, she'd been doing a fairly good job of making Tess feel she was equally to blame.

It was a long afternoon. She had a couple more customers, one of whom actually bought a painting of the pretty resort of Portofino further up the coast. The other was a young Frenchman, who was evidently on holiday. His main interest was in flirting with Tess, and she guessed Ashley had enjoyed this aspect of her job.

But she didn't. She was in no mood to be flattered and she became impatient when he refused to go. She eventually resorted to blackmail, picking up the phone and threatening to call *la polizia*. She wouldn't have, of course, but thankfully her ploy was successful.

She closed the gallery early, not wanting to risk Silvio coming round to offer her dinner. She couldn't help thinking she'd never been so popular in her life. Of course, at home her work kept her busy and the men with whom she worked were not her type. Those that weren't married were often too boyish. Her friend, Maggie, always said they were like overgrown school kids themselves.

Tess had only had one real relationship and that had been with a boy she'd met at college. They'd kept in touch for a couple of years afterwards, but Tess's moving to Derbyshire had put paid to their affair. He'd eventually written that he'd found someone else, and Tess remembered she had been more relieved than sorry. Maybe she just wasn't cut out to find a partner, she thought as she drove back to Ashley's apartment. The quintessential schoolmistress, that was her.

An image of herself and Castelli on the beach flashed into her mind, but she quickly pushed it away. Apart from the fact that she'd initiated that encounter, it was obvious he'd only been humouring her. He was a virile man and perhaps he'd been flattered at a younger woman coming on to him. Even if he'd felt sorry for her, and that was not an alternative she wanted to consider, it hadn't been hard for him to fake a convincing response.

He'd certainly convinced her, she thought bitterly. Her

stomach still quivered at the memory of the feelings he had aroused inside her. She could still taste his kiss, still feel the heat of his tongue in her mouth. She knew he'd been physically aroused. That was something he hadn't been able to hide. Yet even so, he'd found it easy to pull away.

And that hurt. She couldn't understand how he'd been able to turn off his emotions like a switch. Or perhaps his emotions hadn't been involved. She'd obviously been wrong to think he'd been as eager as she had. While she'd been anticipating how exciting making love with him would be, he'd had an entirely different agenda.

But what agenda? If he hadn't avoided the subject of Ashley all the way back to San Michele, she'd have suspected that finding her sister had still been his principal concern. He could have thought that seducing her might produce some hitherto unspoken confession. That she'd be so bemused by his lovemaking, she'd betray any confidence she'd been given.

But she'd been wrong about that, too. While she'd been aching with longings now suppressed, Castelli had spoken of his interest in wine, and the grape harvest, and how lots of people were leaving the towns to start a new life in the country. He'd behaved as if nothing untoward had happened, as if he was totally unaware of how she was feeling.

She was sure she'd never forgive him for that. Being rejected was one thing; being ignored was something else. But, with Ashley's example to follow, what had she expected? Castelli didn't want anything more from her than information. He didn't care about her. He only cared about his son.

CHAPTER NINE

TESS bought some chicken and vegetables on her way home and stir-fried them for her supper. She wasn't particularly hungry, but there was no point in starving because she'd made a fool of herself over a man. She wasn't the first woman to do that and she wouldn't be the last. And she at least had the satisfaction of knowing that Castelli hadn't been totally indifferent to her.

She'd bought some wine, too, but, although she left it on the counter, she didn't open the bottle. It was one thing making herself a decent meal for once. Drinking a whole bottle of Lambrusco on her own was something else. Instead, after making a gallant effort to enjoy the food, she made herself a cup of instant coffee and carried it out onto the balcony adjoining the bedroom to drink.

It was almost dark and already a string of lights had sprung up along the waterfront. She could smell the aromas of food cooking, of garlic and other herbs, and hear the sound of voices from the street below. Somewhere a saxophone was playing a haunting melody, bringing the unwilling brush of tears to her eyes. This should have been such a simple visit, she thought miserably. When had it all started to go wrong?

She knew the answer, of course. It had been wrong from the beginning. Andrea wasn't ill; Ashley hadn't been called home to look after her. Instead, she'd taken off with a boy who was far too young for her, causing embarrassment to her sister and distress to his family.

Tess caught her breath as another thought struck her. It was Friday tomorrow, and, remembering what Ashley's mother had said, she was surprised she hadn't heard from her again. She prayed it wasn't because Andrea had decided to make good on her threat and come to Italy herself.

Oh, God, that was all she needed, for her stepmother to show up unannounced. Where would she stay? The apartment wasn't really big enough for two people and Tess could well imagine that she'd be the one expected to find alternative accommodation.

A burst of laughter from the courtyard below was reassuring. Obviously some of her neighbours were having a party and she envied them their careless enjoyment. She thought if she'd lived here, like Ashley, she'd have made an effort to make friends with the other tenants. She'd noticed a couple of younger people going in and out of the building and they'd looked friendly enough. It would have been fun to brush up on her Italian, too. Fun, also, to invite someone in to share her supper. Someone who, unlike Silvio, would not expect anything more than good food and casual conversation.

She was considering opening the wine, after all, as a compensation for standing here all alone, when everyone else seemed to be having such a good time, when there was a knock on her door.

Tess froze for a moment and then took a swift look at her watch. It was after nine o'clock. Far too late for a casual caller. It had to be Andrea, she thought in dismay. Who else could it be?

She was tempted to pretend she wasn't in. Ashley's mother didn't have a key, obviously, and she doubted the old caretaker would let a complete stranger into the apartment. But she would have to face her sooner or later and she didn't have the heart to send her away. Depositing her empty coffee-cup in the sink, she composed herself and went to open the door.

It wasn't Andrea. The man standing outside was probably the person she'd least expected to see, and she stared at him in total disbelief.

'You should have checked who your caller was before

you opened the door,' Castelli said roughly, by way of a greeting. 'Who were you expecting?'

'No one.' Tess was too shocked to lie to him. 'I wasn't *expecting* anyone.' Then, in an attempt to regain the initiative, she added defiantly, 'What are you doing here, *signore*? Slumming?'

Castelli's mouth compressed. 'I will not dignify that remark with a response,' he declared harshly. Then, with a glance beyond her into the apartment, 'Are you alone?'

Tess caught her breath. 'What's that to you?' she retorted, in no mood to respect his feelings. The image of his regretful—no, pitying—expression when he'd pushed her away from him on the beach was still painfully acute. How dared he come here and behave as if he had any right to question her behaviour? Unless this visit was to get her to apologise for what she'd said to his mother. If it was, he was wasting his time.

He sighed now. 'May I come in?'

'Why?'

'Because I wish to speak with you,' he said patiently. 'And I would prefer it if we could speak privately.'

Tess felt mutinous. 'I don't think I want to speak to you tonight, *signore*,' she said, squashing the little spark of hope that he might have come to apologise himself. Besides which, it was better if she didn't spend any time alone with him. Crazy as it was, she didn't trust herself where he was concerned. She waited a beat and then added defensively, 'I was just going to bed.'

His expression was sceptical. 'At nine-fifteen? I do not think so, *cara*.'

'Don't call me that.' Tess was angry. 'And it's really none of your business what I do, *signore*. I'll be at the gallery in the morning. If you have anything to say to me, perhaps you could save it until then?'

'Tess!'

His use of her name was almost her undoing. His voice had softened, deepened to a dark, persuasive drawl. It caused a quiver in her stomach, an aching need that spread to every part of her body. Despite herself, emotions stirred inside her, and she had to lift a hand to the frame of the door to support her shaking legs.

But somehow, she found the words to say, 'If this is your way of getting me to apologise for what I said to your mother, you're going to be unlucky.' She straightened her spine. 'I meant what I said, and you can tell her from me that I don't think much of the way she left without even closing the door behind her.'

Castelli's brows drew together. Then, before she realised what he intended to do, he swept her hand aside and stepped across the threshold. She was forced to move out of his way to avoid coming into contact with his hard body and he used the opportunity it gave him to slam the door.

The sound reverberated round the apartment and she was gearing herself to demand that he get out of there, at once, when he said, 'What the hell are you talking about? I did not even know you had met my mother.'

Tess's lips parted. She didn't want to believe him but there was something so convincing in his gaze that she couldn't help herself. 'I—she came to the gallery,' she said stiffly. She lifted her shoulders. 'I thought you knew.'

'Well, obviously, I did not.'

'No.' Tess conceded the point. 'I'm sorry. I naturally assumed that was why you were here.'

Castelli made a strangely defeated gesture. 'Naturally,' he said flatly, walking across the living room to stand staring down at the lights of the harbour below. 'What other reason could there be?'

Tess caught her lower lip between her teeth. She would not feel sorry for him, she thought. That way lay danger. And, as she didn't have a satisfactory answer for him, she indulged herself for a moment by pretending he really had come here to see her.

With his back to her, she was able to look at him unobserved and her eyes lingered on broad shoulders, shown to advantage in a close-fitting black polo shirt. His black draw-string trousers were tight over his buttocks but only hinted at the powerful muscles of his legs. Taken as a whole, his outfit didn't look like something he would wear to a social gathering. Which meant what? That he had come here to see her, after all?

The breath she was about to take caught in her throat and all her bones seemed to melt beneath her. A purely visceral surge of longing gripped her, but before she could say something foolish, comprehension dawned.

'Ashley,' she said quickly before her panicked breathing could betray her. 'You're here about Ashley.' She paused to take another calming gulp of air. 'Have you found out where they are?'

He turned then, pushing his hands into the pockets of his pants as he did so, tautening the soft cotton across his thighs. In spite of herself, Tess's eyes were drawn there. She dragged them away again as he said, 'No,' in a flat, ex-pressionless voice. Then, as if he too was finding it hard to speak casually, he continued, 'Verdicci has had no luck in Genova. If your sister has hired a car, she has hired it under another name.'

'Oh.' Tess swallowed. 'Could she do that?'

'If she had an accomplice,' replied Castelli carelessly. 'Do you know if she has any friends here in San Michele?'

Tess shook her head. 'Not as far as I know,' she replied, sure that Ashley had never mentioned any particular friend to her. Certainly no one who might be willing to assist her in doing something that sounded vaguely illegal. 'She's only lived here for nine months. Hardly long enough to get that close to anyone.'

'Except Marco,' Castelli observed softly, and Tess felt his frustration. Then, his eyes intent, 'Tell me about my mother. I assume she came to ask you about your sister. What did she say to upset you?'

Tess shrugged. 'Why do you think she upset me?' she

argued defensively, and a faint smile tugged at his lean, attractive mouth.

'You said that if I had come for an apology, I would be unlucky, *no*?' he responded drily. 'Please, humour me. I would like to know her reasons for speaking with you.'

Tess sighed. 'Oh—you know. She thought I might know more than I'd said.'

'That you might know more than you had told me?' he suggested shrewdly, and she nodded.

'Something like that.'

'Mmm.' He withdrew his hands from his pockets and crossed them over his chest, tucking his fingers beneath his arms. 'I guess she was unhappy with the results I had achieved. Did she tell you what a disappointment I had been to her as both a husband and a father?'

'No!' Tess was shocked. 'She didn't say anything like that.'

'But she did imply that I was to blame for allowing Marco to become involved with your sister?'

'No.' Tess shook her head. 'It was Ashley she vilified, not you. Or Marco. She said that Ashley had corrupted her grandson. That he was just a child. And when I said that boys of sixteen were not considered children in England, she criticised that, as well.' She paused. 'You—you were hardly mentioned.'

Castelli was sardonic. 'You disappoint me.'

'Well, I'm sure she didn't approve of you associating with me,' Tess appended swiftly. She pressed her hands together at her midriff, aware that she'd changed into an old pair of denim cut-offs when she'd got home from the gallery and they were hardly flattering. 'She probably thinks that I'll corrupt you, too.'

Castelli regarded her with mild amusement. 'Do you think that is possible, *cara*? I am not an impressionable boy to be dazzled by a woman's looks. In my experience, a pretty face has a limited appeal. If I had to choose, I would pick brains over beauty every time.'

'How noble of you.' Tess couldn't hide her bitterness. 'Is that why your wife left you? Because she couldn't live up to such high ideals?'

It was an unforgivable thing to say, but Tess refused to feel any remorse. She resented the fact that he'd come here, that he'd felt he had the right to force his way into the apartment on some pretext she had yet to discover. All right, the way she'd behaved on the beach had probably given him the notion that she'd be willing to do just about anything he asked of her. But that had been a moment of madness that she had no intention of repeating. Ever.

Castelli moved then and she had to steel herself not to put the bar that divided the kitchenette from the rest of the room between them. But all he did was rub his palms over his spread thighs. He seemed to be more thoughtful than angry. It was as if he was considering her words and deciding how to answer her. Perhaps she'd been a little too close for comfort, she thought eagerly, feeling a momentary surge of revenge.

When he said, 'I do not wish to discuss my wife with you,' she felt almost euphoric. And when he continued, 'Her reasons for leaving me are not part of this equation,' she was sure she had bloodied a nerve.

'So I was right,' she said, amazed at her own temerity. 'You're just like your mother and Maria. You Castellis think you're never wrong!'

'No!' The word was harsh and angry and for the first time Tess was aware that they were alone. 'You are not right,' he said, coming towards her. 'Gina and I did not separate because of any high ideals on my part. Not unless you consider the fact that she preferred to sleep in other beds than mine no justification.'

Tess did retreat behind the bar then.

She felt mortified and ashamed. She'd been so intent on scoring points, she hadn't considered the wounds she might have been inflicting.

'I'm sorry,' she said unhappily. 'I shouldn't have said

that.' She spread her hands along the bar, nails digging into the plastic rim. She licked her lips and when he didn't speak she added, with a weak attempt at humour, 'Blame your mother. I got used to defending myself with her.'

Castelli's lips tightened. 'You do it very well,' he said, facing her across the narrow divide. 'But you are wrong about me. My opinion of my own character is very poor.'

'Is it?'

Tess couldn't prevent the rejoinder and, because it seemed as if she couldn't speak to him without being provoking, she picked up the bottle of wine she'd left on the counter earlier. The label meant nothing to her but she pretended to examine it anyway. Anything to avoid looking at him, from responding to that dangerous sexuality that he wore as naturally as his skin.

'It seems you had the last word. As far as my mother was concerned,' he said after a moment, and she wondered if he was trying to defuse the situation, too. It made it even harder to remember why she'd been so angry with him. But at least talking about his mother seemed harmless enough.

'It was only because she got upset,' she admitted now, putting down the bottle and opening a drawer. Rummaging around for the corkscrew gave her another excuse not to look at him. 'I suggested she went into the office to compose herself. Then she let herself out the back without even closing the door behind her.'

Castelli snorted. '*She* got upset,' he echoed disbelievingly. 'That does not sound like the woman I know. *Cara*, Lucia does not get upset. Not unless it is for some purpose of her own.'

'Well, perhaps she wanted to spend some time alone in the office,' offered Tess, finding the corkscrew and pulling a rueful face. 'I—well, I'm not absolutely sure about this, but I think she might have searched Ashley's desk.'

'*Non credo!*' Castelli was shocked, she could tell. 'No. Lucia may be many things, *cara*, but she is not a thief!'

'I believe you.' Tess sighed. 'But I think she was looking for something all the same.'

'*Cosa?*' What?

Tess shrugged, and then, because she'd succeeded in finding the corkscrew, she felt obliged to use it. She was fitting the screw into the cork when Castelli came round the bar and took the implement from her. 'Let me do that,' he said, with obvious impatience. 'Then perhaps you will explain what you are talking about.'

Tess didn't argue with him. Stepping back, she let him have his way. But the kitchenette was tiny and he was now much too close for comfort. She couldn't get past him. Not without rubbing up against him. And that was the last thing she wanted to do in her present state of emotional upheaval.

Instead, she kept her gaze riveted on his hands in an effort to distract herself. But she was uncomfortably aware of the strength in his chest and arms, the way his tight shirt outlined the taut muscles of his stomach.

He was all male, all man, and she wouldn't have been human if she hadn't responded to it. Particularly after what had happened between them before. Her breasts puckered in anticipation of a caress they were not going to receive, and she crossed her arms across her body in an effort to hide her reaction from him.

Her mouth was dry and, realising he was waiting for an explanation, she said quickly, 'I think your mother was looking for information about Ashley. Perhaps she thought I'd missed something when I looked through the desk myself.'

Castelli pulled out the cork before replying. Then, setting the bottle down on the counter, he said, 'So did she find anything?'

'Not as far as I know.' Tess was wary. 'Why? Do you think she did?'

Castelli made a dismissive gesture. 'Until this moment, I did not even know she had visited the gallery,' he said drily. He frowned. 'But I have not seen her today, so who knows?'

Tess's lips parted. 'I hope you don't still think I've been keeping Ashley's whereabouts a secret from you,' she exclaimed indignantly, and Castelli gave her a speaking look. 'You needn't deny it,' she continued hotly. 'That's why you've come here, isn't it? Because your mother's disappeared and you think I might know where she's gone?'

'Do not be so ridiculous,' he told her impatiently. 'I have just told you, I did not even know Lucia had been to the gallery when I came here.'

'So you said.'

'What is that supposed to mean?'

'Well, I only have your word that you didn't know about her visit,' said Tess challengingly. 'And you must admit, you haven't given me a good reason for coming here yet.'

Castelli leaned back against the counter, resting his hands on the worn plastic at either side of him. Then, with gentle irony, he said, 'Well, obviously I am not here at your invitation. Let us be honest with one another. Do you want me to go?'

Yes!

But she couldn't say it. Didn't want to say it, if she was completely truthful with herself.

'I'm sure you know exactly what I want,' she said at last, turning away to open the cupboard door above her. But as he'd opened the wine, it would be churlish not to offer him a glass. 'I think there are some glasses in here somewhere. Why don't you have some wine before you go?'

'Do I have a choice?'

She started, almost dropping the two glasses she'd found in the cupboard. The words had been spoken immediately behind her, his warm breath fanning the damp curls that nestled at her nape.

Looking down, she saw he had placed a hand on the unit at either side of her now and she was successfully trapped within the barrier of his arms. If she turned around, her face would only be inches from his. Goodness knew if there'd be room enough to take a breath and she didn't feel confident enough to try.

'What are you doing?' she asked instead, amazed her voice sounded almost normal. 'Do you want some wine or don't you?'

'If it is anything like your coffee, perhaps I will pass,' he chided lightly. And then, with sudden passion, '*Dio*, Tess, are you ever going to forgive me for what happened yesterday? I know I hurt you. Do not bother to deny it. And I want you to know I have suffered for it ever since.'

CHAPTER TEN

SHE didn't believe him.

'You flatter yourself,' Tess said now, taking a shaky breath. She despised the feelings of weakness his lying words evoked. 'I've forgotten all about it.'

'I do not think so.' He was inflexible. 'If you had forgotten all about it, *cara*, you would not be standing here, afraid to turn and face me.' He paused, blowing on her neck. '*Non abbia paura.* Do not be afraid of me, *cara*. I will do nothing you do not want me to do.'

Tess felt a momentary twinge of cynicism. He could say that because he thought he knew what she was thinking, what she was feeling. And perhaps he did, but he would never know it. She had no intention of letting him make a fool of her again.

Steeling herself against his flagrant magnetism, she put the glass down and forced herself to turn then. But she pressed her hips against the unit behind her, taking shallow little breaths to avoid the inevitable brush of her breasts against his chest. Fixing her gaze on some point beyond his right ear, she said stiffly, 'And if I want you to go?'

His sigh was heartfelt. 'Then I will do as you wish,' he said heavily, his hands falling to his sides. 'But before I do, there is something I have to say to you.'

'What?' Tess was uneasy, not least because she was still trapped by his powerful frame.

'You asked why I had come here,' he answered her softly. 'Will you believe me if I say that my only reason for doing so was because I wanted to see you again?'

'No!' The word burst from her lips and this time she had no compunction about pushing him aside and escaping

113

across the room. She should have known better, she thought. He would use any means to get his own way and she was making it easy for him. It seemed tonight that he'd decided to take her up on her oh-so-unsubtle advances and she'd almost given in. 'I think you'd better go, *signore*. Before I call the *custode* and have you thrown out!'

Which was ridiculous considering the old caretaker was seventy if he was a day.

He shook his head now. 'I do not think you will do that, *cara*,' he said flatly. 'You would not wish to make a scene.'

'Don't bet on it.' Tess hated it that he could read her so easily. 'I know you think that because Ashley appears not to have any scruples, I'm the same. But I'm not. What happened on the beach was a mistake. It was sensible to stop it as you did.'

He sighed. 'You may be right,' he said wearily, raking a resigned hand through his hair. 'And it was probably a mistake to come here. Put it down to a moment of weakness. I wanted to see you and I did not stop to think how it might look to you.'

'Oh, please.' Tess had heard enough. 'We both know why you came here and it wasn't to beg my forgiveness or anything as high-minded as that. You were at a loose end and you remembered how easy I'd been to seduce. I can't exactly blame you for that but I don't have to prove it.'

Castelli gave a harsh exclamation. 'You are so wrong,' he said vehemently. 'Wrong about the reasons I came here and wrong about what happened on the beach.'

'I don't think so,' she began, but her words were overridden by his.

'What?' he demanded bitterly. 'Do you think if I was the kind of man you seem to think I am, I would have been so *galante*? And by the way, I did not seduce you, *cara*. I wanted to. Ah, *sì*, I admit I wanted to. Why not? You are a very desirable woman. But, contrary to your beliefs, I do not make love with women who are only a few years older than my own daughter. I have standards, too, and I know I am too old for you.' He shrugged. 'That is all I wanted to tell you.'

Tess stared at him. 'So why come here? Why make a special journey just to tell me something I don't believe and which I don't think you believe either.'

Castelli's lips twisted. 'You are a hard woman, Tess,' he said heavily. 'And perhaps you are right. Perhaps I did come here hoping you might be glad to see me. I like you. I like being with you. And if you think I wanted to let you go the other afternoon…' He sighed. '*Dio*, I do not think even you can be that insensitive.'

Tess felt the force of his words deep in the pit of her stomach. Her body hummed with the sexual energy he was generating and, although she was trying so very hard to remain unmoved by his appeal, there was something disturbingly vulnerable in his face.

'So—so what are you saying?' she asked, despising herself for giving him an opening. 'That the only reason you let me go was because you believe you're too old for me?'

'Not entirely.' His response flattened a momentary spurt of excitement. 'I was thinking of myself, too.'

'Why am I not surprised?' Tess shook her head. And then caught her breath when he strode forward and grabbed her wrist.

'*Stammi a sentire!*' he commanded harshly. 'Listen to me!' His thumb pressed hard on the fine veins on the inner side of her wrist. 'You think you are the only one with something to lose here, but you are wrong. And I am not willing to provide a romantic diversion for someone who is only looking for a holiday affair.'

Tess swallowed. 'I—I see.'

'Do you?' He was sardonic. 'And do you also see that touching you like this is a mistake?'

Tess quivered. 'Then let me go.'

'To do what?' He arched his dark brows, his eyes insistent, disturbing, intent. 'Leave you with the impression that I am not strong enough to control my own feelings? *Dio*,

Tess, this was not meant to happen. You are my connection to my son. That was supposed to be the only reason why we spent any time together.'

'And it was,' said Tess breathlessly, intensely aware of the sinuous yet immensely strong hold he had on her wrist. The heat from his fingers enveloped her arm, spread unchecked into her shoulder. She licked her dry lips, hardly aware of what she was doing. Then, persuasively, 'Why don't we have a glass of wine? I think we both need some time to cool off.'

'Do we?' With a twist of his wrist, he pulled her towards him, taking her wrist behind his back, pressing it into the taut curve of his spine. Then, exerting an increasing pressure, he bent his head and covered her lips with his.

His kiss was electric. As soon as their mouths fused, a devastating weakness almost buckled her knees beneath her. A frisson of alarm slid down her spine, a warning that she had no defences where he was concerned. But then his tongue slid between her teeth and she couldn't bear to pull away.

Her lips parted beneath that sensual assault, and it was incredibly difficult to keep her eyes open when all she wanted to do was close them against the searching hunger in his. He was watching her, she thought fancifully, watching how easy it was for him to subdue her. But his predator's eyes were also hot and mesmerising, causing goosebumps to shiver over her flesh.

His mouth hardened, grew more demanding, and he released her wrist to place possessive hands on her hips. He drew her against him, letting her feel his heavy arousal throbbing against her stomach, leaving her in no doubt that, whatever his misgivings, he was as aroused as she was herself.

Tess's hands fisted at her sides for a moment, but the desire to touch him became irresistible. With a little moan of submission, she lifted her arms and linked them behind his neck.

His response was to urge her even closer, their bodies melding together from chest to hip. His hands burned on her thighs as he cupped her buttocks and lifted her against him, and she wound one leg about his calf as he rubbed himself against her.

The effect of that sexual abrasion was incredible. Tiny synapses of energy fused her nerves, ran unchecked under her skin. Her breasts felt tight and a tiny trickle of sweat ran down between them. She wasn't wearing a bra and she knew the dampness must be moistening the thin chemise top.

'*Tu voglio,*' he whispered unevenly, the roughening stubble on his jawline scratching her chin. His teeth fastened on the tender curve of her nape. She felt his suckling tongue right down to her core. 'I want you,' he repeated harshly, lifting his head to look down at her, his eyes darker now and strangely guarded as he met her startled gaze. 'And I am just crazy enough tonight to cast caution to the winds. So—if you have any doubts about this, stop me now.'

As if she could, Tess thought weakly. Her own needs were like a consuming fire inside her. She knew what he was saying, that he was taking all and promising nothing. But she doubted she had the will to resist him when this might be the only chance with him she had.

'I'm not a child,' she said, trying to sound blasé and failing dismally. 'I'm not a virgin either,' she added, as if he cared. 'You needn't worry about me. I—I know what I'm doing.'

Castelli's eyes softened. 'Do you?' he murmured, one hand curving over her cheek before slipping down to cup one firm rounded breast. Her nipple peaked, and he stroked his thumb back and forward across it. 'The question is, do I?'

Tess trembled, his caress causing a melting in her bones. But his words disturbed her, hinting as they did of some ambivalence on his part. With a convulsive swallow, she said, 'You're not having second thoughts, are you?'

Castelli shook his head, his hand finding the hem of her chemise now and sliding beneath it with unexpected ease. He watched her reaction as he touched the underside of her breast and then found the sensitive peak he'd been stroking earlier. And Tess thought how much more erotic his thumb felt against her bare skin.

She quivered then, leaning into him, and with a gruff sound he said, 'I am not made of ice, *cara*. Do you think I can touch you like this without wanting to see you also?' A trace of self-derision flickered in his eyes, but his expression didn't change. 'I may not know what I am doing. But I know I cannot stop myself. I have wanted you since the first day I saw you.'

Me, too, thought Tess fervently, though she didn't have the courage to say it. Instead, she stepped back from him and took his hand, linking her fingers with his. 'Would you like to see the bedroom?' she asked, amazed at her own temerity, and, with a sensuous narrowing of his eyes, he inclined his head.

It wasn't until she'd opened the door that Tess remembered she hadn't made the bed that morning. The sheet, which was all she usually used to cover her, was twisted, the pillows still bearing the indent of her head. Releasing his hand, she hurried to straighten the bedding. But Castelli caught her before she could do much more than pull the sheet aside and tugged her into his arms.

'Stop panicking,' he said, and she guessed he could feel her heartbeat hammering in her chest. 'We have all night,' he went on, dipping his head to nuzzle her shoulder. Then he brushed the straps of her chemise aside and drew it over her head.

It was hard not to feel some embarrassment as he stared at her. But her breasts were firm and high and she had no reason to feel ashamed of them. Nevertheless, she felt a quiver deep in her belly when he lifted his hands and cupped them almost reverently. And when he bent his head and buried his face in the moist hollow of her cleavage, she clutched the back of his neck and hung on for dear life.

When he lifted his head again, her face was flushed, damp strands of hair clinging to her neck and cheeks. He nudged her legs with one thigh and she parted them obediently. Castelli moved between them, rubbing sensuously against her sensitive core.

'You know we are wearing too many clothes, *fare lo non*?' he asked huskily, and, releasing her, he peeled his shirt over his head. Now her breasts brushed against the triangle of dark hair that angled down to his navel, hair that curled across his chest and shadowed his olive skin.

Tess stared. She couldn't help herself. She'd already guessed his body was taut and athletic and now she could see for herself. His nipples were pointed, his stomach flat and muscular, and below his navel another line of dark hair arrowed beneath the drawstring waistband of his pants.

The cord that hung from his waistband was irresistible. Before she could stop herself, Tess had reached out and pulled it free. Almost immediately, the soft trousers shimmied down to his ankles, and she was left to face the biggest erection she'd ever seen.

'You can touch me,' he said, kicking his trousers aside and tossing his deck shoes in the process. 'But do you not think we should lose these shorts first?'

His fingers easily disposed of her zip and the button that secured her waistband, but when he would have eased them down she grabbed the two sides in alarm.

'I—I had a shower when I came home,' she said. 'I—I didn't bother with any underwear.' She took a deep breath. 'Shouldn't we draw the curtains first?'

A glimpse of amusement touched his lean face at this evidence of her prudishness. 'Why?' he asked softly. 'Who can see us here?'

You can see me, Tess thought, releasing her hold on the shorts reluctantly. But what the hell? she thought. He was going to see her sooner or later anyway.

The denim cut-offs pooled around her ankles. Now it was Castelli who stared and she shifted uneasily under his gaze. *'Lei sono bello,'* he said hoarsely. 'You are beautiful, *cara*. Do not be ashamed of your body. It is *perfetto* in every way.'

Tess knew *perfetto* meant perfect, but she didn't believe him. She wasn't overweight, it was true, and her legs were slim, but she was a long way short of being ideal. Castelli on the other hand was magnificent. She wondered why he'd never married again. It was not for want of offers, she was sure.

'Now you help me,' he said, and her mouth dried instinctively. She wasn't used to such uninhibited behaviour and the idea of stripping his boxers from him was too much for her to take in.

But she did want to be close to him, and, hooking a finger into his shorts, she pulled him nearer. Which served the dual purpose of pretending to do as he asked and hiding her face as well.

'Ehi,' he said softly, gripping her waist and holding her away from him. 'Do not be afraid, *cara*. It will not bite.'

'I'm not afraid,' said Tess staunchly. 'It's just that I'm not used to—used to this.'

He gave a soft laugh. 'Oh, *amatissimo*,' he said, his voice rough with emotion. 'Do you think I do not know that by now? Here.' He took her hand. 'Let me show you. It will please me very much to be your tutor.'

He covered her fingers with his and used them to push his shorts down over his jutting manhood. It sprang free, thick and heavy and pulsing with heat. There was a smear of moisture at the tip that Tess found fascinating. She found herself itching to taste it and her breath came swiftly as he curled her palm around his silken length.

Her fingers moved automatically, and Castelli made a hoarse sound in his throat. Then his mouth was on hers again and she was pressed even closer and now there was no barrier between her and his naked frame.

Aching needs stirred inside her. She clung to him tightly, rejoicing in the freedom he had given her to do as she wished. His erection touched her mound and she arched her back instinctively. She couldn't wait to have him closer still.

When he released her mouth again, she made a sound of protest. But he swung her up into his arms and carried her to the bed. The cotton sheets were cool against her back as he came down beside her, and her legs parted almost involuntarily, inviting him to enter her and end her mindless need.

But instead of lying between her legs, he stretched out beside her, propping himself up on one elbow, seemingly content just to look at her. She shifted restlessly trying to let him see what she really wanted, but, although he obviously knew how she was feeling, he merely brushed her shoulder with his lips, his thumb brushing sensually over her mouth.

'Castelli—'

'Rafe,' he corrected her softly. 'My name is Rafe. I want you to use it. I am tired of being only Castelli to you.'

'Rafe, then,' she said obediently. 'Rafe—please! Don't you want to make love to me? I ache—' her hand flicked herself '—here; inside me. Do you know what I mean?'

'I have a faint inkling,' he teased her huskily, and now he bent and bit the soft skin above her breast. He tugged the flesh between his teeth and the feeling was erotic. Tess trembled violently. *Oh, God,* she thought, *I don't know how much more of this I can stand.*

But although she fretted beneath his hands, they were intensely pleasurable. While he suckled on her breast, his fingers trailed down over her stomach, raising little shivers as they went. They lingered in the hollow of her navel, then dipped into the curls at the apex of her legs. He was driving her to the brink and she was sure he knew it, could feel her essence hot against his hand.

He used his thumb to rub against the swollen nub of her womanhood, ignoring her protests as he inserted two fingers into her cleft. His fingers imitated the act of mating, and in no time at all she was writhing beneath him, far beyond the limits of her own control.

Her orgasm, when it came, was shattering, drenching him in moisture, bringing a look of raw satisfaction to his face. She wondered if this was all he wanted: to play with her without any real participation on his part. Then he removed his hand and replaced it with his mouth.

'No, please,' she said desperately, feeling herself responding again. Pleasurable as this was, it was not what she wanted. She pushed herself up on two elbows, trying to stop him. But Castelli only continued his sensual assault. She climaxed again, almost immediately, clutching his head instead of pushing him away.

He waited until she'd collapsed onto the pillows before moving over her. 'It was good, yes?' he asked huskily, and she tossed her head helplessly from side to side.

'It was good,' she agreed. And then, because she couldn't help herself, she reached up and ground her mouth against his with a tearful lack of restraint.

The kiss was as hot and passionate as before but he must have felt her tears against his cheek. He drew back to rest his forehead against hers and swore gently, frowning down at her. 'Why are you crying?' he asked softly. 'What did I do wrong?'

'You didn't do anything wrong. You just didn't do—anything,' she confessed unhappily.

She couldn't go on and Castelli captured an errant tear with the tip of his tongue. 'I told you,' he said. 'We have plenty of time. I am not going anywhere, *cara*. Relax. I just want you to remember tonight.'

He didn't say, 'When I'm gone,' but the words were implicit in what he had said. As if she would ever forget, thought Tess, with a wistful sigh. She wondered if she'd regret it when she got home, but that was not something she wanted to think about. This was a night out of time. A memory to console her in years to come.

He moved between her legs, positioning himself above her, but when she attempted to caress him with her lips he drew back at once. 'Not now, *cara*,' he said hoarsely. 'I am only human. And I want to be inside you when—well, you know what I mean.'

Tess didn't argue. She was desperate for him to be inside her, too, and she urged him on with real hunger in her eyes. She had been half afraid she wouldn't be able to take all of him, but her body stretched almost languidly, tightening about his length as he eased into her.

She felt a fullness then, a wholeness, a delicious anticipation of events still to come. And, although she'd been sure she couldn't be aroused for a third time, he soon proved that he was right and she was wrong.

She also realised the iron control Castelli must have been exercising over his emotions. He was breathing unevenly and his upper lip was filmed with sweat. His hands slipped beneath her bottom, lifting her against him. And when he began to move, the moist sounds their bodies made were sensuous to her ears.

'Dear God,' she moaned, giving voice to the wild emotions roiling inside her, and almost instinctively she wound her legs about his hips. She'd never dreamt she could feel like this, never dreamt she could be so uninhibited with a man. The inadequate experiences she'd had before had never prepared her for Castelli's lovemaking.

'Look at me,' he said once, causing her to gaze up at him with unguarded eyes. 'I want you to know who is with you. I want you to know we are together.' He looked down at where their bodies were joined, his eyes darkening with feeling. 'I don't want you to know where your body ends and mine begins.'

She nodded then, too emotionally aroused to use words to tell him how she felt. Instead, she reached up with her hands and pulled his face to hers, giving him her answer with her lips.

His movements quickened, and she felt her own emotions

spiralling upward. She hadn't believed she could feel anything so devastating after what she'd felt before. She looked at him again, saw the way his eyes grew unfocussed, and then reached that seemingly unattainable pinnacle as he found his release....

CHAPTER ELEVEN

TESS awakened next morning feeling a little sick and achy to the sound of someone hammering on the door.

She'd drunk too much wine the night before, she thought, half prepared to believe the hammering was in her head. But she knew her headache was just a minor symptom of what was really wrong with her, and, although she knew she ought to see who it was, she buried her face in the pillow instead.

Castelli hadn't left until it was almost daylight. They'd spent most of the night together, and, although they'd done very little sleeping, Tess had thought it was the most wonderful night of her life.

While she'd been recovering from their first bout of love-making, Castelli had gone into the other room and returned with the wine and two glasses. Comfortably at home in his skin, he'd knelt beside her on the bed, offering her wine and kisses, and the erotic delight of drinking it from his lips.

His uninhibited behaviour had been catching and pretty soon she'd been sitting up, knees drawn up to her chin while he'd reclined beside her. But then his hand had become too tantalisingly familiar, and they'd shared that incredible magic again.

They'd made love twice more, the last time as slow and languorous as she could have wished. Her body had been aching but it had been a sweet torment, and one that she would have willingly suffered for the rest of her life.

But that would not happen. She knew that. Had known it before she'd invited him into her bedroom. Castelli had given her no commitment, made her no promises. When he'd departed early this morning, he'd said nothing about seeing her again. And although she guessed they might have to be in contact when Ashley and Marco turned up, she didn't kid herself he'd find it difficult to walk away afterwards.

The hammering came again and she pulled the sheet over her head to shut out the sound. It didn't work, but it did shut out the morning sunlight streaming through the unguarded windows. Which reminded her anew of what had happened the night before. Making love by moonlight, the most romantic memory of all.

She knew she had to think about getting up and going to the gallery. She was still Ashley's deputy, at least until the beginning of next week. The fact that she would have been happiest to stay where she was for the rest of the day didn't figure. She was committed to doing what she'd been asked, even if no one else seemed to care about the rules.

Some people would say she'd been a fool, she thought ruefully. Ashley certainly would, if she ever found out. Her sister would never have behaved so recklessly, not without providing a safety net first.

Her sister!

Tess groaned. Oh, God, what time was it anyway? There was always the chance that Andrea might turn up as she'd threatened to do. She could imagine what her stepmother would say if she arrived and found Tess still in bed.

Pulling the sheet away from her face, she struggled up onto her pillows. Blinking, she managed to bring the clock on the bedside cabinet into focus. It was almost eleven, she saw with horror. She must have gone back to sleep after Castelli left. She had been very tired, but that was no excuse.

She could hear someone shouting now. The knocking was still going on, but it was accompanied by an angry voice calling her name. 'Tess,' she heard. 'Tess Daniels, are you in there? Will you unlock this door, dammit? I can't get into my own apartment.'

Ashley!

Tess's jaw dropped. And before she'd thought it through

she was halfway to the door. She remembered bolting it after Castelli left, never expecting anyone to try and get in with just a key. But then she remembered she wasn't wearing a stitch to cover herself with. Not even the man-sized tee shirt she usually slept in.

She and Castelli had slept in one another's arms, she recalled unwillingly, hurrying back into the bedroom to find her robe. Naked and unashamed, she thought, wondering why that now sounded so—so sordid. She grimaced. It was because Ashley had come back and now any chance of seeing him alone again had been removed.

She found her robe hanging on the back of the bathroom door and she slid her arms into the sleeves, wrapping it about her and tying the cord as she hastily retraced her steps. Ashley wasn't giving up and Tess guessed she'd been to the gallery first to find her. When Tess wasn't there, she'd guessed she must be here.

It wouldn't occur to her sister that Tess might have spent the night anywhere else. That she might have been to a party and been invited to spend the night. Despite what she'd told Silvio, Ashley wouldn't expect her to make friends here. Least of all…Tess arrested the thought. Castelli was not a friend.

'I'm coming, I'm coming,' she called now, half afraid the noise Ashley was making would encourage the old caretaker to call the police. She drew the bolt and turned the key, almost in unison. Then, pulling open the door, she said, 'I'm sorry. I slept in.'

'Didn't you just?' Ashley was not appeased by her apology. She strode into the apartment, looking about her as she did so, and Tess wondered if she suspected she wasn't alone. 'Get my case, will you?' she added, shedding a bulging backpack onto a chair. 'I've had to haul it all the way from the gallery. I expected you'd be using my car and I could collect it.'

'Sorry,' said Tess again, rather less meekly this time. But as Ashley went to fill the kettle and plug it in she obediently wheeled the case into the apartment, before adding, 'Perhaps if you'd told me that you were coming back, I could have arranged to pick you up at the airport.'

'There was no need.' Ashley was offhand, pushing her hair behind her ear with a careless hand. 'I got a cab from the airport. I thought you'd be relieved I was back.'

'Oh, I am.' As her sister stood there, casually making herself a pot of tea, Tess felt her temper rising. 'How is Andrea, by the way? I really ought to give her a ring myself.'

'Don't bother.' Ashley cast a wary glance over her shoulder and Tess wondered if she really thought she'd got away with it. 'She's okay. You know what she's like. Always exaggerating her illnesses.'

Tess pushed her hands into the pockets of her robe, feeling them ball into fists. 'You've spoken to her, then?'

Ashley looked at her again. 'Why?' Then, 'Of course, I've spoken to her.' She turned back to the kettle. 'What are you talking about, Tess? I've been staying with her for the past week.'

'Have you?' Tess steeled herself for the confrontation. 'That's funny. She says she hasn't seen you.'

'You've spoken to her?' Ashley swung round again, and this time her face was flushed with anger. 'What were you doing, Tess? Checking up on me? Dammit, now she's going to wonder what's going on.'

'As we all are,' observed Tess coldly. 'Did you really think I wouldn't find out? My God, Ashley, you never cease to amaze me.'

Ashley's mouth was sullen. 'You had no right to go checking up on me,' she declared. 'What did it matter to you where I was? You offered to look after the gallery while I was away.'

'You *asked* me to look after the gallery,' Tess contradicted her shortly. 'You told me your mother was ill and needed you. What a crock that was!'

'Well, you appear to have been having a good time any-

way,' countered Ashley, gesturing towards her bathrobe.
'Obviously you haven't stuck to the letter of our agreement
either. How often has the gallery stayed closed until lunchtime? That's my livelihood you're messing with, you know.'

'Oh, please.' Tess regarded her contemptuously. 'The gallery is the least of your problems and you know it.' She
paused. 'Where's Marco? Did you drop him off at the villa?'

Ashley stared at her, open-mouthed. 'What do you know
about Marco?' she demanded. Her brows drew together in
a scowl. 'Oh, God, you've seen his father, haven't you?'

Tess felt sick. Until that moment she'd clung to the hope
that there might have been some misunderstanding, that
Ashley hadn't abducted Castelli's son and taken the boy
away. But it was obvious from her sister's face that Marco
had been with her. And like Castelli, she could only think
the worst.

'Did you think the Castellis wouldn't try and contact
you?' she asked now, incredulously. 'Dammit, Ashley,
Marco's only sixteen!'

'He's almost seventeen,' said Ashley impatiently. 'Only
his family doesn't seem to recognise that. They keep that
boy in a glass case, Tess. No wonder he can't wait to break
out.'

Tess blinked. 'So you decided to help him, did you?' she
exclaimed bitterly. 'Whatever you say, whatever excuses
you come up with, he is still only sixteen, Ashley. Did you
honestly expect his father would approve of you—running
off with him?' She shook her head. 'I thought you'd have
had more sense.'

Ashley scowled now. 'What do you mean, running off
with him?'

'Well, you did, didn't you? An investigator Cas—his
father hired saw you get on the plane to Milan almost a
week ago.'

'So?'

Tess gasped. 'So—where the hell were you going? You
weren't on the plane when it got to Milan. They checked.'

Ashley looked mutinous for a moment and then she turned to make the tea and Tess was obliged to wait. What was she doing? Tess wondered. Concocting a convincing excuse or deciding how much to tell her? She didn't want to know all the intimate details. Heaven forbid! But she would like to know how they had avoided being found.

With the tea made and a cup poured to her satisfaction, Ashley crossed the room and sank down onto the shabby sofa with a sigh of relief. She sipped the tea, nodded appreciatively, and then turned to Tess again. 'Don't look at me like that,' she exclaimed. 'I'm not a pervert, if that's what you're thinking.'

Tess clenched her teeth. How could Ashley talk about what had happened so carelessly? She dragged a chair out from the table and perched on the edge, regarding her sister intently. 'All right,' she said. 'So tell me. What has been going on?'

Ashley shrugged. 'We've been in Genoa,' she replied, taking another sip of her tea, and Tess acknowledged that Castelli had been right about that, at least.

'But you bought tickets for Milan,' she pointed out, still waiting for an explanation. 'If it was an entirely innocent trip, why do that?'

'To put his family off the scent, of course,' said Ashley impatiently. 'We didn't want his father turning up and ruining his chance to get some real tuition for once.' She shook her head. 'His father won't even allow that he has any talent. When Marco told him he wanted to go on a painting holiday, he wouldn't even consider it.'

A painting holiday! Tess was nonplussed. 'And you think his father knew about this?'

'About his interest in painting? Of course.'

'No, not that.' Tess was impatient now. 'About this painting holiday or whatever it was? Because I don't think he did.'

'Well, Marco told him all about it,' asserted Ashley firmly. 'But we decided not to tell him where it was being held for obvious reasons. I didn't want him sending his goons after us.'

Tess caught her breath. 'I don't believe it,' she said incredulously and Ashley frowned.

'What don't you believe? That his family might have tried to stop us? Come on, Tess, you said yourself that Marco's father had hired an investigator to check up on him.'

'Because he was worried about him,' declared Tess vehemently. 'And whatever you believe, Marco couldn't have told his father where he was going. I doubt if he even mentioned a painting holiday to his family. When his father came to the gallery looking for you, he accused you of kidnapping his son!'

Now Ashley gasped. 'You're joking!'

'No, I'm not joking,' Tess retorted grimly. 'His family thinks you're having an affair.'

Ashley's face was difficult to read then. Tess thought she was dismayed. She hoped she was. But there was something strangely secretive in her expression.

Then she saw Tess watching her, and she shook off whatever she was thinking. 'You can't be serious,' she said, getting to her feet and striding across to the windows. 'For heaven's sake, Tess, what do you think I am?'

'So it's not true, then?'

'No.' But Ashley wasn't looking at her as she made the denial. She seemed to be intent on what she could see out of the window, the roofs of the small town and the harbour far below. 'You shouldn't believe everything you hear.'

'I'm only telling you what Marco's family thinks,' said Tess defensively, hoping Ashley wouldn't question how she came to be so knowledgeable all of a sudden. Now that her sister appeared to be exonerated, her own behaviour seemed even less justifiable.

Ashley turned then, wrapping protective arms about her midriff, causing the short skirt of her slip dress to rise high above her knees. She'd kicked off her high-heeled sandals when she'd come into the apartment, but her long legs were still shown to advantage. Tanned and slender, they complemented her shapely frame, making Tess feel small and insignificant beside her.

'Can I help it if that fool boy thinks he's in love with me?' she demanded suddenly, and Tess's eyes widened at this sudden shift in emphasis.

'You mean, you are involved with him?' she asked faintly, and Ashley gave her a scornful look.

'Haven't I just said I'm not interested in schoolboys?' she demanded. 'But that doesn't mean Marco doesn't have—expectations.' A slightly sensual smile tugged at the corners of her lips and Tess's doubts were rekindled. 'He's crazy about me, you know. That's why his father is so worried about him, I suppose.'

'Then what on earth possessed you to take him on a painting holiday?' protested Tess, disturbed by her sister's attitude. 'As soon as you realised how he felt about you, you should have kept out of his way.'

'Why?' Ashley was mocking. 'Just because his family don't approve?'

'Because he's only sixteen,' repeated Tess staunchly. 'For heaven's sake, Ashley, what are you trying to do? Alienate him from the Castellis completely?'

'That will never happen,' retorted Ashley positively, bending to pick up the cup of tea she'd deposited on the floor when she got up from the sofa. 'As you've obviously found out for yourself, Marco is the most important person in his father's life. He's a divorcee, you know, Signor di Castelli, and, according to Marco, he's got no intention of getting married again. So there'll be no other sons to pass on the family name.'

As if she didn't know, thought Tess painfully. But Ashley was waiting for her to say something and that definitely wasn't it. 'Do you know him?' she asked instead, which seemed a reasonable question. After all, Ashley would never expect Castelli to have shown any interest in her.

'I met him once, at the grape harvest last year,' her sister replied, confirming Castelli's comment. 'He's quite a hunk, isn't he? Or didn't you notice?'

'He's—quite attractive,' conceded Tess, realising that to say anything else would sound suspicious and Ashley gave her a scornful look.

'Quite attractive,' she mimicked. 'Tess, the man's gorgeous. Do you think I'd care what Marco's ambitions were if Rafe di Castelli was interested in me?'

She finished her tea and carried the empty cup into the kitchenette as Tess absorbed her last statement. But it wasn't what Ashley had said that really disturbed her. It was what she hadn't said that caused a shiver of apprehension to feather her spine.

'What do you mean?' she asked now, needing some further reassurance that she was mistaken. 'What does—Signor di Castelli have to do with you?'

'Can't you guess?' The face Ashley turned towards her was impatient. 'Oh, grow up, Tess, what do you think this is all about?' She rinsed out her teacup and set it on the drainer, drying her hands on a paper towel. 'I haven't wasted time on Marco just for his well-being. And if the Castellis want me to leave town when the gallery closes, it's going to cost them. That's all.'

Tess was appalled. But all she could find to say was, 'You know the gallery's closing?'

'Of course.' Ashley was complacent. 'I'm not stupid. The gallery's not making any money and Scottolino's no bleeding heart, believe me. He won't do anything to cushion my retirement. Not when I've only been working for him for less than a year.'

Tess swallowed as her aching brain kicked into action. 'And you think the Castellis will?'

'I'm sure of it.' Ashley nodded. 'I think they'll do almost anything now to get me out of their hair. Of course when I suggested this week at Carlo Ravelli's studio, I had no idea Marco would decide to keep the whole thing a secret. That's a bonus. I suppose I was surprised when there wasn't more opposition. But then nobody was supposed to know exactly when we were going.'

Tess stared at her. 'And don't you care that they were worried about Marco?'

'I'm sorry if I've upset anyone.' Ashley shrugged. 'But it's really not my fault. Besides, I don't owe the Castellis any favours. When Silvio took me to the villa last year—and that's some villa, let me tell you—the whole family behaved as if they were the aristocrats and the rest of us were just peasants!'

'Ashley!'

'Well…' A look of defiance replaced her complacency. 'It's true. They are an arrogant lot. All except Marco, that is. He and I hit it off immediately.' She smirked reminiscently. 'He came down to the gallery to see me the very next day.'

'And you encouraged him!'

'I didn't have to.' Ashley walked across to where Tess had left her suitcase and lifted the strap. 'I think I was the first person who'd taken his aspirations seriously. You've met his father and he has no time for his talent, and his grandmother treats him like a kid.'

'He is a kid.'

'He's a teenager,' retorted Ashley shortly. 'How many teenagers do you know who have to get their parents' permission to leave the house?'

'I'm sure that's an exaggeration.'

'Is it? You know nothing about it. I'm surprised Marco's father contacted you personally. He usually gets his assistant to do stuff like that.'

'Perhaps he was more worried than you thought,' remarked Tess, not wanting to get into her association with Castelli. 'Isn't it true that Marco has never shown any interest in painting before he met you?'

'Is that what his father said?' Ashley frowned. 'That must have been quite a conversation you had with him. What else did he say? Did he mention me at all?'

Tess had had enough. 'Does it matter?' she asked, getting up and wrapping her robe closer about her naked body. She needed a shower, she thought. She needed to check that Castelli hadn't left any visible marks on her skin. 'Perhaps you ought to ring your mother,' she went on, weary of the whole affair, including her part in it. 'She's been worried about you. I told her you'd ring as soon as you could.'

'Oh, yes. You went and grassed on me,' Ashley accused her grimly. 'Couldn't you at least have kept your suspicions to yourself?'

'I didn't grass on you,' retorted Tess. 'I told her I must have made a mistake about where you'd said you were staying. I didn't entirely drop you in it, though I don't honestly know why not.'

'Because you love me,' said Ashley at once, her expression lightening. She dragged her suitcase towards the bedroom. 'You know, it's good to be back. Now I'm going to have a long cool shower. I think I deserve it, don't you?'

Tess shook her head. 'What about ringing your mother?' she protested.

'Oh, I'll do that later,' replied Ashley dismissively. 'Why don't you get dressed and go and get us something for lunch?'

'Because I need a shower, too,' muttered Tess under her breath as Ashley went into the bedroom. But, of course, she'd have to wait. It was Ashley's bathroom, after all.

And it was then she remembered the tumbled bed and the empty wine bottle and glasses standing on the bedside cabinet. She had hardly time to register what her sister's reaction was likely to be before Ashley let out an angry yell.

'What the hell?' Ashley appeared in the open doorway again, brandishing the empty wine bottle, her face flushed and dark with anger. 'Who the—who have you had in here?' she demanded, practically flinging the bottle at her sister. 'And don't tell me you were drinking alone. The place stinks of alcohol and sex!'

CHAPTER TWELVE

LUCIA DI CASTELLI arrived at the villa soon after eleven o'clock that morning.

Rafe was in his study, trying to concentrate on the latest batch of sales figures, when his mother erupted into the room.

'I know where they are,' she announced triumphantly. 'I know what they've been doing. They're in Milan, at the home of some minor painter called Carlo Ravelli. He runs these semi-educational holidays. You know the sort of thing. People pay a certain amount of money for tuition and the rest goes on meals and accommodation. A house party, in effect, but one pays for the privilege.'

Rafe put his pen aside and looked up. 'I know,' he said evenly, and Lucia stared at him as if he'd suddenly grown two heads.

'You know?' she echoed. 'How do you know? How long have you known? If you've been keeping this from me—'

'I know because Marco arrived home half an hour ago,' Rafe interrupted her wearily. 'He and his companion flew back to Pisa this morning. He could have phoned and I would have gone to meet them. But they each chose to take a cab. He's upstairs right now unpacking his bag.'

His mother's jaw sagged and, groping behind her, she found a chair and dropped into it. 'Just like that?' she asked disbelievingly. 'The boy comes home and you have nothing to say to him? He disobeyed you, Rafe. He disobeyed both of us. Surely you're not going to let him get away with it?'

'I have no intention of cracking the whip, if that's what you expect,' Rafe replied civilly. 'Have you considered that

136

it might be because we've been too hard on him that he feels it's necessary to rebel?'

'He's just a boy, Rafe.' Lucia was infuriated. 'When you were his age, you were still in school.'

'As is Marco,' Rafe reminded her. 'Just because I refused to let my son be educated in Rome, as I was, does not mean the college he attends locally is any the less adequate.'

Lucia pursed her lips. 'What you mean is, you had no intention of permitting Marco to train for the priesthood. You knew it was my dearest wish and you dismissed it out of hand.'

'Priests are born, Mama, not made,' retorted Rafe shortly. 'I can't honestly see Marco embracing the celibate life.'

'Well, not now, obviously,' muttered his mother. 'And what about this woman he went off with? Are you going to let her get away with it, too?' She snorted, and before he could reply she added angrily, 'We don't really know what they got up to, do we? Attending a course that's held in the home of an artist, of all things, can hide a multitude of sins.'

'I know that.' Rafe was irritated now, and he threw his pen down on the desk. 'Be assured, I will not allow Miss Daniels to get away with anything. Nor do I intend to make things easy for her.' He paused. 'Right now, she will be expecting me to turn up at the gallery, breathing fire. Instead, I shall do nothing for the next couple of days. It will do her good to—what is it the English say?—to stew for a while. Then, when I am ready, I will make my move.'

Lucia sniffed. 'And what is that move likely to be, exactly?'

'I don't know yet.' Rafe took a thoughtful breath and lay back in his chair. 'I have been asking myself what Miss Daniels intended to get out of this. Now that we know she was not lusting after Marco's body, it is an interesting question, is it not?'

His mother pursed her lips. 'How do you know she hasn't—I refuse to use that disgusting word you used—how do we know she hasn't seduced him anyway?'

'We don't,' said Rafe honestly. 'Except that Marco does not behave like a boy who has lost his virginity.'

'Raphael!'

'Oh, please.' Rafe sighed. 'Let's not use euphemisms here, Mama. Marco seems decidedly—subdued. As if—dare I say it?—he has been disappointed in love.'

'Well, that certainly sounds a lot better than losing his— um—innocence,' declared Lucia firmly. 'I just hope you are right and that Miss Daniels has the sense to leave him alone from now on.'

'I didn't say that,' said Rafe resignedly. 'I said I didn't think she and Marco had slept together, yet.'

'Yet?' His mother was scandalised. 'You can't think there's still a possibility of that happening, Raphael. He's home, apparently safe and sound. What more can she do?'

'I suppose that's what we're supposed to find out,' remarked her son shrewdly. 'I don't think we've heard the last of Miss Daniels, Mama. That's why I say I intend to give her time to consider her options. It's always best to know your enemy. Attack isn't always the surest form of defence.'

Lucia grumbled some more but she eventually had to concede that Rafe was probably right. And besides, she was eager to tell him how she'd found out where Marco was.

'I went to the gallery myself,' she said, not noticing that her son's features had stiffened. 'I wanted to speak to her sister, but in the event she had nothing new to tell me. She insisted she didn't know where they were. Can you believe it? Anyway, I pretended to get upset and she invited me to recover in the office.'

Rafe's mouth compressed. 'Really?'

'Yes, really.' Lucia pouted. 'Don't look like that, Raphael. I have my methods, as you should know by now. Anyway, the stupid girl left me alone and I took the opportunity to look through the drawers of the desk.' Her eyes sparkled. 'I found Ravelli's leaflet among a pile of similar leaflets for painting courses in various parts of the country. So I went to Pisa and saw your investigator, Signor

Verdicci. It was a simple matter for him to ring round all the agencies and find out if the Daniels woman had booked into any of them.'

Rafe breathed heavily. 'You took a leaflet?'

'I took several, actually,' said Lucia airily. 'Most of them in this area, as we knew they'd taken a flight to Milan. They're not of any value, Raphael. And if everyone had their rights, they probably belong to Augustin Scottolino. You needn't look at me like that. They don't belong to the Daniels woman, so don't fuss.'

'Nevertheless, you stole the leaflets,' said Rafe flatly, imagining how Tess would have felt if she'd discovered they were missing. 'You took advantage of Tess's kindness. And then left like a thief in the night.'

'How do you know I didn't put the leaflets in my handbag and leave like anyone else?' demanded his mother at once, and Rafe cursed himself for having a big mouth.

'Because I spoke to Tess yesterday,' he said. 'She told me you'd visited the gallery. She said you'd been upset, but she doesn't know you as I do.'

'Oh, don't be tiresome, Raphael.' Lucia regarded him impatiently. 'In any case, you seem to have become very friendly with this young woman.' Her disdain was evident. 'Have you forgotten that the woman who kidnapped your son is her sister, her flesh and blood?'

'I think we've established that no one kidnapped Marco,' Rafe retorted shortly. 'And, as I've said before, Tess is nothing like her sister.'

'How do you know?' His mother wasn't prepared to let it rest there, and Rafe guessed she was using his involvement with Tess to take the heat from herself. 'Because she says so?'

'Because she's a decent person,' said Rafe harshly, feeling an unwilling twinge of guilt at his own duplicity. 'In any case, we weren't talking about Tess, we were talking about your behaviour. I think you owe her an apology, don't you?'

As he'd expected, Lucia didn't linger long after that suggestion. His mother seldom apologised to anyone and she rarely admitted her mistakes. Although her own parents had only owned a *taverna*, she'd adopted her aristocratic bearing when she'd married Rafe's father, and over the years she'd put those humble beginnings out of her head.

Rafe sighed now, reluctant to admit that his mother's departure had resurrected his own misgivings. Although he'd felt tired and pleasantly sated when he'd arrived back at the villa, he'd known it was only a matter of time before his conscience reasserted itself. He'd managed to keep his thoughts at bay to begin with, and while he'd been dealing with Marco he'd had too much else on his mind. But the lethargy had cleared now and he was forced to face the truth of what he'd done.

The trouble was, he didn't want to acknowledge how he felt about it, felt about her. It was no use pretending he hadn't wanted to make love with Tess when, from the moment she'd opened the door in that thin camisole and skimpy cut-offs, it had been the only thing on his mind.

And before that, he admitted, deciding there was no point in trying to delude himself. He hadn't been lying when he'd said he'd wanted her from the first time he'd seen her. He realised now that that was why he'd been so hard on her in the beginning. Because at first he'd thought she was her sister—with all the baggage that had entailed. And later, because he'd realised that she could be dangerous to his peace of mind.

She was the first woman who had invaded his consciousness, to the extent that he couldn't get her out of his head. He thought about her, he dreamed about her, dreams he hadn't had since he was a teenager. He was worse than Marco, he admitted ruefully. Lusting after a woman he barely knew.

Yet it didn't seem like that when he was with her. There was a familiarity between them he'd never felt with anyone else. His obsession was such that he was able to fool himself that she wanted him, also. But, although they'd made love, he was no closer to finding out how she really felt about him. He should have had more sense and kept away from temptation. What was that he'd said about the perils of a holiday affair?

Ashley was outraged that Tess wouldn't discuss who she had been entertaining with her. She flounced into the shower, threatening all manner of reprisals, and Tess spent the time she was away changing the sheets and making the bed. The things she had done—like balancing the gallery's books and spring-cleaning the apartment—would mean nothing to her sister. As far as Ashley was concerned, Tess had behaved abominably and even the prospect of the revenge she intended to take on the Castellis was no compensation.

Not that Tess was anxious to have a heart-to-heart with her sister. Even talking about the gallery brought back too many painful memories of Castelli and the time they'd spent together. When Ashley emerged from the bathroom, Tess took a shower, too, albeit a cold one, and then dressed and went out to do some food shopping as Ashley had suggested.

She didn't mention the gallery. If her sister wanted to open up, that was her affair. After the way she'd behaved, Tess felt little responsibility towards her. She refused to feel guilty if the gallery remained closed all day.

When she returned to the apartment, she was half prepared for Ashley to have packed her bags in her absence. Tess had already faced the fact that she was unlikely to see Castelli again. If he went to the gallery, it would be Ashley he'd want to speak to, not her.

She entered the apartment in some trepidation. If Ashley was still here, there was no certainty that Castelli wouldn't be here, too. He might have come to the apartment, if the gallery was closed. She assumed he'd be eager to confront her sister with what she'd done.

But although Ashley was there, Castelli wasn't. Nor was there any sign that he'd visited while she was out buying lunch. However, to her surprise, Ashley's attitude had changed entirely. Instead of asking if Tess had booked her flight home, she astonished her by asking if she'd stay on for a few more days.

'I was hasty before,' she said, perching on a stool at the bar as Tess prepared a light meal of melon and ham and freshly baked rolls. 'I forget, you have your own life to lead. I guess I was jealous. Here I've been nursemaiding a love-struck teenager, and you've been getting it on with some sexy Italian.'

Tess winced. The description was too apt, and she couldn't avoid remembering how Castelli had cornered her in the kitchenette the night before. 'It doesn't matter,' she said, taking butter from the fridge and setting it on the bar beside her. Then, after adding knives and forks to the im-promptu settings, she handed Ashley a plate.

'Thanks.' Ashley helped herself to salad before continu-ing. Then, after adding several slices of melon and some of the spicy ham to her plate, she lifted her head. 'This looks delicious, Tess. And I have to admit, I'm starving. They offered us coffee and rolls on the flight, but you know what airline food is like.'

Tess managed a slight smile and took the stool opposite. She didn't know what had caused Ashley's sudden change of heart, but she didn't trust it for a minute. Something had happened. Either Castelli had been here and Ashley thought she needed a bodyguard, or she'd found out who Tess had spent the night with and intended to use it to further her own ends.

'I'm not sure it's a good idea for me to stay on,' she murmured, after a minute's deliberation. 'I mean, you only have one bedroom and the apartment's really only big enough for one.'

'It's a double bed,' Ashley pointed out quickly. 'As I'm sure you were grateful for last night.' And then, perhaps because she thought that approach wouldn't win her any favours, she went on persuasively, 'You and I have shared a bed before.'

Tess pressed her lips together. The temptation to stay on for a few more days was attractive, but she was only kidding herself if she thought that seeing Castelli again was a wise thing to do. Wasn't it painful enough already? And did she really want to get involved in whatever scheme Ashley was planning?

'It's—kind of you to ask me,' she began at last, but Ashley interrupted her.

'You're not going to say no, are you?' she protested. 'Please, you've got to give me a chance to make amends.'

Tess shook her head. 'It's not that. I'm due back in school next Thursday,' she said. 'And I've got things to do, stuff to sort out, washing and so on, when I get home.'

'Then stay until Tuesday.' Ashley was persistent. 'You can do your laundry any time.'

'Ashley—'

'You've got to stay.' Ashley's tone had changed again and Tess regarded her warily. 'I need you. I can't handle this on my own.'

'You've handled things pretty well on your own up till now,' observed Tess, not inclined to be sympathetic. 'I don't want to get involved in this, Ash. We don't have that kind of relationship.'

'We never will, if you don't allow it to happen,' retorted her sister sulkily. 'What's wrong with you? I'm offering you a holiday and you're turning me down.'

'I'm sorry—'

'All right, all right.' Ashley hunched her shoulders and regarded her broodingly. 'There is another reason why I want you to stay on. I phoned my mother while you were out and she suggested coming out for a visit. I don't want her here now. God, surely you can see that? So I told her you were staying on and that I didn't have any room.'

'Ashley!'

'Well, it was all I could think of on the spur of the moment. And if you go back to England now, she's sure to find out.'

'How?' Tess blinked. 'We never see one another.'

'Oh, I don't know.' Ashley spread her hands expressively. 'I wouldn't put it past her to check up on you. Particularly after you'd rung to ask if I was there.'

'Which reminds me, did you tell her I'd suggested you'd take this job in Italy,' Tess asked, remembering Andrea's accusation.

Ashley shrugged now. 'I may have done.' And then, as Tess looked appalled, she tried to justify herself. 'You know the old lady always wants to know what I'm doing. As I couldn't afford to get a place of my own, it seemed a good idea to say you were in favour.'

Tess shook her head. 'You amaze me. You really do. Do you ever consider anyone but yourself?'

'Oh, come on, Tess, I'm not that bad really. Please, say you'll stay on.'

'But your mother won't get in touch with me. She knows you're back now.'

'Yes, but she's still suspicious. I had to tell her my mobile was out of order to explain why she hadn't been able to reach me.'

'And where did you say you'd been?' Tess asked. 'Just in case she asks me.'

'In Venice,' said Ashley offhandedly. 'I said Signor Scottolino had asked me to check up on one of his artists while I was there.'

Tess stared at her sister disbelievingly. 'The lies just roll off your tongue, don't they?'

'I think on my feet, that's all. As I say, I can't have my mother coming here.'

'And you really think a few more days will make a difference?'

'I'll think of something else,' said Ashley. 'I can always tell her I'm losing my job, remember? If I tell her I'll be flying back to England soon, she won't want to waste money coming here.'

'You are totally unscrupulous, aren't you?'

Ashley shrugged. 'I'd call it practical. You don't get anywhere if you don't assert yourself, Tess. But I don't expect you to understand.'

Yet she could. Tess bent her head over her meal, picking idly at a thin curl of ham. If she hadn't asserted herself last night, Castelli would have left without touching her. It was she who had decided to be self-indulgent for once in her life.

And staying on? Wasn't that another form of self-indulgence? She knew Ashley wasn't to be trusted. She ought to catch the next flight back to London and safety. It was foolish to think that she could exert any influence over her sister. And Castelli wouldn't forgive her for being a party to Ashley's deceit.

So why was she even considering her sister's offer? It wasn't for Ashley's sake. She'd meant what she'd said. Ashley could take care of herself. And she surely didn't think Castelli would want her sympathy. As soon as Ashley told him what she had in mind, he'd want nothing more to do with either of them.

'I'm sorry,' she said at last, her appetite deserting her. She pushed her plate aside. 'I don't want to get involved in your schemes.'

'You won't.' Ashley was definite. 'Why should you? Signor di Castelli will want to see me, not you. He'll probably come to the gallery tomorrow. You can be sunbathing on the beach while I deal with him.'

Tess sighed. 'Ashley—'

'Well, say you'll stay until Monday at least,' pleaded the younger girl persuasively. 'What's a few more days? You'll be doing me a big favour and what harm can it do? It's not as if you've booked your flight, and if I hadn't got back you'd be staying on anyway. One more weekend. Pretty please. Then you can go back to your old boring life in Buxton.'

Tess objected to her life being called boring. Though she had to admit that, compared to the life Ashley led, it did seem rather dull. But safe, she reminded herself firmly. And predictable. These few days in Porto San Michele had been exciting, but she preferred a more secure existence.

Didn't she?

CHAPTER THIRTEEN

IN THE event, Tess couldn't get a flight until Tuesday. It was nearing the end of the Easter holidays and all the flights were fully booked. As it was, she was only on standby, and she had been asked to ring the airport Tuesday morning to check availability. The booking agent seemed to think that she would make it, but Tess was less convinced.

She refused to think what she'd do if she couldn't get a flight before Thursday. She could imagine what Mrs Peacock, her head teacher, would say if she wasn't back for the start of the new term. Mrs Peacock lived and breathed for East Vale Comprehensive, and unfortunately she expected her staff to do the same.

Ashley, of course, was delighted. Although her delight was decidedly muted by the end of Monday when she hadn't heard from either Marco or his father.

'They're keeping him away,' she said angrily, storming into the apartment after the gallery had closed, her face flushed with frustration. 'Well, they needn't think they're going to get away with it. I'll go to the villa, if I have to. Marco has a right to see whoever he likes.'

'It's not Marco you want to see, though, is it?' Tess remarked shrewdly. 'If you ask me, you've been lucky that his father hasn't contacted the police. Taking a minor away from his family is probably an offence here, just as it is at home.'

'That's rubbish!' Ashley didn't want to hear Tess's argument. 'Marco came with me of his own free will. His father knows that as well as you do.'

'All the same...'

'All right, all right. You may have a point. But that still

doesn't alter the way Marco feels about me.' She frowned as she considered her options. 'Somehow I've got to see him, to talk to him. Maybe if you could get in touch with his father—'

'No!' Tess was adamant. 'I told you I didn't want to get involved in your schemes.'

'And you won't be.' Ashley gazed at her appealingly. 'Come on, Tess. All you have to do is ask him to come to the gallery. I'll take it from there.' She spread her hands. 'I think you owe me. You were so determined to leave, but you're still here, enjoying my hospitality. I could have thrown you out.'

'No.' Tess turned away, and as she did so she heard someone knock at the door. She stiffened, her mouth going dry. 'I—I think you've got a visitor.'

'At last!'

Tess barely had time to conceal herself in the bedroom before Ashley had the door open. She tried not to listen, but she couldn't deny the longing she felt to hear Castelli's voice again. But the voice was younger, lighter, definitely not a man's voice, and her spirits sank accordingly. Marco, she thought dejectedly. Ashley would be rapt.

She sat down on the bed, expecting a long wait, but only moments later the door opened. Ashley came into the room, carrying a white embossed envelope. 'It's for you,' she said shortly, tossing it at her sister. 'A delivery boy brought it. It's got the vineyard's logo on the back. So, tell me, why would Signor di Castelli be writing to you?'

Tess's stomach hollowed. 'I don't know,' she said. And she didn't, although she doubted Ashley would believe her. She turned the envelope over, curiously reluctant to open it with her sister standing there, watching her. 'Ms Teresa Daniels,' she read, half disbelievingly. Yes. It was definitely for her.

'Open it,' said Ashley irritably, unaware of her ambivalence. She had no way of knowing that the letter filled Tess with a mixture of expectation and dread. She'd thought she'd dealt with her feelings for Castelli, but the way she felt about this letter proved she hadn't. And she dreaded the disappointment she was sure was to come when she read it.

'Hurry up,' Ashley persisted. 'It's probably about me. I want to know what lies they're telling about me. And how did they know you were still here?'

'Well, I didn't tell them,' said Tess, resenting the implication, though that thought had occurred to her, too. She ran a nervous finger under the flap and eased it open. 'I have no idea why—why any of the Castellis would write to me.'

'Just open it, Tess.' Ashley was impatient. She waited with obvious agitation for her sister to pull the sheet of notepaper out of the envelope. Tess did so, unfolding it with shaking fingers. 'Well?' the other girl prompted. 'What does it say?'

Tess read the words once, then read them again, hardly able to believe what she was seeing. 'I—we're—invited to dinner at the Villa Castelli,' she said weakly. 'The invitation's for tomorrow night.'

'Really!' Ashley didn't bother to curb her sarcasm, leaning over Tess's shoulder and reading the letter herself. 'What do you know? An invitation to the villa! I told you they'd want to see me again.'

Tess shook her head. 'Well, I can't go.'

Ashley scowled. 'Why not?'

'Because I'm going back to England tomorrow,' replied Tess steadily. 'According to the airline, I should be able to get a seat on one of the afternoon flights.'

'You can't be serious!' Ashley stared at her disbelievingly. 'If you think I'm going to lose my chance to speak to Marco's father just because you think getting back to your prissy job in England is more important, you're mistaken.'

'I'm not stopping you from going,' protested Tess defensively.

'It was sent to you. How will it look if you don't turn up?'

Tess told herself she didn't care. That even the thought of going to the villa filled her with trepidation. She didn't know why Castelli had invited them, but she doubted it was going to be a social occasion. The mention of dinner was just a lure, an incentive to Ashley. He had no intention of allowing her to get away with what she'd done.

'I can't go,' she repeated now, folding the letter again and pushing it back into the envelope. 'I've got to get back to England. I can't afford to lose my job.'

Ashley was desperate. 'If you go, I'll never forgive you,' she said threateningly. 'I'll—I'll do something terrible to myself and I'll make sure my mother knows that you're to blame.'

'Then do it,' said Tess wearily, too distressed to care if she was hurting the other girl's feelings. 'Ashley, if you think I'm going to the villa knowing that you intend to ask for money, forget it. I've supported you this far but no further.'

'Tess!'

Ashley's wail of anguish was drowned out by the ringing of her mobile phone. The strains of Beethoven's 'Moonlight Sonata' sounded incongruous in the small apartment, but Ashley had evidently come to the same solution Tess had and she hurried into the other room to find the phone.

'Marco?' Tess heard her say excitedly. And then, 'Oh. Oh, I see. Yes. Yes, she's here.' By the time Tess had reached the bedroom door, Ashley was already coming back to her. 'It's Marco's father,' she hissed, with her hand over the mouthpiece. 'If you blow this, Tess, I'll make sure you regret it.'

Tess pulled a face at her as she took the phone. But her hand was shaking and she guessed Ashley attributed it to what she was threatening to do. 'H-Hello,' she said. And then, refusing to let Ashley intimidate her, she closed the door in her face. 'Signor di Castelli?' She moistened her lips. 'What do you want?'

'Oh, *cara*, is that any way to greet a lover?' he mocked gently, and she was tempted to disconnect the call there and then. He had no right ringing her here, no right to send her invitations to the villa. Just what game was he playing? Divide and conquer?

'I received your invitation,' she said tersely, deciding now was as good a time as any to tell him she wouldn't be accepting it. 'I'm sorry, but I'm flying back to England to-morrow.'

'Surely not.' His voice was low and disturbingly familiar. It couldn't help but stir the memories she was trying so hard to forget. '*Cara*, I want to see you again. Do not tell me you do not wish to see me also.'

Tess's breath came unevenly. 'I think the person you want to see is Ashley,' she said, keeping her voice steady with an effort. 'And—and she wants to see you, too, so that's all right. I—don't want to get involved. It's nothing to do with me. I've got to get back to England. I—I'm sorry if this disrupts your plans, but I think it's the best way, don't you?'

Castelli sighed. 'I cannot believe you can dismiss the night we spent together as if it never happened,' he said softly.

'It shouldn't have happened,' Tess responded, her palms becoming moist at the thought.

'No?' He sounded regretful. 'Me, I do not believe that. I remember every moment of it, *cara*. How it felt to touch you, how it felt to be inside you—'

'Stop it!' Tess couldn't bear to listen to any more knowing he didn't mean it. This was just a ploy to get her to agree to accompany Ashley to the villa, so she'd be there to pick up the pieces when he blew her sister apart. 'I—we agreed there were no commitments, on either side. It—it was—fun, but it didn't mean anything. You know that.'

'You wound me, *cara*.' His voice sounded strangely

harsh now and she guessed he hadn't expected her to see through his deception. 'And we did not agree to anything, as I recall. All I told you was that I was not prepared to offer you a holiday affair.'

'Nevertheless...' Tess felt out of her depth, but she refused to let him persuade her that the night had meant something to him when for the last three days she'd heard nothing from him. 'I know you're just using me to get at Ashley. Well, she can take care of herself. She doesn't need me to hold her hand.'

'You are perhaps concerned because you have been having some difficulty in getting on a flight back to England,' he went on, as if she hadn't spoken.

'How do you know that?' she demanded, but he didn't answer her.

'You are afraid you will not be back in time to start the new term at your school.' He paused. 'I can personally guarantee that if you accompany your sister to the villa tomorrow evening, you will be flown back to England the following day.'

Tess gulped. She would not be manipulated like this. 'No!'

'*Molto bene.*' Very well. His tone had hardened now and when he spoke again there was no expression in his voice. 'If you persist in adopting this attitude, then I am forced to take sterner measures.' He sucked in a breath. 'If you will not accept my invitation, then you leave me no choice but to contact the police.'

Castelli had said he would send a car for them and the sleek black limousine arrived promptly at half past seven. Tess had thought of arguing, of saying that as Ashley had a car they could drive themselves to the villa, but she decided not to bother. What was the point? Whatever she said, he'd do what he wanted. For the first time she was beginning to see what Ashley had been dealing with.

Not that she could forgive her sister for getting her involved in this. Not even Ashley's assertion that Castelli deserved everything he got was any compensation at all. But her sister was right about one thing: the Castellis were a law unto themselves. If they wanted something, they got it, and despite Ashley's confidence she doubted this was going to be an easy few hours.

Nevertheless, Ashley had been delighted when Tess had told her she was going to the villa, after all. She didn't care about all the murky details, the fact that Castelli had practically threatened them with arrest if they didn't obey his orders. Such things meant nothing to her.

'He'd never do it,' she said, when Tess voiced her own doubts about the proceedings. Then, judging that her sister might change her mind, Ashley added, 'Well, he might. I suppose we can't give him the chance, can we?'

In consequence, Ashley had spent all the next day searching for a suitable dress to wear that evening. She'd suggested that Tess should do the same, but she'd refused to waste time and money on such an event. She was convinced the whole evening was going to be a disaster. Why should she get dressed up?

As she was applying a bronzed eye-shadow to her lids, however, she half wished she'd done as Ashley suggested. There was no doubt that the white sheath her sister was wearing gave her the confidence of knowing she looked her best. And Ashley did look good, tall and slim and darkly beautiful. She made Tess feel like a pale shadow of herself.

Now, sitting in the back of the limousine, Tess accepted she could never compete with Ashley. Although she'd abandoned her first choice of a long skirt and basque top in favour of a black slip dress, she still felt underdressed. Her bare legs were nicely tanned, but they bore no comparison to Ashley's, which were much longer. And where Ashley's hair was smooth and sleekly styled, Tess's was a spiky blonde halo around her head.

It was about thirty kilometres from Ashley's apartment to the Villa Castelli. The chauffeur, a man of middle years, wearing a navy blue uniform and a peaked cap, informed them it would take about half an hour.

'No speeding tickets for him, then,' whispered Ashley drily, pulling a face at her sister. But after experiencing some of the hairpin bends on the road, Tess had to admit she was relieved.

And, no matter how prepared she'd thought she was, the Villa Castelli was so much more than she'd ever imagined. It seemed to float above a valley, where the mist rising from a lake that was hidden among trees gave it an eerie insubstantiality. The purpling shadows of evening were massing behind it, looking like mountains in the fading light. It was beautiful and remote, more like some fairy-tale palace than a house.

'What do you think?' asked Ashley in an undertone as the chauffeur turned between stone gateposts and they started up a steep, curving track towards the villa. They drove between cypress trees and flowering oleander, the vineyard dropping away below them in terraces where the budding vines would eventually ripen in the sun.

'It's—impressive,' said Tess, aware of the inadequacy of her words. 'Do you think so?'

'You forget, I've been here before,' Ashley reminded her. 'Not to go inside, I grant you. But I was pretty stunned by the house and grounds.'

'Hmm.'

But Tess was feeling more and more apprehensive. The beauty of the place, its very atmosphere, was intimidating, and no amount of encouragement on Ashley's part was going to make her feel any different. She didn't belong here; they didn't belong here. She felt like one of the Christian prisoners must have done before they were thrown to the lions.

'That's the loggia at the side of the house,' Ashley pointed out as they drew nearer to their destination. 'Marco and I had a glass of wine there. He was showing me the view.' She gave an expressive sigh. 'He's quite sweet, in his own way.' She lifted her shoulders. 'I could get used to living like this, you know.'

Tess glanced half apprehensively at her. 'That's not why we're here,' she warned, half afraid the younger girl was thinking of changing her mind.

'I know that. But I can dream, can't I?' Ashley retorted. 'In any case, I'd probably get bored after a while.' She pulled a face. 'But the money would be nice.'

Tess shook her head, dreading the evening before her. She felt as if she was dealing with three—or possibly four—people all of whom had their own agenda. How did Marco feel about his father's intervention? What kind of reception had he received when he'd got home? And would Signora di Castelli be there, casting a malevolent eye over the proceedings? Had she told her son about her visit to the gallery? Or was Tess supposed to behave as if she'd never seen the woman before?

So many questions; so few answers. The car was slowing and Tess felt totally unprepared for what was ahead. For the first time in her life she wished she could be more like Ashley. Her sister was enjoying this. She was actually looking forward to going head-to-head with Castelli himself.

The first impression Tess had was of grace and elegance. As she stepped out of the car beneath a pillared portico she was instantly enchanted by the building's sun-bleached walls and sloping roofs. A long veranda, made bright with hanging baskets and planters filled with flowering shrubs, gave access to a lamp-lit foyer, where more flowers sat in vases or spilled from urns across the floor.

The floor of the foyer was tiled in a rich pattern of white and gold and navy, and set about with chairs and sofas in matching shades. White walls, archways supported by sculpted columns, and yet more greenery, overflowing from pots and climbing up the walls.

A uniformed manservant had met them on their arrival, and it was he who escorted them inside. Then, with a murmur of apology, he left them to let his employer know that his guests had arrived, and Tess was left to wonder again why she had ever agreed to this.

Beyond the foyer a splendid apartment invited inspection. But although Ashley peered into the room, Tess remained firmly where she was. She could see enough: polished maple floors, soft hide sofas, chairs upholstered with tapestries embroidered by an expert hand. There were tall cabinets filled with artwork, low tables and oriental rugs. And raw silk drapes at the long windows that faced a huge fireplace with a carved marble surround.

It was the home of a rich man, thought Tess ruefully. As if she hadn't known that already. Was that why Ashley had been invited here? Because Castelli wanted to intimidate her with his wealth? Not that she really believed he needed any assistance. He was a master manipulator. She was here tonight because he'd insisted she should be. Instead of flying home to things that were familiar and safe, she was standing here waiting for the proverbial axe to fall.

Footsteps sounded on the stairs that led down into the foyer and she turned her head abruptly. But it wasn't Castelli who appeared. It was a much younger man. He was tall and slim, dressed in an open-necked white shirt and navy pants, and he looked so much like his father that Tess knew this must be Marco.

'Hey.' It was Ashley who spoke first, going to meet him as he reached the hall. 'What about this place?' she said, apparently realising he didn't look particularly pleased to see her. 'I had no idea it would be so—grand.'

'Didn't you?' Marco's smile came and went so swiftly Tess almost missed it. But then he was turning towards her, his hand extended in greeting. 'You must be the other Miss Daniels,' he said. 'My father asked me to come and meet you. Unfortunately, he has had to take a phone call. He will join us shortly.'

Tess allowed him to shake her hand, and then said, 'It's Marco, isn't it? You look so much like your father, I can't be mistaken.'

'Of course, this is Marco.' Ashley didn't like being ignored and she immediately went to his side and slipped her arm through his. 'Are you okay, sweetie?' she asked, deliberately attempting to invoke an intimacy between them. 'I hear you didn't tell your father about our trip.'

Marco looked down at her momentarily, a curious expression playing about his mouth. 'No, that was a mistake,' he said, politely removing himself from her possessive hold. '*Adesso*, will you come with me? There are drinks waiting on the loggia.'

Tess could see that Ashley liked this even less. Her dark brows drew together and she looked decidedly put out. For her part, Tess had to wonder if her sister had been mistaken about Marco's infatuation for her. Unless, the painting holiday—or his father—had opened his eyes.

CHAPTER FOURTEEN

THEY bypassed the elegant salon and entered another reception room, with a high frescoed ceiling and a cool marble floor. The furnishings were a little less formal here: cane-backed chairs, painted tables, cool statuary between windows that were open to the air. Mesh screens prevented insects from investigating the tall lamps that stood beside a grand piano, but Marco pushed them aside to allow them access to the loggia beyond.

The first person Tess saw was Lucia di Castelli. As Marco closed the screens again she saw Castelli's mother watching them from the comfort of her chair. She was not alone, however, and the elderly gentleman sitting with her rose to his feet politely. Unlike Marco, he was wearing a velvet dinner jacket and Tess hoped this wasn't going to be a very formal occasion.

His smile was welcoming, however, unlike Lucia who looked decidedly put out. *'Chi e questo?'* he said, speaking to Marco, and the boy quickly made the introductions.

'This is an old friend of my *nonna's.* The Count Vittorio di Mazzini.' He glanced at Tess and then continued. 'These are the two Miss Daniels we were telling you about, Tio Vittorio.'

A count! Tess digested this as the old man bowed over her hand. *'Piacere, signorinas,'* he said. And then continued with less fluency, 'Welcome to Italy. You are enjoying your visit to San Michele?'

'Tess is visiting. I live there,' remarked Ashley, before Marco could explain the situation. Her gaze moved to the other occupant of the loggia. 'And you must be Signora di Castelli, Marco's grandmother. Am I right?'

Tess winced at the brash way her sister had insinuated herself into the conversation and Lucia got regally to her feet. 'I am Lucia di Castelli, yes,' she said. 'Do I take it you are the young woman who works for Augustin Scottolino?'

The omission of any other reference was conspicuous. In those few words, Castelli's mother had successfully removed any connection between Ashley and her grandson. Tess could see the count absorbing this, perhaps wondering why the Castellis should have invited them to the villa. But he was too polite to ask the question and Lucia patted his hand understandingly.

'Are you not going to offer our guests some refreshment, Marco?' she asked as Ashley fumed over the deliberate slight. 'I hope your father will not be too long. It seems cooler this evening. Do you not think so, Vittorio?'

The count nodded as Marco said, 'That was my intention, Nonna.' He gestured towards the tray of drinks on a cabinet close by. 'What would you like, Miss Daniels?' He addressed himself to Tess again. 'Would you like wine, or a cocktail? Or perhaps you would prefer something stronger.'

'I think Tess would like wine, Marco,' remarked another voice behind them. Tess turned to find Castelli closing the screen door. 'White wine, am I right?' he asked, causing Ashley to transfer a wide-eyed gaze to her sister. Then, 'I am sorry I was not here to greet you. My *avvocato*—my lawyer—called at just the wrong time.'

Tess didn't know whether the mention of his lawyer was deliberate or not. She didn't know what to think with him standing there staring at her with that intent searching gaze. Another ploy? she wondered. Another gambit? Another attempt to put both her and Ashley on their guard? What was Ashley thinking? Was this what she had expected? Tess rather doubted it, but you never could tell.

'It doesn't matter,' she said now, realising they were all waiting for her to answer him. 'And—and a glass of wine would be very nice.' She paused, and then continued bravely, 'But I'd prefer Chianti. White wine tends to give me a headache.'

Ashley's eyes narrowed at this and Tess realised that she hadn't been too wise. It had been an empty bottle of white wine that Ashley had found in her bedroom. Now all it needed was for her sister to connect the two.

'*Veramente?*' Tess was glad it was getting dark and she hoped only she had noticed the sardonic arching of his brows. '*Bene, Marco. Chianti per la signorina, per favore. E Ashley? Un bicchier di vino, sì?*'

'No, thanks.' Ashley spoke offhandedly, and Tess wondered what she thought she'd achieve with that attitude. 'I'd prefer a gin and tonic, if you have it. Just show the gin the tonic, Marco. You know how I like it.'

The insinuation was plain and Tess accepted her glass from Marco and turned away. Lucia and the count had resumed their seats and were talking together, so she moved to the edge of the loggia, ostensibly to admire the view.

Even in the fading light, the lake glimmered below them like a jewel set among the trees. Stars were winking out and the sky grew darker as a sliver of moon appeared. A moth swooped past, bent on its own destruction, its destination the dozens of candles that illuminated the terrace.

'Do you like it?' murmured Castelli, and she realised he had come to stand beside her. He was wearing black trousers and a black silk shirt this evening and his sleeve, rolled back over his forearm, brushed her skin. If she was surprised he chose to make his interest in her so plain, she chose not to voice it. This was just another way to anger Ashley, she thought. He wanted her to bring the battle to him.

'It's beautiful,' she replied coolly. What else could she say? He had probably been complimented by more sophisticated guests than her. She moistened her lips and then decided there was no point in avoiding the issue. 'Why have you brought me here, Signor di Castelli? And please don't insult my intelligence by pretending you wanted to see me again.'

'But I did,' he told her softly, turning and propping his hips on the stone balustrade. 'And my name is Rafe, as I've told you several times already.' She could see his face now, his tawny eyes darkening and smouldering with an emotion she didn't want to identify. 'Come on, *cara*, say you are pleased to see me. Is this not a more civilised way of spending an evening than exchanging insults?'

Tess shook her head, her wine forgotten. 'I don't understand,' she said, wishing he wouldn't look at her that way.

'You will in—what is that expression?—in the fullness of time, *no*?' He lifted his hand and rubbed her arm with proprietary familiarity. 'You are cold. Would you like to go inside?'

'What I'd like is for you to stop treating me like an idiot,' she blurted in an undertone. 'You have no right to touch me, no right to—to jerk me around to satisfy some perverted desire to score points.' She swallowed, setting her glass aside, admitting that she really had no love for Chianti. 'Why have you invited Ashley and me to dinner? I know— I just know you don't really want us here.'

'I want you here,' he contradicted her, his voice playing on her senses. 'If to achieve that I have to be civil to your sister, also, then so be it.'

'No.' Tess was insistent in her denial. 'Dammit, you know nothing about me.'

'But I want to know more,' he essayed smoothly, his words rippling across her flesh. 'I want to possess you, *cara*. Not just your body, no matter how delectable the experience was, but your soul also.'

Tess trembled. A film of dampness enveloped her. Her stomach contracted and tiny beads of moisture trickled between her breasts. Did he know how she was feeling? Of course he must. He'd done this before. But she hadn't, and she was agitatedly aware that she was out of her depth.

A breeze wafted the scent of pine onto the loggia, and the draught of air stirred her awareness of his warmth, his heat. Despite what she'd said, she recognised the scent of his aftershave. It was as familiar to her as the clean male aroma of his skin.

She wondered if his sensual words had had an effect on his emotions. Though she had to remember that a man didn't need to involve his emotions to become aroused. Nevertheless, the thought took root, a disturbing compulsion she had to fight against. Much as she wanted to, she didn't dare let her eyes drop below his waist.

She had to get away from him, she told herself unsteadily. Before she did something really stupid like grab a handful of his shirt and jerk him towards her. Or maybe she would lean forward and wrap herself around him. Wouldn't his mother get a surprise if she did something as outrageous as that?

'Do it,' he urged her huskily, and she realised she had been staring at him for fully half a minute. And, dear God, it seemed he really could read her mind.

'Go to hell,' she snapped, grabbing up her glass again and marching back to where Ashley was still talking to Marco. Though, judging by her sister's expression, she was no happier with their conversation than Tess had been with his father's.

Marco seemed pleased to see Tess, however, and immediately asked if she wanted another drink. 'Nothing else, thank you,' she replied as Ashley turned to look accusingly at her. 'I'm not usually much of a drinker. I only have a glass of wine now and then.'

'Except when she has male company,' observed Ashley maliciously, finishing her own drink and offering her glass for a refill. 'Isn't that right, Tess? Even you have been known to break your own rules.'

Tess felt a wave of colour rising up her throat. 'I expect so,' she said, not wanting to argue with her in this mood. 'You have a beautiful home, Marco. Did this view inspire your desire to paint?'

'Oh, I would not say so,' murmured the boy, busying himself with replacing bottles on the tray.

'Marco's decided he doesn't have what it takes to become a painter,' Ashley put in scornfully. 'Or perhaps his father has decided for him. Who knows?'

'Marco knows that if he wants to continue with his painting studies, he has my permission,' declared Castelli, strolling across the loggia to join them. 'But now, I suggest we go and have dinner. Antonio has been trying to attract my attention for the last ten minutes.' He gestured towards the screens. 'Shall we go inside?'

To Tess's relief, there was no formal gathering to go into the house. Castelli led the way, with Ashley and Marco following on behind. The two older people made up the rear, and Tess was grateful when the count spoke to her about England. It was easier to think of going home and the enormous relief that would be.

The dining room they used was smaller than she'd expected, though she guessed it wasn't the only dining room in a house of this size. Nevertheless, its partly panelled walls and many small paintings made it less imposing, a huge chandelier suspended over the ebony table highlighting silver cutlery and Venetian glass.

The chandelier wasn't lit, however. Instead, silver candleholders, set at either end of the table, flickered with a mellow light. Scarlet hibiscus set among dark shiny leaves provided an exotic centrepiece and red wine, poured into tall decanters, looked rich and dark.

The table was set for six and Tess was relieved to find that Marco was sitting beside her. Castelli and his mother occupied the places at either end of the table, with Ashley and the count opposite. It should have been a pleasant occasion, but Tess was full of tension, a headache threatening at her temples. Only the count seemed unaware of the atmosphere—and Castelli, himself, who seemed able to divorce himself from any situation.

The food was exquisite: tortellini, filled with parsley and ricotta; tender chicken sautéed in a lemon sauce. There was a green salad to cleanse the palate before a selection of rich pastries and Italian cheeses were offered, and as much wine as she could drink, which wasn't very much.

In fact, Tess ate very little either. She was conscious of both Castelli and his mother watching her, and Ashley was obviously nurturing her resentment as she kept allowing the man who served them to refill her glass. Tess hoped her sister wouldn't drink too much and say something that would embarrass them all. Castelli's surprising acknowledgement of his son's interest in painting had evidently rankled.

Marco spoke little, answering his grandmother when she asked how soon he had to return to college, and exchanging the occasional few words with the count. When Ashley spoke to him, he seemed strangely noncommittal, and Tess could see that her sister resented his detachment.

Just as Tess was beginning to hope that they might get through the meal without a scene, Ashley turned to her host and said, 'I suppose you think you're very clever, don't you?'

'Ashley!'

Tess was appalled. Clearly the wine had loosened her sister's tongue and she dreaded what she might say next.

But, although Lucia di Castelli looked mildly dismayed, Castelli was unperturbed. 'Not clever at all,' he demurred, getting up from the table. 'But if you wish to speak to me, I would prefer it if you did not embarrass my guests.'

'I bet you would.' Ashley made no attempt to get up from the table, and Marco cast his father a worried look.

'I think Ashley's had too much wine,' he said, and Tess admired his courage for saying it. He looked across the table at the younger woman. 'Would you like to get some air?'

'With you?' Ashley drawled, narrowing her eyes suggestively, and Tess wanted to die at that moment. She had guessed this was coming, but there'd been nothing she could do to stop it. She just hoped Marco had more sense than to play into her sister's hands.

'Yes, with me,' said Marco, pushing back his chair and getting to his feet.

'But perhaps I'd prefer to be escorted by your father,' Ashley declared, apparently deciding Marco wasn't going to give her what she wanted. 'How about it, Signor di Castelli? Would you like to show me the gardens by moonlight?'

'Papa!'

'Ashley!'

Marco and Tess spoke almost simultaneously, but Castelli was already helping Ashley up out of her chair. 'I will be delighted to show you the gardens, *signorina*,' he said, 'if your sister will agree to accompany us.'

Tess looked up then, right into his eyes, and her heart felt as if it turned a somersault right there in her chest. Oh, God, she thought, why was he doing this, why was he tormenting her? Why didn't he just tell Ashley he wasn't playing her games and send them home?

'I don't need a chaperon, *signore*.' Ashley swayed a little and caught his arm and Tess almost groaned with frustration.

But, 'I do,' was all he said in reply, and once again he was looking at her. '*Bene*, Tess,' he said. 'Will you come with us?'

Tess pressed her lips together for a moment, and then she nodded and got abruptly to her feet. 'If you insist,' she said, refusing to acknowledge the angry stares Ashley was casting in her direction. This wasn't her choice, surely her sister knew that.

'Shall I come, also, Papa?'

Marco was obviously disturbed by this development and Ashley gave him a contemptuous look. 'Oh, yes,' she said scornfully. 'Why don't we make this a family party? Are you coming, Lucia? Count? Let's all go outside and have ourselves an orgy.' She gave a harsh laugh. 'That sounds like a plan.'

Tess was mortified, as much by Ashley's disrespect towards the older woman as by what she'd actually said. She'd had no idea that the wine would have such an unfortunate effect on her sister. She seemed totally out of control.

Castelli said nothing. He merely took Ashley's arm and guided her across the room. It was only when Ashley tried to jerk away that Tess realised her sister wasn't cooperating. But as Tess knew for herself, Castelli was immensely strong.

'Papa…'

Marco spoke again, and Tess could see that the boy was unsure what to do in the circumstances. 'Order coffee,' said his father without pausing. 'Tess! Are you coming?'

What choice did she have? thought Tess, casting an apologetic look at Castelli's mother and the count. Then, 'Excuse me,' she said, ducking her head, and hurried after the others.

Once again, they emerged onto the loggia, but this time Castelli led Ashley down the steps to the formal gardens that surrounded the house. The night air was cool and lightly scented with orange blossom. Tess thought she would never encounter that smell again without thinking of tonight.

But at least the night air seemed to bring Ashley to her senses and lamps, set among the greenery, illuminated their path. When they were far enough from the villa for their conversation not to be overheard, she succeeded in wrenching her arm from Castelli's grasp. Then she glared at both of them with equal dislike.

'What is this?' she exclaimed. 'What do you know that I don't, Tess? You insisted you didn't want to come here, so I don't think you're involved in this conspiracy. Or are you?'

Castelli took a deep breath. There was a stone fountain close by and he leaned back against the rim. 'There is no conspiracy, Miss Daniels,' he declared after a moment. 'I thought it was important that you should hear what Marco has to say. I have not threatened him and I am not threatening you. I have been extremely tolerant. And your sister is here because I invited her. I wanted her to know exactly what was said between us.'

'Oh, really?' Ashley sneered. 'What are you afraid of, *signore*? Don't you think you're big enough to handle a red-blooded woman like me?'

As Tess cringed at Ashley's crassness their host shrugged indifferently. 'I have no desire to handle you at all, Miss Daniels,' he remarked and Ashley's face flushed with anger at his dismissal. 'But I do not trust you. You are, I think, quite unscrupulous in your desire to achieve your own ends.'

Ashley snorted. 'It sounds as if you think I might charge you with assaulting me,' she retorted. 'That's not a bad idea, accusing the arrogant Raphael di Castelli with rape.' She looked at Tess, whose mouth had dropped with horror. 'How do you know she won't support me? Just think how much more convincing it would be if we both told the same story.'

'For pity's sake, Ashley!'

Tess started to protest, but Castelli's words overrode her. 'Tess wouldn't do it,' he said. 'And I think even you have more sense than that. This is not a game, Miss Daniels. It is my son's life you have been toying with. And I should tell you, you are only here now because I have no desire to hurt your sister.'

Ashley's eyes narrowed. 'So Tess is involved.' She made a contemptuous sound. 'I might have known it. What has she been telling you? That I wouldn't touch your darling boy, if I had a choice.'

'I've said nothing,' Tess exclaimed, stung by Ashley's willingness to shift the blame onto her shoulders. 'Let's go home, Ash. Can't you see you're wasting your time here?'

'Not yet.' It was Castelli who spoke now and they both turned to look at him. 'I think it is time I came to the point of this discussion.'

'I wish you would.' Ashley ignored her sister. She parted her lips and allowed her tongue to appear in silent provocation. 'Poor Marco will be wondering where I am. Just because he's decided he doesn't have a talent for art doesn't mean we can't still see one another. He's been a little subdued this evening. I think it's time I showed him how to have some fun.'

Castelli's lips curled. 'I think Marco has realised he made a mistake going away with you,' he said levelly. 'He tells me you and this man, Carlo Ravelli, got to know one another rather well.' Tess caught her breath and turned to her sister, but Castelli wasn't finished. 'Marco is not a fool, Miss Daniels. You may have thought you were very discreet, but he is not too young to notice what was going on.'

Ashley looked furious now. 'Are you saying that little rat was spying on me?' she demanded.

'Not spying on you, no.' Castelli shook his head. 'But, as I am sure you have told your sister, Marco was infatuated with you. Do you blame him if he was concerned that Ravelli was becoming too familiar? He wanted to protect you, Miss Daniels. He thought the man was annoying you. Imagine his surprise when he found Ravelli slept in your bed.'

Tess was stunned, and even Ashley looked a little sick at this revelation. 'He was mistaken,' she said hastily. 'Carlo was just—just pretending he was interested in me.'

'Oh, I believe you.' Castelli was sardonic. 'I imagine a man like Ravelli makes many conquests. You were just one more. But you made a mistake, too, Miss Daniels. Just now, when you said Marco would be missing you, you knew he would not. A young man's feelings are easily hurt. And you hurt Marco. You made a fool of him, *signorina*. He will not forgive you for that.'

'You mean, you won't let him,' snarled Ashley, and Tess knew she could see all her carefully thought-out plans going down the drain. 'Well, we'll see, Signor di Castelli. I'm not planning on going anywhere. Marco may change his mind when I explain it to him.'

'I do not think you will have time to explain anything to

Marco. You will not be staying in San Michele, Miss Daniels,' he declared, spreading his hands. 'As of tomorrow, the gallery is to be closed. I have spoken to Augustin Scottolino and I have his word on that.'

'You—you—'

'Careful, *signorina*. You have not heard all that I have to say and you may regret it if you are too reckless in your anger.' Castelli glanced at Tess briefly, and then went on with heavy emphasis. 'I am prepared to make your—what shall we say?—your redundancy more tolerable. If you agree to leave San Michele and return to England, I will pay forty thousand pounds into your bank account. Not all at once, of course, but in instalments: ten thousand pounds a year for the next four years.'

CHAPTER FIFTEEN

TESS was teaching a year nine class when Mrs Peacock sent for her. One of the school secretaries came to give her the message and Tess felt an immediate sense of apprehension. Mrs Peacock did not drag one of her teachers out of class unless something pretty drastic had happened. Had either Ashley or her stepmother been taken ill or involved in an accident? Heaven forbid! If not, she couldn't imagine that she'd done anything wrong.

Not that she could be absolutely sure of that. Although the private jet the Castellis had provided had ensured that she'd been back home in plenty of time for the start of term, Mrs Peacock had chided her for being unavailable for the whole of the holidays. She had tried to get in touch with her, she'd said. Certain assignments hadn't been handed in before the end of term, and the head teacher had decided to make it her business to find out why. The fact that Tess had been able to assure her that she had all the assignments and was marking them hadn't pleased her. Particularly as Tess had had to admit that she still had some marking left to do.

All the same, that had been over three weeks ago. Since then, Tess had done everything she could to complete her work on schedule and keep out of Mrs Peacock's way. This summons now was really depressing. She was beginning to think she hadn't been cut out to be a teacher, after all.

Looking after the gallery in San Michele while Ashley was away had probably unsettled her, she decided. It had been an emotional roller coaster from start to finish and even now she couldn't think of what had happened without regret. Regret for Marco, who had discovered firsthand what it felt like to be betrayed, and for herself in allowing Ashley to ruin her life.

Pursing her lips, she hurried along the corridor towards Mrs Peacock's office. That was over-dramatising things, she told herself. Ashley hadn't ruined her life; she'd done that for herself. She'd known from the beginning that it would be madness to get involved with Rafe di Castelli. Yet, she'd let him get close to her; had encouraged him, in fact. And when the inevitable had happened and he'd made love to her, she'd allowed herself to fall in love with him.

And how pathetic was that?

The only blessing was that Ashley hadn't guessed how stupidly she'd behaved. Even with the evidence of the wine bottle and the fact that some man had spent the night in the apartment, Ashley hadn't associated that with him. Or perhaps she'd had more important things on her mind when they'd got back from the villa. Like how soon she could start spending Castelli's money. And how she could now afford to rent a small flat in London instead of living with her mother.

For her part, Tess had been too disgusted at the turn of events to make much conversation, and she guessed her sister had assumed she was to blame for Tess's black mood. And, in part, she was. Tess had been sickened by the way Ashley had accepted Castelli's offer. No wonder he thought money could buy anything. Yet, he was to blame, also. She found it hard to forgive him for making her an unwilling witness to her sister's greed.

He'd tried to speak to her after Ashley had gone back to the house to collect her belongings. He'd blocked her path when she'd tried to follow her sister, saying desperately, 'Please: do not go like this.' And when she still refused to speak to him, to look at him even, he became angry. '*Dio mio*, Tess,' he burst out. 'What did you expect me to do?'

'I don't want to talk about it,' she told him stiffly. 'I don't see any reason why you had to involve me in this sordid affair.' She darted a glance his way and then wished she hadn't when she saw the haunted look on his face. 'Were you really afraid that Ashley might accuse you of assault if you spoke to her alone? Or did you just want me to see for myself how ruthless you can be?'

'Ruthless? No!'

He seemed stunned by her accusation. And she guessed that in his world what he'd done was no big thing. Paying off a mistress was probably acceptable. And if Ashley hadn't actually been Marco's mistress, that didn't matter. In fact it was a plus, and it still got her off his hands.

'Cunning, then,' she said, refusing to feel any sympathy for him. 'Giving Ashley the money in four instalments. I suppose you're hoping that by the time Marco is twenty-one, he'll have more sense than to get involved with her again.'

Castelli sighed then. 'I do not believe Marco would be so foolish as to care what your sister does, with or without the money,' he said flatly. 'And if your sister was the only one involved, I think I would have taken that chance. I am not buying Marco's freedom, Tess. I was hoping I was making the problem of Ashley go away, for both of us. And I knew it would be easier if she thought she had won.'

Tess didn't know what to think then, except that he was cleverer than even she had imagined. Somehow, he'd turned the situation around and made it seem as if he'd done it all for her. As if, she thought bitterly. How could he even imagine she would condone his behaviour? He was powerful, and ruthless, as she'd said, and he was determined to have his own way.

Somehow, she pushed past him then and hurried along the path back to the villa. Ashley was waiting and Signora di Castelli was happy to summon the chauffeur to drive them back to Porto San Michele. Only Marco seemed to care that his father wasn't there to bid them farewell. But Tess put his concern down to anxiety that their plan might not have worked.

Since then, Tess had spent many sleepless nights wondering why she'd been so eager to think the worst of him. Perhaps the truth was, it had been the only way she knew to get out of there without breaking down completely. Whatever he'd said, whatever he'd done, she'd known there was no future in their relationship. Allowing he had only had the best interests of all concerned at heart only made it impossible to bear.

Outside the corridor windows, it was raining. A steady drizzle had fallen for most of the last week, which hadn't helped. East Vale, which lay on the northern outskirts of Buxton, was a pretty place, and Tess used to like living here. But now her job had become her only lifeline in a future that stretched ahead of her, cold and bleak.

Mrs Peacock's office door stood ajar and Tess halted rather uncertainly. The older woman was a stickler for protocol and her door was always shut. She usually made her staff knock before being summoned into her presence. Tess thought it gave her a feeling of importance and that usually worked to her advantage.

Now Tess tapped at the door, only to find it opened inward at her touch. 'Mrs Peacock?' she said, half alarmed at this development. Surely the woman wasn't ill. She would hardly have sent for Tess if she were.

Her alarm increased at the sight of a man standing by the window. He had his back to her and, for a moment, she wondered if he was an intruder. But there was something unbelievably familiar about the way his dark hair brushed the collar of his leather overcoat, a disturbing recognition that she knew him.

'Come in, Tess,' he said, without turning, and her mouth dried at the realisation that it was Castelli. She'd thought it might be; no, she'd known it *was*. What she couldn't get her head round was why he should be here.

'Um—where's Mrs Peacock?' she asked. A stupid question, but it was the only thing she could think to say. The real questions like, *Why are you here? What do you want?*

were simply beyond her. She had neither the courage, nor the right, she conceded, to ask him anything.

'She has gone to organise some coffee,' he said, and now he turned to face her. The incongruity of that statement, the fact that Mrs Peacock never organised coffee for her guests herself, went over Tess's head. She was staring at him, noticing how much thinner he looked, the lines beside his mouth that hadn't been there before. 'How are you, Tess? You look well,' he continued, his hands pushed deep into his pockets. His lips twitched as he looked at her, too. 'You are letting your hair grow.'

Tess put an uncertain hand to her head. Then let it fall to her side. 'I—yes. Yes, it used to be long, but I cut it before—before the Easter holidays.' She moistened her lips. 'How are you? How's Marco? Your mother?'

'Marco is back at school, working hard, I believe. My mother?' He shrugged. 'She and Vittorio have gone on a cruise.' He paused. 'Me, I am surviving. I think that is the expression.'

Tess let out the breath she had hardly been aware she was holding. And then, realising she was still hovering in the doorway, she stepped rather tentatively into the room. 'Surviving?' she said, not sure how to take that and deciding he was probably being sarcastic. 'I'm sure you're in no danger of extinction.'

'You think not?'

His words disconcerted her and for a moment a wave of fear swept over her. 'You're—you're not ill, are you?' she asked, moving to the desk and staring at him across its width.

'Would it make any difference to you if I was?' he countered, making no attempt to leave his position by the window.

She tried to gauge if he was serious. Then, 'Of course it would,' she said, feeling her nails digging into her palms at her side. She swallowed. 'But you're not ill, are you? That was just a trick question. What are you doing here, Castelli?

If you're looking for Ashley, I've told you she doesn't live near me.'

His dark face hardened. 'I did not come here looking for your sister,' he said harshly. '*Dio*, Tess, must every conversation we have include that woman's name? At the risk of being ridiculed again, I came to see you. My assistant and myself had no easy task to find you. Do you know how many schools there are in the Buxton area? I can tell you, more than a few.'

Tess glanced nervously behind her. She had left the door to the corridor open and she could imagine Mrs Peacock coming back and hearing this and wondering what on earth this annoying member of her staff had done now.

'She will not return,' said Castelli, as if reading her mind. 'We are alone, Tess. Now—perhaps you will tell me how you felt when you discovered I was here.'

Tess took a deep breath. 'I—I was surprised,' she murmured inadequately.

'Surprised?' His dark brows arched in inquiry. 'So, you do not hate me any more?'

'I never hated you.' The words broke from her. 'I never said I hated you.'

'But you did not like me much when you left the villa,' he reminded her softly. 'I have found it very hard to live with that.'

Tess felt a quiver in her stomach. 'I'm sorry,' she said, not knowing how to answer him. Had he come all this way to gain her forgiveness? It was probably the kind of thing he would do. 'I—I think after what happened, I just felt— humiliated. But—but afterwards, I understood that you thought you were protecting your son.'

Castelli swore then, dragging a hand out of his pocket and raking it across his scalp. 'My son can take care of himself,' he said harshly. 'It was you I was concerned about. That was why I wanted to make sure you did not leave Italy until I had had a chance to speak to you. You seemed so—

loyal, so vulnerable. I wanted you to see how unscrupulous your sister was and—in your terminology—I blew it.'

Tess really didn't know what to say now, and she could only shake her head helplessly. It was obvious he blamed himself for what had happened and she wished she had some trite reassurance to give him.

'It doesn't matter,' she said at last. 'I've gotten over it.' She pressed her hands down on the desk, trying to keep the emotion out of her voice. 'Um—are you staying in England long?'

Castelli blew out a breath. 'That is the question, is it not? How long am I staying?' His lips twisted. 'What shall I say? As long as it takes to persuade you to come back to Italy in the summer?'

Tess blinked. 'Well, I would like to visit Italy again,' she began, but he interrupted her.

'Perhaps I did not make myself plain,' he said. 'I want you to come back to Tuscany and stay at the villa with me.' He paused as her eyes widened, her lips parting in confusion. 'Marco is spending the summer in France, working at a vineyard in the Loire Valley. We will be completely alone and, if that scares you, I will ask my mother to act as chaperon.'

Tess could only stare at him. 'Why would you want me to stay at the villa?'

Castelli didn't answer her. Instead, he went on, 'Lucia is already of the opinion that I am crazy to think you might agree. She says you only see me as Marco's father, that I am too old for such nonsense. And I know she is right, but still I had to come.'

Tess drew a trembling breath. 'Why do you want me to stay at the villa?' she asked again. 'Castelli—Rafe—what exactly are you offering? A holiday in the sun, or some crazy compensation for what you think I think about what you did for Ashley?'

He bent his head, his lean cheeks hollowing as he composed his answer. 'I am offering neither,' he said, his voice rough with emotion. 'It is my unskilled way of asking you if you will give me another chance.'

Tess was really trembling now. 'Another chance for what?' she asked unsteadily, needing him to spell it out, and he lifted his head, his face haggard in the grey morning light.

'To show you how much I care about you,' he said simply. 'To give me time to prove I am not the arrogant fool you think I am.'

Tess couldn't believe what she was hearing. And some of that confusion must have shown in her face. But this time Castelli's sixth sense was sadly lacking. Because instead of understanding how she was feeling, he carried on.

'If—if you think I am too old for you, as my mother says, then I would have to agree with you. Or there may be some man in England who has a prior claim to your affections. If there is, then so be it. But you understand I had to come here. I had to know—'

'Don't!' Tess cared about him too much to allow him to continue. 'Please, Rafe, don't go on.'

'No?' His eyes darkened, their tawny brilliance clouded now and dull with fatigue. '*Bene*, at least that is honest.' He made an obvious effort to gather himself. 'Perhaps you would give my thanks to Mrs Peacock for allowing me to use her office.'

'No, you don't understand!' Before he could move, before he could talk himself out of the room and out of her life, Tess had to stop him. She sidestepped the desk as he came towards her, virtually forcing him into a partial retreat. 'Oh, God, Rafe, I thought I was never going to see you again.'

He looked stunned now, staring at her as if he couldn't quite believe what he was hearing. He lifted his hands as if to grip her arms and then let them fall. 'You mean, you will come to the villa?' he asked hoarsely. And when she nodded she saw that the hand he raised to grip the back of his neck shook a little.

It made her want to touch him. It made her want to take hold of him and silence any doubts he still had with her mouth. Even the idea of kissing him again caused an explosion of need in her belly. She'd wanted him so badly, she realised. Could she really believe he wanted her, too?

'You—you will stay for how long?' he probed, and she wondered what he was thinking.

'How long would you like me to stay?' she countered softly, knowing that as she spoke her warm breath was fanning his chin. She'd stepped closer so that there was barely a hand's breadth between them. The sides of his coat were parted and she felt his heat envelop her despite the fine silk of his shirt.

'For ever,' he suggested harshly, and then shook his head as if impatient with himself. And, before she could respond, he changed his answer. 'Um—you have six weeks' holiday, do you not? If I say four weeks—'

Tess could hardly speak. He actually wanted her to live with him at the villa. Any limitations to be put on it, she would put there herself. She took a breath, knew that the next few minutes were probably going to be the most important minutes of her life. With a daring she hardly recognised she said huskily, 'For ever sounds better.'

Castelli made a strangled sound in his throat. 'You mean—you want to stay with me?'

'As long as you'll have me,' she whispered, lifting her hand to cup his cheek. 'Is that what you wanted to hear?'

'*Dio, mi amore,* it is what I wanted to hear,' he said, his voice breaking with emotion. He covered her hand with his and turned his face into her palm. She felt his tongue against her skin, shivered in anticipation. And then he bent his head to hers and his mouth touched her lips.

Tess clutched the front of his coat, pressing herself against him. She could feel his heart hammering in his chest, sensed the wildness in his kiss that he was trying so hard to control. But he was hungry for her; they were hungry for each other. And what began with sensitivity and tenderness quickly developed into a passionate assault that seared her soul.

He stepped back, taking her with him, and with the wall to support him he transferred his hands to her breasts. Her nipples peaked at the first brush of his fingers over the white blouse she was wearing, and she desperately wanted him to pull the hem of the blouse out of her skirt and touch her skin.

The scratch of his stubble scraped her cheek as he explored her earlobe, his teeth catching the soft flesh and dragging it into his mouth. Tess felt consumed by her senses, at the mercy of her body's gnawing hunger, and when he finally pulled away she gave a plaintive cry.

'Rafe—'

'*Cara*, I want you,' he told her fiercely. 'How can you doubt it? But not here. Not in this office.' He gave a half-smile. '*Per di pui*, I think that would be too much for your Mrs Peacock, *no*?' He ran his tongue across her parted lips to console her before putting her from him. 'Come, show me where you live. You said you had an apartment, did you not?'

Tess's apartment occupied the ground floor of a Victorian town house about half a mile from the school. To her surprise, she discovered Castelli had leased a car, a small compact, much different from the cars he drove at home.

'I know the Peak District a little,' he said as they covered the short distance to Hawthorn Terrace. 'I did some pot-holing here when I was a young man.'

'You're still a young man.' Tess hesitated for a moment and then squeezed his thigh with unfamiliar intimacy. 'I still can't believe you're real, that you've actually come all this way just to see me.'

'Not just to see you,' Castelli corrected her softly. 'To tell you I want you in my life.'

Tess had her keys in her hand as they went up the short path to the entrance of her apartment. But her hands were trembling so much, she couldn't open the door. Eventually, Castelli took the keys from her and succeeded in unlocking it, and then they were inside and she turned automatically into his arms.

The kiss they exchanged was all too brief before he gently nudged her ahead of him down the long narrow hall. 'Show me where you live,' he said, and she led the way past the bedroom and the living room into the kitchen-cum-dining room, keeping up a rather breathless patter as they went.

'I've lived here for almost nine years,' she said as he paused in the doorway to the kitchen. 'I'm responsible for the décor. I painted it myself. And do you like my plants? I grow herbs because they have such a lovely scent.'

'It is—charming,' he said, and, although she knew it was much different from what he was used to, she had the feeling he meant it. 'I have tried to picture your home many times in my imagination.' His smile came and went with a gentle sweetness. 'I knew it would be as neat and efficient as you.'

'You make me sound very dull,' she said, turning away to switch on the concealed lights to brighten the small apartment. She wasn't sure of him any more, she realised. Bringing him here had probably been a mistake. The kiss they'd exchanged had hardly been the passionate encounter she'd envisaged. There seemed to be a hesitation between them now, which she didn't know how to breach.

But while she was fretting over this, bustling about, filling the kettle and setting out cups for instant coffee she doubted he'd like, he came behind her. He had shed his coat, she discovered as he slipped his arms about her waist.

'*Cara,*' he said huskily, 'there is nothing dull about you. You are everything I have ever wanted in a woman. But are you prepared to give up your life in England to come and live with me?'

Tess caught her breath. 'I thought I'd already proved that,' she exclaimed, twisting in his arms until she was facing him. She framed his face with her hands. 'I'll do anything you want. You know that.'

'But it is a big step,' he said, and she acknowledged it was when he was obviously making no formal commitment. What had Ashley said? That Marco had insisted his father would never get married again?

'If you want me, I'm yours,' she said simply, casting any lingering doubts aside as she gazed up at him. If she lived with this man for a year, or a month, or a week, it could never be enough. But she would take what she was given and be grateful for it.

'*Mi amore!*'

Castelli's hoarse words of endearment were his submission. His mouth sought hers as his hands pressed her even closer to his taut frame. The feel of him, the smell of him, the taste of him surrounded her, and she tore his shirt apart and burrowed next to his skin.

'*Dio*, Tess, these have been the longest three weeks of my life,' he muttered, unbuttoning her shirt with unsteady fingers. He exposed the lacy bra she was wearing, and a look of pure indulgence crossed his lean face. '*Bellissima,*' he said, bending to bury his face into the moist hollow between her breasts. 'You are so beautiful, *innamorata.*'

Tess trembled beneath his hands and even Castelli seemed a little shaken by the strength of their feelings for one another. Glancing behind him, he saw one of the dining chairs pulled out from the table and sank down into it with obvious relief.

He had taken her with him, and she could feel his erection hard beneath her now. Hitching up her skirt, she straddled him to bring him even closer to the pulse that was beating between her legs.

Castelli had loosened her bra and his teeth tugged almost painfully at her nipple, but she knew it was only an indication of how desperate to be with her he was. His shirt was open now and she peeled it off his shoulders, running her tongue over his warm flesh, revelling in the taste of him.

Touching him like this was such a turn-on. So much so that she couldn't resist unbuckling his belt and unzipping his pants.

'Tess,' he groaned, but he didn't stop her, though when she started to caress him he had to protest. 'Remember I am only human and I want you very much,' he said thickly. 'Unless you do not want me inside you when I come you had better not touch me any more.'

Tess hesitated only a moment, and then, sliding off his lap, she quickly dropped her skirt and panties to the floor. 'Is this better?' she breathed, positioning herself and then sliding down slickly onto him, and Castelli caught her mouth in a savage kiss.

'*Molto meglio*. Much better,' he said hoarsely, and with a triumphant little smile she rose above him again.

'And this?' she whispered as his hands clung to her hips to guide himself deeper into her, and he nodded and buried his face between her breasts, unable to speak.

It was soon over, and when they were both weak and breathless from their passion Castelli sealed their lovemaking with a tender kiss.

'*Ti amo*. I love you,' he told her huskily, making no attempt to separate himself from her. 'I want you to come back to Italy with me. I cannot wait for another two months to elapse before you are free.'

EPILOGUE

THREE months later Tess was quite used to living at the Villa Castelli. Marco seemed quite happy to have her around and, although Maria still had reservations, because Tess had made her father so happy she was prepared to give her the benefit of the doubt.

Castelli's mother was another matter. Tess knew she didn't approve of her son living with a woman who was not his wife. But, like Maria, she had had to accept that Rafe was obviously in love with his English mistress, and Tess guessed she thought that in time he'd get tired of her as he had of other women he'd dated.

For herself, Tess didn't look too far to the future. It was enough that she was here, that Castelli apparently doted on her. She certainly doted on him, and if at any time the prospect of what she would do if he became tired of her impinged on her consciousness, she determinedly fought the demons of that particular despair.

Travelling back to Italy with him had been so exciting. At first she hadn't known how Castelli had persuaded Mrs Peacock and the board of governors to let her leave halfway though the term, but eventually he'd confessed that he'd made a donation to the school, a fact he'd kept from her, he'd said, because he'd been afraid she wouldn't approve.

Which had been rather foolish, she'd conceded, kissing him. That was one occasion when she'd been grateful for his financial contribution. Giving up her apartment had been harder. But, as Castelli had said, there'd been no point in continuing to pay rent when she wasn't coming back.

Well, not immediately, she amended now, waking to find the bed empty beside her. She and Castelli had their own

183

suite of rooms and she slid out of bed and padded naked into the bathroom without any fear of being observed. Who knew what the future held? She had already stayed longer than she knew her stepmother had expected. Andrea had been very scathing when she'd explained what she was going to do.

Ashley was in the United States at present. Although she, too, had been scornful of Tess for giving up her teaching post and moving to Italy, she was too busy with her new career in advertising to care. Tess suspected what she was doing was not quite as glamorous as she would have them believe but she wished her sister every success anyway.

Tess was in the shower when she saw a shadow in the bathroom, and she wasn't surprised when, moments later, Castelli slid open the shower door.

'I hoped you would not yet be up,' he said, and she saw he was just wearing his boxers. 'I went downstairs to get something out of the safe.'

Tess turned off the shower and stepped out into the folds of the fluffy towel he was holding. 'I thought you'd gone to work,' she said. Castelli spent most mornings in his office at the winery, and Tess had got into the habit of giving English lessons to the children whose parents worked on the estate while he was away.

'It is Saturday,' he said, and she pulled a face at the realisation.

'I'm still half asleep,' she confessed ruefully. 'That's why I was taking a shower.'

'We will both take a shower later,' said Castelli, walking back into the bedroom, and Tess followed him, feeling an anxious tingling in her stomach. He hadn't kissed her, she thought. He hadn't made any attempt to touch her after wrapping the towel around her. Another morning he would have joined her in the shower. Was something wrong?

His words came back to her. He'd been downstairs, he'd said, getting something out of the safe. Oh, God, she thought weakly. Was he going to pay her off now? She trembled.

She had been too optimistic, she thought, imagining their relationship was permanent. Just because he'd said he loved her, she'd believed that it would last.

She hardly noticed the bedroom that had once inspired such delight in her. The marble floors, strewn with Chinese rugs, and the enormous four-poster bed. The windows stood wide to their own private balcony, where sometimes they had breakfast together. She could see that the maid had already delivered orange juice and coffee. The two jugs were standing on the white linen tablecloth that covered the table on the balcony, a basket of warm rolls and creamy butter just waiting for them to taste.

But Castelli didn't go out onto the balcony. Instead, he sat down on the side of the bed and gestured for her to sit beside him. Tess gathered the towel closer about her, feeling absurdly shy all of a sudden. If he was going to send her away, she thought, she didn't want any money from him.

'So,' he said at last, turning to look at her, and she had to force herself not to reach for him, to bestow a warm kiss on his lean, tanned cheek. There was a look of detachment in his eyes, a wary frown that defined her uncertainty. 'I have something to tell you,' he continued. 'I was going to tell you last night, but I—what do you say?—ducked out, yes? At the last minute.'

Tess was certain she knew what he was going to say now. The night before they'd had a romantic dinner together on the loggia, and afterwards they'd danced to the music from a trio of musicians who also worked on the estate. It had had all the makings of a special occasion—or a last evening, she acknowledged painfully. And instead of spoiling it by telling her their affair was over, he had taken her to bed and made frantic love to her for half the night.

Yes, she should definitely have realised that something was different, she thought despairingly. Would it make it easier for him if she told him she wanted to go? But no. She had to hear it from his lips. Even if it was the last thing he said to her. There must be no mistakes, no pre-emptive tears to make him change his mind.

Now she looked at him, keeping her tears at bay with an effort. 'Go on,' she said huskily. 'What is it you want to say?'

Castelli bent his head. 'It is not easy, Tess,' he said. 'You know I love you, do you not? Well, now I find that is not enough.'

'No?'

The word was barely audible, caught as it was by the tightness in her throat. 'No,' he said unevenly. 'I realise these weeks—months—together have been magical. But— I need more. I need to know you are mine. Not just physically but spiritually as well.'

Tess stared at him. 'I—I don't know what you mean,' she stammered.

'This is why I went down to the safe,' he said, producing a small box from beneath the satin coverlet of the bed. 'It is a ring, *cara*. It once belonged to my grandmother. I would like you to wear it. It is a betrothal ring, of course, and I know what that means.'

Tess swallowed. 'Does it mean you want to marry me?' she asked disbelievingly, and he nodded.

'But I will understand if you say no.' He caught her hand and took it to his lips. '*Cara*, I know we have never talked of marriage and it is a big step for you to take, but I would like you to consider it. You do not have to decide right away,' he added, seeing her stunned expression and mis-understanding its meaning. 'You can have all the time in the world.' His lips twitched. 'Well, the rest of the day, perhaps.'

'Oh, Rafe!' With a strangled cry she flung herself into his arms, laughing and crying together. 'I thought you were going to break up with me. I couldn't think of anything else you might want to say to me.'

'Break up with you?' He drew back to look into her face, and she saw his eyes were dark with emotion. 'I wanted to ask you to marry me weeks, no, months ago. But I wanted to give you time to be sure that this was what you really wanted, too.'

'Oh, Rafe!' She kissed him soundly and then drew back to let him put the ring on her finger. It fitted perfectly, and he gave a smug little grin.

'I had it sized,' he admitted, and she remembered how he had once pretended to admire her signet ring. 'So—will you marry me, *mi amore*? Will you live with me and be my love?'

And, of course, she said yes.

THE SICILIAN'S BOUGHT BRIDE

BY
CAROL MARINELLI

Carol Marinelli recently filled in a form where she was asked for her job title and was thrilled, after all these years, to be able to put down her answer as writer. Then it asked what Carol did for relaxation and after chewing her pen for a moment Carol put down the truth —writing. The third question asked—what are your hobbies? Well, not wanting to look obsessed or, worse still, boring, she crossed the fingers on her free hand and answered swimming and tennis, but, given that the chlorine in the pool does terrible things to her highlights and the closest she's got to a tennis racket in the last couple of years is watching the Australian Open—I'm sure you can guess the real answer!

CHAPTER ONE

'THEY wouldn't have suffered.'

'Of course they wouldn't have.' Catherine could hear the bitterness in her own voice, see the flicker of confusion in the young nurse's expression, but she was too raw, too exhausted, and frankly too damn angry to soften the blow, to spare anyone's feelings.

'My sister and her husband refused to suffer anything. Why worry when you can have a drink? Why dwell on your problems when there's always family to bail you out?' She shook her head fiercely, pressing her fingers against her eyeballs and trying to quell the scream that seemed to be building up inside her.

She knew the poor nurse didn't have a clue what she was going on about, that she was just trying to be kind and say the right thing, and that the car accident had happened in an instant, that it had been over for Marco and Janey before the skidding vehicle had even halted—but her words simply weren't helping. Instead they were touching nerves so raw that every last word made Catherine flinch as she tried and failed not to envisage the final moments of her sister's short life.

Maybe later, Catherine told herself, taking deep breaths and trying to calm herself. Maybe later, when she could think straight—maybe in a few weeks—those words might bring some comfort. But sitting alone in the hospital interview room, exhausted and shellshocked, trying to fathom all that had happened, they brought no comfort at all.

'I really am sorry.' The nurse handed her a small manila envelope and Catherine held on to it tightly, feeling the hard shape of the metal inside it.

'So am I.' The bitterness had gone from her voice now, and Catherine gave the nurse a small nod of thanks. 'You've all been wonderful.'

'Is there anything else I can do for you?'

Catherine shook her head, couldn't even manage an answer, and again she was left alone. Tearing the brown paper, she slid out the contents, staring curiously dry-eyed at the three pieces of jewellery in her palm, tracing the outline of each precious piece as every one told its story. An awful sense of *déjà-vu* descended as she eyed the solitaire diamond ring Janey wore, that had belonged to their mother—the same ring that had slid out of an envelope and into her hand eight years ago. But familiarity brought no comfort. The crash that had killed her parents and the lessons it had taught offered no barrier to the pain she felt now.

It was actually eight years and two months ago, to be precise.

Eight years and two months since she had been handed her parents' belongings along with more responsibility than any nineteen-year-old deserved. But the endless meetings with solicitors and accountants as they attempted to unscramble the chaos her parents had left in their wake had been the easy part.

Dealing with a wayward sixteen-year-old—her sister Janey—had proved the greater feat.

Catherine stared at the ring for a long moment and suddenly she was back there, standing at her mother's dressing table, wishing her thick, dark, curly hair could be as smooth and as straight as her mother's and Janey's, wishing her solemn brown eyes could sparkle blue like theirs.

Instead she had inherited her father's looks—his personality too.

Well, most of it. She was serious, studious, yet she wasn't weak as her father had been, didn't cave in the way he had. One giggle from their mother, one tiny pout of her pretty mouth and John Masters had been lost—would agree to whatever his lovely Lily wanted to put the smile back on her face.

And Janey had been the same—she had possessed the certainty that her looks would get her whatever she had wanted, the same take it or leave it attitude that had held men intrigued, the same inner confidence that someone would always pick up the pieces of the chaos she created—and up till now it had worked.

The glint of the massive sapphire that caught her eye next reminded Catherine so much of her sister's blue eyes that for a second it hurt, physically hurt, to hold the engagement ring Janey had worn with such glee. She had been sure it was her ticket to the fast lane, an end to the financial mess she had got herself into, a way out of the problems that had been just too big for Catherine to sort out this time, however hard she tried.

'Marco's amazing!' Catherine could hear Janey's dizzy, slightly breathless voice as clearly as if she were in the room now. 'Oh, Catherine, you should see where he lives. It's right on the beach—and when I say on the beach, I mean it's literally on it. You step out of the patio and on to the sand. His garage alone is as big as your flat.'

Catherine couldn't have cared less what size Marco's garage was, but she had let Janey ramble for a while, listened to her excited chatter, hoping that it would calm her, that if she let her go on for long enough the euphoria might somehow wear off and that she could find out some more important answers.

'What does he do?' When Janey didn't answer she pushed further. 'For a living—what does Marco do?'

Janey gave a small shrug, tossed her hair and poured herself a drink.

'He has fun.' There was an edge to Janey's voice, a defiant look in her eyes as she stared at her older sister. 'His mother died when he was a teenager,' Janey explained, but without a hint of compassion. 'Just as ours did; only the difference is Bella Mancini actually left something for her children…'

'You mean she left money!' Catherine's voice held a warning ring. Lily might not have been the most conventional mother, but her love of life and her passion for her children had left a void that could never be filled, and no amount of inheritance would have lessened the pain of losing her.

For Catherine at least.

'Oh, spare me the speeches,' Janey spat. 'I don't want to hear again how money isn't important. I don't want to hear again how you worked two jobs while you went through teacher training college—but didn't mind a bit just as long as we were together. If our parents hadn't forgotten to pay their life insurance premiums you wouldn't have had to work so hard. You wouldn't have had to sell the family home and move into a pokey little flat…'

'I didn't mind,' Catherine insisted.

'Well, I did,' Janey snapped, her eyes narrowing. 'I hated being poor and I have no intention of spending the rest of my life chewing my nails over bills. Marco can look after me now, the same way his mother looked after him. Bella Mancini was a property developer, and when she died the business went to her children.'

A flash of recognition offered a ray of hope. The Mancini empire! Oh, Catherine wasn't exactly into reading the business pages of the newspaper, but even without a shred of business acumen she'd have needed to live in a cave for the last decade not to know about the Mancini empire and the stranglehold it held on the Melbourne property market.

The drive along Port Phillip Bay was littered with their latest acquisitions—the smart navy signs telling anyone who cared to see, that this bayview property was being developed by Mancini's.

To make it in the cut-throat world of property development would take stamina, intelligence and, dare she even say it, responsibility. Which, Catherine realised, were the very things Janey needed in a man to keep her on the straight and narrow.

'So Marco's into property development? He's part of the Mancini chain?' Catherine asked, trying not to sound too keen. She had learnt long ago that her approval was the kiss of death for any of Janey's relationships. But the hope that Janey's latest boyfriend might actually posses a scrap of responsibility was doused as quickly as it flared.

'Marco's sold his share of the business to his brother Rico,' Janey corrected, with a note of irritation that Catherine refused to acknowledge. She was determined to find out more about the man Janey was involved with, and was liking him less with each revelation. 'When Marco turned eighteen he was all set to go on board, but by then Rico had decided that he wanted to ''grow'' the business, to work sixty-hour weeks—'

'That's what people do, Janey,' Catherine interrupted, but Janey tossed her blonde hair and took another slug of her wine.

'Why?' she asked, with a glint of challenge in her eyes. 'Why would you bother when you've already made it? Marco's rich in his own right; he doesn't need to work and so he doesn't—it's as simple as that.'

'So he lives off his inheritance?' Catherine shook her head, bewildered. 'He's never even had a job?'

'You sound just like his brother,' Janey sneered. 'And I'll tell you the same thing Marco tells Rico. He doesn't sponge off his family; the money is his to spend.'

'But what sort of a man—?'

'Oh, what would you know about men?' Janey spat back spitefully, 'Who are you to give me advice?'

'I'm your sister.' Cheeks flaming, she had tried to keep her voice even, determined not to rise to the venom that appeared every time she tried to reel Janey in. 'I care about you, Janey, and whether you like it or not I'm concerned about you. Since Mum and Dad...' Her voice trailed off for a second. She didn't want to rake up the past, didn't want to go over those painful memories, but knew that now it was called for. 'I've done my best for us, Janey. I've tried as hard as I can to be there for you, and I'm asking you to listen to me now. I just think it's all too soon. You've only known this Marco for a couple of months. Why are you rushing into things? Why not wait a while and see how things—?'

'I'm pregnant.'

The words were enough to still Catherine, enough to shed a whole new different light on the rumblings of their argument. But even though the news had floored her Catherine deliberately didn't look shocked; she even managed to bite her tongue as Janey took a long sip of wine, knowing now wasn't the time for a lecture.

'Then I'm here for you,' she said again. 'We can sort this out, Janey. Just because you're pregnant it doesn't mean you have to marry him. You don't have to do anything you don't want to do.'

'You really are stupid, aren't you?' The sneer on Janey's pretty face was like a slap to Catherine's cheek. 'For a schoolteacher you really are thick—do you know that? As if I'd get knocked up by *accident*.'

'Knocked up?'

'Pregnant.' Janey gave a malicious laugh. 'Don't think for one moment, Catherine, that I don't know what I'm doing. Don't for one second think that this baby is an accident.'

'Janey, I'm sorry.' Catherine stood up. 'I wasn't suggesting you don't want your baby. I just never thought you…' She struggled helplessly for a second. 'You've never shown any interest in babies.'

'And I don't intend to start.' Janey's eyes narrowed spitefully. 'Do I really have to spell this out, Catherine? I've never had it so good. I can go into a shop, *any* shop— and not look at the price tags. I can walk into the best restaurants without checking the prices. And if you think I'm going to let it end then you don't know me at all.

Maybe Marco does love me, maybe this would have carried on indefinitely, but I'm not prepared to take the risk. So I've created my own little insurance policy.' She patted her stomach, but without a trace of tenderness, laughing mirthlessly at Catherine's shocked expression. 'And if you're worried about my lack of maternal instincts, then don't waste your time; Marco can afford the best nannies. I won't have to do a thing. So you can save the big sister lectures, save the boring speeches—because I don't need you, Catherine.'

Even a year later the words hurt.

The shiny cool gold of Janey's wedding band held its own batch of memories—only this time they weren't exclusive to Janey.

Rico, smart in his dark suit, pausing a fraction too long before handing the rings over, his hand hovering over the Bible before dropping them down in an almost truculent gesture. For Catherine had come the welcome realisation that she wasn't alone in her doubts about this union...

'How are you doing?'

The nurse was back, providing a welcome break from her painful memories, and Catherine gave a tired smile, standing on legs that felt like jelly and smoothing down her skirt as she picked up her jacket.

'I'm fine, but I think I'd like to go to the children's ward and sit with Lily.'

Lily.

A wave of bile threatened to choke her as she thought of her niece, orphaned and alone in the children's ward, and for a moment she wrestled with a surge of hatred— hatred for her sister that was surely out of place now she was dead.

'They said they'd call down when they were ready. It shouldn't be too much longer. I know you must be exhausted, dealing with all this on your own, but at least we've finally managed to locate Marco's parents. Apparently they're holidaying in the States; that's why it's taken so long.'

'His father and stepmother,' Catherine corrected. 'His mother died a long time ago.'

'Well, they've been contacted.'

Catherine gave a weary nod. She hadn't expected the Mancinis to drop everything, and even though she knew a lot needed to be organised and a lot of choices needed to be made, secretly she was relieved nothing would be done tonight.

Tonight was hard enough.

'Someone called Rico's coming, though; he rang on his mobile and said for you to wait here… Are you all right, Miss Masters?' Catherine could see the nurse's mouth moving, the concern in her face as Catherine swayed slightly.

'I'm fine. It's just…' Her pulse seemed to be pounding in her temples and her tongue was dry as she ran it over her lips. Legs that had just found their bearings seemed to be collapsing beneath her again as the nurse pulled the chair nearer and guided Catherine into it.

'Take some slow, deep breaths, Miss Masters, and keep your head down. That's the way. You're just a bit dizzy, that's all, which isn't surprising after all you've been through. I'll get you some water. Just wait there. It's all been such a shock for you it isn't any wonder you're feeling faint.'

Catherine gave a weak nod, burying her head in her

hands and feeling a vague stab of guilt at the nurse's kindness.

Today hadn't really been a shock.

It was agony. It hurt more than she could even begin to bear. But the nurse was wrong again. The sad end to these lives hadn't been a shock. The way Marco and Janey had lived their lives, flaunting society's rules, sure that money would protect them, that rules didn't somehow apply to them...today had been inevitable.

It wasn't the accident and its aftermath that had caused her near-faint—although, Catherine admitted, it would certainly have contributed to it—it wasn't even the long interviews with social workers, trying to map out a tentative path for Lily, and it had very little to do with the fact she hadn't eaten since breakfast. It was all down to the fact that Rico was coming. After all these months she was finally going to see him.

'Rico,' she whispered his name out loud, dragging in the stuffy hospital air and closing her eyes, allowing her mind to drift away for a slice of time, drift away from this awful room and the awful day to the beauty she had once witnessed. The horrors of the days receded as his face came into focus—a face she had pushed out of her mind for a year now, refused to dwell on, forcibly removed from her consciousness, but a face that had always been there, slipping into her dreams at night, supposedly unwelcome but shamefully, gratefully received.

He had made her laugh.

The wedding she had dreaded had turned out to be the most exhilarating, heady night of her life, and it had all been down to Rico.

It had been Rico who had come up to her as she'd sat,

seemingly aloof but actually tense and awkward at the head table, watching confused and bewildered as Janey and Marco made a mockery of everything sacred and twirled around the dance floor.

Rico who had turned her world around.

'I need you to talk to me!' The urgency in his voice had caught Catherine completely off guard.

'Me?' Turning, she had opened her mouth, questions bobbing on her tongue as to why the most eligible of eligible bachelors should suddenly be paying attention to her. 'Why?' Catherine asked rudely.

'I'll tell you in a moment, but I really need for you to talk to me,' he insisted. 'I know this is probably the last thing you need right now, but I want you to look as if you're engrossed.'

She already was! It wasn't hard to give Rico Mancini her full attention, wasn't exactly a feat to stare into those dark, dark eyes and appear mesmerised. He had turned his chair so he was facing her. His knees casually apart he dragged her chair forward an inch or two, effectively caging her in, an earnest look on his face as he moved in closer and begged in low, urgent tones for her to stay put.

'What on earth's going on?' Catherine giggled, embarrassed and pleased and suddenly excited all at the same time.

'Would you believe me if I told you the minister's wife was coming on to me?'

'Esther?' Her mouth dropped open and her eyes automatically flicked across the room to gape in open disbelief at the paragon of virtue, dressed in twinset and pearls, her newly set hair lacquered firmly in place. She was scarcely able to believe Esther was capable of coming on to anyone. Mind you, Catherine mused as Esther's gaze wandered anxiously in their direction, from the effect two minutes up close with Rico was having on her, maybe even ministers' wives weren't immune.

'Don't look!' He put a hand up to her cheek, forcing her attention.

'I'm sorry.' Catherine was flustered, jumping a mile as he touched her, her cheeks stinging red as a blush worked its way upwards. She desperately tried to keep her voice even. 'Surely you've misread things!'

'That's what I told myself,' Rico agreed. 'That's what I kept on telling myself as she started fiddling with the buttons on my jacket....'

'She didn't!'

'That's not the half of it.' He gave a small shudder and Catherine started to laugh. 'If your sister had settled for a good Catholic wedding, then none of this would have happened.'

'That's Janey for you,' Catherine said dryly, and for a second so small it was barely there they shared a knowing smile.

'I excused myself, of course—said I had to get back to my girlfriend; so if you don't mind I'm going to have to borrow you for a while.'

'Borrow away.' Somehow she smiled. Somehow she accepted the champagne glass he offered with hands that were amazingly steady, given her heart-rate!

It had been the best night of her life—even if it had been a false togetherness; even if it had been just for Esther's benefit he'd made her feel special. Made her feel as if she was the only woman in the room.

Later, alone in his hotel room, those dark, brooding and

suspicious eyes had softened, gazing into hers as that strong, inscrutable face had moved in to kiss her. She could still almost taste the velvet of his lips, smell the heady tang of his cologne, feel her fingers in that jet hair as she had drowned in his kiss, responded to his urgent demands in a way she never had before. His kiss had fueled responses, unfamiliar, yet achingly welcome. Her breasts had pushed against his chest, her groin had pressed into his as his hand had worked the buttons of her dress, his frustration mounting as the tiny pink buttons proved too much for the frenzy of emotions that had gripped them. He'd ripped the pale pink tulle till her shoulders had been exposed, and she hadn't cared—hadn't cared he'd ruined her dress. She had hated it anyway, hated Janey for forcing her to wear it.

She had stood exposed but curiously excited, her dilated pupils struggling to focus, as one olive-skinned hand moved the fabric apart. The contrast of his dark skin on her soft white breast had caused her breath to catch in her throat, a tiny groan of ecstasy escaping as he'd buried his face in her bosom, his lips hot on her stinging nipples, flicking them with a firm tongue. The blood had rushed down—not to her breasts, though, down to her groin, and then the flicker of her first orgasm, as impatient hands slid up her legs, tearing the tiny panties aside. His fingers had snaked inside her wet warmth, his breath hot and hard as he sucked on her breasts, and she'd shuddered in the palm of his hand, lost in the frenzy of it all, stunned at how easily her body had responded, scarcely able to fathom how she could yield so much to him.

He had seemed to understand how overwhelmed she

had been, had held her afterwards, and for that slice of time, for one tiny moment, life had felt safe.

'We have to go back down,' he whispered into her hair as the world slowly drifted back into focus, seemingly understanding that this was alien for her, that she was feeling overwhelmed by the frenzy of emotion that had gripped her.

But even Rico's tender embrace wasn't enough to stop cruel reality invading, the sting of shame to prickle her senses. She barely knew this man, had met him only that night, and yet here she stood in his arms dishevelled, her groin still curiously alive, eyes glittering, cheeks flushed. Her arousal was still only a whisper away, yet he quelled her doubts in an instant, reading her mind as if she were a book.

'Don't regret this.' His voice was a low, delicious throb of reassurance in her ear. 'You are beautiful—this was beautiful.'

'I shouldn't have—'

'Hush.' His own arousal still pressed into her and she felt a stab of guilt: No longer the situation, but at her own selfishness, sure all the pleasure of the moment had been hers.

One woefully inexperienced hand tentatively moved down, clasping the steel of his erection, terrified of her own boldness, yet sure it was expected.

'Catherine, no.' His voice was breathless, his hand clamping over hers like a vice, and she flushed with embarrassment, terrified she had hurt him, sure he could feel the inexperience of her touch. 'We must go back, I am the best man and you are the bridesmaid. It is my brother's and your sister's wedding.'

'But I haven't...' She swallowed hard. 'You didn't...'

'There is time for that later.' His accent caressed her like a warm blanket on a cold night, and the glimpse of tomorrow, of another time, satisfied her craving in an instant. 'After the bride and groom leave I have to go to the airport, I have to go to the States, but before then we will talk—arrange to see each other again.' He kissed her then, slow and hard, but laced with tenderness.

She held onto his words all night, like a precious jewel clasped close to her chest, and it made the night bearable—made the night she had dreaded suddenly exciting.

'Well, you've changed your tune.'

Helping Janey out of her wedding dress and into her leaving outfit, Catherine was barely able to keep her hands still enough to undo the zipper.

Rico was downstairs waiting for her. In an hour or so she would be in his arms again.

'See—I knew if you actually let your hair down you might enjoy yourself.' Turning, Janey stared for a moment, taking in the dark, dishevelled curls, the glittering eyes and flushed cheeks. 'How come you changed your dress?' Her eyes dragged over the simple rust silk tunic Catherine had changed into, watching her sister's cheeks darken.

'Pink tulle really isn't my thing,' Catherine answered as blithely as she could with her heart in her mouth.

'Well, it's certainly Rico's thing. He couldn't take his eyes off you.' Calculating blue eyes narrowed thoughtfully. 'Where did you two disappear to after the speeches?'

'I don't know what you're talking about.' Catherine

was flustered, appalled that her sister might know. 'Come on, Janey, you'll miss your flight.'

'It will wait,' Janey said airily, 'When you've got your own private plane it doesn't leave without you.' Her voice dropped then, suddenly serious, and her eyes were wide with an urgency that made Catherine suddenly nervous. 'Play your cards right, sis, and all this could be yours.'

'Don't be ridiculous…'

'It really could. I've paved the way for you, Catherine, do you know how hard I had to work to convince Marco I wasn't just after him for his money? That I wasn't some cheap little gold-digger?'

'I don't want to talk about it, Janey.'

'But I *am* a cheap little gold-digger.' Janey gave a malicious smile. 'And now I'm married to a *very* rich man. You could do it too, Catherine.' She gave a dry, mirthless laugh as her sister shook her head and covered her ears, her voice rising in excitement as she pulled Catherine's hands away, enjoying her sister's embarrassment as she warmed to her subject. 'You hate your job, hate working with those awful children, hate your poky little flat…'

'Janey…' Catherine gave in then. Gave up trying to reason with her sister. Janey would never believe that even though she moaned about staff shortages and even her students at times, she loved her work—truly adored it. And, yes, her flat might be small, but it was home.

Tears were threatening now, at a vision of her sister so alive, so excited—such an appalling contrast to the cold, lifeless body that lay just a few rooms away. Balling her fists into her eyes, Catherine held them back. There was no point in tears, none at all. There was no one to wipe them—hadn't been since the day her parents had died—

and there was no one to comfort her tonight. Her memories flicked back in a second to the awful reality she faced—a reality she had to accept.

Janey was dead.

Rico despised her.

CHAPTER TWO

'CATHERINE.'

Gripping the jewellery tight in the palm of her hand, she stilled, her breath hot in her lungs. Even her heart seemed to stop for a second, then thudded back into action, tripping into a gallop as the scent that had fuelled her dreams for a year reached her nostrils, as the low drawl of one single word catapulted her senses into overdrive.

'Catherine?'

This time she looked up, praying somehow that the passage of time might render her impervious to his beauty, that a year might have dimmed the passion in those dark eyes, that somehow she might see that her imagination had been working overtime, had built him up to a status that cold reality would knock down. But if anything, Catherine realised, her imagination had underplayed his exquisiteness. Hadn't quite captured the haughty, effortless elegance, the razor-sharp cheekbones, the jet-dark hair, superbly cut, the tiny fan of silver at the temples that accentuated those inscrutable coal eyes.

'I came as soon as I heard.'

She didn't respond—*couldn't* respond. His presence was too overwhelming to allow for speech. Instead she gave a small nod, struggled with lips that didn't seem to know how to move any more.

'How long have you been here?'

'Since five.' Her voice was a croak, the two words all she could manage, but as his eyes bored into her Catherine realised more was called for and she cleared her throat, knowing he deserved the facts. It was his brother who was dead, after all. Their one night of passion and bitter parting had no place in this conversation, this was no time to rake over their past. 'I came back from work and the police were at my door. They drove me here.'

'Have they told you how it happened?' When she didn't answer he pushed harder. 'I know there was an accident. I know that Marco and Janey are both dead and that Lily is on the children's ward, but that is all I know.' His fists were bunched in tension. Catherine could see a muscle galloping in his taut cheek and she knew how hard it must be for a man like Rico, who always knew what was happening, always had everything in control, to be in the dark—to know that for once there was absolutely nothing he could do to put things right.

'I have tried to speak with the doctors and the police, but everyone who dealt with it directly is off duty. I will of course speak with them in the morning, but for now I would appreciate it if you could fill me in.'

His voice was supremely polite, as if he were addressing a stranger, and Catherine realised with a stab of sadness that that was exactly what she was to him—a stranger who had passed by once, no more and no less.

'Of course.' Again she cleared her throat, opened her mouth to speak, but his rather forebidding stance wasn't inspiring and she dragged her eyes away, resting her head in her hands and massaging her temples for a moment, willing eloquence to come.

'I need to know what happened, Catherine.' There was an impatient note to his voice.

'I'm trying to tell you, if you'd just—'

'I need to know *now*!' His fingers snapped in her face, an impatient Latin gesture that held no charm at all, and Catherine blinked and jumped back as Rico raised his voice. 'I am sorry you have had to deal with this—sorry you have had to face it all. But that is not my fault. I was in a closed meeting, my phone was off, and my secretary had taken an early flight back to Melbourne. I came as soon as I heard. I have been stuck in traffic, held up at the airport, and sitting on a plane going out of my mind with worry. I need some answers!'

The fire suddenly seemed to go out of him, his eyes taking in her shocked expression, the reddened rims of her eyes, the pale and trembling lips. 'I know it has been hard for you today, and I am sorry you have had to face this alone, but I am here now and I will take care of everything.'

'Take care of everything?' An incredulous laugh shot out of her pale lips, the anger that had simmered since the tragic news had been delivered, unleashed now. And however misdirected, however much this wasn't Rico's fault, he was the nearest target and Catherine turned a furious glare on him, her words coming out staccato, her body trembling with rage. How dare he waltz in here and demand answers? Swan in past midnight and say he would deal with it now when it had been she, Catherine, dealing with it—she alone facing the police, the social workers. She alone who had stood and identified the bodies.

'I have taken care of everything, Rico!' she shouted. 'Just as I took care of everything when my parents were killed. I should be used to it by now, I suppose. I guess I'm an old hand at identifying bodies and filling in forms!'

He didn't move a muscle, just stood in grim silence as her outburst continued, and his inaction incensed her, spurred her on to new levels of anger.

'I've been in this hospital for seven hours taking care of things, so don't you dare march in here and expect an eloquent detached statement, then snap your fingers in impatience if I don't speak quickly enough for you!' She looked up at him, her eyes furious and her chin jutting defiantly. 'I am not a member of your family, Rico, and neither am I one of your staff. You have no right to demand anything from me, no right at all. However, if you will sit down and exercise some patience I will tell you, as best I can, what little I know.'

For a second she thought he might hit her. Anger blazed in his eyes, the pent-up frustration of what must have been a hellish few hours undoubtedly exacerbated by her venom. But just as she thought she'd pushed him too far his wide shoulders slumped in an almost dejected fashion, and almost imperceptibly he gave a small nod, his Adam's apple bobbing a couple of times as he looked around the room, as if seeing it for the first time. Registering the fake leather chairs, he chose one next to her and sat down, raking a hand through his short hair, over the dark stubble of his chin, before turning to face her.

'I came as soon as I could,' he said again, but this time, his words were quiet, raw with emotion—apologetic even—his eyes utterly bereft as he stared at her, and for a tiny slice of time she caught a glimpse inside the beautiful head of Rico Mancini. Understood the pain behind the inscrutable mask he wore so effortlessly for she felt the agony of this senseless loss too.

'They went out for lunch,' Catherine started, her voice almost a whisper. 'They took Lily because apparently their nanny, Jessica, had walked out on them this morning.'

He opened his mouth, then closed it quickly, and Catherine gave a grateful nod. She would answer the whys in her own time.

'I went round last night, Rico.'

'You were there last night?' His eyes widened and she could almost hear his brain whirring into motion, almost foretell the questions on the tip of his tongue. But somehow he managed to hold them in, to let her tell her tale in her own time.

'I was at a parent-teacher night at school. It didn't finish till after nine, and for some reason—for some reason I...' Her fists clenched in her lap as the pain became almost more than she could bear, and only when he took her hand, only when he held it in his, was Catherine able to go on. 'I went round,' she whispered. 'I just couldn't be a bystander any more. What Janey and Marco got up to might have been their business, but if it was affecting Lily I couldn't just sit back and watch...'

Her eyes met his, imploring him to understand, and she was rewarded with a small nod. 'Of course they weren't at home, but I decided to wait. I spoke to Jessica—I wanted to find out if things were as bad as I feared or if I was just imagining it—and believe me she was only too happy to unload. Apparently she was sick of the way they carried on—the wild parties, the mess, and the fact they consistently *forgot* to pay her didn't help. It was supposed to have been her night off, but yet again Janey and Marco had gone out without telling her.'

Catherine was staring at their hands now, their fingers interlaced, and the contrast between them had never been more obvious. His dark and strong, a heavy watch on his wrist, such a contrast to her pale and trembling hands, an inkstain on her fingers, her nails short and neat but certainly not as groomed.

'We both waited for them to come home.'

For an age he said nothing, just held her hand tighter before gently saying, 'There was a confrontation?'

'I believe that would be the polite term for it.'

She screwed her eyes closed, the images of last night too horrible to relive. The harsh words she had spoken in anger were out now, with no hands of time to soothe them over the years.

'Jessica said she was leaving in the morning. That as soon as they'd sobered up enough to take responsibility for Lily she was going to get out of there—which is presumably why they took Lily to lunch with them,' Catherine carried on. 'You would have thought that might have slowed them down, forced them to behave responsibly...' Her voice trailed off, and this time when Rico broke in it wasn't unwelcome.

'They were drinking.' It wasn't a question, more a statement, but Catherine shook her head.

'I'm not sure what they were doing. According to the blood test Marco wasn't over the limit, but the police have ordered a drug screen. Apparently Marco was stumbling when they left the restaurant, and the doorman said he was utterly incoherent as they walked out. The *lunch* went till four. The only sensible thing they did all day was make sure that Lily was strapped in her car seat before they took off.'

'Who was driving?'

'Marco.'

'Was anyone else…?' His questions weren't rapid now, and they were no longer unwelcome. The whole sorry mess was easier shared.

'No one else was hurt. It seems Marco lost control or fell asleep at the wheel. They shot through the safety barrier onto the other side of the road, but thankfully they didn't hit anyone else.'

'Did they…?' Rico's eyes screwed closed and his fist balled again, only this time not in anger.

'Apparently they didn't suffer.' She repeated the nurse's words, hoping they might bring Rico the comfort that had eluded her, but the wry twist of his mouth told her the effect was about the same.

'They left that part to us.'

Us.

Even in the depths of despair the word offered a shelter for her mind to run to and hide for a while from the onslaught of the day and she took welcome refuge. Rico's hand tightened harder around hers; his grip warm and strong and it helped—helped her get through the next few seconds at least.

'Sorry to interrupt.' The nurse was back now, standing hesitantly at the door, a sympathetic smile on her young face and as Rico's hand dropped hers like a hot stone, cruel reality invaded.

There is no us, Catherine reminded herself. There never has been.

She was in this alone.

'I'm going off on my break in a few minutes. Would you like me to walk you back up to the children's ward before I go? It's a bit of a maze…'

'That won't be necessary, thank you.' Rico stood up, the tenderness she had briefly witnessed flicking off like a light switch, as he asserted his authority in an instant. 'I have already been to the children's ward and seen Lily. I explained to the sister in charge that Miss Masters and I will be staying at a nearby hotel tonight and will be back first thing in the morning. Thank you,' he said again crisply, effectively dismissing her, and as the door closed Catherine blinked at him a couple of times.

'You've been to see Lily?'

'Of course.'

Of course. The words played over in her mind. Of course he would have been to see her first. Marco and Janey were dead, there was nothing he could do there, why wouldn't he rush to see his niece? It made perfect sense, but a chill of foreboding crept over her as she met his dark, brooding stare, saw his eyes narrow suspiciously as he watched her.

'I don't want to go to a hotel and leave her.' Catherine stood up, relieved that her legs, although still trembling, seemed at least to be holding her now. 'I don't think she should be alone tonight. If she wakes up—'

'The nurses will deal with her,' Rico said crisply 'And if there is a problem we are only two minutes away. That is why I have booked into a hotel rather than go home; we will be literally across the road.'

'But I'd be next to her here,' Catherine pointed out. 'Just because you're too grand to sleep on a roller bed it doesn't mean that I am.'

'I make no apology,' Rico clipped. 'I would like to shower, I would like a very large drink, and...' Whatever else he wanted, Rico wasn't sharing it. He stared haughtily back at her. 'I'm sure the nurses will be able to cope with her.'

'But she needs—'

'What?' Rico broke in, his word a pistol shot. 'Needs what? You can't miss what you don't have, and I doubt that baby has ever seen her mother after six p.m. In the six months Lily's been alive she's already had to get to know five nannies, so I'm sure a nurse feeding her in the middle of the night isn't going to send her into a frenzy. Your sister made quite sure Lily got used to strangers.'

Your sister. He had spat the words at her accusingly but Catherine refused to rise.

'I want to be with her,' Catherine stated calmly. 'If you want to go to a hotel—fine. But I'm not leaving.' Picking up her bag, she headed for the door, but the slow hand-clap resounding from Rico stilled her. Tossing her head, she turned to face him, her eyes questioning.

'Bravo,' he sneered. 'If I didn't know you better you'd almost pass for a grief-stricken aunty.'

'I just want to do the right thing by Lily,' Catherine responded, utterly bemused, with no idea where this was leading.

'Of course you do!' She heard the sarcasm dripping in his voice, but it merely confused her. 'Possession is nine-tenths of the law and all that.'

'I don't know what you're talking about.' Whatever Rico's problem was she didn't want to hear it. She didn't want to do this now. She was exhausted, physically and mentally exhausted, and even though she'd only been promised a roller bed by Lily's cot the thought of stretching out, of closing her eyes on this vile day, was the only thing keeping her standing. 'I'll speak to you in the morning.'

'You'll speak to me tonight.' His voice stayed low but there was a menacing note that had the hairs rising on the back of her neck. 'You'll tell me everything that's happened.'

'I've already told you,' Catherine responded hotly. 'What the hell does it matter how it happened, Rico? They're dead, and going over and over it doesn't change anything.'

'Oh, but it does.' His eyes bored into hers. 'The fact they're dead changes everything. Why didn't you tell me you'd spoken to social workers, Catherine? Why did you omit to mention that you've told them you are taking Lily home with you when she's discharged? That you are applying for guardianship?'

Her mind was working nineteen to the dozen now, realisation dawning as his savage eyes met hers, as she registered just how low he thought she was prepared to stoop.

'You've got it all wrong,' she insisted. 'It wasn't like that. The hospital needed a name, a next of kin, someone to sign a consent form if Lily needed an operation.'

'And you were only too happy to provide it.'

'Of course I was,' Catherine responded hotly. 'As much as you mightn't like it, Rico, as much as you might want to wipe me out of your life, I have as much right to be here as you. I am Lily's aunt just as you are her uncle, and given the fact that her parents have just been killed it makes us her next of kin. I had every right to sign that form and I resent the implication that I had some sort of ulterior motive. She's seems okay now, but we didn't know. She has bruises from the car seat and the doctors thought there could be some internal damage. You weren't here, Rico! What was I supposed to do? Refuse to sign?'

'Okay,' he conceded reluctantly. 'But you told them you are taking Lily home with you when she's discharged, told them you are prepared to look after her...'

'And I am,' Catherine wailed, her patience flying out of the window as she faced this impossible, mistrusting man. 'She's my niece and I want to look after her—in the short term at least.'

'That's not what you said to the social workers.'

'Oh, come on, Rico. Janey died this afternoon. I can barely comprehend what's happened, let alone make long-term plans! As if I know what I'm going to do.'

'Don't lie,' he spat. '*Poor little Lily.* I can just see you laying it on with a trowel to the social workers. I can almost hear the little sob in your voice as you said it!' His eyes narrowed, his lips contorting as he eyed her distastefully. 'Only she's not so poor, is she? As of this evening, Lily's incredibly rich. You must have been rubbing your hands in glee when the bloody Mancinis couldn't even be bothered to make it to the hospital—rubbing your hands in glee when no one was there to stop you when you said you'd take care of her.'

'It wasn't like that!' It was Catherine's voice rising now. 'How dare you? How dare you accuse me of trying to profit from my sister's death? How dare you suggest I would use my niece as a pawn? Why would I—'

'I'll tell you why.' His voice was low, a contrast to hers, his eyes forbidding as they stared back at her coldly. 'Because you hate your life, Catherine. Because you'd go to any lengths to change it.'

'You're disgusting.' Pulling her arms away, she attempted to wrestle it from his hand, but his grip only tightened. 'Let go of me, Rico. I'm going to my niece.'

'Over my dead body.' His face was as white as marble in the fluorescent light, his cheeks jagged, his lips set in grim determination. 'You're coming back to the hotel with me, Catherine. Tonight we talk.'

CHAPTER THREE

THEY drove in silence.

Angry denials were bobbing on her tongue, but the set of his jaw, the grip of his hands on the steering wheel told her now wasn't the time.

They needed to face the situation calmly, talk things through rationally. Lily's future was too precious to be relegated to a heated row in a hospital corridor, and given the day's events a high-speed sports car wasn't exactly the ideal spot either. That was the only reason Catherine had given in and agreed to go back to the hotel, allowed him to lead her through the endless hospital corridors and out to the car park, and she held her tongue now, biting back smart replies, determined to do things properly.

His sleek, low silver car purred through the night streets. The windows thankfully were open, and Catherine welcomed the cool breeze that whipped her cheeks, blowing away the nauseating stench of the hospital. As they slowed at the lights a tram clattered past. A couple of young lovers were kissing in a doorway, and the early editions of tomorrow's papers were already bundled outside a newsagents'. It was hard to comprehend that the world was carrying on as normal, hard to fathom that those same newspapers probably contained a line or two, maybe even a photo, summarising the tragic end of Janey and Marco for those who wanted to know.

The concierge greeted Rico as if he had been waiting

up only for him to arrive, making impatient gestures in Reception to hurry things along.

'Mr Mancini, this is such an unexpected pleasure. I was just saying that we haven't seen you or...' His warm greeting was barely acknowledged and even in her numb state Catherine felt a sting of embarrassment at Rico's cool treatment of the staff.

'I would like to go straight up, please.'

'Your bags are already on their way up, and the house-keeper is turning back the bed as we speak. It will be just a moment—'

'I don't have a moment.' Rico's voice was pure, un-adulterated snobbery. 'Miss Masters is tired, I am tired, and I'm going to my room!' Striding to the lift, he beck-oned a furiously blushing Catherine to join him, punching the top button and closing the door on the poor concierge.

'You really think you're better than everyone, don't you?'

For once Rico didn't respond, for once a smart reply seemed to elude him, and Catherine warmed to her subject as the lift door slid open on the heady heights of the penthouse. She watched as he dismissed the frenziedly working staff with one flick of his hand and let out a low snort, shaking her head as he poured himself a drink, not even bothering to offer her one.

'You haven't even booked a room here, yet you expect one to be waiting for you—for people to jump just be-cause you deign to grace them with your presence.'

'What do you expect me to do, Catherine?' He downed his drink in one, slamming the crystal onto the silver tray, his eyes finally meeting hers. 'Tell me how you expected me to behave down there.'

'You could have shown some manners, to start with,' Catherine replied hotly, and even though the argument was meaningless, even though it was so far removed from all that had happened, she prolonged it. Maybe it was easier than facing the real reason why she was here. 'The concierge was being nothing but pleasant—'

'He's paid to be pleasant,' Rico broke in. 'He's paid to remember my name, to remember that this is where my brother and I come for lunch when my schedule allows, that sometimes I choose to stay here rather than drive home.'

'Maybe he is paid to remember, but surely you can still be polite when someone greets you!'

'My brother is dead,' Rico snapped.

'So is my sister. But I don't use it as an excuse to snub people. I didn't treat the nurses and doctors like dirt on my shoe...'

'If I hadn't interrupted him he would have asked about Marco, asked how he was doing, when they could expect to see him again. Did you want me to tell him, Catherine? Did you want me to stand in the foyer and tell the world my brother is dead when any moment now they're going to find out anyway?'

He looked at her bemused face and shook his head disbelievingly. Picking up a remote control, he flicked on the television, watching her expression as the images shot into focus, hearing the tiny strangled sob as the mangled wreckage of a car filled the screen, then Marco and Janey's wedding photo, superimposed on the top right corner. The news reader droned on, regaling supposed facts Catherine simply wasn't ready to hear, and her hand shot to her ears in a childlike gesture, her eyes screwing

closed against the horrible images that seemed to be chok-
ing her.

'I asked the hospital not to release their names until we
left.'

His explanation wasn't helping, and she opened her
eyes, stared at him, bemused.

'A Mancini is dead.'

'Two Mancinis,' Catherine corrected. 'My sister counts
too.'

'Your sister counts for nothing,' Rico sneered. 'But,
yes, I stand corrected. Technically two Mancinis are dead,
Catherine, and that is news. No doubt the *poor concierge*
you were so worried about is now either kicking himself
for his insensitivity or ringing the press to tell them I am
here.' He gave a small shrug. 'Frankly, I don't give a
damn which one it is.'

'But why would the press want to speak to you?'

'Are you stupid, Catherine? Or just a really good actress?'

His words barely touched the sides. Pain was already
layered on top of pain—another dash of scorn, another
dose of humiliation from Rico was not much in the
scheme of things.

'I'm not stupid, Rico.' Her brown eyes met his. 'I read
the papers, I watch the news when I get home from work,
and I know how powerful the Mancinis are, I know that
the stockmarket rises and falls depending on your company's profits. But Marco wasn't a part of the family business—Marco never worked a day in his life. I really can't
see why the press are getting so excited. His death isn't
going to affect the company—'

'Do you think the press will care about a small detail like that?' Rico broke in, 'Marco is rich, he has a daughter—'

'*Was* rich,' Catherine corrected, and for a second so small it was barely there she was sure she saw a flicker of pain in those dark eyes, saw the haughty, bland mask slip for a tiny second, but she continued anyway. '*Had* a daughter.'

'Which is why I've brought you here.'

'You didn't bring me here,' Catherine pointed out. 'I chose to come. I'm not stupid, Rico, but possibly I've been a bit naïve. Maybe the world isn't going to stop because of Janey and Marco's deaths, but it's certainly going to pause for a few days' reflection, and I can see that Lily's future will be debated vigorously by people who don't give a damn about her. But I for one don't care what the newspapers have to say, because at the end of the day everyone will get on with their lives. We're the ones who are going to be living it; we're the ones dealing with the issues.'

'I don't give a damn what the press say, either,' Rico responded. 'But it is not only the press who will be having their say…' His eyes narrowed thoughtfully and he stared at her for the longest moment, as if deciding whether or not to continue. 'My stepmother is not going to let you have Lily.' A tiny gasp of protest escaped Catherine's lips, but she swallowed it back. Rico's words were too important for interruption. 'I can tell you now that she won't allow it to happen. She will not allow Lily's inheritance to leave the family.'

'But why?' Catherine asked, bemused. 'Surely she doesn't need the money? Surely…?'

'Too much is never enough, and the way my stepmother spends money this unexpected windfall will not be given up without a fight.' His mouth set in a grim line. 'My stepmother is the coldest woman on this earth. She is the reason Marco went off the rails, the reason he drank himself—'

'That's an excuse,' Catherine broke in. 'I had the same argument over and over with Janey, when she tried to blame our parents for whatever scrape she found herself in. You had the same family as Marco, the same pressures, yet you still managed to hold down a job, manage your affairs. Marco may have been disadvantaged by his stepmother, but he still had a lot more opportunities in life than most people dream of. You do him no favours by blaming your stepmother.'

'Perhaps,' Rico conceded. 'But it is not always black and white, Catherine. People are different. I am stronger than Marco; I am tougher.' There was no superiority in his words, just the cool deliverance of fact, and this time Catherine chose not to remind him that Marco was now in the past tense. She just listened as he continued to talk. 'Antonia is a nasty piece of work, and till the day I die I will blame her in part for the fact Marco is now lying in a mortuary…' His voice wavered slightly, his fists clenching in salute by his sides, and Catherine was shocked to see what was surely the glint of tears in those dark eyes. But just as soon as his pain registered, like a light flicking off, the impassive mask returned. 'I will not allow her to mess up Lily the way she messed up Marco.'

'Then what was all that about back at the hospital?' Deliberately she kept her tone even, refusing to be intimidated by him. 'Given what you've just told me, surely I'm the better option to raise Lily? And before you insist

I only want her for the money, let me tell you, Rico, you are wrong. Her inheritance never entered my head—not until you came tonight.'

He stared at her, disbelief etched on his features, but his shrug was almost weary. 'Maybe you want both. Maybe you do care for Lily, and I guess there is no shame in wanting to be rich.' She opened her mouth to argue, but Rico carried on talking. 'I cannot let Lily go with this woman, Catherine.'

'Then let me have her.'

'It is not that simple. Antonia will go to every court in the land, use every means available to discredit you. She'll have the most expensive lawyers. You are a teacher, Catherine. The reality is that you survive on a schoolteacher's wage. Against her you won't stand a chance.'

His words made sense, and a dark feeling of foreboding shivered through her. Though it galled her to ask for his assistance, Catherine knew she had no choice, and the words were out before the idea had even formed. 'You could help me.'

'Why would I help you, Catherine? Why wouldn't I just apply for custody myself?'

'Go ahead,' Catherine said airily, though her heart was in her mouth. She registered the surprise in his expression and it gave her a small surge of triumph. Her eyes met his defiantly, fighting fire with fire as she carried on talking. 'But don't try and scare me off, Rico, with talk of money and lawyers. I'll sell my home if I have to, and when the money has gone I'll apply for legal aid. I'll tell you this now, and I'll tell each Mancini in turn if they care to ask: I have as much right to Lily as anyone. Unlike you, I've actually played a part in her short life. As much as I loathed the way Marco and Janey carried on I still went round, still made sure I was there for Lily…'

'I've been busy with work,' Rico argued. 'And watching those two made me—'

'Save it,' Catherine snapped. 'Tell the court how you couldn't even get away for her christening, how you saw your niece for two minutes at the hospital the day after she was born and that you haven't seen her since.'

'There are reasons!' Rico roared, but Catherine just glared back.

'Excuses,' Catherine flared. 'They are nothing but excuses! And now you have the gall to tell me you want custody of Lily—a baby you've barely met. Well, I'm not going to let you do it, Rico. I don't give a damn about the Mancini fortune, and your power doesn't frighten me. I will fight for her, and deep down I think you know that I'm the best person for her.'

'*You?*'

She heard the scorn and contempt in his voice and deliberately kept hers even. 'Yes, me, Rico. I will fight for Lily. I will do whatever it takes to ensure her future. Whatever it takes,' Catherine repeated, just to be sure he understood. 'I know you don't think much of me, Rico. You made that abundantly clear on the night of the wedding—'

'That night has no bearing on this discussion.'

'Oh, but it does.' The sting of embarrassment brought a flush of colour to her pale cheeks, but Catherine refused to be silenced. Lily's future was too important for her to dodge behind embarrassing facts. 'You were the one who treated me like a cheap tart, Rico.' She saw him wince at her brutal words, but ploughed on anyway. 'You were the one who walked out of the reception without even a good-bye...' Her cheeks were red now, but not with embarrassment. Instead it was with a year's worth of humiliation and anger at this man who had treated her with such contempt. 'I ran after you, Rico. I came to your car and knocked on your window and you refused to even look at me...'

'Because you disgusted me.'

Her recoil was so visible he might as well have hit her. The colour that had suffused her cheeks drained, and tears that had stayed buried all day, were stinging now, but Catherine bit them back, refusing to let him see her cry, to allow him the glory of her utter humiliation.

'Might I remind you, Rico—' her voice was strained but dignified, her lips barely moving as she struggled to hold it together '—that it takes two? And if you're going to try and use that night to discredit me in court then it won't work. You were very much a participant in what happened.'

'What are you talking about?' he sneered.

'Presumably you're one of those chauvinist men who assume it's okay for men to behave in such a fashion but that's it somehow different for women?' He opened his mouth to speak but Catherine overrode him, her voice coming louder now. 'And maybe you're right, Rico. Because try as I might I cannot justify what happened that night. I cannot explain to anyone, let alone myself, how I ended up in a hotel room with a man I barely knew. Yes, I behaved like a cheap tart—so you see, Rico, you can't hurt me with your cruel words, can't shame me any more than I shamed myself that night. I may disgust you, but I can assure you I disgust myself more.'

They stood in bristling silence, her words resonating like an awful echo until Catherine could no longer bear it—couldn't bear to stand there a moment longer. Her eyes scanned the luxurious room for an exit, settling instead for the safety of the bathroom, and only when she'd closed the door did she let out the breath she had been inadvertently holding. Her jaw was aching from gritting her teeth together.

How could she explain to him that to her dying day she would never be able to fathom how she had so brazenly allowed him to touch her, hold her? That even a year on she could scarcely comprehend the intimacies she had shared with a virtual stranger that night? But he hadn't seemed like a stranger, Catherine recalled, resting her burning face against the mirror as she remembered the passion that had gripped her, that had sullied her sensibility and overridden her normal reservation.

How could she explain to Rico what she couldn't understand herself?

Peeling off her clothes, Catherine stepped into the shower, the welcome bliss of water on her body soothing somehow, giving her a few moments to compose herself, to sort through the jumble of events today had thrown at her. She wished she could stay there for ever, wished she could hide from the world for just a moment longer, but somehow she had to be strong, had to go back in that room and face him.

For Lily's sake.

Pulling on a thick white robe, she tied it firmly before filling the sink to wash her stockings and knickers. Luxurious as the hotel might be, it didn't come with a fully stocked wardrobe—and anyway she was glad of the chance to prolong the discussion a few moments longer.

'What are you doing?'

Appalled, she swung round, scarcely able to believe his gall.

'How dare you come in here without knocking?' Eyes blazing, she met his gaze. 'How dare you come in here? I could have been naked…'

'You are dressed in a robe,' Rico pointed out, clearly unmoved at her protests. 'We need to talk, and instead you are hiding in here.'

'I'm not hiding,' Catherine lied, but Rico just shook his head.

'Why are you washing your clothes like some gipsy in the river, then?' he sneered. 'You *are* hiding, Catherine…'

'You really are the limit—do you know that? For your information, I didn't stop to pack an overnight bag when the police arrived at my door.'

'Send your washing down to Housekeeping, then.' Rico shrugged.

'I have some pride,' Catherine retorted. 'Not much, I admit that—you've managed to obliterate most of it—but if you think I'm going to hand my underwear over to be washed and ironed then you've got another think coming.' Very deliberately she turned away, rinsing out her washing and draping it over the bath ledge, making sure she took her time, sensing his bristling impatience yet refusing to be rushed, refusing to turn as he commenced the discussion she had hoped to delay.

'If Lily were older undoubtedly we could ask her what

she wanted. But given she is only six months old, that is of course impossible.'

She could feel his eyes on her, but she didn't turn, just gave a small nod as Rico continued.

'So perhaps we should ask ourselves what her parents would have wanted?'

His words made sense, and reluctantly she turned to face him, willing to at least listen to what Rico had to say.

'Marco and I may have rowed on occasion, and I may have alienated myself from him to some degree because I didn't approve of his lifestyle, but we still met up regularly. As I said before, we came to this hotel for many lunches, and whatever trouble he was in Marco knew he could always call on me. I know that he did respect me.' His voice thickened and he swallowed hard before continuing. 'I know in my heart that he loved me, Catherine, and I also know he would have wanted me to raise his child. So now it's your turn. What about Janey?'

His eyes never left her face, taking in every flicker of reaction as his question reached her. 'What would Janey have wanted for Lily?'

'She'd have wanted me to have her…' Her voice trailed off, her startled eyes blinking rapidly, and Rico leapt in, sensing weakness and exploiting it in an instant.

'Because she loved you?' His voice was so silken you might almost have missed the derisive sneer, but Catherine was like a radar where Rico was concerned, and she flinched at his insensitivity. 'Janey would have wanted you to have Lily because she adored her big sister Catherine?'

'She did love me; I was her sister.' Her lips were impossibly dry and she ran her tongue over them, her head spinning as he relentlessly continued.

'You don't have to love your sister, Catherine,' Rico pointed out mercilessly. 'You don't even have to love your husband—and Janey didn't love Marco, did she? *Did she?*' He roared the words the second time—the roar of a lion defending its territory, of a beautiful animal to be admired from a distance, but that could turn in a second. 'In fact Marco was just a walking, talking chequebook to his young bride…'

'Rico, please…' Catherine started. She wanted him to stop, wanted to end this horrible interrogation, didn't want to sully the few precious memories she had with the awful truth—didn't want to admit even to herself how little Janey had thought of her.

'Janey wanted the fast cars, the nice home, the maids, the lifestyle—and I don't doubt she'd have wanted the same for her daughter.'

'Janey would have wanted me,' Catherine insisted, but the lack of conviction in her voice truly terrified her. 'You've got it all wrong, Rico.'

'Have I?' His eyes narrowed thoughtfully. 'Which part?'

'All of it,' Catherine whispered, pleating the tie of her robe with trembling fingers. And she knew there and then that she could never admit to the truth. Rico was right, damn him, and it hurt to admit it. Janey hadn't loved her; Janey had hated her. More damaging than that, Janey had blatantly admitted she had married Marco for his money. If it ever got out, if Catherine ever admitted the truth, what chance would she have against the family courts?

What chance would she have against the might of Rico Mancini? It would all be over bar the shouting.

Lily would be gone from her life as surely as she was standing here now.

A lion Rico might be, but the lioness in Catherine emerged then—proud and wary, sleek and refined, and willing to do whatever it took to protect those she loved. To her dying breath she would deny it. She would take Janey's words to the grave. Would lie through her teeth if that was what it took.

Lily needed her.

'Janey loved Marco.'

'She told you that?'

Dragging in air through her clenched teeth, she wrenched her eyes from the floor and forced herself to do the hardest thing she had done in her life—look Rico in the eye and lie.

'Yes, Rico. She told me that she loved him. Janey loved Marco and his money had nothing to do with it. I know in my heart that—'

'Save it.' A well-manicured hand flicked in the air. His eyes were more shuttered than ever, his voice almost weary, and for once there was economy in his actions, the usual extravagant Latin temperament curiously subdued as he halted her speech. 'It is time for bed.'

'I thought we were going to talk,' Catherine protested, following him out of the bathroom, confused at the sudden change in his demeanour. She had braced herself for confrontation, adrenaline pumping through her veins as she geared up to defend herself, to do whatever it took to keep Lily near. But all the fight seemed to have left Rico now. Suddenly all he looked was exhausted. 'I thought we were going to talk, Rico,' she said again. 'That is why I came here after all; we need to sort something out.'

'And we will,' Rico affirmed. 'But I realise now is not the time. We cannot decide anything tonight; we are both tired and it has been an emotional day.'

She almost laughed—almost laughed at his detached summing up. The man who stood before her seemed curiously void of emotion.

'Here.' He handed her a crisp white shirt. 'I always have a spare in my briefcase. You can sleep in this.'

'Rico?' Even as the word was out Catherine knew she would get no response. His apathy unnerved her and, though she was loath to admit it, somehow she preferred the angry, volatile man she was starting to get used to.

'It is time to sleep, Catherine. You can have the master bedroom; I'll take the other.'

It should have been uncomfortable, awkward—in any other circumstances sharing a suite with the man who had so carelessly broken her heart would have sent Catherine into a spin. But not tonight.

Tonight was for Janey.

By the time she had popped back into the bathroom and pulled on the shirt Rico had left the lounge, and she stood for an uncertain moment before heading to the open door of his room; he was already stretched out on his bed, his hands behind his head, staring fixedly at the ceiling. Catherine knew his averted gaze had nothing to do with the heated words they had shared, or the problems they faced. Knew that his pensive shift in tempo had grief written all over it.

'Goodnight, then.' She hovered by his door, awaiting a

response that never came, before gently closing the door and heading for her own room.

As the light flicked off and darkness descended the oblivion she so desperately craved didn't come, but the horrors of the day did recede slightly as she drifted to the gentle past...

Suddenly she was away from the sullied world Janey had created, back to two little girls, one dark, one blonde. The Janey she chose to remember danced in her mind— Janey before their parents' death, Janey before money and greed had taken over. The little sister she had grown up with was ready to be mourned now, and Catherine drifted back to the beauty of a past when the world had seemed good and safe. Suddenly she was scared to go there, scared of the depth of her pain, scared to take the lid off her grief, terrified of what she might find. The past a mocking reminder of the void left today.

An involuntary sob escaped her lips and she bit it back hard, gulping into the darkness, her breath coming in short, ragged bursts as she struggled to hold it in—hold in eight years of agony, eight years of pain, eight years of being alone and having to be the strong one.

She had learnt long ago the folly of tears, the loneliness of weeping into the night with no one to wipe them away.

And she would *not* cry now.

'Catherine?'

She heard the concern in his voice but she didn't answer, just lay frozen in the darkness, her ears on elastic as he crossed the room, feeling the indentation of the mattress as he lowered himself onto the bed.

'Catherine, are you okay?'

She nodded, her hand shielding her eyes as he flicked on the light.

'You are allowed to cry, you know,' Rico offered gently, but she shook her head.

'Crying won't bring them all back.'

'All?' When she didn't answer he carried on gently. 'You're not just talking about Janey and Marco, are you, Catherine?'

She didn't respond, but he pushed on gently. 'What happened to your parents?'

'They died,' she said simply.

'Tell me about it.'

She was about to say no, to shake her head and turn away, but something stopped her. A need to share, to delve a little into her past—a past she simply couldn't face alone tonight. And even if Rico despised her, even if this conversation would be forgotten, or even held against her in the cold light of day, tonight the simple fact that it was another human being, reaching out in the lonely abyss of grief, was enough to make her open up.

'My mother was beautiful.' Catherine's voice quivered, and she cleared her throat before going on. 'Her name was Lily as well, and my father would have done anything for her.'

'Like Janey and Marco?'

'In some ways,' Catherine admitted. 'Although my father was always very sensible where the children were concerned. Just not with my mother.' She gave a wry laugh, but it held no malice. 'My mother decided she wanted to go skiing, just like that. She saw an advert on the television and demanded my father take her to the snow. It didn't matter to her that it was a five-hour drive, didn't matter to her that my father had never even seen snow, let alone driven in it, or that they didn't have chains for the car; she wanted to go and that was all there was to it.'

Rico's hand moved across the bed, capturing hers as she screwed her eyes tightly closed, and somehow his touch gave her the strength to continue, to tell her sorry tale.

'Needless to say they never made it. The police turned up at my home just as they did today, said just what the nurse did this afternoon—''They wouldn't have suffered.'''

'But you did.' His free hand moved to her face, brushing away a heavy dark curl then lingering there, tracing the apple of her cheek, the high arch of eyebrow, before capturing her face in his hand. She ached to turn to him, his touch a comfort she craved, but still she lay there frozen. 'What happened then?'

'Their affairs were a mess.' Catherine closed her eyes for a second, the tension and the agony of those times still painful even now. 'I took a couple of jobs to support Janey and I...'

'You still went to college, though?'

Catherine nodded. 'Maybe I shouldn't have. Maybe I should have been there more for Janey. I just thought if I could get my training over, forge a decent career, then eventually we'd both be okay. Clearly I was wrong.'

'Janey chose how to live her life,' Rico suggested gently, but Catherine refused to be comforted.

'Eventually I sold the house.' Her lip quivered slightly. 'I just couldn't handle the mortgage repayments. I put a deposit on a flat with my half; I hoped Janey would do the same with hers. She didn't,' Catherine added needlessly. 'Instead she blew the money on fancy clothes and restaurants, renting apartments she could never afford. No matter how I tried to reel her in, no matter how I tried to slow her spending down, she spun out of control.'

Tears were precariously close now, but still she bit them back, clenched her eyes closed, raked in some air in an effort to hold on. When she opened them Rico was still there, his eyes not mocking now, infinitely patient as he sat there.

'You have lost so much, Catherine; there is no shame in tears.'

'There's no point either.' She gave a tired shrug. 'I learnt that eight years ago, Rico. Tears don't change anything.'

'I don't agree,' Rico murmured. 'Sometimes it is better to feel pain than to feel nothing.'

And Catherine wished perhaps more than she had ever wished for anything that she could do it. Could let out some of what she held in. But as the silence lingered on, as her tears stayed firmly away, it was Rico who broke the loaded silence, Rico who summed it all up in four simple words.

'I will miss him.'

Still she didn't respond, just lay there staring as Rico softly continued. 'It hurts when I think of Marco. It is agony to know that he is never coming back…' His hand was still on her face, and as he spoke this time she did turn her cheek, nestle a little in the warmth of his touch. 'Marco was born in this country.' Rico smiled gently. 'I used to look after him. I didn't want him to go through what I went through.'

When Catherine's eyes narrowed, Rico's smile widened a touch. 'When I started school I spoke no English. I was the little Sicilian boy with the lunch that smelt. Salami and forty-degree heat is not a good mix. And I suppose Marco looked up to me for a while, came to me if he was in trouble.' There was a wistful note to his voice, then a tiny swallow before he continued. 'I only wish he had carried on looking up to me; carried on coming to me for advice instead of going off the rails. But even though I knew he did stupid things, knew he made mistakes, still I loved him. He wasn't always bad.'

'Nor was Janey.' She saw his shoulders stiffen, a denial undoubtedly bobbing on his tongue, but instead he nodded, afforded her the right to remember her sister as she saw fit.

He sat just a breath away, his presence no longer intimidating, but strangely comforting. The lamplight drew dark shadows on his torso, highlighting the magnificence of his shoulders, defining the quiet strength of his muscular body, imparting confidence. A weary five o'clock shadow dusted his jaw now, but there was veracity in each and every tear that glittered in those brooding eyes—not mocking now, not clouded with suspicion, just infinitely understanding, giving the acquiescence she needed to continue.

'I was thinking about when we were little—how we used to play, how she used to make me laugh. She was always the naughty one...' a sob caught in her throat, 'I can't believe she's really gone.'

He pulled her towards him then, scooping her in his arms and wrapping them around her, a shield, a rock to cling to. 'Let it out, Catherine. Now is not the time to hold back.'

Oh, how she wanted to. How badly she wanted to give way to the tears that were threatening. This glimpse of his tenderness was taking her back to their first night together, when emotion had won, when feelings had been followed, and she was grateful to him—grateful to Rico for crossing the room, for taking her in his arms and telling her that he hurt too, for allowing her to glimpse that behind the cool façade beat a mortal heart that hurt too sometimes, that got broken, that mourned.

But she couldn't quite go there. Couldn't give in to the tears that threatened to drown her. So instead she held him, held him ever closer. There was something about grief that suspended morals, something about loneliness that broke all the rules—because she didn't want to be alone tonight and knew that neither did he. She didn't want the light to go off, to be plunged back into the hell of the twilight zone she had inhabited moments before, and as he held her, caressed her, she was aware, achingly aware, of the shift in tempo. His caress was not so much comforting now, but urgent. His body beneath her fingers was now not so safe and reassuring. There was a tingling awareness of his skin against hers, his lips tracing her cheeks, and it was far easier to drown in his kiss than to face a night alone. Far easier to seek solace in the escape his touch afforded than face cruel reality…

Oh, she might regret it, might see the folly of her ways later, but she craved oblivion now—craved the balmy bliss only Rico could provide. And as his tongue slid inside her parted lips, as his hand cupped her breast through the crisp cotton, she knew Rico craved it too.

Her body arched towards his, long legs coiling around his hips, and he impatiently pulled at the shirt, kicked off his boxers until she could feel his manhood against her, swollen and urgent against her thighs. His lips were hot and urgent over her stomach as she lifted her arms, allowing him to slide the shirt away, and then he pushed her gently down, parted her legs with his hands.

She stared, mesmerized, as he knelt before her, a knot of fear, excitement, anticipation welling as she eyed the velvet steel of his erection. Its sight was more intoxicating than any drink, blurring her senses into one, transfixed on this moment. Her pulse fluttered in a throat that seemed to constrict and she dragged her eyes to his, her whole body on high alert as he lifted the peach of her buttocks slightly from the sheets, held her aching and impatient in his hands and guided her towards him. A stab of pain so delicious she cried out for a moment. Her legs were coiling around him, dragging him deeper, moving against him.

Hot breath burned on her shoulders as he moved inside her, his muscles taut beneath her touch, and she surrendered herself utterly. Focusing only on him—his skin, his smell, the salty, heady taste of him. She could hear her own gasps growing louder, could feel the rise and fall of her breasts as they moulded into him. The flush of her orgasm was whooshing up her cheeks, a dizzy, heady glow, and her thighs trembled convulsively. She could feel him growing more inside her, his breathing uneven, a low groan building inside as he bucked against her, his buttocks taut as she dragged her nails over him, in an animal frenzy as they climaxed together, contracting with an intensity more than merely physical. She could hear him call her name, but it seemed to be from a distance. She called his too, searching for him in the darkness, both calling out as they found the emotional haven they craved, and for a second she knew he needed her—that this release was as necessary as it was wondrous.

And after, as he held her, as he reached over and turned out the light, she no longer feared the darkness. For no dark imaginings could hurt her with Rico by her side.

CHAPTER FOUR

FOR a moment it was all okay.

For one stolen moment between awakening and opening her eyes the world seemed right, but a strange sensation gripped her, a horrible sense of foreboding, and Catherine mentally tried to fathom what was wrong. The truth dawned with a sickening thud as her eyes snapped open.

Janey was dead.

'Here.' A cup of coffee was placed on the bedside table and, pulling the sheet around her, Catherine sat up, taking a grateful sip of the liquid as she tried to fathom all that had happened. She'd never had a hangover, but from Janey's description this must come precariously close, and she eyed the dripping percolator, already planning her second cup. She could see the crumpled shirt lying on the floor, Rico's dark boxers beside it—evidence if ever it was needed of what had taken place. Under any other circumstances it would have overwhelmed her, but not today. Her grief was too overwhelming to allow much else.

'My father just called. He and Antonia are at the airport; they'll be here tomorrow.'

Catherine looked up briefly. She'd only ever seen Rico in a suit, but now he stood unshaven, a towel wrapped around his waist. From the guarded look on his face the intimacies they had shared last night had been eradicated, and he stared back at her coolly.

'I thought they weren't coming until the funeral.'

'They want to be here for Lily. At least that is what my father said.'

Lily!

A wave of guilt washed over her. She hadn't even given her niece a thought since she had awoken. Catherine turned anguished eyes to his, replacing her cup in the saucer and spilling most of the contents. 'I should ring—'

'I already have,' Rico broke in. 'The bruising is more extensive than they first thought, so they would like to keep her under observation for the next few days. She is fine,' he added, as Catherine opened her mouth to ask. 'The doctor said there is no need for concern; it is just as a precaution. I also get the impression they are assessing her social situation closely. The newspapers are full of it this morning, and though the doctor didn't say as much I have a niggling feeling Antonia has rung from the States and let her feelings be known on the subject. As I feared, it would seem the battle for Lily's future welfare is already gearing up.'

He paused for the longest time. 'Now, we really do have to talk, Catherine.'

She didn't want to talk, didn't want to go over and over things, yet she knew they had to—knew things needed to be sorted and that time wasn't on their side.

'This time tomorrow my family will be here. We cannot stop this from turning ugly. Antonia isn't going to take it lying down, but if we can at least put on a united front with the social workers—if we can at least get the legal ball rolling—we can hopefully prevent Antonia from taking Lily from the hospital.'

'She has no right,' Catherine responded immediately. 'She's not even a blood relative.'

'But my father is,' Rico pointed out. 'And my father will do whatever Antonia tells him, believe me.'

Oh, she did believe him, as much as she might not want to. It had been the same with her own parents, and Catherine swallowed nervously. Only now was the magnitude of what she faced truly registering.

'Look, Rico.' She kept her voice deliberately even. 'I understand your doubts about motives, but that aside, surely you cannot question my suitability? I'm a teacher, I work with children, I'm Lily's aunty…' She reeled off her possible attributes but he remained unmoved. 'Surely after last night, after what we shared…' Her voice trailed off as his face darkened. The fury in his eyes was more painful than any slap, the anger in his voice so visible she recoiled into the pillows, her eyes widening as he spoke, fury blazing in every word.

'I wondered how long it would take you.' He glanced at his heavy gold watch. 'But you even surpassed my expectations. I thought you'd at least last five minutes, but you couldn't even hold out that long.'

'I don't know what you're talking about.'

'You think last night changes anything? Well, it doesn't.' His finger jabbed accusingly at her. 'You warned me yesterday you'd do whatever it takes to get Lily, and I should have bloody listened. So if you think you can use your feminine wiles to win me round you're wrong. We had sex last night. That was all.'

'You really are the limit, Rico.' So blind was her fury,

Catherine didn't even bother to wrap the sheet around her, just stood up out of the bed and reached for a robe, tying the belt furiously around her. She stood before him, bristling with anger. 'Do you really think I orchestrated last night? Do you really think I was lying there hoping you'd come to me? Well, you're wrong. Last night we needed each other. Last night we wanted each other. There was no master plan intended. My God—' Her voice was rising now, and her hand raked through her hair, utterly appalled at his slant on things. 'Sleeping with you was the last thing I expected when I lay down on that bed. You know that, Rico. *You know that,*' she repeated, grabbing his arm and trying to rattle some sense into him. But he flicked it away. 'If we'd thought about it undoubtedly it would never have happened. We didn't even—' Her hand shot up to her lips, trembling, as an impossible thought came into focus.

'Go on.' Rico's voice was like ice, and when Catherine said nothing it was Rico who continued for her. 'We didn't use any precautions, is that what you were about to say?'

She gave a small, worried nod, wincing at the bitterness in Rico's voice. 'Why aren't I surprised that you're not on the Pill, Catherine? Why aren't I surprised that, just like your sister before you, you had unprotected sex—?'

'With a very rich man,' Catherine finished for him, her voice a pale whisper. *'You bastard.'*

Very slowly he shook his head, his eyes menacing as they held hers. One hand touched her cheek, one finger traced her cheekbone, but utterly without tenderness. 'There are no bastards in the Mancini family. You know that, Catherine. Just as Janey did. There are no bastards in the Mancini family because, like the traditional Sicilian family we are, we always pay for our mistakes—and, my God, you'd make me pay, wouldn't you?'

The vileness of his accusation was almost more than she could comprehend. The fact that he could think she would stoop so low ignited the anger that had simmered unattended since the first knock at her door from the police.

'We didn't have sex last night, Rico. We made love. You think I engineered it? You think that while my sister lay in the mortuary I was planning to ensure a link with the Mancinis?'

'You glimpsed wealth.' Rico shrugged. 'For a few hours you saw how your life could be…'

'So I seduced you?' She shook her head fiercely, scarcely able to comprehend what he was accusing her of. 'I summoned you to my bed in the vain hope I might conceive?'

'Just as your sister did with Marco.'

Anger boiled within her, blurred her sense and took away her constraint. 'Haven't Sicilians heard of contraception, Rico? You make out I am some sort of tart when the truth is I have had only two relationships in my life and—as fleeting as it was—you were the second.' She watched his face pale, almost took back what she had just said, lied to save herself. But she was beyond rationality now. Pride intermingled with hurt—a dangerous cocktail. 'So, no, I'm not on the Pill, and I didn't have a condom in my handbag just in case some six-foot-four Sicilian chose to make love to me. You'll have to forgive me for my naivety, Rico, but the question really is, what's your excuse? How come *you* didn't think to take precautions?'

To her utter exasperation he didn't answer.

'Because maybe, just maybe you needed me last night?' Catherine suggested for him. 'Because maybe you needed to be with another person? Needed—'

'I needed sex.' Rico shrugged. 'It helps me sleep.'

'What are you scared of, Rico? Why do you have to sully everything with your own warped take on things?'

'Nothing scares me,' he said proudly, but the lack of conviction in his voice was audible to Catherine.

'Oh, yes, it does. You're scared to believe that last night might actually have been about emotion, that maybe just for a moment in time you needed another human being. But don't worry, Rico, I'm not about to trap you...' Her mind was working overtime, tossing up answers to questions she hadn't even considered. 'There's a pill I can take. I can see a doctor today...'

'There will be no pills.' His eyes narrowed menacingly. 'Put that out of your mind this instant. And, contrary to what you just said, I do need you.'

I do need you. His admission stilled her, but his lack of emotion told her this wasn't going to be the declaration she secretly craved.

'You're right. You are a teacher, a supposed upstanding citizen, and on paper you probably look good. And at the end of the day Lily needs a mother figure in her life.'

'So you won't contest it when I apply for custody?' She could scarcely comprehend it would be that easy, that Rico would give up with barely a fight. But he nodded and she felt her breathing even, her pulse-rate slow down as Rico's eyes met hers and he gave a small smile.

'Of course not.' For a second she relaxed—a stupid move when Rico Mancini was in the room, for he struck like a viper the second her defences were down. 'Why would I fight with my wife when we want the same thing?'

'Your wife?' Bewildered eyes met his, her mouth opening and closing as speech evaded her.

'My wife,' Rico confirmed, a malicious smile carving his strong features. 'That is what you want, after all.'

She moved to deny it, opened her mouth to protest, but the words died on her tongue before they were even formed. Rico was right. That *was* what she wanted—for the last year it had been all she had wanted, all she had secretly craved. But not like this. Never, ever like this.

'Antonia and my father can afford the best lawyers—'

'So can you,' Catherine cut in, but he withered her with a stare.

'This could go on for years. Years,' he repeated, making sure she understood. 'And in that time Lily would be dragged between us. But if you and I unite, if we tell the social workers we are married, that Lily is our first and only priority, we would stand a chance. At the very least I'm sure we'd gain custody. and it would be up to my father and Antonia to try and prove we were not fit.'

'But marriage… I can't believe you're suggesting…'

'Oh, but this isn't a suggestion,' Rico corrected. 'This is what we will do.'

'You can't order me to marry you.' She gave an incredulous laugh. 'You can't drag me up the aisle screaming, Rico.'

'There will be no aisle; there will be no church. I think a quick discreet service would be more appropriate.'

'You really think you've got it all worked out, don't you?'

'Of course I have,' Rico said with annoying patience,

as if he were addressing a petulant two-year-old. 'A young professional couple will certainly appease the family court judges.'

'And I suppose once it's all sorted we arrange a discreet divorce?' Her words were laced with scorn. 'What would happen to Lily then?' Catherine fired. 'I suppose I'd have her during the week and you'd rock up at the weekends?'

'She's not a parcel to be passed around; we will do the right thing by her.'

Catherine shook her head, brown eyes blazing, appalled that he thought it could all be so easy. 'A loveless marriage isn't the right thing, Rico. A convenient divorce isn't the right thing by Lily. She deserves better.'

'And she will get it.' He didn't raise his voice, but something in the icy deliverance of his words told Catherine he meant business. She stepped back slightly, swallowing nervously as he walked over and took her none too gently by the shoulders, fixing her with a menacing stare. 'You are the one who mentioned the word divorce…'

'You can hardly expect me to sign my life away for ever.'

'But that is what happens when you have a child,' Rico pointed out. 'That is the commitment you make. Yesterday you told me you wanted custody, that you wanted to do the right thing by your niece.'

'And I do,' Catherine protested, but not quite so forcibly. 'But, Rico, what is a marriage without love?'

'Ha!' He gave a scornful laugh. 'Love is for fools.' Seeing her shocked face only egged him on further. 'Love is a false state of mind, a fantasy one chooses to live in.'

'You don't believe in love? You don't believe a man and a woman can love each other?' She truly couldn't comprehend the magnitude of his words, but Rico was only too happy to enlighten her.

'Of course they can.' Rico shrugged. 'If they choose to mess up their lives. Look at Janey and Marco. Marco loved her, adored her, and in the end it killed him.'

'But surely...?' Catherine started, but Rico was on a roll now.

'My parents.' He held up his hands then clapped them together. 'Sham! My father and Antonia.' Again he clapped his hands. 'Sham!' Picking up the newspaper, he waved it for an angry moment before tossing it aside. 'I bet this is full of happy couples telling the world how love saved the day. Only this time next year we will be reading how she drank too much, or he hit her.' He clapped his hands together again. 'More shams! Love is for fools, Catherine,' Rico said firmly. 'Love leaves you bleeding. The last thing I want or need in my life is a marriage that is a sham. But this way...'

His eyes narrowed and he eyed her thoughtfully, his voice low and husky but utterly determined as he continued. 'You and I—well, I believe it could work. For centuries my ancestors decided their children's fate, chose their partners for them. There was no love there, no stars in their eyes, no promises that their passion might conquer all—and there was no divorce,' he added triumphantly. 'No fools believing that love would get them through. They made a commitment, worked at their marriage, stuck at it even when times were hard. Maybe the old ways had some merit—'

'Your argument is utterly, utterly flawed,' Catherine interrupted. 'Nobody got divorced in those days unless they were incredibly brave or incredibly rich. But it didn't mean they were happy!' She closed her eyes for a second, massaging her temples as she tried to assimilate Rico's strange logic into the twenty-first century. 'And it isn't our parents choosing a suitable match; it's two people—'

'Two people who want the same thing,' Rico broke in, refusing to move an inch. 'Two people with a vested interest. Love doesn't have to come into it. Love *cannot* come into it. There is too much at stake to lose our heads. This is the right thing,' he added. He was speaking more softly now, but there was no mistaking the determination in his voice. 'Lily needs a mother figure, needs some security, and if we don't unite and present a proper case Antonia and my father will pull out all the stops to ensure a bloody, messy court battle. This is the only way.'

'But the social workers will never believe that our marriage is anything other than one of the shams you so vehemently abhor.'

'Why?' He was almost shaking her now. 'When it isn't one? We both know the rules from the start. No talk of love, no promises we can surely never keep. We will tell them the truth—that there was an instant attraction when we first met a year ago and it flared again last night.' His hands tightened their grip, his face so close she could feel his breath on her cheek. But there was nothing tender in his touch, no affection in the arms that held her. 'Of course we won't shatter their illusions with the seamier side of your nature, Catherine. Naturally they don't need to know that you are merely following in your sister's footsteps, ensuring that your future will be very much taken care off. Apart from that, there is no lie.'

But there was.

One touch, one look from Rico and she was a gibbering mess. With just one show of tenderness, one crook of his finger she had tumbled into bed with him. To deny that love was involved was the biggest lie of all...for Catherine, at least.

'We both care for Lily,' Rico continued, taking her distraction as a motion to continue, 'so we decided to accelerate things—build on our attraction to provide Lily with a stable home. When they hear that you are prepared to give up work—'

'No!' Her response was immediate, a knee-jerk reaction, and the single word came out with more force than she'd intended. As his eyes narrowed Catherine took a deep breath, adjusting her tone, but though her voice was softer there was no mistaking her determination. 'I'm not giving up work, Rico. Maybe I don't make millions, like you do, but my job is equally important. I'm a teacher,' she insisted to her unreceptive audience. 'I can't just walk out mid-term.'

'So teachers don't have children?' Rico asked with annoying logic. 'Are you telling me that teachers around the world plan their pregnancies to fit in with term time?'

'Of course not,' Catherine wailed in frustration. 'You're impossible, Rico,' she shouted. 'Impossible and—and...'

'And what? Come on, Catherine, say what you have to.'

'Contrary to what you choose to believe, Rico, I'm too much of a lady to say what I really think of you. But tell me this—why does it have to be the woman who gives up work? Why *should* it be the woman?'

'Do you really expect me to play house husband!' It

was Rico laughing incredulously now. 'You expect me to walk away from my job to change nappies and go to the park each day to feed the ducks? I am a Mancini,' he said pompously, as if his surname alone closed the discussion. But Catherine refused to be silenced—refused to be intimidated by his arrogant name dropping, even if the name was Rico's own.

'And I'm a Masters.' Her brown eyes flared and Rico's mouth snapped closed. 'And I've worked just as hard as you to get where I am. Maybe I don't make millions, Rico, maybe it won't appear on the news if I decide to walk away from my work. But I have twenty-eight students relying on me to give them an education and I happen to believe I'm making a difference. So don't try to belittle me, Rico. Don't assume I measure my self-worth by your cold standards.'

'I apologise.' For a nanosecond she thought she'd won, thought she had actually made a dent in that cold black heart, but as her eyes flashed to his Catherine knew her victory was short-lived. 'Of course you will work. You will carry on living in your tiny cramped flat and go on living the life you so clearly relish.' Sarcasm dripped off every word as he mercilessly continued. 'But tell me, Catherine, how do you intend to pay for all this? Surely if you work Lily will need full-time care?'

'There are day-care centres,' Catherine retorted. 'Crèches. Lots of women juggle babies with a career!'

'Do you know the price of full-time childcare?'

'Oh, and you do?' Catherine snapped.

'Yes.' His smile was anything but friendly. 'Contrary to what you undoubtedly believe, I pride myself in looking after my staff. Along with their other perks, I decided some years ago to subsidise my working mothers' childcare. It made good business sense: not only do I retain good workers, I am repaid tenfold by their loyalty.'

Damn!

She'd walked into that one. But Catherine consoled herself—it wasn't her fault. Never in a million years could she have seen it coming. Rico Mancini and the reputation that preceded him didn't exactly conjure up the words 'caring' and 'sensitive'. How the hell could she have known he was in the running for the Employer of the Year Award?

But Rico hadn't quite finished twisting the knife.

'Now, call me pedantic if you will, but occasionally I even manage to run an eye over the cheques I sign. So you see, Catherine, I am well aware of the cost of *good* childcare. So I'll ask again—how do you intend to fund this latest acquisition? How are you going to make the jump from single professional woman to single professional working mother?'

'I'll find a way,' Catherine insisted, her mind racing.

'How?'

'I don't know.' Her fingers raked through her hair as she stalled for time, frantically trying to come up with an answer. 'I'll manage—women do. Lily will have some…' Her eyes widened in horror, the steel of the trap Rico had laid for her closing around like a vice.

'Some what, Catherine?'

Colour was whooshing up her cheeks now. Like a trapped animal she darted her eyes around the room, desperate for escape, for some breathing space. The percolator was still dripping, but instead of images of second cups it reminded her of Chinese water torture—relentless questions that demanded answers, Rico twisting and turning the facts until his truth was fashioned.

'Shall I finish that for you, Catherine? Lily will have some money. Is that what you were about to say?' She didn't respond. Not that Rico gave her much option. 'There will be no childcare.' Rico's eyes were menacing now, his hands gripping her wrists as he spelt out the rules. 'That baby has had enough of being palmed off, enough of strangers caring for her. If we do this then we do it right, Catherine. You will have a nanny, a housekeeper—all the staff you need. But Lily's day-to-day care will be provided by you. You will not work.'

'I'm not even discussing this.' Shaking his hand off, she moved away, refusing to look at him as she worked the room, picking up her clothes, trying to locate her shoes, shaking her head in furious disbelief when Rico relentlessly continued.

'We have to show the court commitment. We cannot expect Lily to slot into our lives with no sacrifices.'

'I'm not afraid of sacrifice,' she called over her shoulder, heading into the bathroom and putting her clothes down over the rail, then wailing in frustration as he came up behind her. 'Why aren't I surprised you followed me in? Look, Rico, you do your best and I'll do mine. But there is no way, no way at all, that a marriage between us could work.'

'Why?' He seemed genuinely bemused, genuinely confused at her outright refusal to even consider it. 'We have a niece who needs a home, we are clearly sexually compatible, and there is a chance you are carrying my child, Catherine. I'd say we have three very good reasons to be married—three very good reasons indeed.'

Suddenly Catherine felt panicky and out of control. Actually, not so suddenly—since Rico had reappeared on the scene her responses could hardly be classed as normal. But yesterday, in the daze of grief, watching Lily with a bleeding heart, it had been so easy to say yes, to put up her hand and say of course she was up to it. But now, in the cold light of day, the ramifications were starting to hit home.

This wasn't a puppy or a goldfish she was thinking of taking on while the owners went overseas. This was a baby, a living, breathing baby, and the commitment was for ever. She didn't even have the luxury of nine months to come round to the idea.

Even though Rico never moved she could almost feel the mental snap of his fingers, forcing her into decision. Time was not on their side.

'Why do all the sacrifices have to come from me?' Catherine protested again. 'I happen to like my life, Rico. I like my job, my flat, my social life, and you're asking me to throw it all away.'

'You almost sound convincing. Come on, Catherine, let's not pretend—this is what you've always wanted.'

'You're so pompous.' A sob of frustration fuelled her words. 'So damned sure that this is what I want.'

'Isn't it?' He gave a mocking smile that only fed her fury.

'You tell me to jump and I'm supposed to ask how high! Why should it be me making all the sacrifices? What are you giving up?'

'Oh, there will be sacrifices on my part.' He gave a malicious smile. 'You have every right to expect fidelity.'

His words hurt more than Catherine expected. The

thought of him with another woman was more vile than she could contemplate; jealousy reared its head just at the mere thought.

'I wouldn't just expect it, Rico—I would demand it.'

'So we are agreed, then?' Triumph glittered in his eyes, but faded as Catherine firmly shook her head.

'I have agreed to nothing.' Still she shook her head, but less firmly now, and there was bemusement in her voice as she carried on talking. 'Why, when you clearly think so little of me, Rico, would you want me for your wife? You said yourself I disgust you, and you think all I want from Lily is wealth, so why on earth would you ask me to marry you?'

He stared at her for the longest time, his eyes holding hers. His voice, when it came, was low and measured. 'Keep your friends close, and your enemies closer,' he said softly, but without any trace of tenderness. 'Surely you have heard that saying, Catherine?'

'When did I become the enemy, Rico?' Catherine asked, perplexed eyes scanning his. Her voice was softer now. She was genuinely bemused at the stranger who stood before her now, such a stark contrast to the caring, gentle lover who had held her last night. The man who had reached out in the darkness and kept her afloat through the loneliest hours of her life. 'You know, I almost feel sorry for you, Rico.' Catherine let out a low, hollow laugh. 'I'm starting to think you'd actually prefer for me to be some scheming little gold-digger than— heaven forbid—a real woman, with real feelings.'

'Save it, Catherine,' he clipped. 'You're not impressing anyone. You see, I know what you really think of me. I know how Janey felt about Marco and I can prove it to you.' His words silenced her, his voice so cold that Catherine swore her heart stilled for a second. 'When I saw you at the wedding, Catherine, so proud, so apart from everyone else, I lost my head.' He gave a wry smile. 'Lost my head over a woman I had never even met. All I knew was that I had to talk to you, to get to know you. I've dealt with a million Esthers in my time, yet I used her as an excuse to come over. I *had* to be with you.'

There was a raw note to his voice now, the urgency she had witnessed in her own emotions, and she blinked back at him, listening as his story unfolded. She was scarcely able to believe that this beautiful, beautiful man could have been so moved, so enthralled that he would engineer a meeting with her—scarcely able to believe that, however fleetingly, however transitory, for a slice of time he had adored her.

'*Had* to be with you,' he reiterated, and Catherine felt her heart trip back into action, flickering like a bird against her ribcage as she recalled that night from his perspective. 'What happened in the hotel didn't disgust me, Catherine. What happened in that hotel room was as inevitable as night following day. From the second I laid eyes on you I had to have you, Catherine. There could only ever have been one outcome. It was what happened after that disgusted me.'

A gasp escaped her lips as the words shot out of his mouth. Hazy, best forgotten recollections came cruelly into focus as Rico gave a poor imitation of Janey's voice. '"Play your cards right, sis, and all this could be yours!"'

Even if the imitation was lousy, each and every shameful word hit its mark. 'Fool I was, I came looking for you,

Catherine—and, my God, I'm glad I did. Glad that I found out in time your true motives. You ask why I stayed away, you ask why I barely went round to see my niece? Well, there is your reason. I knew Janey was using my brother, knew because I'd heard it from her own mouth, and if I'd spent more than five minutes in the same room as Janey I'd have told Marco—told him that his lovely young wife was nothing more than a cheap, conniving tart.'

'I'm sorry.' Appalled, she stammered as she spoke, 'Sorry that you had to hear all that—sorry that you found out that way.'

'I'm not,' Rico responded coolly. 'In fact, though I admit I was disappointed at the time, I'm glad I heard Janey's take on things. 'Those were Janey's words,' Catherine pointed out, but Rico remained unmoved.

'Perhaps, but I didn't hear you putting up too much of an argument.'

'Just because she felt like that it doesn't mean that I do too. And whatever you heard, whatever was said, deep down, I believe that Janey did love him—that somewhere in her heart…' She shook her head slightly. Janey and Marco faded temporarily into the distance as a deeper realisation hit home. 'You came looking for me?'

He gave a curt nod—such a contrast to her stumbling confusion.

'But why?' Catherine begged. 'Why did you come looking for me?' Her mind was skidding into overdrive. Her focus had shifted now, a million rights wronged as a lens clicked and Rico's perspective of the night shifted into focus. Suddenly the world was clearer, finally his indifference was explained—but the hope that shone in her eyes was doused in an instant by the utter contempt in his.

'I was hoping to finish what we'd started.' His lips curled cruelly around each and every word, singeing her hope with a vile hiss as he relentlessly continued. 'What?' he snapped as she recoiled in horror. 'Did you really think it would be for anything else? That Rico Mancini could really want anything more from you?'

His hand snaked along the nape of her neck, his fingers tangling in the mane of hair, pulling her towards him. But there wasn't a shred of tenderness behind his movements, and his eyes were black and cruel, oblivious to her pain as he twisted the knife deeper in her bleeding heart. 'We had unfinished business, Catherine. That is the only reason I came back, and don't ever forget it.'

'So now that's out of the way, can I go ahead and arrange the wedding?' She would not allow him to see how much he had hurt her. Proudly, defiantly she stared back, refusing to be intimidated, refusing to let him see the black hole her heart had once been. 'Well, you certainly know how to propose in style, Mr Mancini.'

'This is the only way you will get Lily, Catherine. The only chance we have against Antonia.'

'So you'll marry a woman you despise for the sake of your niece? A woman you loathe, who under any other circumstances wouldn't be fit to be your wife?'

'Absolutely,' Rico responded, without missing a beat. 'To keep my family safe I would do anything, and Lily is my blood, Catherine.' He smiled then, but there was nothing reassuring about it. 'You put yourself down, though, Catherine. I never said I loathed you, never said I despised you—in fact I have a grudging respect for a woman who knows what she wants, a woman who just like me is prepared to do anything to get it. Your words,' he added, his hand still working the nape of her neck.

Inexplicably, after the most vile of accusations, the cruel deliverance of his speech, a stinging awareness remained, and his touch was a guilty pleasure she would never admit to.

'Despite that rather uptight exterior you're a hot little thing, aren't you, Catherine? Maybe a marriage of convenience might have some compensations after all.'

Her first instinct was to lash out, to slap that taut cheek, to leave tangible evidence of the scorching shame that imbued her. But somewhere deep inside something moved her: somewhere deep inside she knew this was not the real Rico that she was witnessing now. The real Rico had held her last night, and the real Rico was so much more than the man goading her now.

It was the only reason she didn't walk away.

'I will think about it.' As his eyes narrowed and he opened his mouth to argue she broke in and something in her voice told him to keep quiet. 'I will think about it,' she repeated, and his hand dropped to his side. She was almost daring him to disagree, because one word, one more pompous show of arrogance, and this discussion would terminate.

Her back might be to the wall, but she would not be rushed.

'I'm going to the hospital now, Rico. I'm going to speak with the doctors and find out how Lily's doing and then I'm going to spend the day with her. Now, if you want to come with me then that's your prerogative, but I don't want to hear another word about marriage.'

He nodded, a small curt nod, and Catherine let out the breath she had been holding. She gave a small nod of confirmation back, relaxing a touch as she finally gained a semblance of control.

'Of course when making your decision there is one other thing you need to consider.'

The viper was back, striking when her defences were down. Grabbing her wrists and pulling her towards him, Rico ran a hand over her stomach in a curiously posses-sive gesture.

'If you are carrying my child, Catherine, you can forget any rubbish about being a single parent. You will put out of your mind in an instant any suggestion of a marriage of convenience followed by an amicable divorce. If you are having my baby, this marriage will be for ever.'

CHAPTER FIVE

SHE'D never felt more cold.

Even with the late-afternoon sun shining on her face, even with Lily in her dark-suited arms, soft and warm, smiling and cooing, utterly oblivious to her devastation, Catherine felt as if ice ran through her veins, shivering as she stood at the graveside, barely taking in the words as the coffins were lowered.

The service had passed in a dizzy, nauseating blur. The outpouring of grief she had witnessed from the Sicilian contingent—the frenzy of Marco's relatives, wailing and sobbing, the sheer exhausting emotion that had filled the church and graveside—was such a contrast to the icy reserve that held her together, yet she envied them. Envied their honesty, the cathartic cleansing their outpouring must surely deliver. Instead Catherine's emotions had seemed to implode within her, immobilising her as she stood dry-eyed at the graveside.

The newly dug ground, the vile earthy stench in her nostrils made her want to call out for them to stop, to say that someone, somewhere, somehow had made a terrible mistake, that surely this hadn't been meant to happen, surely some master plan had gone seriously wrong. There was so much left unsaid, so much life still to be lived, so many wrongs to put right. But what good would it do? Even if it had been a mistake, even if the powers that be had this time got it wrong, it was a mistake that would have to be swallowed.

No rewind button to be pushed. Too much had been done to change things.

And somewhere in the abyss of her grief she could feel Rico's hand holding hers, closing in around her icy flesh, squeezing just a little too tight, and she held on, loath to let him know just how much she needed him, but powerless to let go.

'It's over, Catherine.'

The crowd was dispersing, heading back to the endless line of black cars, but still she stood, not wanting that to be it, not wanting Rico's words to be true. It was hard to fathom that this was how it all ended.

'Lily needs to be fed.' It was the first time she had spoken, and her lips shivered around the simple sentence. 'Maybe I should…'

'Jessica will take her home now.' She watched him raise his hand, watched as Jessica came over, smiling awkwardly as she took her charge.

Jessica couldn't yet meet Catherine's eyes, and both women were uncomfortable in each other's presence. The furious row with Janey and Marco was still uppermost in their minds, that last meeting too near to be relegated to history just yet, but too raw and painful to explore with any hope of objectivity. As Catherine handed Lily over she felt guilty at the relief that flooded her. Guilty at how relieved she was that Rico had been able to persuade Jessica to come back and care for Lily. Grateful she wouldn't have to deal with Lily just yet, when it was still taking a supreme effort just to remember to breathe.

Today was too hard.

'We need to face my family now.' Rico broke into her thoughts. 'It is best Lily is not present for this.'

She wasn't up to this today, but Catherine knew they had no choice. Antonia had already made her feelings clear on the subject. The spiteful rows at the hospital were still ringing in her ears, and the venom of her verbal attack when Lily had been discharged into Rico and Catherine's temporary care was as horrible in hindsight as it had been in the present. With a weary nod she walked back to the waiting car, quietly grateful his hand still held hers.

'This isn't going to be pleasant,' Rico warned as she stared blindly out of the window, tears pricking her eyes at the sight of the two lonely mounds of earth, the flowers already wilting in the hot Australian sun.

'None of this is pleasant.'

Under any other circumstances arriving at Carlos Mancini's family home would have been intimidating, to say the least. In Toorak, one of Melbourne's most affluent suburbs, the huge mansion was barely visible from the street. Huge boxed hedges dwarfed the massive black gates that slid open as the limousine approached, but today her mind was too full of all that had been lost to let its opulence overwhelm her. Today the vast stone walls covered with creeping ivy only reminded Catherine of the tombstones in the graveyard and the wreath she had just laid.

Accepting a brandy, Catherine sipped on it. She was not a big drinker, not a drinker, but the warmth of the liquor seeped through her and she braced herself for the inevitable small talk—the awful low murmurs about how well the service had gone, how awful it was to meet under such circumstances. She was determined to hold up her end, for Janey to have a presence here today, no matter how small.

'*Dovè Lily?*' Antonia's voice carried across the large foyer, and even though Catherine spoke not a word of Italian in this instance no translation was needed. Everything stilled, the hushed reverence normally reserved for such events changing instead to a strained silence as every eye turned to Rico and Catherine.

'She was tired.' Rico shrugged, carefully choosing a drink from a passing waiter. 'After all, Antonia, she was only discharged from hospital this morning.'

'Well, she should be here,' Antonia responded, matching Rico's English. 'It's her parents' funeral, after all.'

'No.' Rico's voice was very calm, but there was an edge to it that had the hairs on Catherine's neck standing to attention, and though it galled her she had a certain reluctant admiration for Antonia when she maintained her disdainful glare towards her stepson. 'She shouldn't be here. No six-month-old should have to attend her parents' funeral.'

'That isn't what I meant and you know it, Rico. Your father is in the study; perhaps we should discuss Lily's future there.'

Catherine's mouth dropped open. Oh, she wasn't naïve, and Rico had left no room for doubt that this discussion was imminent, but she'd been sure there would be at the very least an attempt at pleasantries.

'Let's get this over with,' Rico murmured, guiding her by the elbow towards a large imposing room. But Antonia clearly had other ideas, shaking her head the second they entered. '*Questo e solo per famiglia, Rico.*'

'Catherine *is* family,' Rico responded easily, refusing to join Antonia's blatant mind-games. 'She's Lily's aunt.'

'Then she'd better get herself a solicitor.' Antonia flashed him a look that was pure malice, and Catherine privately wondered if this conversation might be best left misunderstood.

'I have no doubt she intends to,' Rico said, with a note of dryness that was clearly for Catherine's benefit. 'But given the fact that Lily has been entrusted into both Catherine's and my care, I suggest it would be prudent if she stays and polite to have this discussion in English.'

'You've only been granted temporary care,' Antonia corrected. 'The social worker was very clear about that when I spoke with her; this isn't finished by a long shot. Heaven only knows what lies the two of you fed that social worker. Why on earth she would think you could provide better care than Carlos and I is beyond me.' This time it was Catherine who was the recipient of Antonia's withering stare. 'Don't think I don't know where you're coming from, young lady.' Her lips curled into a sneer. 'You're a guttersnipe, just like your sister.'

She flicked her eyes away, clearly ready to move on to seemingly more important things, but for the first time since entering the house, Catherine found her voice.

'I can understand that you have issues with me, Antonia.' The voice was shaky, but her resolve was steel. 'However, Marco wasn't the only person buried this afternoon. It was my sister's funeral also, and, given that it is my sister's daughter we're discussing, I'd ask that you all show Janey some respect, at least where Lily's concerned.'

Her words seemed to reach Antonia. Her expression

softened slightly and she gave a brief nod that Catherine took as an apology before turning her attention back to Rico.

'Your father and I have discussed this at length,' Antonia stated. 'In fact we've barely slept since the accident.'

'How exhausting for you,' Rico drawled, but his sarcasm was wasted.

'It has been,' Antonia agreed, fishing a small lace handkerchief from her heavily tanned bosom and dabbing at a tear Catherine couldn't see. 'But that's not the issue. The issue is Lily's welfare.'

'Agreed,' Rico said, but his expression was anything but receptive.

'Lily needs security.' Antonia looked over to her husband, who smiled warily back. 'And your father and I are the ones who can give her that.'

'Are you sure it isn't the other way round?' Rico's voice cut like a knife, his black stare withering, and Catherine was eternally grateful that for once she wasn't the recipient of his simmering anger.

'This has nothing to do with money,' Antonia insisted, gesturing to the opulent study, with a beautifully manicured hand, then fingering the heavy jewels around her neck. 'Your father and I are hardly in the poor house.'

'But you *are* heading into financial trouble.'

'Don't be ridiculous!' Antonia's eyes were bulging and her well made-up face reddened as Rico eyed her disdainfully.

'I'm not the one being ridiculous,' Rico replied without a trace of emotion. 'I'm not the one jetting around the world in my own private plane with an entourage of staff.

I'm not the one flying to Paris to update my wardrobe or deciding on a whim to head over to New York to see the tennis.'

Even in her numb state of grief Catherine felt a surge of shock at the sheer lavishness of Antonia's existence.

'You're living beyond your means,' Rico said, his voice darker now.

'How would you know?' Antonia flared, but Rico merely shrugged and for the first time addressed his father.

'I know because I bought out your portion of the business. I know because I still do your accounts, Dad, and at the end of the day valuing properties is my bread and butter. As nice as this is, as divine as your Queensland holiday home might be, and all the other little nest-eggs you've got stashed away, the simple fact of the matter is that you cannot afford this lifestyle indefinitely. Some day in the not too distant future something will have to give.' The harshness left his voice then, and a note of exasperation crept in as he implored Carlos to listen. 'Have you read any of the paperwork I gave you, Dad?'

'I haven't had time.' Carlos Mancini's voice was still heavily accented. 'And today is not the day for money talk. Today I lay my son to rest.'

'Fair enough.' Rico nodded, but from previous experience Catherine knew the conversation wasn't over—knew Rico wasn't going to just walk away now. 'If it really isn't about money then let's make a deal before the solicitors get involved—before this leaves the family and becomes open gossip for every journalist in Australia.'

He paused for an age before continuing. The heavy clock on the mantelpiece ticked so slowly Catherine would have sworn it was faulty, so long did each passing second drag.

'We all agree that Lily's money stays in trust for her until she's twenty-one, and that whoever gets custody finances Lily's upbringing by their own means.'

'Lily will need an education.' Antonia was choosing her words carefully but her agitation was palpable. 'You can hardly expect your father and I to fund—'

'The sad thing is,' Rico broke in, 'I don't expect a thing from the two of you. The saddest part of this whole discussion is that Lily is nothing more than a means to an end for you, Antonia.'

Catherine simply didn't know where to look, it was horrible watching as Antonia flushed ever darker, her mouth pursing. Rico's father was fishing in his suit for a handkerchief and wiping his brow, and she felt sorry for him, remembering that at the end of the day, Carlos Mancini had buried his youngest son today. But Rico clearly wasn't taking that into consideration, for he didn't let up, was ruthless in his pursuit as he carried on talking. 'Lily would provide a nice little pension for the pair of you, as well as getting you out of the hole you've dug yourself into.'

'Oh, we didn't dig,' Antonia soon recovered and stood up, her eyes bulging as she faced her stepson, veins standing out in her neck as she choked out the words. 'You buried us, Rico. You put us in this hole the day you bought your father out of the business for a pittance.'

'Hardly a pittance,' Rico drawled but his icy reserve only exacerbated Antonia's fury.

'You knew the company was about to take off.' Antonia was practically purple now. 'You knew the fortune it was going to make, and yet you bought out your brother and father for a tenth of what you would now. And you have the gall to stand there and gloat, the tenacity to breeze in and tell us that we're in financial trouble when *you're* the one with blood on your hands.'

Catherine's eyes shot to Rico as she waited for him to say something, for him to defend himself against Antonia's vile accusations. But he just stood there, his face impassive, not a bead of sweat on his brow, and not for the first time Catherine wondered what she had got herself into, wondered at the lengths Rico was clearly prepared to go to in order to claim what he assumed was rightly his.

'So far, Antonia, you've said two things that merit comment.'

Finally, Catherine thought. Finally he's going to put her in her place, clear the slur on his name. But the hope that flared was extinguished as Rico continued.

'The issue *is* Lily's welfare, and, yes, Lily, *does* need security, which I'm more than capable of providing.'

'You!' Antonia sneered. 'A man who has had more girlfriends than I've had hot dinners? A man who spends fifteen hours a day in an office? When are you supposed to see her, Rico? Are you intending to e-mail her a couple of times a day? Read her a bedtime story over the telephone?'

'And you're such an expert on parenting suddenly, Antonia?'

This time Rico's sarcasm didn't go unnoticed.

'You were eighteen when I married your father, Rico. Hardly an age for fairytales and nights around the fire with a cup of cocoa. So cut it with the sob stories. I was good to you.'

'You were good for nothing, Antonia!' Rico's voice was pure venom. 'And, yes, I was eighteen. Yes, I was old enough to get on with my life, to walk away from the woman who had destroyed not only my mother's marriage but ultimately her life. But Marco was twelve—a twelve-year-old boy you treated like dirt on your shoe. You moved in and he was shipped out to boarding school the next month. *The next month,*' he repeated, emotion finally rearing its head, his voice a loud roar. 'Is that what you intend for Lily?'

'She's a baby,' Antonia retorted. 'She's years away from school. It's not even an issue at the moment. You're not having her, Rico. I'll sell the plane if I have to, but I'll fight you till the end for her.' Her eyes met Catherine's, locked on them for an uncomfortable moment, and suddenly everything didn't seem quite so crystal-clear any more. The picture Rico had painted of a money-hungry woman was suddenly not quite so plausible. 'Your sister would want the best for her daughter—surely you can see that?'

Catherine gave a small nod.

'Let's put the money aside for a moment.' Antonia's voice bordered on reasonable, and again Catherine nodded, determined to hear all sides, to make a rational decision when all the cards were on the table. Lily's future was too precious for egos and finances to get in the way. 'Children should have two parents. That might sound old-fashioned, but I firmly believe it—as I'm sure the courts do—'

'For once we agree on something,' Rico's voice broke in, and Catherine shot him a furious look.

'Antonia was talking, Rico. I think we should at least hear what she has to say.'

'I'm tired of listening to her crap.' Taking Catherine's hand, he held it for a moment, slowly turning it over in his palm before holding it up. 'Notice anything?' His malevolent tones had shivers running down Catherine's spine, and there was nothing tender in the way he held her. 'Aren't you going to congratulate us, Father?' When Carlos just sat there in stunned silence he addressed his stepmother. 'Antonia? Aren't you going to welcome the newest addition to the Mancini family?'

'You see, you're right Antonia. Children *do* deserve two parents, and I figured with you damaging my reputation, coupled with the hours I put in at the office—well, it might go against me if I were in sole charge. But given I've got a loving wife at home—a loving, educated wife, I hasten to add, with not a single skeleton in the cupboard—well, I'm sure the courts will understand that I need to provide for my family. I'm sure the courts will have no hesitation in giving Catherine and I full custody.'

The room was icy cold. Antonia was opening and closing her mouth like a goldfish as Rico's hand snaked around Catherine's face and he planted a kiss on her cheek in a curiously triumphant gesture before addressing his family. 'Antonia, Father—' Rico smiled in turn at them both. 'Allow me to introduce my wife.'

'Your wife?' The incredulity in Antonia's voice wasn't born of affection; Catherine could almost taste her disgust as it permeated the room. 'When did this happen?'

'This morning.' Rico's voice was insolent. 'You'll understand there wasn't exactly time to send out invitations, and naturally we don't expect a present, but surely congratulations should be in order?'

'Never!'

Antonia was shuddering with an unleashed fury which Rico clearly wasn't going to hang around to witness. As he stalked out of the room, Catherine knew her supposed place was by his side, but her legs were leaden as she turned to go. She was truly torn by what she had witnessed.

'He's using you.' Antonia almost ran to catch up with her. Pulling at Catherine's suit, she turned her around, and Catherine waited—waited for confrontation, for accusations of what she didn't know. But more bewildering was a look from Antonia that bordered on sympathetic, a touch that was almost maternal as she squeezed Catherine's arm. 'Maybe you think you're using him as well, Catherine. Perhaps you've agreed to use each other. But I'm telling you: you won't come out of this unscathed.'

'Please, Antonia,' Catherine warned her, 'don't threaten me.'

'I'm not threatening you, my dear.' Antonia shook her head. 'It's not me that you have to fear; I only want what's best for Lily.'

'So do I.' Catherine's throat was dry, her mouth like sandpaper, and she could see Rico out of the corner of her eye, waiting impatiently for her to join him. But still she held her ground. 'And I truly believe that this is the best way.'

'Can I at least see her?' Tears were filling Antonia's eyes now, and Catherine was appalled at what she had been reduced to. She had read about grandparents being kept from their grandchildren, had moaned with her colleagues about children being used as a weapon in bitter custody battles, and to think she was capable of it truly appalled her. 'Please don't keep us away from her while the court case goes on. Whatever happens between the families, surely we should still be able to see her.'

'Of—of course,' Catherine stammered. 'Lily needs people who love her.'

'And I do love her.' Antonia gulped. 'Whatever Rico says about me, I do love her. All I'm asking is that you remember that.'

Oh, she didn't want to remember that—didn't want the rules to suddenly change. It had all been so much easier when Antonia was the enemy—a cold, heartless woman who would stop at nothing—but suddenly she didn't look so cold. Right now she looked like a grandmother having her heart stamped on.

'I have to go,' Catherine said. 'Rico is waiting…'

'It's Rico you need to watch out for,' Antonia warned, her eyes boring into her, almost mesmerising in their clarity. 'He's using you, and when he's finished with you he'll toss you aside, the same as he did with his father, the same as he did with his brother. You'll be left with nothing.'

'I'm Lily's aunty,' Catherine said, with a conviction that wavered as Antonia shook her head slowly.

'You're a pawn, darling. A pawn in one of Rico's games.'

CHAPTER SIX

'I KNOW it all seems a bit strange, but you'll soon get used to it.'

Catherine didn't even deign to give a response as she clipped along the marble entrance hall in her high heels, her dark suit matching her sombre mood. Antonia's words were still ringing in her ears as she tried to fathom the new world she now inhabited.

And he watched.

Watched from a distance as she explored her new surroundings, quietly proud of her detached dignity as she adjusted to yet another new page in the book of her life, again faced the challenges the world seemed only too willing to provide this resilient woman.

You have to let her come to you.

How many times over the last days had he heard that?

Every time Lily had arched her back, sobbed in protest as he held out his arms to her, the social worker had repeated those words. 'She's confused, scared—it's all too much for her to take in. If you can just be there for her, and try not to expect too much, then in time she'll come to you.'

But it wasn't Lily worrying him now; tonight his concern was purely for Catherine.

How he longed to go over to his new bride, to shower that pale, strained face with kisses, to make things better with just a smile. But this wasn't a baby to be won over with a smile; this was a woman...

In every sense of the word, Rico thought, then attempted a retraction, mentally slamming closed a window that simply couldn't be opened tonight.

He wanted to tell her—tell her what was in his heart—but surely now wasn't the time. Catherine had enough to deal with, without clouding the issue with his pointless declarations.

A loveless marriage.

That was what they had agreed and that was how it must be. For now at least.

Yet no matter how he fought it, no matter how he tried to feign aloofness, still he found himself admiring those legs that seemed to go on for ever, silhouetted by her sheer stockings as she walked the length of the house. He took in the soft curve of her stomach, so much more appealing than the flat, concave gamines he usually dated.

But though he adored her with his eyes, they narrowed in concern as she made her way back to the entrance hall. She faced him head-on for the first time that day, and he couldn't help but notice the dark smudges under eyes that had lost all their sparkle, the luscious hair tied back in a severe knot. Only her lips added a splash of colour, but even they seemed to have paled, and he ached, physically ached to take her into his arms and kiss away all the hurt, to somehow let her know that he understood the hell of today—the funeral, the awful confrontation with his family. But something in her stance told him he was neither wanted nor needed.

'I'd better check on Lily.' Even her voice seemed to have lost its fire. 'Listless' was the word that sprang to mind. Her eyes didn't even flick to his as she headed for the stairs.

'Jessica said she was sleeping,' Rico pointed out. 'Maybe it's best not to disturb her.'

'Jessica's the nanny.' Catherine shrugged. 'I thought nighttime kisses and fairy stories were my department.'

'Catherine.' He came up behind her, taking the stairs two at a time till he stood beside her, one hand reaching for her shoulder. But he saw her stiffen before he even made contact and pulled it away. 'You've just lost your sister, moved out of your home—'

'And just got married!' Her eyes glinted dangerously at him. 'You failed to mention the fact we got married this morning, Rico. But then why would you? It was hardly the ceremony of the century.'

'Which was what you wanted,' Rico pointed out. 'What you insisted upon.'

And it had been, Catherine conceded. But only to herself. She'd never been one of those women who'd dreamed since childhood about her wedding day, but a draughty, bland register office in the middle of the city, a ceremony snatched between meetings with lawyers and funeral preparations, certainly hadn't been envisaged either.

'I just didn't expect it to be so—'

'Look,' Rico quickly interrupted, 'I know it wasn't much of a wedding—I know that it was all a bit rushed. If you want, we can do it again—do it properly. When things have settled down we can have the wedding you want, the wedding you deserve. I'll get my secretary to find you the best wedding planners; they can put you on to designers, anything you want…'

He was trying to help, Catherine told herself. Rico Mancini was used to waving a chequebook to fix things, used to plastering over cracks. But her pain ran too deep.

He simply didn't get it.

He'd probably never get it.

The bland surroundings, the lack of grandeur, her crumpled clothes, the impassive celebrant—they didn't matter a jot.

Had Rico only loved her, had his eyes adored her as he'd taken her as his wife, had his hand only reached for hers as they'd signed the register, the wedding would have been all she'd ever hoped for.

Her wedding would have been magical.

'I'm going to check on Lily.'

'Leave Lily for now.' Rico was insistent. 'Jessica seems very responsible and her room is just next door to Lily's. Why don't you come and have a drink?'

'I don't want a drink.'

'Well, a bath, then.'

She gave a low laugh. 'I would, except I don't even know where the bathroom is.'

'Catherine, please.' She could hear an impatient note to his voice and gave a wry shake of her head—her allotted two minutes of understanding were clearly up.

'What's wrong, Rico?' Accusing eyes turned to his, for even though she was as much a participant as Rico, a willing partner in the sham they had engineered, somehow she couldn't help but blame him.

Blame him for not loving her back.

'Aren't I playing the part of new bride to your satisfaction? Are you disappointed I didn't want to be carried over the threshold to satisfy the photographers? Were you hoping I might have a nice bath and then slip into something more comfortable?'

'Of course not—' Rico started, but Catherine hadn't finished.

'You've got what you wanted, Rico. I've kept up my end of the deal. But don't for one second expect me to be happy about it.'

Even as she spoke Catherine regretted her harsh words. She didn't want to be like this, didn't want to be mooching around like a surly teenager, making this uncomfortable situation worse for both of them. But it was as if she couldn't help herself.

Antonia's dreadful accusations were still buzzing in her ears. How she longed to escape for a few days, to check out of the world and digest all that had happened, assimilate it into some sort of order—something she could deal with. But at her own bidding she was a mother now. And not one part of her life was familiar. Her possessions had been cleared from her flat in a single day, compassionate leave arranged from work with one phone call—even her name was different: Catherine Mancini.

Catherine Mancini, who lived in a huge, imposing house, with servants and nannies. Catherine Mancini, who had a baby to care for. Catherine Mancini, wife to a husband who under any other circumstances wouldn't have deigned to marry her.

'Leave Lily,' he said again, and the tone of his voice told Catherine he wasn't about to be argued with. 'If you wake her now it will take ages to settle her, and we're both exhausted.'

'Fine.' Her mouth barely moved. 'Maybe I will have a

bath after all, and then I think I'll go to bed. Could you show me where I'll be sleeping?'

'Of course.' He led her up the stairs, his hand resting gently on tense shoulders that stiffened even more as he pushed open the large mahogany door. He registered her sharp intake of breath as she eyed the vast bed, the massive floor-to-ceiling windows that took in the shimmering Melbourne skyline. 'I will even run a bath for you.'

Run a bath. He made it sound such a supreme effort, and for Rico it probably was, Catherine mused as he walked across the room. No doubt this was a first. She watched as he stood for a moment by the vast sunken spa, eyeing the bottles of oil, then flicking a switch. She stood, seemingly transfixed by the swirling bubbles but struggling against a surge of panic, wishing more than Catherine had ever wished in her life that she could do it. Could slip off her clothes with the confidence his numerous other lovers had undoubtedly had, smile up at him through her eyelashes and suggest he join her. But she felt as if her feet had been nailed to the floor, a shadow of what Rico undoubtedly expected his wife to be—a mere solution to a problem, a wife of convenience in every sense.

'There must be another room.' She ran a tongue over her dry lips, watched his eyes narrow, the muscles on his face quilting as he turned to face her. 'I mean, it might make things easier for both of us…'

'Easier?' His voice was menacingly quiet and she had to strain to catch it over the noise of the running water. 'You think my wife sleeping down the hallway will make things easier? Tell me how so, Catherine?'

'I think it would be easier if we had a bit of space. We both know this isn't a true marriage; we both know we don't...' She swallowed nervously. Lies were hard work, even at this dangerous stage.

'Don't love each other?' Rico finished the sentence for her, the words snapping out through his taut lips, and the air crackled with tension as Catherine gave a nervous nod, consoling herself that it was a lie by omission only.

To love each other took commitment from both sides, a commitment Rico had vowed he would never give. But though she loved him she hated him too—hated his presumption, his arrogance, the way he walked over people he should care about.

The questions that had saturated her mind since the wake could be voiced now; answers were needed before she could even contemplate continuing this charade. Forcing herself to take a calming breath, finally she spoke. 'Is it true what Antonia said? Did you know that the business was going to take off when you bought out your brother and father?'

He didn't answer for a moment, and when he did despite his blithe response Catherine knew she'd hit a nerve. 'I knew it was a possibility.'

'But Antonia said—'

'Forget Antonia.' His voice was like the crack of a whip, his nonchalance disappearing as Catherine pressed on. 'She is poison—evil. I told you not to listen to a word she says.'

'And that's supposed to be enough for me?' Catherine flared. 'You tell me not to listen and I'm supposed to comply? Am I not allowed to form my own opinions, Rico? Are you going to remind me again of the good old days, when wives took their husbands' opinions as gospel? The good old days when wives meekly complied with the master's orders?'

'You are twisting my words; I am telling you that woman is no good,' Rico growled, grabbing her wrist and pulling her towards him to force her to listen. But Catherine pulled her hand away, standing tall and proud, looking him square in the eyes.

'I heard you the first time, Rico.' Catherine was shouting now. 'And you can scream it from the rafters, swear it to be true, but so far all I see is a grandmother with her back to the wall—a grandmother fighting to raise her orphaned grandchild.'

'Step-grandchild,' Rico corrected, but Catherine refused to buy it.

'Now who's twisting words, Rico? We'll never be Lily's biological parents, yet that doesn't mean we won't love her as if we were! And you still haven't answered my question. Did you pay off your brother and father knowing that the business was about to explode into an empire?'

'It was years ago.' Rico's hands were working furiously now, tossing in the air with exasperated gestures, and again he reminded her of a lion—but trapped now, pacing the cage restlessly, his simmering anger ready to explode. 'Why the hell do we have to drag it up? Why go into things that don't have any bearing on the here and now? They didn't have to sell.'

'The same way I didn't have to marry you?' She gave a low, mirthless laugh. 'I bet you ensured that they had no choice but to sell—the same way you gave me no choice. And despite what you say it does have a bearing on us. How you treated your family in the past is a pretty good indicator of how you're going to treat me in the future, Rico. There's a lot of unfinished business there. A lot of pain—'

'Oh, there's pain,' Rico said darkly, his eyes narrowing as he looked at her. 'But go on, Catherine. Finish what you were saying.'

She swallowed hard. Something in his voice merited deeper exploration, but she had to see this through, could not be dragged from the path again by Rico's clever bidding. 'I'm not sure I want to be married to a man who could cheat his own family.'

A compressed hiss escaped his lips. So savage was the fury in his eyes that Catherine braced herself for impact, for that incurable Latin temperament to bubble over into a blind torrent of rage.

All of that she could have dealt with.

Could have fought his fire with her own.

Only it never came. For an age he didn't answer, just calmly walked over and flicked off the taps she had forgotten were even running, and when he straightened up, when he turned to address her, his voice was incredibly even, his icy demeanor more chilling than any heated confrontation.

'You make it sound as if you still have a choice, Catherine. You make it sound as if you are still considering the proposal I made back at the hotel.' He held up his left hand, the heavy gold band she had placed there catching the light as he crossed the room towards her. 'Might I remind you that we have a legally binding commitment to each other? The register you signed wasn't a birthday card, or a casual letter you can rip up and forget about.' His face was so close she could feel every word he uttered skim along her cheek, feel the tension in every muscle as he stood before her, body taut, eyes blazing. 'You are my wife now, Catherine, with all that that entails.'

'Surely you can't expect us to share a bed? Surely after all that's gone on you don't expect us to sleep together?'

'Back at the hotel I remember us sharing a bed together. I don't remember you needing space then!'

'That was then,' Catherine retaliated. 'I was confused, lonely…' Pleading eyes begged him to understand, and if he'd just taken her in his arms, told her it was all okay, that it wasn't just for appearances' sake he wanted her in his bed, she'd have gone to him without hesitation— would have settled, even, for a convincing lie. But Rico was a closed book. Not one flicker of his face betrayed how he was feeling. Every emotion was guarded fiercely behind the mask he so readily wore.

'I can't do it, Rico. Please don't make me.'

Her plea was genuine, for with one crook of his finger she knew she would dissolve like jelly in hot water—fall into his arms and betray herself with the words he didn't want to hear. Or maybe he did, Catherine realised.

After all, if she loved him, he won.

'We don't have a choice.' He nodded to the window. 'Did you notice the press when we came home, Catherine? Are you foolish enough to think that they've got their pictures and gone home now?' He gave a mocking laugh. 'They don't believe in fairytales any more than I do, and each and every one of them will want to be the first to prove their point—lights flicking on in the guest room will do just that. And if by some chance we manage to fool them on that score, how long do you think it will be before one of the staff decides Christmas should come a bit early?'

'I don't understand...'

'Trust no one, Catherine,' Rico said darkly, a mocking smile curving on his lips. 'Except maybe me.'

'And that's supposed to make me feel better?' Her pulse was pounding in her temples now—not gently, though. A nauseating throbbing would be a more apt description. Her hand moved up, massaging her temples, and she wondered how best to play this.

'Don't tell me...' His voice was dripping with sarcasm. 'You're getting a headache?'

'Isn't that what wives normally get?' Catherine bit back, but Rico's riposte was just as swift.

'I believe so. Though generally after the marriage is consummated.'

A low laugh escaped her pale lips. 'Worried the contract is not quite legally binding, Rico? Are you worried that until we've slept together I might be able to ask for an annulment?'

'I never worry about small details. Why would I when I have an army of solicitors to do it for me? And I believe, off the top of my head, that a request for an annulment wouldn't stand up too well in court when only days before the wedding the bride was not only sleeping with the groom but begging for it.'

'I never begged.'

'Oh, no?'

He never moved, his eyes stayed fixed and not a muscle flickered in his body, but she could almost taste the sudden sexual tension. The suggestion in his words was enough to cast her mind back until she could almost see her head on the pillow, thrashing in frenzied passion as she wept for him to enter her, and she knew he was thinking it too. The knowledge caused a ripple of lust to dart through her traitorous body—just the memory of his touch was enough to instigate instant arousal.

'That's not how I remember it, Catherine.'

His words should have shamed her, but she was beyond that now. His scorn should have hurt, but Catherine was beyond pain. She had buried her sister today, sworn at Janey's graveside she would do her best for Lily, and if standing tall and proud, quelling her fears and fighting back was the order of the day, then somehow she'd do it. This was Rico Mancini she was up against—a man who would use her to further his cause. She had to remember that, had to keep her head however much she wanted to lose it, had to stay strong.

For Janey and for Lily.

'Then I'm not the only fool in this room.' The derisive note in her voice, the clarity of her speech, surprised even Catherine. And when she saw the dart of confusion in his eyes it was all that was needed to spur her on further.

One tiny victory when all had seemed lost.

'Contrary to your orders, I haven't quite burnt all my bridges—I didn't hand in my notice, Rico, I'm on compassionate leave. So I can walk back into my old life at any given moment.' She stepped back slightly; the fire was back in her eyes now, a soft pink dusted her pale cheeks and her chin set determinedly as she carried on talking. 'But then why would I bother when there's always the divorce card to play? Even the *ex* Mrs Mancini would have more clout in a courtroom than Miss Catherine Masters.'

'That's why you said yes?' Rico's voice was a pale whisper.

'That's the *only* reason I said yes,' Catherine said firmly.

'You wanted me that night,' he insisted, but though his voice was resolute there was flicker of doubt in his eyes.

'I wouldn't be so sure, Rico.' As she turned Catherine smiled softly at him, but it was a smile laced with danger, a curious cocktail of seduction and menace.

The gentle, sweet woman was gone now; instead a bewitching temptress smiled back at him. He stood frozen, watching transfixed as she loosened her hair from its confines, pulled off her jacket and worked the buttons of her black lace blouse, undressing slowly, but utterly ignoring him at the same time, absolutely refusing to let him see the effect he was having on her, determined not to be intimidated.

For the first time in their strange relationship Catherine knew the power of being a woman, learnt the lessons her mother and Janey had unwittingly imparted.

Knew for once she had the valuable upper hand.

'What proud Sicilian would like his lack of sexual prowess played out in court? What proud Sicilian would want the world to know that one night with a woman was enough to make her ensure it was the last?'

Unzipping her skirt, she let it fall around her ankles. Under any other circumstances she would have felt stupid, utterly stupid, standing in stockings and high heels, her creamy breasts spilling out of black lace. But his well-cut suit wasn't enough to hide his furious arousal, and Catherine flicked a superior eye downwards before turning her triumphant gaze back to him as she discarded her bra.

'You lie.' He cursed the words at her, but she deliberately didn't flinch. 'You enjoyed every moment.'

'Did I?' Slowly she walked over to the bath, and slowly she lowered herself in—grateful for the heated water as an excuse for her flaming skin, grateful for the bubbles that covered her jutting nipples. 'I'm sure Marco was equally convinced when Janey called out his name.'

His eyes found hers then.

'You bitch.'

'Why act so surprised, Rico? All along you've accused me of being a gold-digger, all along you've insisted I'm only here for the money, and yet now you've finally got me to admit it you don't seem very pleased all of a sudden.' Dragging her eyes away, she concentrated for an age on the bottles, before selecting one and massaging its contents into her hair. He stood rigid beside the bathtub, his face livid, anger blazing in every taut muscle.

'Lily is my sole priority, Rico. Not this marriage and definitely not you. And if you think you can use me as some sort of pawn in your game and I'll just comply—'

'You believe Antonia?' Rico demanded. 'After everything I said, still you choose to believe her?'

'I believe no one,' Catherine said resolutely. 'But believe this, Rico. If you think you can brush me off like some smudge on your suit when it all dies down, that I'll walk away without a fight, then you'd better think again. Catherine Masters has long gone now, I'm Catherine *Mancini*, with everything the name entails.'

CHAPTER SEVEN

SHE waited for morning.

Lying in the massive bed, feeling the bristling hatred emanating from him, she ached, literally ached to go over to him, to lay her head on his chest and to feel his arms around her, to take back all she had said. But there was too much at stake, too much to lose in a weak moment. So instead she lay there, the room as light as day as the full moon drifted past the massive windows, listening to the creaking house, every nerve taut as finally his breathing evened out.

One heavy arm moved towards her, almost instinctive in its directness, caressing the curve of her waist until she turned towards him. She'd never seen him asleep before, never witnessed the beauty of his face without tension. The taut mouth was relaxed, full, sensual lips slightly parted, dark eyelashes fanning his haughty cheeks, and he looked younger, softer, but so desirable she had to bite back the urge to kiss him, to place her lips on his. Instead she adored him with her eyes, stealing this time away from his accusing glare to absorb his beauty, to capture the delicious image of a husband who was hers in name only.

Her eyes drifted down to the rumpled sheet that lay precariously over his manhood, and she had to clench her fists, such was her desire to move it, to unwrap the parcel and claim the prize. And what terrified her most was that she knew, just knew, he would respond. There was an undeniable attraction that overrode all else. In sleep, his body would yield to her, that tumid length would harden, would awake in her hands. But what then…?

Could a marriage survive on sex alone? Was attraction enough to carry them through whatever lay ahead? Oh, *she* had love—but was it enough for both of them?

Such was her pain that for a moment she thought the piercing cry that filled her ears had come from her own lips. It took a moment to register it was Lily.

Quietly she slipped from Rico's embrace. Wrapping her bath towel around her, she crept down the passage, arriving at the nursery door just as Jessica did.

'I'm sorry she woke you, Mrs Mancini. I was just warming a bottle. I'll take care of her now.'

'I'll do it, Jessica. I don't mind getting up to her at night.'

'Oh!' Jessica gave her a slightly startled look. 'Janey always…' Her voice trailed off and Catherine did nothing to resurrect the conversation, the words hanging in the air as she opened the nursery door and padded in. She was curiously nervous about what exactly it was she was supposed do, and smiled awkwardly at Lily, who had her arms outstretched, tears streaming down her angry red cheeks as she sobbed in anguish.

'Hush,' Catherine begged, picking her up and trying to cuddle her. But despite her best efforts she simply refused to take the bottle, refused to be comforted. It was almost a relief when a hesitant Jessica reappeared at the door.

'I think she wants you,' Catherine admitted, curiously defeated by Lily's rejection, tears glittering dangerously in her eyes as Jessica came over.

'It isn't me Lily wants; she just likes to be changed first.' Registering Catherine's frown, Jessica gestured to the change table. 'She likes her nappy changed before she has her bottle, then she settles right down.'

'Of course.' Catherine's movements were wooden her gestures awkward as she laid Lily down on the changing table, and even though she wanted Jessica to go, even though she wanted her fumbling to be unwitnessed, Catherine was silently terrified of being left alone with Lily; the full weight of the responsibility that she had fought for, starting to descend on her tense shoulders. 'All these poppers.' She let out a nervous laugh, pulling the legs of Lily's baby suit closed over the clumsily applied nappy.

'You'll soon get used to them,' Jessica said kindly. 'I'll leave you to it, then.'

It took a moment to register she hadn't gone. Only when Catherine looked up did she realise Jessica still stood there.

'Mrs Mancini?' Her voice was hesitant, and under any other circumstances Catherine would have moved to reassure her. But, knowing what was coming, she simply couldn't do it. 'About that night—about the row we had with Janey…'

Deliberately Catherine didn't turn her head; deliberately she concentrated on the poppers.

'I feel so guilty.'

'You have nothing to feel guilty about.' Catherine's voice was high, her gestures subtly dismissive as still she focused on the blessed poppers. 'Neither of us have anything to feel guilty about, come to that. Janey and Marco were out of line, and something had to be said.'

'But if I hadn't walked out on them that morning...'

'This isn't your fault.' Finally she met her employee's eyes. 'And going over it doesn't change a thing. It's Lily who is important now.'

'I know,' Jessica mumbled. 'Except...'

Oh, God, she didn't need this now—didn't want to be standing here at two a.m., lifting the lid on Pandora's Box. But she wasn't quite ready to close it either.

'Except what?'

'Janey begged me to stay.' Tears were streaming down Jessica's cheeks unstopped, and Catherine felt like joining her. But she knew she had to be strong if ever she were to survive. 'Janey swore she was going to change, that they both were. She said...'

'That thing's would be different?' Catherine shook her head ruefully. 'That it really was the last time? Well, let me tell you, Jessica, I've lost count of how many times Janey said the same to me—lost count of the times she swore things were about to change. The last thing either of us deserves is another dose of guilt. Janey made her own choices, and unfortunately we're the ones living with them. You have *nothing* to feel guilty about.'

She watched as Jessica nodded, saw her dejected shoulders as she turned to leave the nursery, and knew she had said nothing to comfort her.

'Jessica?' Catherine called her back. 'This wasn't your fault and it wasn't mine. I don't want to hear another word about what was said that night, or what happened the morning after. We did nothing wrong.'

If only she could believe it.

Blinking back tears as the door closed on Jessica, Catherine settled back in the rocking chair she and Rico had hastily chosen, along with the rest of the nursery furniture. It felt like a film set—everything new, everything staged for tonight's main show—and at that moment Catherine felt like the worst actress in the world.

Lily let out a low whimper which Catherine quickly countered, pulling the baby in closer. But she could barely feign affection as she held the hot body of her niece close, the soft downy hair tickling her neck as she cuddled her.

A poor substitute for a mother.

CHAPTER EIGHT

SEEING her empty pillow, Rico's first reaction was to panic, but he forced himself to lie there for a moment, ears straining to hear her voice, waiting for the bathroom door to open, for Catherine to come back to him. Running a hand along the bed confirmed what he knew. The uneasy sleep, the vague discomfort he had awoken with, were all explained as he felt the cool sheets.

He had been sleeping alone.

Deliberately he moved slowly, taking his time to shower, to dress, resisting the urge to find her, to demand to know where she was hiding.

Opening the nursery door, he stepped inside, staring for a moment at the two new ladies in his life. Lily was comfortable and contented, sleeping the innocent sleep of babies, with nothing more on her mind than where her next feed would come from. For a second his stern features melted, but it wasn't Lily's beauty that held his gaze, instead it was Catherine.

Rico frowned in concern. Her face was so pale, her posture awkward in the hard chair, and though his stomach still churned from their row last night, though his mind was still buzzing from her spiteful words, in the grey morning shadows the woman who had taunted him last night seemed but a distant memory. She was almost as childlike as Lily in her innocence—dark hair tumbling around her shoulders, the bulky rings on her finger looking out of place on such slender hands.

Moving quietly, he picked up the slumbering Lily, placing her gently in the crib and covering her before turning his attention back to his reluctant wife. Her eyes flicked open, and he watched as she accustomed herself once again to her new surroundings.

'So this is where you have been hiding.'

'Lily woke—' Catherine started, casting her eyes anxiously around the room, and Rico registered her fear and moved to reassure her.

'She's back in her cot.'

Catherine let out a low sigh of relief. 'I thought I'd dropped her.'

'Don't be silly.'

She was massaging her neck, stretching her spine, like an oriental cat awakening. One hand was raised behind her head, causing her gown to open just a fraction, allowing a glimpse of creamy bosom. Rico felt the breath still in his lungs. The child was gone now, the woman was back, and his features quilted. He straightened his back as his resolve returned and with a supreme effort he forced his attention away, focused instead on the sleeping baby.

'Are you going to work?'

It was a silly question really, for he stood in a dark suit, a heavy cotton shirt enhancing his dark complexion, a tie expertly knotted. Everything about him screamed wealth and success. His cufflinks caught the morning rays as he pulled the bunny rug higher around Lily's shoulders. 'I just came to give her a kiss before I leave. I will be home around seven this evening, ask Jessica to save her bath for me.'

Catherine gave a vague nod, staring fixedly at the wall in front of her as Rico tenderly kissed the sleeping babe.

'What will you do with yourself today?' Rico asked, straightening up but still refusing to look at her, and Catherine gave a brief unnoticed shrug, rocking idly in the chair and wishing this uncomfortable meeting was over.

'We might go for a walk, I suppose—do some shopping.'

'Here.' He handed her a wad of cash which Catherine didn't accept.

'When I said shopping, Rico, I meant for an ice cream or something. I'm sure even I can stretch to that.'

'Don't be ridiculous, Catherine. I'll arrange for some cards to be made up in your name, but for now you'll have to use cash.'

Still she refused. 'I've got my own money, Rico.'

'So what was that little lecture about last night?' Rico asked shrewdly, watching as the colour returned to her cheeks. 'I thought you said you were a Mancini now?'

'Mrs Mancini—you haven't been in here all night, I hope?' Jessica gave a worried frown as she bustled in, and heeding Rico's words about trusting the staff Catherine shook her head.

'Of course not. I thought I heard something and I was just checking she was okay. Rico wanted to give her a kiss before he went to work.'

'I'll be off, then.' He moved to go, but changed his mind midway. Turning, he fixed her with a black smile and walked over, ignoring the furious warning signs blazing from Catherine's eyes.

'Goodbye, darling.'

God, he deserved an Oscar.

Jessica, clearly used to being ignored, stood politely as he pulled Catherine into his arms, buried his face in hers and kissed her way too thoroughly. Mindful of her unbrushed teeth, burning with embarrassment at their audience, she stood stiff and unyielding in his arms. But Rico didn't seem to mind a bit. His tongue probed her lips, his hand lazily working its way under her hair, fingers massaging her tense neck. She could feel the cool metal of his watch, smell the fresh crisp scent of him, and as he pulled away Catherine changed her mind—it was she who deserved the Oscar, for it had taken every ounce of will power to keep from kissing him back.

'Bye, then.' That triumphant glint was back in his eye.

He's enjoying this, Catherine thought darkly. *Enjoying my utter humiliation, enjoying watching me squirm. Well, two can play at that game!*

'Sweetheart?' Her voice was pure honey and she saw him frown quizzically as he turned back from the door, clearly bemused at the change in her. 'You said something about leaving me some money...'

She watched his face darken, but her smile stayed fixed and she held out her hand as he handed over the cash, a malicious glint in her eye to mask the tears.

'Hurry home, Rico.'

CHAPTER NINE

IT SHOULD have been perfect.

Day after lonely day she reminded herself of the fact.

A beautiful home, Lily growing more divine by the second, a husband she loved, everything there for the taking.

So why did she feel like a prisoner?

It looked good on paper.

Rico had already given her the answer, Catherine realised. On paper she had everything, but it counted for nothing. Hovering behind the curtains, watching the endless camera lenses still mercilessly trained on the house, she was scarcely able to believe that after two weeks public interest hadn't waned.

But then why would it? Catherine thought with a wry smile. She was as guilty as anyone of devouring the glossies, and the Mancinis certainly made for a good centre spread; the upcoming legal battle, and Antonia, grim and determined, giving endless interviews which Rico read without comment then promptly deposited in the bin.

Naturally, after he'd left for work, Catherine retrieved them.

She was desperate for some insight, frantically trying to join together the jumble of dots that made up Rico. Her heart just melted at the sight of a photo of him, dark and brooding, climbing into his car, his lips set in a grim line, eyes

114

hidden behind dark glasses, the proverbial no comment all he had to say on the matter.

All he had to say full stop.

Since their first night back at the house enemy lines had been drawn, and night after lonely night she chided herself for her part in it. Day after day Catherine berated herself for her handling of things. Time and again she attempted to talk to him, to somehow fashion a path out of the stalemate they'd locked themselves into.

Time and again he pushed her away.

'Lily's grandparents are at the front door.' Jessica's nervous voice broke into her thoughts. 'I didn't know if I should let them in or not.'

Her first instinct was to say no, to let the staff sort it out, even to ring Rico and ask him what she should do. But Catherine reminded herself she was made of sterner stuff than that, and perhaps if she was ever to make an informed opinion she should listen to what they had to say—stop relying on magazines and find out the real story.

'Show them through.'

The sight that confronted her was one she hadn't expected. Bracing herself for the garish, overdressed woman she had seen at the funeral, she was somewhat shocked to see Antonia Mancini dressed in casual trousers and a pale jumper. Her make-up was minimal and her smile seemed genuine.

'Catherine.' She swept across the room in a moment and pulled her into an embrace as Catherine stood awkward and unsure. 'I'm sorry—too tactile for my own good sometimes. I'm just so pleased that you let us in.'

'I don't want to keep Lily from her family.' Catherine

smiled at the baby on the floor as Carlos and Antonia knelt down beside her and tickled her toes. 'Tactile' wasn't the word that sprung to mind after Rico's stern description of Antonia, but the effusive woman playing with Lily now seemed a world away from the person who had greeted her with such distaste at the funeral.

'She's beautiful, isn't she?' Antonia was positively crooning, and she flashed an embarrassed smile as Catherine stood there rigid.

Picking up the infant, Antonia waited patiently as Carlos sat himself down and then held his hands out, and nothing Rico could say would ever convince Catherine that the love that blazed in the elderly man's eyes as he took his granddaughter wasn't genuine.

'I think I've got a competitor for Carlos's affections.' Antonia smiled. 'Can I see the nursery?'

It was an obvious request, Catherine told herself, the sort of thing any doting grandparent would ask, and after only a brief hesitation she nodded. But Lily's grizzles halted the women at the door.

'Here.' Handing Carlos a book of nursery rhymes, she gave an embarrassed smile. 'She's due a bottle, but I've found if I read a few of these to her I can generally hold her off for a little while.'

Carlos took the book and eyed it distastefully before depositing it beside him on the couch.

'We will manage.'

'Of course.' Catherine frowned, taken aback by the abruptness of his gesture when she had only been trying to help.

'Carlos will be fine,' Antonia soothed as they made their way up the stairs. 'No doubt he'll be singing some

Sicilian lullaby to her by the time we go back down. He's been so looking forward to seeing her. Me too,' Antonia added as they walked into the nursery. 'I love babies—girls especially.'

'Did you have any? I mean…' Catherine was flustered. 'Do you have any children of your own?'

Antonia shook her head. 'My first husband and I weren't blessed, unfortunately. When Carlos and I married I thought…' Her voice trailed off for a moment, and there was a wistful gleam in her eye as she looked around the nursery. Her hands lingered a moment on the heavy wooden cot, and she stared at the picture of Janey and Marco Catherine had placed on a small table by the night-light. 'I was naïve, I suppose. I assumed I could step right in and take over, but Bella Mancini was rather a hard act to follow—at least in her children's eyes.'

'It must have been hard for you,' Catherine ventured, her mind working nineteen to the dozen. She didn't want to be taken in, but as she sat down in the rocking chair and listened as Antonia told her tale she found herself slowly warming to the older woman.

'It was,' Antonia agreed. 'Oh, not that I'm complaining. Carlos was marvellous, and once Marco went to…' She gave a helpless shrug and Catherine jumped in.

'Why did you send Marco to boarding school?' It sounded like an accusation, but Catherine deliberately didn't apologise watching Antonia's reaction closely, determined to hear the facts, to make up her own mind.

'Marco was out of control.' Antonia's eyes fixed on hers. 'Bella, their mother, had let them run wild—she was a working mum.' Watching Catherine's shoulders stiffen slightly, Antonia changed tack. 'I'm not against working mums, you understand, but Bella spent her whole time in the office and made up for it with her chequebook. Anything the children wanted they had—except their mother. Rico was an insular young man; there was no reaching him. He was eighteen years old by the time Carlos and I got married. Oh, I tried to get close. But—well, I'm sure I don't have to explain to you how guarded he is...'

She didn't. 'Guarded' certainly was an apt description, and trying to picture Rico as a young man was an almost impossible feat. He seemed born mature.

'As for Marco, he was heading for trouble—twelve years old and with no authority figure. Carlos adored him, but he was never very good at saying no to him. I thought if he went to boarding school, got some sense of worth instilled in him, discipline...'

Antonia was fishing for her hanky now, only this time her tears seemed real. Catherine suddenly felt sorry for her—there really were two sides to every story.

'Maybe I did make a mistake, maybe I should have hung in there a bit longer, but at the time...' She picked up the photo, staring at it for an age before softly replacing it. 'I was hoping to do things better with Lily—show Carlos and Rico that I can be a good mother and maybe somehow make things up to Marco. I know Rico will not be pleased you let us in, but I want to thank you, Catherine—thank you for letting Carlos and I have some time with Lily.'

'You're welcome.' Catherine went to stand, but the room suddenly seemed to be shrinking. Antonia's eyes bored into her as she held firmly onto the cot rail, steadying herself against a sudden overwhelming nausea.

'My dear, are you all right?' Antonia asked, pushing Catherine gently back down in the seat. 'You look ever so pale.'

'I'm fine,' Catherine croaked, and then righted herself.

'I'm fine,' she said again, only this time more forcibly. 'Just a bit tired.'

'You must be exhausted.' Antonia picked up her bag and as Catherine again went to stand she gestured for her to sit. 'I can see myself out, Catherine; you just sit there and rest a while.'

'I'm fine,' Catherine insisted, suddenly feeling foolish.

'You're worn out, my dear.' Antonia patted her shoulder in an almost motherly gesture. 'And undoubtedly you've got a lot on your mind.'

That was the understatement of the millennium.

Left alone, Catherine creased her forehead in concern, her hands fluttering to her stomach. The eternal calculator women reverted to sprang into action as she tried to remember a landmark—she'd been at work—no, shopping—the twenty-second... Her fingers drummed on the side of the rocking chair as she did the maths, trying to ignore the gnawing possibility that seemed to be gaining momentum, trying to push away a truth that couldn't be ignored no matter how she might want to.

How long she sat there she wasn't quite sure. But Jessica had long since taken Lily for a walk, and late-afternoon shadows had long since started creeping in when, chilled to the core, Catherine took herself to her room and lay on the lonely marital bed like a wounded animal, trying to fathom Rico's reaction when she told him.

Trying to fathom her own reaction to the news that was only now starting to hit home.

Her marriage was now for ever.

CHAPTER TEN

'I THOUGHT one actually had to give birth to suffer from postnatal depression!'

Flinging open the curtains, Rico looked down at her, and Catherine stared back, unblinking, watching his cat-like elegance as he started to prowl the room. He threw open the wardrobe and pulled out one of the many expensive dresses that had miraculously appeared. 'Or don't tell me—you're tired again!'

He had a point. Much as it galled her to admit it, Rico had every right to be scathing. Since Antonia's visit most of her days had been spent in the bedroom, trying and failing to work out some sort of plan, trying and failing to summon up the courage to tell Rico what was really on her mind.

But it wasn't just Rico's reaction troubling Catherine, it was her own take on things that terrified her the most. How could she even begin to contemplate having another baby when she'd barely adjusted to having Lily? How could a heart that already seemed stretched to capacity falling in love with one, fall in love with two?

'I'm bored, Rico.' Sitting up on the crumpled bed, Catherine refused to look him in the eye, woefully aware of her rather shabby appearance compared to his—the unkempt hair, the dark bags under her eyes, the shiny unmade-up face.

120

'Well, why aren't you at the park with Lily?' Rico protested. 'It's a beautiful day.'

'It's been a beautiful day since eight a.m.,' Catherine said with an edge to her voice. 'And I've been to the park—twice. I've been for a coffee at the bakery you told me about, and I've even been to children's storytime at the library—much to Jessica's horror. We're both falling over ourselves to find something to do.' When he didn't respond Catherine pushed harder. 'I want to go back to work, Rico.'

'You are *not* working.'

'I'm going out of my mind.' Catherine attempted to run a hand through her hair, but to her eternal shame—and Rico's rather obvious contempt—a knot midway prevented her.

'You could try going to the hairdresser's,' Rico responded nastily. 'Try making a bit more of an effort with yourself.'

His words stung. Catherine was painfully aware she had let herself go over the past couple of weeks, but with Rico leaving at the crack of dawn, only to reappear late evening, it was hard to summon up the enthusiasm to look gorgeous. Invariably he'd arrive home and roll up his sleeves, lavish attention on a receptive Lily, then disappear into his study. She could be dressed in a sack for all the attention he gave her, and now he had the audacity to stroll in unannounced at five p.m. and demand a sleek sophisticate purring on the couch and eagerly anticipating her master's return.

Well, she damn well wasn't going to jump.

'I'm not cut out for this, Rico.' She kept her voice even, tried to keep the note of urgency away. 'I've always worked, the same as you, and I enjoyed my career. Imagine if you suddenly had to give it up. Imagine if you were left alone in this house all day.'

'You're not alone, though,' Rico pointed out. 'You've got Lily.'

'I know that.' Catherine whistled through gritted teeth. 'But I truly think I'd be a better mother if I could work—even part-time.'

'Because we really need the money?'

His sarcasm wasn't helping.

'Because I really need something else.'

'No, Catherine.' He shook his head fiercely. 'This is a pathetic attempt to show me you're not after me for my money—a half-hearted attempt to show me you actually liked your life.'

'I did like my life.' She was shouting now, as she confronted this impossible man. 'I liked it a damn sight more than I like it now. I'm tired of being waited on, tired of staff hovering and attending to my every whim, tired of rattling around a massive house all day with nothing to do. I want to work, Rico, I want to cook my own meals now and then or ring for a pizza if I feel like it...' she shook her head in sheer frustration at his non-comprehending expression, desperate for him to understand. 'Rico, I just want to get used to my new family in my own way, to try and feel like a normal wife and mother.' For a tiny slice of time she seemed to reach him, registered something in his eyes that bordered on understanding, and she stood trembling for a moment, willing herself to continue, to bring things out into the open. 'I know what's worrying you, Rico. I know what you're scared of and I promise you that if I did go back to work then I wouldn't be like your mother.'

For an age there was silence. Catherine scarcely recognised the dark stranger staring back at her. 'That goes without saying.' His voice was a snarl. 'Because at least my mother knew how to treat her husband. My mother managed to make an effort. But tell me, where does my mother come into this, Catherine? What crap have you been listening to now?'

'There's no need to swear.'

'Oh, there's every need,' Rico snarled. 'You bury your head in magazines, you insist on having Antonia over, despite my express orders…'

She jumped back slightly, eyes widening as she realised Rico knew.

'You think I don't know that Antonia has been here? You think I don't know that you have let her in this house?'

'She's Lily's grandmother.'

'She's my father's *putana*. Nothing more, nothing less.'

His anger was palpable, a simmering rage that might explode at any moment, but Catherine was past caring. She had to get through to him—couldn't carry on this sham of a marriage. And even though Rico had crossed that line, the boundary that normally kept their rows decent, and opened the borders to a place Catherine wasn't sure she was ready to explore, she knew now was the time—knew there had to be changes if ever they were to move ahead.

'I want to go back to work, Rico.' Catherine's voice was firm. 'I'd still be here for you and Lily.'

'You're not here for me, though, are you?' His words

were like pistol-shots. 'You haven't been a wife to me since that ring was put on your finger. And you're certainly not here for Lily. You're lying up here, mooching around and feeling sorry for yourself. I've tried—my God, I've tried—to give you space. I've tried to understand you're grieving for your sister, and the wrench all this has been, but you don't make things easy.'

'Antonia said that your mother—'

'Don't mention her name in the same breath as my mother,' Rico roared. 'I can just imagine what Antonia said—just imagine the lies she's been feeding you when you've let her in. You'd rather believe her than your husband? You are my wife, Catherine, and you're going to start acting like one. You will go and have a shower, do your hair, and tonight we will go out.'

'No.' Her response was instant. Going out was the last thing she wanted to do tonight. 'Please, Rico, I really don't feel well.'

Instantly his expression changed, his anger evaporating, his face a picture of concern. 'What is wrong?'

'I just…' She hesitated a fraction too long, and Rico's grip tightened around her wrist as she tried to walk away.

'Just what, Catherine? Come on—you will tell me. If you are sick I will call a doctor.'

She almost laughed—almost, but not quite. A doctor was the last thing she wanted or needed right now. A simple kit from the chemist would be more appropriate. Oh, God… A bubble of panic welled inside her as she imagined his face if she told him the truth.

Imagined his features hardening as she confirmed what he had suspected all along—that she had set out to trap him.

'I don't need a doctor.' Shrugging his hands away, she headed for the bathroom.

'But if you are ill...'

'I'm not *ill*, Rico. I just...'

'Your period?' It seemed strange for someone so overtly chauvinist to say the word so easily; she had expected a rather more vague attempt—but then Rico was making great strides in being a New Age guy at the moment, rolling up his sleeves each evening and bathing Lily with an enthusiasm Catherine wished she could muster.

Turning, she gave a wan smile. 'It's due; that's why I was having a lie-down, I just didn't feel so good.'

'I'm sorry.' There was an expression she couldn't read in his eyes, a certain woodenness in his movements as he gave a small smile. 'I should have been more considerate, I guess...'

'It's no big deal.' Catherine's smile was equally false. 'I'm probably being a bit precious.'

'Catherine, if there is something you need to tell me...'

'There isn't.' Tears were brimming now and she blinked them back, but not quickly enough for Rico's shrewd glare.

'When you say it's due, what exactly do you mean?'

'That it's due.'

'When?'

She swallowed hard, scared to tell him but too terrified to keep it in. 'A few days ago.' In an effort to stop her tears Catherine's nose started to run, and a rather ungracious sniff was the only follow-up to her words. She couldn't bear to look at him—couldn't stand to see the knowing look in his eyes, the confirmation, if ever he'd needed it, that she had trapped him.

'So you could be pregnant?'

'I don't know.' Deliberately she kept her voice light. 'I'm a few days late, and given all that's happened—'

'You must see a doctor.'

Catherine shook her head. 'It's too soon—too early...'

'No!' Still she couldn't read his mood. His face was pale, but his gestures were decisive. Picking up the dress he had earlier discarded, he handed it to her. 'I will telephone the surgery now and have the staff bring the car around. We need to know, Catherine.'

He didn't wait for her response, assuming as he always did that Catherine would oblige, and left her standing as he marched out of the room. But Rico was right, Catherine admitted as she showered and quickly dressed. They did need to know. They needed to know where they stood—needed to work things out once and for all.

It was their first outing together since the funeral, and the mood in the car was just as lively. Time and again she opened her mouth to speak, to ask Rico about his take on this, but nerves overtook and she shrank back in her seat, staring instead at the parched gardens and trying to fathom her own feelings on the situation.

A baby was the last thing they needed. She knew that—knew their relationship, if you could call it that, was tenuous to say the least. And yet...

Glancing sideways, she took in his profile, her breath catching as it always did at the mere sight of him. It was so easy to remember being held by him, so easy to remember how he had adored her, the delicious place he had taken her to with his skilful lovemaking. That night was etched in her mind indelibly, but it took on more meaning now, and she dragged her eyes away from Rico, staring down at her stomach and trying to imagine a life within, her stomach swelling, ripe with Rico's child. As mistimed as it was, as calculating as he might deem it, inexplicably it excited her.

'We're here.'

Waiting for the driver to open the door, she could scarcely catch her breath, and her legs were like jelly as she stepped out of the car. Clutching Rico's hand, she walked into a large house, and it was nothing like any doctor's surgery Catherine had ever seen. But this was Rico's world, she reminded herself. No crowded waiting rooms for him. No thumbing through ten-year-old magazines or catching a cold from your fellow patients. Instead they were whisked through to an office, where they sat in massive leather seats behind a huge mahogany desk and a doctor introduced himself—a doctor who was as assured and confident as Rico, and, Catherine noted with relief, who didn't appear to be intimidated by him.

'Rico, it is good to see you!' Malcolm Sellers shook hands, smiling at Catherine as he did so. 'And this must be your lovely new wife.' He sat down. 'I was actually about to call you, Rico. Have the police been in touch with you, Catherine?'

Frowning, she shook her head. 'I haven't been home since the funeral—but why would they…?'

'Why have you been calling, Malcolm?' Rico's question was direct, and Catherine was grateful for it.

'The autopsy results are in.' He let the news sink in for a moment before carrying on. 'Naturally I don't have Janey's results, but with your permission, Catherine, I can ring and have them sent over, if you would like to go through them both together?'

'That is not what we're here for.' Rico's accent sounded more pronounced and, turning, Catherine saw his hands gripping the sides of the chair, his knuckles white under the strain. 'We are here for another matter entirely.'

'Even so,' Sellers pushed, 'it might be better for you both to go through the findings with me. There's going to be an inquest, and knowing the results prior to that might make things just a touch easier when hearing the whole thing played out in court.'

'We are not here to discuss our siblings, Malcolm. When we choose to do so will make an appointment.'

'If that's the way you want it.' Malcolm Sellers sounded resigned, and Catherine guessed he was all too used to Rico's stubbornness. 'But if you do have any questions then you know I'm always here. Now—' he forced a smile '—who's the patient?'

'Catherine,' Rico answered even as she opened her mouth to do so. 'We would like to arrange some tests.'

'What sort of tests?' Dr Sellers's eyes were on her, but again it was Rico who answered.

'A pregnancy test.'

'Rico.' Catherine smiled at Dr Sellers politely before turning to him. 'I can speak for myself.'

She couldn't be certain, but she was almost sure a dusting of colour crept up Rico's cheeks, and he snapped his mouth closed, reverting to the surly pre-adolescent manner he assumed when he didn't get his way.

'My period is late, Doctor.'

'And you're usually regular?'

It was Catherine flushing now, the boldness of before leaving her as she attempted to discuss her monthly cycle with this difficult audience. 'Well, I wouldn't set my watch by it,' she said quietly, scuffing at the floor with her foot. 'But I am definitely a few days late. Though I know it's probably too soon to tell.'

'Not these days.' Dr Sellers's voice was kind. 'Though I should warn you there can be a down side to finding out too soon.'

'Such as?' Rico asked, and Dr Sellers shot him a rather irritated look.

'Rico, I'm going to need to examine Catherine. Perhaps you could wait outside?'

Rico's eyes darted to Catherine's and he blinked a couple of times when she nodded.

'It might be better.'

Rico clearly wasn't used to being asked to leave, and Catherine half expected him to protest, but surprisingly he agreed, shrugging his shoulders in a curiously nonchalant gesture before strutting outside.

'Someone's getting a bit over-excited.' Dr Sellers smiled as the door closed none too gently behind him.

Catherine didn't respond. 'Furious' would be a more apt description. 'Trapped' might be another. Dragging her mind away from Rico, she concentrated on the issue in hand.

'You said there was a down side to finding out too soon. What is that?'

'A very long nine months, for one thing,' Dr Sellers said dryly, but then his expression turned more serious. 'This is a very fragile time in a pregnancy, Catherine. Sometimes I suggest that my patients come back in a week or two if nothing has happened.'

'I understand what you're saying, Doctor,' Catherine

answered, equally serious. 'But I don't really need the test to tell me I'm pregnant.'

She didn't. From the moment their stars had collided Catherine had felt different. From the second Rico had cruelly suggested the possibility it was as if she had known the outcome—had almost envisaged the moment in her mind. 'This is really just a formality.'

'So the test is for Rico's benefit?'

Catherine didn't answer. Instead she handed over her specimen bottle as Dr Sellers opened his drawer.

'I can't imagine he'd be one to settle for feminine intuition. Even as a teenager he questioned me on everything.'

'Rico?' Catherine was smiling now, enjoying the small talk, grateful not to have to listen to the ticking clock as her fate was decided. 'I can't imagine him as a sickly child.'

'He's never had a sick day in his life; it's taken all my powers of persuasion just to get him to have his cholesterol checked. Disgustingly normal, of course.' He gave a smile, glancing at his watch, then back to the tiny strip of blotting paper before him. 'No, I'm talking about when his mother died. Rico grilled me for hours, sure there must have been something I could have done, should have foreseen.'

'How did she die?'

For a second she thought he wasn't going to answer, but after a brief pause he gave a tight nod. 'She had a stroke. I'm not breaking any confidences by telling you—it was all over the papers, much like now. Rico wanted answers, and unfortunately there weren't many I could give him. No one could have foreseen it. It was especially hard for Rico. Carlos's English wasn't very good, and Marco was so much younger. It was Rico who had to deal with the press, the paperwork—Rico who dealt with it all, really.'

Tears were pricking her eyes now. This was another side of Rico she had never envisaged—a young man trying to do the right thing, terrified, but having to be strong.

'It's a shame he's not being so pedantic where his brother is concerned.' Doctor Sellers's voice forced Catherine's attention, and he caught her eyes and held them. 'I really think Rico should come and see me regarding Marco's results. As I said, Bella's death couldn't have been foreseen, but...' His voice trailed off and it was Catherine who filled in the gap, the hairs on the back of her neck suddenly standing to attention. There had been something in Dr Sellers's voice that unnerved her.

'What did the autopsy show?'

'Catherine, I'm sorry. I cannot discuss this any further with you. Marco was my patient; Rico is his family...'

She nodded her understanding. 'Do you know anything about Janey?'

Malcolm shook his head. 'I can ring through to your doctor, though—explain that you're seeing me now?'

Catherine thought for a moment. She liked Dr Sellers, liked his directness, the way he handled Rico, but despite her curiosity she actually understood where Rico was coming from. She needed some time to prepare herself, to brace herself before she heard about Janey's injuries.

Today simply wasn't the day.

'Can I have some time to think about it?'

'Take all the time you need.' Dr Sellers was pushing the test strip towards her now, watching her expression

132 THE SICILIAN'S BOUGHT BRIDE

with knowing eyes. 'I'd suggest this is enough to be going on with for now. Are congratulations in order?'

She couldn't answer, her throat constricting, her stomach clenching as she eyed the test.

'Catherine, I do read the papers. I know a little of what you've been through, and if this result isn't what you were hoping for...' He gave a small cough. 'You are my patient, Catherine. Nothing that is said in this room goes further. You have been under a lot of stress, and as you know stress manifests itself in many ways. If you choose, then that can be what we tell Rico.'

'Thank you.' Her voice was a tiny whisper. 'And you're right. I'm not sure if this is the result I wanted.' She gave a small laugh, but it changed midway and came out as a sob. 'But deep down I knew it was the one I was going to get. I'll be all right, Doctor. There's no question of ending the pregnancy.' She went to stand, but Dr Sellers gestured for her to sit.

'In that case, I haven't finished with you yet. In fact, I've barely even started.'

CHAPTER ELEVEN

RICO was practically climbing the walls by the time she emerged, a good twenty minutes later, glassy-eyed, a touch pink around the cheeks, but relatively composed.

'What the hell took so long?'

'He wanted to examine me, take some blood—that type of thing.'

'You went for a pregnancy test, not a roadworthy test. Bloody doctors. Why can't they just do what you ask?'

'He did do as I asked.' She tried to summon more words, tried to carry on the conversation, but she simply couldn't do it.

'Well?'

'If you snap your fingers, Rico,' Catherine warned him, 'I swear I'll…' Her eyes lifted to his, the answer blazing there for all to see, and she saw his mouth open as he registered her hesitant face. She braced herself for some scathing response, waited for his scorn, but it never came.

'You're definitely pregnant?'

'I'm sorry if this isn't the news you wanted, Rico. Sorry—'

'Never, ever be sorry,' Rico broke in. 'Catherine, this is wonderful…'

'Is it?' She stared up at him, utterly bemused at his reaction. 'It's too much, Rico, too soon. You think you're happy now, but one day you'll throw it back at me, say that I—'

'Forget the past, Catherine,' he demanded, and how she wanted to—how she wanted to put it all behind her. But it simply wasn't that easy. Too much had been said for instant resolution. 'Whatever your motives, whatever the reason…'

'My motives?' An incredulous laugh shot out of her lips. 'Two minutes into this pregnancy, Rico, and you already throw it back at me…'

'What I'm trying to say…' He was silenced as a nurse walked past, and he shook his head proudly. 'This is not the place.'

He took her to a restaurant, one of those tiny dark buildings people wandered past unwittingly, a hidden gem in the middle of the city, and once inside led her to an alcove, waiting till she was seated before speaking.

'What I was trying to say—' Rico resumed the conversation as if they had only just left it '—is that this is not a conventional marriage.' His words were without malice, and Catherine nodded, glad they could acknowledge that truth at last, glad they were finally talking. 'Whatever has gone on in the past, surely now is the time to put it aside, to start afresh? We are having a baby, Catherine. Something good, something positive has come from our loss—why can't we just move forward?'

'Without even glancing back at the past?' Catherine questioned. 'I'm not like you, Rico. I can't just move ahead without a backward glance. You won't discuss your past; you won't even discuss what happened to Marco with the doctor…'

'Cannot today be just about us?' he asked. 'I know this marriage is for Lily, but surely…' He picked up her left hand, played with the heavy gold band for a moment before continuing. 'Can we make a fresh start, Catherine? Start this marriage over again?'

'For the baby's sake?'

Rico shook his head. 'For all our sakes. Catherine, I want you to be happy. I want us all to be happy. With commitment on both sides surely we can make it work? We have to make it work,' he finished, more urgently.

'I know we do, Rico,' Catherine agreed. 'Which is why I want to go back to work.' She watched his shoulders stiffen, but chose to ignore it. 'I'm struggling, Rico. Struggling to find my place in a world that's so unfamiliar. I need something more, need my friends around me now more than ever—and, yes, I admit that maybe I do somehow want to prove that I'm not totally dependent on you, but it isn't just about that. My work is important to me,' Catherine insisted softly.

'My mother hated working.' His admission startled her—not his words so much, but the fact he was for the first time volunteering information, and about his mother, no less. 'No one knew that. Even my father assumed she adored it, and I guess for a while she did. She started the family business,' Rico added proudly. 'One of only a handful of women who made it in the property business, at least in those days. She barely spoke English when she first came here.'

'She must have been very clever.'

'She had an amazing eye.' Rico shrugged. 'I have inherited it. I see an old property and it is as if I know how it should be. I don't have to consult books. It is as if my mind's eye can see it in its former glory. When we first arrived in Australia my parents scraped together enough money to buy an old townhouse in Carlton. My father was a labourer and under my mother's guidance they re-built it, and then they sold it. That was just the start. Soon my mother was hiring people, buying pockets of land for next to nothing. They are now worth millions. I think my first words were ''bayside views''. He gave a low laugh. 'That is a lie. I spoke only Italian till I was five.'

Catherine found herself smiling. 'What about Marco?'

'He was born here.' Rico shrugged. 'He was always an Aussie. I spoke to him in English, so by the time he went to school he could speak both.'

'So things were easier for him?'

Rico shook his head. 'I love my first language, Catherine; hell at school was a small price to pay. I can still remember being picked up from kindergarten and driving along the beach road looking for properties. They were good times.'

'She took you with her?' He heard the question in her voice.

'Antonia no doubt tells a different story,' he responded, ignoring her furious blush. 'But, yes, she took me with her—and later, when the business was bigger, when I was at school and my mother was working the same ridiculous hours I do now, she still came home every night; she still kissed us goodbye each morning.'

'So what went wrong?' Catherine pushed gently, seeing the wistful look in his eyes, and slamming her fingers between the shutters she just knew were about to come down.

'One day it became a job—not a labour of love, not a passion. Just a job. She had obligations—houses, cars, boats—and as you can imagine Antonia didn't come cheap.'

'Antonia?'

'My father was having an affair. He had barely worked a day in his life. It was my mother who provided for us and he got bored. That was my father's excuse anyway. The night before my mother died she had a headache. She was more tired than I've ever seen a person, and yet she still had to make calls, had to go and check out a property. I found her crying in the study. That was when I discovered she knew about my father's affair. She said she was tired, that she just wanted to lie down and sleep, that after the Christmas break she would sort things out... She died the next day. A stroke, the doctors said. It could have happened at any time. But I know different. If she hadn't been working—hadn't been pushing herself—'

'You don't know that, Rico,' Catherine broke in, but she knew her words fell on deaf ears—knew there was no room for manoeuvre. But just when she thought it was over, just when she thought the conversation was closed, again Rico surprised her.

'Part-time, Catherine. You can work part-time if that's what you want.' His eyes implored her to listen. 'And the day it gets too much—the day you feel you shouldn't be there...'

'I'll stop.'

'You have nothing to prove to me, Catherine, but if this is something you feel you have to do...'

'It is.'

And now that he had given a little—now that he had allowed her to glimpse a tiny piece of him—perhaps for the first time since the police had arrived at her door Catherine allowed herself to relax, allowed herself to just sit back and take in the world around her.

Rico was amazingly good company. When he wasn't being superior, when he actually let up, he had a wicked sense of humour, and as the dessert plates were cleared away Catherine was amazed to hear that the laughter filling the tiny restaurant was coming from her.

'You should laugh more often,' Rico said, taking her hand. 'It suits you.'

'It feels good,' Catherine admitted.

'I want you to be happy, Catherine; I want us to be happy. You, me and Lily.'

'I want that too.'

On Rico's instructions the driver had long since gone, and they walked hand in hand along the Yarra River, following its majestic curves. The warm, still night air was filled with hope, and for a while they blended in—and Catherine had never been more happy to do so, never been more happy to seem two young lovers on the threshold of their future.

'Thank you.' She turned her gaze to his. 'For understanding.'

'Marriage is supposed to be about give and take,' Rico said lightly, but there was an edge to his voice. 'Hopefully I do a better job than my father.'

'Don't be too hard on him, Rico.' In the moonlight they stood, her eyes searching his, imploring him to listen. 'It must have been hard on him too. He was an immigrant, a labourer; I bet he was a proud, hard-working man.'

'He was,' Rico admitted, albeit reluctantly. 'Mind you, once my mother started making money he was only too happy to give up and reap the benefits of *her* hard work.'

'Are you sure he was happy?' There was a long silence, and Rico made to walk away, but Catherine pulled on his

sleeve and after a slight hesitation he turned back, ready
to listen to what she had to say. 'Normally it's the other
way around—isn't it, Rico? Especially in Sicilian families. Normally the husband is the breadwinner; look at
how opposed you are to me working.' He opened his
mouth to argue, but Catherine was too quick for him. 'The
man is supposed to be the provider while the wife stays
at home?'

'Then why didn't he work? Why didn't he join her in
the business, take over the books, do something to ease
her load?' Rico countered, and Catherine hesitated before
answering. Her answer was not one she was sure Rico
was ready to hear.

'Your father can't read, Rico.'

'Don't be ridiculous.' Rico's laugh was derisive, the
superior scathing man back now, but Catherine refused to
be intimidated.

'I'm sure of it, Rico.'

'He's a clever man...'

'I'm sure he is,' Catherine responded. 'And a proud one
too. Can you imagine how hard it must be for him, Rico?
How hard not to be able to read his bills, the snappy little
letters you send him? The small world he must live in
when he can't even look at a newspaper?'

'You're sure?'

'I'm sure.' Catherine nodded. 'Please, Rico, try not to
view him so harshly, try and understand your father's side
too.' He gave a small nod which, however tentative,
Catherine took as a sign of encouragement. 'Maybe it
wasn't so easy for your dad to sit back and do nothing.
However much I don't condone it, maybe in some way
having an affair made him feel a man again. Who knows

what goes on in people's lives, Rico? Only your mother and father know the full story.'

'And Antonia,' Rico added bitterly.

'Antonia knows your father's version,' Catherine said thoughtfully. 'And, however much you might loathe her, your father clearly loves her. Surely that must count for something?'

He didn't respond—Catherine had never really expected him to—but this time when he walked away he reached for her hand and took her with him, walking in pensive silence along the river. And despite the lack of conversation, despite the endless problems that lay between them, never had Catherine felt closer to him.

CHAPTER TWELVE

'YOU'LL be okay?'

Standing in the hallway, almost bristling with excitement at the day ahead, Catherine picked up her briefcase.

'I'll be fine.' She laughed. 'Yesterday was wonderful.'

'You were tired last night,' Rico pointed out. You fell asleep on the sofa after dinner.'

'It was my first day back,' Catherine answered, buttoning up her jacket and checking her reflection in the mirror.

She could scarcely believe the smiling face that stared back. Going back to work had truly been a godsend. With the eternal teacher shortage, her school principal had welcomed her back with open arms—and Catherine had been only too pleased to run. Rico might not understand her need for independence, but even he had reluctantly agreed last night that she seemed happier. Oh, she wasn't stupid, knew that the money she would be earning would be like loose change to Rico, but it was *her* money, the independence she craved. It was a reason to put on her lipstick in the morning, a chance to use her brain, to escape the undoubtedly luxurious but nonetheless stuffy confines of the house. And even though it was early days she felt as if she now had so much more to give. Even though she had been physically tired, Catherine had been imbued with a curious high when she arrived home last night. She had played with Lily with the same gusto Rico managed to muster on his return, even woken to give her

141

·her two a.m. feed. Going back to work was surely the right thing, and she moved quickly now to reassure Rico, terrified of having her new-found freedom taken away, determined to prove she could do it all. 'I've only got today to do, then I'm finished till next week; I'm hardly slaving away.'

'You realise you're in the newspaper?' He pulled the paper out of his briefcase and handed it to her, but Catherine shook her head.

'I don't need to see it, Rico. I know the journalists followed me to school yesterday, but they'll soon get bored; they'll soon find another family to hound.'

'It doesn't look good,' Rico insisted, but Catherine merely laughed.

'So the company shares are sliding because a Mancini woman is actually going out to work? We're in frantic financial trouble and relying on my part-time teacher's wage to support us? Come on, Rico, they're clutching at straws to make a story out of it—and anyway, it was your mother, a *mere* woman, who founded the company. Remind them of that when you blast them this morning.'

'You really don't give a damn what people think, do you?'

'Do you?' Catherine asked.

'Normally, no. But I am worried about what the social worker is going to say.'

'The social worker happens to be called Lucy,' Catherine said with a slightly weary edge. 'Lucy has two children herself, and if you'd bothered to find out you'd also know that her husband happens to be one of the leading consultants at the hospital. So she more than anyone understands that women need to work for so much more than money these days, Rico.'

'I never realised you were such a feminist!'

'Get used to it.' Catherine grinned. 'And if this so-called newspaper's article moves the sisterhood on an inch then I'll be a happy woman indeed.'

'Happy's good,' Rico said softly, and Catherine felt her smile fade, replaced instead with a nervous lick of her lips as their eyes locked. Tension seeped in, but not the head-on, angry confrontation that had become so much a part of them—this time it was a thrum of togetherness, a sexual awareness that had never really gone away, just faded a touch from neglect. And when Rico moved a step forward she shivered with excitement as he moved closer.

'Are you both off, then?' They both jumped as Jessica came out to the hallway, holding a bleary-eyed Lily, her hair all sticking up. Catherine felt her heart trip. The eyes staring back at her melted her for a second so fleeting, so fragile, Catherine was almost scared to acknowledge it—almost scared to comprehend that the maternal instinct the social worker had promised would ensue might actually be stirring.

Last night she had come home, tired but elated after her first day back at work, and as she had climbed the stone steps of her new home a curious bubble of elation had welled inside her—almost a need to get inside, to see the little girl she hadn't even realised she'd missed.

'I'll be back around five,' Catherine responded. 'Though I can't vouch for Rico.'

'Seven,' he quipped, but his face softened as he made his way over to Lily. 'So save her bath for me, Jessica. And as for you, little lady...' He tickled the baby's chin, and Catherine watched as her face lit up, a smile breaking on her sleepy face. 'Make sure Jessica chooses a good bedtime story for me to read to you—preferably one with no songs!'

'Is that what that awful droning was last night?'

He didn't answer, his face concentrating intently on Lily before he turned to Catherine with an incredulous smile. 'I think she's getting a tooth!'

'Really?' Making her way over, Catherine peered at the gummy mouth. Rico tickled Lily to ensure she laughed enough for a good view. 'She is too.'

Such was the happy atmosphere in the hallway Catherine was almost reluctant to leave it. For a while there they almost looked like a normal family, celebrating one of life's tiny milestones, and most amazingly of all she relished it. But Jessica was a stickler for the clock, and soon pointed out that if they didn't get a move on they'd both be late.

'I'll see you this evening.' Catherine smiled, kissing the plump cheek almost without thinking about it, taking in the soft baby smell and lingering just a second before turning away.

Now came the difficult part.

For the staff's sake, appearances were always kept, and every morning as Rico left for work they always kissed—only on this morning it didn't feel so staged; on this morning it felt like the most natural thing in the world. But though it might feel natural, it didn't lessen her awkwardness. A furious blush darkened her cheeks as she lifted her face to his, and something in the way his hand snaked around her waist, something in the way his lips dusted hers, held hers for just a moment too long, told Catherine this wasn't a kiss for the cameras. This kiss was loaded with the passion that had lingered unchecked for so long, loaded with the tenderness that was starting to tentatively grow between them.

'I'll see you tonight.' His voice was gruff, his pupils dilated as he stared down at her pink cheeks, taking in her glittering eyes, feeling her chest rise and fall against his. His head moved a fraction, so when he spoke his words were for her ears only. His hot breath tickled her ears, making her toes curl just at the sound of it. 'You can save your bath for me too.'

'No songs,' Catherine teased, but her eyes grew serious, the magnitude of tonight starting to take shape in her lust-dazed mind.

'No songs,' Rico said softly. 'But maybe we could put some music on, have dinner up in our room…' Reluctantly he let her go, but took her hand as they left the house, walking towards their cars. Rico's driver nodded and held the door open as Catherine dived into her rather less impressive, infinitely unreliable but much loved car, winding down the window as Rico knocked on it.

'I'm going to be late, Rico!' she warned.

'Will your feminist principles object to me buying you a decent car?'

'Not a bit.' Catherine grinned. 'You see, the wonderful thing about being a woman in the twenty-first century means you really can have it all. But nothing too flash,' she added hastily.

'Mustn't outshine the principal,' Rico said dryly, but his eyes were smiling. 'Here.' Tossing the newspaper through the window, he gave her one final knowing smile. 'You know you're dying to see yourself.'

'I couldn't be less interested,' Catherine lied, but she didn't hand the paper back.

'Suit yourself.' Rico shrugged, turning to go, then halting again. He swung around on a smart heel, a mischievous smile inching across his lips. 'And next time the press are around do up your blouse!'

Determined not to give him the satisfaction of knowing he'd piqued her curiosity, Catherine pointedly started her car and headed out of the long driveway into the peak hour traffic.

She didn't get very far.

Pulling into a side street, she almost tore the newspaper in her haste to get to the said article, scanning the photo with a critical eye and letting out a groan as she saw the rather vast expanse of cleavage, courtesy of a forgotten button. A loud toot had her practically jumping out of her skin, but her annoyed look faded into laughter as Rico's car slid past, with Rico giving a knowing wave as the headlights flashed.

Truly caught, there was nothing for her to do except smile and rather sheepishly wave back.

As she pulled off the handbrake, the smile stayed put.

Oh, it wasn't much—in the scheme of things it barely added up to anything—but sharing a laugh was always good: their history in the making, a tiny step in the right direction…

Her glow didn't last that long. Somewhere mid-afternoon, Catherine's elation at being back at work wore off. Her back ached and so did her head, with the children's raucous laughter growing more grating by the minute. Lily's two a.m. feed, was clearly catching up with her.

Even the thought of a night in Rico's arms barely lifted her gloom as she cleared up the classroom and pulled her bag over her shoulder. All she really wanted to do was get home and soak in a bath alone for an hour and sleep.

'It's good to have you back on board, Catherine.'

Marcus Regan caught her as she dashed out of the staff-room. With his glasses perched on the end of his nose, he was a typical principal in every sense, and though she dearly wanted to get home, Catherine adored her boss and would never dismiss him.

'It's good to be back, Marcus. I'm sorry it's only part-time, I know how short the school is.'

'We are at that.' Marcus scratched his grey hair and Catherine could see the worry lines on his kind face. She hadn't told him about her pregnancy—it was still early days yet—and wasn't looking forward to it, if the truth be known. Staff were scarce on the ground, and the way Marcus's voice had lit up when she'd rung to see if work was still available had spoken volumes. 'Some mornings I wonder if we're actually going to have any staff to run the school. Still, it's good to have you back, Catherine. How's married life treating you?'

'Wonderfully.' Catherine smiled. It was a lie she was so used to telling it came without thought, but remembering the way Rico had held her this morning, she was able to impart it with at least a semblance of honesty.

'Well, I'd better not keep you. We'll see you Monday morning.'

Lily was seriously getting more gorgeous by the day, and her little face lit up as Catherine dashed through the door. She held out her fat little arms for a cuddle, but the gush of tenderness that had filled Catherine on her return yesterday was markedly absent. Catherine literally felt as if she were going through the motions as she played with the little girl. Guilt tore at her heart, and she was eternally grateful when Rico appeared bang on seven to give Lily her customary bath. Catherine perched on the edge of the tub, watching with a quiet smile as the slick sophisticate disappeared before her eyes. She was almost tempted to invite the inevitable photographers outside to come in and witness Rico in tender mode. That superior face was softer now, his expensive silk tie ruined for evermore as it dangled in the soapy water, his five o'clock shadow dotted with bubbles as Lily splashed and squealed in delight, moaning in protest when Catherine finally declared the water was getting cold and Rico should lift her out.

'Now comes the hard part.' Rico held up Lily's sleepsuit, frowning as he wrestled two fat legs and two wriggling arms into the garment.

'Don't ask me to help with the buttons.' Catherine shuddered. 'No matter how hard I try to get it right, Jessica comes in and promptly re-does them.'

'Done,' Rico said proudly, handing her the now sleepy infant as Jessica appeared with a bottle.

'I warmed this for you.'

Taking the bottle, Catherine noticed that Jessica's usually shining scrubbed face was beautifully made up, and the smart shorts and blouse she usually wore had been replaced with a rather slinky little dress.

'You look nice.'

'Thank you.' A blush crept across her young face. 'Mr Mancini gave me the night off.'

'Oh.' Catherine forced a smile. How badly she wanted

to peel off her suit, dive in the shower and have some time to prepare for dinner. This was supposed to be a romantic night—what was the point in having a nanny if Rico was going to give her time off when they really needed to be together?

Left alone with Lily, Catherine held her, fed her, trying so hard to love her—but the familiar panic, heavily tinged with guilt, was gushing back now. She tried to push it away, tried to remember the tenderness she had felt only this morning, tried to recall the social worker's wise words.

Give it time.

But time wasn't on her side. Lily was here and now.

'She's asleep.' Rico crept in, picking up the sleeping babe and placing her tenderly in the cot before turning his attention to Catherine, his smiling fading as he registered her tense features. 'What's wrong?'

'Nothing,' Catherine lied. 'I'd better have a shower before dinner.'

'Dinner is down to us tonight,' Rico said easily. 'I gave the staff the night off.'

'All of them?' Catherine groaned, standing to her feet.

'All of them,' Rico confirmed. 'You said you wanted to be more *normal*, that you were sick of being waited on, wanted to do the normal things a wife and mother does, so I figured I'd give them the night off and it would make you happier. Come on, I'm starving.'

She'd asked for it, really. In fact, Rico probably thought he was being nice, was doing her a favour, but a weary sigh escaped her lips as she headed out of the nursery. Her back was really aching now, and the thought of peeling a load of potatoes just to feel normal frankly did nothing to raise her spirits.

Heading for the staircase, she frowned when Rico took her by the arm and led her to the bedroom.

'I thought you said you were starving?'

'I am,' Rico said mysteriously, opening the door and letting her walk in, watching in amused silence as she took in the rather poorly laid table and massive pizza box.

'Pizza?' A smile played on the edge of her lips.

'Rung for by yours truly.' Pulling a chair out, he sat her down before proceeding to cut her a rather too large slice. 'You said you wanted to be normal, needed some junk food—well, here it is.' After pouring some cola he helped himself to a slice. 'So, like I said, I've given all the staff the night off,' Rico explained further, 'and tonight we do what couples the world over do on a Thursday night when the wife is too tired to cook and the baby is finally asleep!'

It was the perfect solution—the perfect meal, actually—and enough to put a smile on her pinched face.

'I needed that.' Catherine smiled as Rico took the last slice. 'You've no idea how nice it is not to have to use a fork.'

'You certainly spoke more,' Rico commented. 'You still don't feel comfortable around the staff, do you?'

'They're nice and everything...' Catherine shrugged. 'I just find it hard to carry on a normal conversation with everyone hovering around me pretending not to listen.'

'They're not.' Rico grinned. 'I'm sure they've got better things to be thinking about than hanging on to our every word. They're probably bored to tears.'

Put like that, he almost had her convinced—but not

quite. Oh, she was sure the staff didn't find her riveting, but Rico had this magnetism, this aura around him, and Catherine simply couldn't imagine anyone being bored in his company. He filled her day, filled her nights—just the sound of his voice could change her mood, a smile from him could lift her spirits. But that was surely not what Rico wanted to hear right now.

'I really am going to have that shower now.' Standing deliberately, Catherine headed for the *en suite* bathroom, but Rico followed her.

'I just want you to be happy, Catherine.' Turning her to face him, he let his eyes meet and hold hers, and for some inexplicable reason she felt the sting of tears behind her eyelids. She wanted to be happy too—was sure she could be, if only Rico loved her. 'I don't want you to feel like a prisoner.'

'Hardly a prison.' Catherine gestured to the opulent room, but her smile wavered as Rico voiced what was clearly on his mind.

'Am I your jailer?'

She pondered his question. At any time she could walk away—she knew that deep down. And perhaps she could fight for Lily from her own corner—maybe with the right advice she could even win—but it wasn't Lily who kept her here, wasn't the child growing within her, wasn't the desire to give her niece a privileged lifestyle. It was Rico who held her within these walls—Rico her mind always drifted back to whenever it wandered—Rico who held her in the palm of his hand.

'Am I your jailer, Catherine?' he asked again, with an expression she couldn't quite read in his eyes. Only this time when she opened her mouth to speak he didn't wait to hear her answer. His lips came crushing down on hers, drowning out her answer, drowning out her own internal questions as she lost herself in his touch.

So much easier to feel his arms around her, to taste his cool tongue, to respond to his masterful touch to pretend for a while that maybe he did love her, than to deal with the impossible dilemmas that taunted her.

He undressed her in a moment, peeling away the suit easily, unclasping her bra, and she felt the groan of his approval as her breasts fell heavy and warm into his waiting hands. She wrestled with his clothes, and for that moment in time Catherine truly didn't care about the rhymes and reasons that had brought them to this point, didn't care she was his wife in name only. There was just a need, a simple primal need, to make love, to be made love to, to feel his naked skin on hers, to feel his arousal, to touch him as a lover, as a woman in a way she never had before.

She heard his gasp as her hands took the weight of his arousal. She marveled in the velvet steel of his manhood as she ran her fingers its length, closing her eyes in ecstasy as it snaked through her fingers—a jewel she had longed for, a jewel that tonight would finally be hers.

He took her softly at first, with kisses working over her neck as he slipped inside. Mindful of her condition, he kept his weight on his elbows, a delicious friction hovering on the outskirts, but then need took over, a natural desire so strong his soft strokes deepened. Like some heavenly feather, he massaged her most intimate depths, and her shivering climax dragged him in deeper until he exploded within her. Afterwards he held her in the matrimonial bed, as a husband should. His arms slid around her and there was nowhere to hide when his words cut the still dark air, the question that had hung over them repeated now, with infinite tenderness this time.

'Am I your jailer, Catherine?'

She pondered her answer a moment, her voice when it came so low Rico had to bring his face closer to catch her response.

'I'm here because I want to be, Rico—though I admit sometimes I wonder what it is I'm fighting for.'

'You are fighting for your family, Catherine,' Rico said softly. 'How we got here is irrelevant. We have to make the best of things.'

He probably thought he was helping, probably thought he was saying the right thing—but staring into the darkness, wrapped in arms she never wanted to leave, Catherine tried to blot out the awful inference behind his words, keep it all together just a little longer. Only when his breathing evened and she was sure he was asleep, did she give in—allowing salty tears that belonged to the night to slip into her hair as she awaited the refreshing sensibility of dawn.

CHAPTER THIRTEEN

'YOU have a phone call.'

Sitting up in bed, Catherine rubbed her eyes and desperately tried to come to. Surveying the room, the open pizza box, the clothes strewn everywhere, she knew it looked as if some sort of wild teenage party had taken place, and with her thumping head and Rico standing over her like some over-possessive parent as she took the call, the analogy only deepened.

'That was Marcus Regan—the principal,' Catherine explained, replacing the receiver and not quite meeting his eyes. Rico still stood there.

'I gathered that,' he quipped, clearly not impressed by the early-morning call. 'And I also gather you have agreed to go in to work this morning, despite the fact you swore this would be a part-time job.'

'It will still only be three days this week, Rico,' Catherine pointed out, pulling back the sheets and trying to feign a spring in her step as she crossed the bedroom, determined Rico wouldn't get a glimpse of just how awful she really felt. Marcus's phone call had caught her completely unawares, and had she had time to think, to register she wasn't feeling the best, she'd probably have refused his plea to come in and cover for a sick staff member. Right now all she wanted to do was crawl back into bed, pull the rumpled sheet back over her head and recall Rico's blissful lovemaking.

Or sleep; either would do.

'You look exhausted; you should be taking things easy…'

Catherine didn't answer, the toothbrush in her mouth not the best precursor to eloquence, but she let Rico rant for a moment or two before rinsing her mouth and smiling at his reflection, scarcely able to believe that the mere sight of him knotting his tie could have her stomach dancing.

'I'm five weeks pregnant, Rico, not eight months, and I think most women would think that I am taking it easy. I haven't even seen an iron since I moved in here, haven't so much as flicked on a kettle, so a day at work isn't going to kill me.'

'It's not you I'm worried about.'

He was flicking the end of his tie through the knot, concentrating as he tightened it, but his black surly mood was palpable.

Not for a second did he notice her paling face. His words were an instant slap to the cheek, and their intimacy popped like a child's soapy bubble in the warm afternoon air. Never before had she been brought down to earth more quickly. She felt as if she were falling, literally falling. The dizzy heights of their lovemaking had taken her to a dangerous place, a place where just for a second Catherine had felt as if she might fly, and now she was being put in her place. Rico, in his cruelly dismissive way, was reminding her exactly where her place was.

The intimacy, the tenderness, the closeness she had experienced had been only for the benefit of his child's mother.

'I have to go.' His voice seemed to be coming at her

from a distance, and when his lips grazed her cheek she yielded no response. She watched, watched from the mirror, as he checked his watch, then stalked into the bedroom and picked up his briefcase. 'I'll see you tonight.'

Somehow Catherine made it through the morning, but it was literally a case of going through the motions. Lily was kissed and farewelled, the traffic snarl as she approached the school negotiated, her colleagues greeted and her students faced. But it was as if she were operating on autopilot, every response made with barely a thought as her mind again wandered back to Rico, headed down that dangerous, forbidden path that constantly beckoned and which for a while she had been stupid enough to follow. Stupid enough to think that Rico Mancini cared for her not just as a surrogate mother to Lily, a solution to a problem and now incubator to the Mancini heir, but as a woman in her own right.

A woman who loved him.

The children seemed to sense her distracted mood, and their lively chatter grew more raucous. Never had Catherine been more grateful for the lunchtime bell, fleeing to the bathroom where she leant her burning face against the mirror as she recalled their lovemaking last night, sordid now instead of beautiful. In one cruel sentence he had reduced her to a tart, a woman who could please him at his will, provide for his needs, but never, ever get close.

She had only just made it to the bathroom in time. Her retching mingled with her tears, humiliation mingled with a pain that suddenly intensified. But not a sharp pain that brought release, just a dull, throbbing pain, familiar to women worldwide—the monthly price of femininity. But there was no comfort in regularity, no comfort in the familiar feeling her body was imparting, just a horrible thud of clarity. The back pain, the sinking mood of the past twenty-four hours, the brink of tears—all a totally normal response she had chosen to ignore. Refusing to acknowledge, till the facts were indesputable that her pregnancy was actually over.

'I'll do some blood tests.' Malcolm Sellers's voice was efficient, but kind. 'I'm not going to examine you at this stage, because if there is a chance you're still pregnant that could only exacerbate things.'

'I've lost it, haven't I?' Catherine was sitting pale and drawn at his desk, wishing she could rewind the past hour, go back to the safety of being with child, the tiny ray of light that had for a while shone, but instead she was sitting in the doctor's surgery. Her taxi had barely been out of the driveway, before the nurse had ushered her in. She was in the Mancini world, Catherine reminded herself. Things moved quickly here—no waiting rooms to mull over the inevitable, no buffers, just straight to the horrible point.

'I think that's what you should prepare yourself for.' Malcolm nodded slowly. 'The fact you have pain, that you no longer feel pregnant…'

His voice trailed off and Catherine found she was frowning.

'I don't know that I actually *felt* pregnant before. Although…' Her eyes sparkled with tears and she accepted the box of tissues Malcolm pushed towards her. 'I did suddenly feel close to Lily, felt as if I was starting to get the hang of things a bit. Could that have been just because I was pregnant?'

Malcolm gave her a sympathetic smile. 'I'm sure those feelings will all come again in good time, but a good dose of hormones generally helps things along. You mustn't forget the terrible strain you're under, Catherine; you've just lost your sister, you have a new marriage, new home…'

She knew Malcolm was trying to be kind, trying to say the right thing, but each and every one of the problems he had outlined she could deal with if only Rico loved her. She missed Janey, missed Janey so badly it hurt, but if only Rico was truly beside her she could bear it. Without his love even breathing seemed an effort.

'I'll get these bloods couriered to the lab, and as soon as I get the results I'll come and see you at home. For now I want you to go to bed and try to rest. If the pregnancy is still viable it's the best thing you can do. Have you told Rico yet?'

'I've tried. His secretary is trying to get hold of him for me; hopefully he'll call soon.'

'I'll get hold of him for you; doctors generally do better with proprietorial secretaries than wives.'

'Shouldn't I have a scan? Isn't there something you can give me to stop it?'

'It's too early for a scan, Catherine—and, no, there's no medicine I can give you at this stage of pregnancy. Normally it's just nature's way of letting go of something that simply wasn't meant to be.'

In true private doctor style he saw her to a taxi, but she barely registered his kindness. A strange numbness seemed to have seeped inside her veins and she stared stonily ahead until the taxi pulled into the drive. Her legs were shaky as she pulled out some notes to pay.

The door opened on her first knock, and she held her private tragedy tightly inside as she headed for the stairwell.

'Mrs Mancini, I wasn't expecting you home…' Jessica stepped forward, the smiling Lily in her arms an aching reminder of what she was losing. 'Actually I'm really pleased that you are; I was hoping we could talk.'

Jessica was following her up the stairs now, an annoying presence when Catherine ached for privacy. 'Jessica, now's really not a good time; I came back from work because I don't feel well.'

'Oh!' Jessica moved Lily to the other hip. 'It's just…'

Still Jessica followed her. They were at the bedroom door now, and Catherine's stomach was cramping painfully.

'Just what, Jessica?' Her words came out too harsh and Catherine instantly regretted them, but she simply didn't have the energy to take them back. She ached to lie on the bed, to close the door on the world, but still Jessica hovered.

'It can wait…' Jessica's voice trailed off, and the young girl swallowed uncomfortably. 'It doesn't matter, Mrs Mancini. I'll let you rest.'

She lay there in the vast lonely bed, trying to relax, trying to give her baby, if it was still there, its very last chance.

Something that wasn't meant to be.

Malcolm Sellers's words rang in her ears.

Everything around her seemed to be slipping away and she was powerless to stop it. This baby meant so much to her—a spark of hope, a bond that would bind her to the man she loved, something good and true and real to cling to—and now, as sure as the night followed day, she was losing it.

No!

From the ashes hope resurfaced, a tiny stirring of the strong woman she was. She would fight this, fight till it was over. Till someone actually told her that her child was gone she would cling on for dear life, do everything possible to protect the life within. Concentrating on keeping her breathing even, she ignored the cramping pain, drifting away to a place that was gentle and kind, melting into the solace she had glimpsed in Rico's arms.

Somehow amidst the ruins she found the haven of sleep, her hands resting on her stomach, trying to hold her child within, fitful dreams causing her to cry out. As if in response she heard Rico's footsteps on the stairs, the bedroom door opening on his pale tense face. Dr Sellers walked in behind him, and one look at the two men's faces dashed her faintly flickering hopes there and then, told her it had all been in vain.

'I'm sorry, Catherine.' Dr Sellers was sitting on the bed, taking one of her pale hands in his. Her eyes darted to Rico, trying somehow to gauge his reaction. But he stared sternly ahead, his eyes fixedly avoiding hers, his jaw set in stone, muscles quilting around his face and his hands clenched by his sides as the verdict was delivered. 'Your hormone levels have dropped since I took your blood last week. They're supposed to go up,' he added gently, as Catherine shook her head against the pillow, pulling her hand away and shielding her eyes with it, trying to block out a world that seemed to relish the dirt it dished out to her.

'It's called a blighted ovum, which means that there was a pregnancy, but only fleetingly. Quite simply, it never progressed beyond the very early stages. As I said in my office, sometimes this is nature's way of letting go and, hard as it is, you have to remember that. It was simply not meant to be.'

Not meant to be.

He could have been talking about her and Rico.

A love that had surely been there, however fleetingly, but that quite simply couldn't grow—no matter how she wanted it to, how she nurtured it, needed it. A love that wasn't meant to be.

'This is no one's fault,' Dr Sellers continued, pulling her hand down and trying to look her in the eye, but as her eyes shot to Rico he turned to him also. 'Neither of you must blame yourselves or each other for what has happened.'

Wasted words.

One look at Rico and she knew she had lost him for ever. One look at his black coal-chip eyes staring stonily ahead and Catherine knew that quite simply it was over.

'It's not you I'm worried about.'

The recollection of his words taunted her now. The baby had been his priority and she had lost it for him— had followed her heart, ignoring her aching, tired body, and gone to work. Rico would never, ever forgive her.

If ever he had despised her that paled into insignificance now, as Dr Sellers left them alone. Rico was a distant figure, standing resolute and unreachable by the bed, and Catherine ached for him to sit beside her, to take her in his arms and tell her it was all okay.

'Rico…' It was all she could manage, but he didn't respond to her lonely cry, just stared fixedly ahead.

Lily's cries filled the hall, and they seemed to pierce her soul, a painful reminder of all she had lost. Rico pulled a blanket from the wardrobe, laid it over her, and for a second so small it was barely there he held her gaze, his eyes laced with pain, confusion, fear, even, and she ached to comfort him, for him to comfort her, for them to hold each other and weep for what they had just lost.

But just as quickly as he'd met her gaze he pulled away, his voice harsh and austere, a world away from the tenderness they had shared last night. 'Try and sleep.'

'Please don't leave me.'

'I have to go to Lily.' Still he didn't look at her, his voice as cold and removed as if he were addressing a stranger.

'Jessica can take care of Lily for a moment.'

'Jessica is at the shops,' Rico responded briskly, but still Catherine persisted.

'What Dr Sellers said about blame…'

'You need to rest, Catherine.' A pounding on the front door was all the excuse Rico needed to walk out, but Catherine called him back.

'Rico, I need you here with me. Surely one of the staff can get the door…?'

'There are no staff.' Rico's voice was void of expression, and she'd have preferred the familiar fiery man than the empty shell that stared back at her. 'Apart from Jessica, I gave them the weekend off; we were attempting "normal" this weekend, remember?'

He didn't slam the door, but still she jumped when he closed it, listening to his footsteps on the stairs. The low, angry voices barely registered as she lay staring at the ceiling, hardly blinking when the bedroom door opened and Rico and Antonia stepped inside.

'Antonia says this can't wait.' Rico's voice was clipped. 'I explained you weren't feeling well, but she was insistent.'

'I'm sorry.' Antonia stood awkwardly at the edge of the bed. 'I thought Rico was making excuses when he said you were unwell, but clearly…' Her voice trailed off and she turned to go, but then changed her mind. 'I'm sorry for intruding. I had no idea Catherine was pregnant—no idea this was anything other than a marriage for appearances' sake. It would seem I misjudged you both.' Her hand reached out and she patted Catherine tenderly on the arm. 'I'm sorry to hear about your baby, Catherine.' Her eyes drifted uncomfortably to her stepson. 'I'm sorry for your loss too, Rico. I know it might seem hard to believe, but I do understand what you're going through.'

The look Rico gave her clearly indicated he assumed Antonia had absolutely no idea, but a wistful note in her voice stirred something within Catherine. 'You lost a baby too?'

Antonia nodded slowly. 'I lost four,' she replied slowly, fiddling awkwardly with her earrings as Catherine stared back. 'And each time I was told not to worry, that there were years ahead for me to have children, that this was just nature's way…' Her voice wavered for a moment before continuing. 'And I know how empty those words sound at the time, so I won't waste your time with them.'

'There was something you wanted to say?' Catherine offered as Antonia turned to leave.

'I'll come back in a few days,' Antonia replied. 'When you're feeling a bit better.'

'I'm fine.' Pulling herself up on the pillows, Catherine forced a brave smile. 'It really was very early days—I'm probably being a bit precious, lying here. If I hadn't known I was pregnant I would have just assumed it was…'

'It's not the physical pain, though, is it?' Antonia said wisely, and not for the first time Catherine found herself warming to her; not for the first time the enemy didn't seem quite so unapproachable.

'I'll leave you two to it,' Rico said uncomfortably, but Antonia called him back.

'You should stay, Rico. What I have to say affects you both.'

Still she stood stiff and awkward, but there was a dignity about her as she spoke, and Catherine listened with both interest and admiration as Antonia addressed her stepson.

'I was wrong to expect you to accept me all those years ago, Rico. I hurt your mother, and you had every right to hate me, but in my defence all I can say is that I did love your father very much. I still do.' Her words were soft and emotive but Rico stood unmoved.

'So money had nothing to do with it?' he asked mockingly, but surprisingly Antonia nodded.

'I liked the money too, Rico. I admit that. I also admit that I was wrong to accuse you of underselling the business. You gave your father and Marco a more than generous price. They weren't prepared to work and, as lucrative as the company was under your mother, it only really turned into the empire it now is once you took it over.'

'I know all that,' Rico said rudely. 'So why are you really here, Antonia? Why the supposed olive branch?'

'Rico!' Catherine broke in, appalled at his rudeness. 'At least hear what Antonia has to say! I'm sorry,' she said, flustered, turning to the older woman, but Rico hadn't finished yet.

'Don't apologise on my behalf, Catherine.' His eyes turned to his stepmother. 'I don't know what your agenda is this time, Antonia, and I don't know what your motives are for coming here. If I appear rude then so be it; I make no apology. I can take what you did to me, Antonia, but it's the hurt you've caused those closest to me I cannot accept, and I will not let you do it again. So I'm warning you, if you're going to say anything to upset my wife, now really isn't the time. I swear to God if you upset her tonight, when we've just lost our child, you'll never set foot in this house again and I'll do whatever I have to do to ensure you have no further contact with Lily.'

'I have no intention of upsetting Catherine.' Antonia stood resolute, but as she spoke her voice wavered, those well-made-up eyes brimming with tears that could never be manufactured. 'And as for Lily—I've instructed our solicitor to withdraw our application for custody.'

Someone gasped, and it took a moment for Catherine to realise it had been her. Her eyes darted to Rico, trying to read his expression, but he stood tense and silent, his jaw firmly set as Antonia tentatively continued.

'Carlos and I have spoken at length and we realise that Lily deserves more than two retirees can give her. As much as we love her, as much as we want to be there for

her—well, with the best will in the world we're in our
sixties…'

'So why the sudden change of heart?' Rico's voice told
Catherine he remained unconvinced, eternally suspicious.
Antonia's tears wouldn't move him an inch. 'You haven't
aged a decade in the last few weeks. What made you
suddenly decide to give it all away?'

'You did, Rico.' Antonia looked across at her stepson.
'You and Catherine have turned your worlds upside down
to provide a home for Lily. Look, I admit that until now
I thought this was nothing more than a marriage of convenience, nothing more than a sham to win round the
judges…'

'And even then you were prepared to walk away?' A
muscle was pounding in Rico's cheek and it seemed to
match Catherine's own heart-rate as Antonia blindly continued.

'Even then.' Antonia nodded softly. 'It hit me how
much you must love Lily, Rico. That you would give up
your own chance of happiness, live in a loveless marriage
to ensure your niece's future; you too, Catherine.' She
turned and smiled, not noticing Catherine's face paling on
the pillow, her hands clenched by her sides as the nails
hammered deeper into the coffin. 'I know I couldn't do
it.'

'You really love my father?' Rico's voice was raw.

'I've always loved your father, Rico,' Antonia replied
softly, 'and I always will. I'm just sorry it caused so much
pain for so many people. I don't expect your acceptance
or forgiveness, Rico. I want it, of course, but I understand
if it's too much to ask. What I do ask though, is that your
father and I can have regular contact. We want to be a

part of Lily's life, Rico—hopefully now for all the right reasons.'

Rico gave a small nod, his expression still wary, but his Adam's apple bobbed a couple of times before he spoke, and when it came his voice was laced with emotion.

'And you shall be.' For the first time he looked at Antonia without malice. For the first time his voice was soft when he addressed her. 'I will see you out.'

How long she lay there she wasn't sure, but darkness had replaced the late-evening sun, the shadows matching her heavy gloom. Lily's heavy sobs flicked into her consciousness and she held the pillow over her head, trying to block out the cries; the pain in her stomach was easing now, and Catherine missed it.

Missed the pain that matched the agony of an ending to what had never really begun, to tentative dreams that had never really stretched their wings.

She held her breath in her lungs as she heard Rico cross the landing, heard the nursery door close. Lily's cries gave way to silence and she waited, waited for him to come to her—if not to make things better, then to make things a little more bearable. But as the lonely moon drifted past her window Catherine knew she had lost so much more than just her baby tonight.

In the scheme of things she knew her loss barely registered a blip, that maybe Dr Sellers was right—yes, she was young; yes, there would be other babies. But she wanted that one, wanted the child she had lost this day, a baby she could almost see, almost feel. This was the baby she ached for, this was the baby she mourned, and if Rico wouldn't come to her now, in the depths of her grief, couldn't mourn the child they had just lost with her, then what was the point?

No point at all.

There were no ties that bound them now. No baby to unite them, no custody battle to pursue, just a mere legality that would be taken care of easily.

A marriage in name only that had been over before it had started.

She dressed in a moment, packing quickly. She hadn't been in Rico's world long enough to accumulate much, except perhaps the broken heart that would surely weigh her down for the rest of her days.

She wandered the lonely house, bracing herself at each door to witness his beauty—in the lounge, perhaps, nursing a whisky, or in the study, working long into the night. Finally she found him, asleep in the rocking chair, hiding from her as she had from him, Lily dozing in his arms.

Lily Mancini.

A smile ghosted across her face at the sight that greeted her.

How she couldn't have seen it she truly didn't comprehend. Lily could be Rico's child—the same long dark lashes swept over slanting cheekbones, the same full, slightly superior mouth, that even in sleep never really relaxed.

And she loved her.

Loved her enough to do the right thing by her.

To give her the life Janey would have wanted for her.

Slowly she ran her fingers over the soft down of the sleeping babe's hair, gazing now not at the child who slept but at the man who held her, meeting his stare as his eyes flicked open.

'I'm going, Rico.'

He stared back at her, taking a minute to focus, his bewildered expression deepening as he took in her clothes, the bag at the door and the utter defeat in her voice.

'Catherine—' He went to stand, but Lily let out a moan of protest and he moved quickly to gently hush her. He lowered her into the cot, soothing the babe with words as his eyes implored Catherine to hold on, to wait so they could talk. 'You can't just go.' Lily was starting to fret now, perhaps sensing the loaded atmosphere, but Rico was facing Catherine, demanding that she listen. 'You should be in bed. You're not well…' He gestured to the crying infant in a final stab at reaching her. 'Lily needs you.'

'No, Rico.' Catherine's voice was a hoarse whisper. 'I thought she needed me, I thought I was the right person to bring her up—convinced myself that was what Janey would have wanted. But Janey hated me. Why do I flatter myself that she'd want me raising her child?'

'Because you know this is the right thing to do!'

'Janey despised me, Rico.' Catherine's words were without pity, without bitterness. 'Janey wanted money and wealth, and she'd have wanted the same for her daughter. I truly thought I was doing the right thing, truly believed that I could do a better job than Antonia.' She shook her head, bit hard on the tears that were now threatening, refusing to break down at this late stage, determined to escape with her last shred of dignity. 'Antonia loves her;

she proved that today. Lily's going to grow up surrounded by people who adore her.'

'She needs you,' Rico insisted, following her out to the hall. 'I need you.'

His words stilled her, but only for a moment. She squeezed her eyes closed as his words ricocheted through her, hating him for making this harder than it needed to be.

'You don't, though, Rico.' She couldn't bring herself to look at him, couldn't bring herself to turn around and witness what she was losing. 'You've won. As long as you allow Antonia and your father to see Lily, you can have her.'

'I need you,' he said again, his hand on her shoulder, turning her slowly around, but his strong features blurred through her tear-filled eyes.

'No, Rico,' Catherine said softly. 'We lost our baby tonight and still you didn't come to me. If you need me so much, why weren't you there?'

'There were reasons, Catherine, and if you will give me a moment I will explain them to you…'

'I'm tired of your excuses, Rico—tired of the *reasons* you conjure up to hide your heart from the world. So I'm going, Rico, because I can't live like this for a moment longer. I can't live in a marriage that isn't about love, and despite what you say, despite the contempt you regard it with, I still believe in love, still believe in the fairytale. Still believe that one day I will be loved as I deserve to be loved.'

'Then stay.' His words were ragged as he followed her to the stairwell, pulled at her jacket in a desperate attempt to stall her. 'Hear what I have to say before you walk out on us...' He grabbed at her handbag as she started to descend the stairs, urgency in his voice, haste in his actions as he tried to reach out to her.

'Rico, please.' She was pulling at her bag now, in a futile tug of war, tears blurring her vision, her head dizzy with emotion. She wrenched it away, the sudden jolt as he let go was all it took for her to lose her footing, and the banister was out of reach as her flailing arm reached for it.

'Catherine!' His shout was one of pure anguish, but his reflexes were like lightning. Instinctively he reached out and pulled her back from the brink, grabbing her into the safety of his embrace—the only thing that stopped her from toppling the dangerous length of the stairwell. As she looked up through startled eyes she registered the horror in his expression at her near fall, and their chests rose and fell in unison as the shock of what had nearly taken place dawned.

It was Rico who recovered first, his voice ragged, his breathing rapid, still holding her trembling body in his arms, still somehow protecting her even as he finally let her go.

'Is that how badly you want to leave, Catherine? That you would throw yourself down the stairs rather than stay and talk to me?'

She hadn't been throwing herself down the stairs, it would have been a simple accident, but she chose not to correct him. A metaphorical door was opening, and Catherine chose to go through it.

'I'll leave in an ambulance if that's what it takes, but I am going, Rico.'

'I'm not your jailer Catherine.' There was a curious

dignity in his voice as he stared down at her, a wounded pride in his manner now he had released her from his arms. 'This was never how it was supposed to be.'

'I know that,' she whispered through pale, trembling lips, then walked slowly down the stairwell, unhindered physically, but with every cell in her body begging her to stay, to return to all she loved. She turned to him with tear-filled eyes, trying to block out Lily's sobs but failing to do so. 'Tell Lily I do love her. I'll call.'

'When?'

She shook her head, too raw to contemplate a future when she could see Rico without breaking down, share in her niece's birthdays and milestones without dying a little inside for all she had lost.

'I don't know, Rico.' She stared up at him, this haughty, brooding man she had loved—yes, loved—from the second she had laid eyes on him. A difficult, complicated man who simply couldn't lower his guard, a man with a brilliant mind who couldn't get his head around something as simple as love, and the distance between them, the safety of the front door open in her hands gave her the strength to finally speak the truth. 'You were right to be suspicious of Antonia, Rico, and you were right about Janey. But you were so very wrong about me. I never wanted this house, Rico, never wanted the servants or the cars. I love you. The only thing I wanted out of this marriage was you, and it was the one thing you weren't prepared to give, the one thing that wasn't up for negotiation. Well, I can't do it—I can't live in a marriage that looks good on paper; I can't survive in a marriage without love.'

'Catherine, please!' He was bounding down the stairs

three and four at a time, taking the impressive stairwell in barely a stride, but she was too quick for him, slipping out of the heavy door like a thief in the night and then slamming it closed.

He didn't follow.

She'd never really expected him to.

It had all just been a game.

CHAPTER FOURTEEN

EXHAUSTION, grief, pain—they had no meaning now. It was as if she had somehow passed through a barrier and come out the other side, numb, almost without emotion, as if Rico had wrung every last drop out of her and left her with a curious void that must surely be her life now—an empty, dark abyss where her heart and her spirit used to reside.

She drove aimlessly, taking the beach road from the city and heading along the horseshoe of Port Phillip Bay, watching the still, inky water. The same moon that had drifted past her window was like a glitter ball above the water, and the stars danced around, inviting her to step out and take in their grandeur, but for a while she ignored the call, driving with more purpose. Her journey had meaning now, and she acknowledged the magnet that had drawn her here. The grief that had never really been explored was a festering wound that needed to be lanced if ever she were to find peace...

Pulling her car in amongst the tea trees, she gazed at the tombstones silhouetted in the moonlight, then wandered through the stony paths till she came to the soft mound of earth that was Janey's. The funeral flowers had long since died, but a fresh sprig lay on top, beautiful in its simplicity, and sinking to her knees she fingered the warm soil, ran her fingers along the petals of the flowers.

She pulled the card out and read it, and her heart seemed to split in two.

> *Sleep peacefully*
> *We will do our best for Lily*
> *Rico and Catherine.*

The fact he had been there, that the detached, distant Rico had been to Janey's grave, blurred the edges of her reality. He had spoken on behalf of them both, signed her name, promising to do their best for a child left alone, and it tore at her very being.

The tears that had always been there were given permission to fall then, and she sobbed into the lonely darkness, her wails guttural, primitive as she wept for the beautiful sister she had lost, the sister taken too soon, wept for the parents she would always miss and for the baby she would never hold.

She cried for Rico too.

For the man who had danced in her dreams, who had allowed her to glimpse all he could be, if only for a fleeting time—the man who had held her, loved her, even if he couldn't admit it to himself.

A man she would mourn now for ever.

'Let it out, Catherine.'

For a second she stilled, frozen for a moment in time as Rico knelt beside her.

'Leave me,' she sobbed, but Rico as usual ignored her, instead wrapping his arms around her, pulling her into his embrace as she struggled like a cat. 'Leave me,' she pleaded again, but she felt him shake his head, and the vice of his grip was curiously comforting, something to hold onto as tears again took over.

'Let it out, Catherine,' he said again, and suddenly the whys didn't matter. Rico was here, and as she wept his arms were around her, holding her, almost an extension of her own body, a rock to lean on. And however temporary, however ill-fated their union, for a moment or two she allowed herself to cling to him, not strong enough to face this moment alone.

'Janey loved you.' He was trying to comfort her, trying to say the right thing, but his words only fuelled her pain, only widened the abyss of her loss.

'She hated me—how can I look after her daughter when she hated me?' Catherine gulped. 'It's time I faced the truth.'

'Is it?' His question forced her attention. Her shimmering eyes flicked up to his, and her sobs gave way to gentle hiccoughs as he stared back at her. 'Tonight I found out the truth, Catherine. Tonight I found out what really happened to Janey and Marco—that is why I didn't come to you. I truly thought you were too weak to hear it, that now wasn't the time.' He took a deep breath, and for a second so small it was barely there she swore she registered tears glistening in the dark pools of his eyes, swore that for once in his life emotion truly had the better of him. 'It wasn't easy to hear, Catherine, but it is something you need to know, whenever you are ready.'

Summoning strength, she stared bravely back at him. 'I'm ready.'

'Not here.' Standing, he pulled her up, led her out from the graveyard, across the deserted street. They wandered through the bracken till she felt the cool crunch of stones beneath her sandals. She gazed out at the water before sitting down on the cool ground and staring up at the stars. He wrapped his jacket around her, his eyes narrowing in concern as he felt her frozen pale cheeks.

'It is too cold here, Catherine. You are not well; you should be at home...' His voice trailed off, the word 'home' had been placed out of bounds by Catherine, and as much as it tore him he had to respect that.

'I can't go back, Rico.'

He nodded, staring at her for a moment, clearly desperate to take her in his arms, to tell her the truths that needed to come out, but her pallor concerned him.

'We could sit in the car; I could put the heater on.'

A tiny shift of her head told him he was wasting his breath.

'Wait there.'

She didn't respond, just stared into the twinkling sky as Rico wandered over the beach, gathering driftwood. Her tears had left her exhausted—spent, but curiously detached. It had been cathartic cleansing so deep she felt almost void of emotion now, as if nothing more could hurt her, nothing more could touch her.

He knelt close by, parting the stones and filling them with driftwood, lighting the leaves and fanning the tiny flames until the wood caught. And still she said nothing, just gazed into the firelight, mesmerised by its beauty. The hint of eucalyptus as the flames licked the heavy logs was comforting somehow, and the heat from the fire warmed her chilled bones as Rico sat beside her.

'They weren't drinking, Catherine.' His words were soft, but very measured. 'And they hadn't been taking any drugs. As I was seeing Antonia out Dr Sellers came back.

We both spoke to him; he took us through the post mortem results.'

'But Marco staggered out of the restaurant; the doorman said he was so drunk he could barely speak…'

'He had a stroke.'

A gasp escaped her lips, a strangled gasp and her hands shot down and held her cheeks. Her mouth opened and shallow breaths came out in a grief so raw, so painful she was sure the scream that resonated around her head must be audible.

'Marco had a stroke—that's why he lost control of the car, that's why everyone assumed he had been drinking. And the saddest part of it is they were actually out celebrating—celebrating the fact they were going to get their lives on track.'

'How do you know all this?'

'I spoke with Jessica; when she returned from the shops we had a long talk. I think she was waiting for me to ask.'

'She probably was,' Catherine admitted. 'She's been trying to talk to me about it, but I kept pushing her away.'

'You should have listened,' Rico scolded softly. 'We both should have listened. Janey loved you, Catherine. She told Jessica that you had both been right to say something, that you in particular had always been right, that she was living life too fast and too dangerously and it was time to slow down. She said she knew it was time to grow up, to take a leaf out of your book and face up to her responsibilities. She was proud of you, Catherine; she wanted to be like you. You should talk to Jessica also,' he added. 'I think it might help you.'

Catherine nodded, staring into the flickering fire for a pensive moment, then turning back to Rico as he carried on talking. 'Jessica gave me some home movies—videos they had taken…' He swallowed hard, his Adam's apple bobbing up and down, and she could feel his hesitation. His usual reserve was battling to take over, but he fought it, dragging his eyes back to her as if she was what he needed to continue. 'I prepared myself for the worst when I put them on—a drunken party, perhaps, Lily crying in a corner… I've no idea what I expected to see, but never in a million years could I have envisaged the love I witnessed.'

'Love?'

She was sure she must have misheard him, somehow misinterpreted the simple yet intricate word, but Rico nodded slowly, that beautiful full mouth wavering slightly as emotion betrayed his usually steady voice. 'They loved each other, Catherine. To anyone else it would have been the most boring home movie ever, but there they were, cooing not just over Lily, but each other. And, as blind as I might appear in matters of the heart, their love was obvious.'

'So why did she say those terrible things?' Catherine asked.

'Maybe it was safer for her to believe them?' Rico suggested gently, taking in the tiny frown that puckered her brow, those delicious brown eyes blinking at the brilliance of new perception. 'Maybe in that messed-up head of Janey's it was easier to convince herself she was in control of her own emotions? Maybe she loved Marco so much that she did trap him, did everything in her power to ensure he married her? I don't know all the answers, Catherine, but one look at the video and you will be convinced also.'

'We can play it for Lily.' Her words were a whisper as bittersweet relief flooded her veins, because something had finally been salvaged from the wreckage, because Lily would have some precious memories to cling to of parents who had, it seemed, loved her after all.

'*You* can play it for Lily,' Rico corrected softly. 'Catherine, I love Lily, but despite your doubts, despite how hard it has been for you, I know in my heart you are the best person for her. You will be a wonderful mother.' His hand dusted down over her stomach, held the hollow where there should have been their child, and it was Rico's tears she witnessed now, with pain, pride, agony etched in each proud tear that scraped the razor of his cheekbones. 'You would have been a wonderful mother to this one too.'

'I'm sorry, Rico. Maybe I did do too much. Maybe going back to work after all I'd been through was just—'

'Hush.' He placed a finger to her lips. 'Don't do that to yourself. I never blamed you, Catherine, not even for a moment,' he whispered. 'I blame myself.'

'But why?' Catherine begged, her mind in turmoil. Seeing Rico, usually so strong, so utterly self-righteous, plagued by doubt, seeing this proud, dignified man in such pain, tore at her very being. The pain they had unwittingly inflicted on each other was almost more than she could bear. 'How could it be your fault?'

'Because when I found out you were carrying my child I was pleased for all the wrong reasons. I wanted you to be pregnant, Catherine—wanted you to be having my child. Not because I wanted another baby, but because I wanted you! But seeing your pain, hearing Antonia talk, it hit me just what we had lost. Our baby, Catherine. Our child. It was only then I realised how much I'd wanted it too.'

And though she ached to comfort him, to say the right thing, her mind stalled on the middle of his heartfelt speech, the rest of the words a blur as those three little words hit home.

'You wanted me?' Her voice was incredulous and she quickly fought to check it—scared, so scared, of raising her hopes only to have them dashed again; sure, so sure, she must somehow have misheard him, misunderstood. But those dark eyes were staring back at her unwavering, with love blazing brighter than the fire that warmed them.

'I've always wanted you,' Rico said slowly. 'I've always needed you. You changed my world, Catherine, made me open my eyes and see things from your wonderful perspective. You see the good in people,' he explained gently. 'You hang on in there despite the punches and somehow you find the best in everyone—even me. Tonight, when you told me you loved me, I wanted so badly to tell you I loved you too—to take you in my arms and weep with you for our baby…'

'You got here in the end.' Catherine smiled bravely, but when he shook his head and the shutters came down again she felt her heart split in two.

'It is too late for us, Catherine.'

'No!' Her shout was instantaneous, a furious yet heartfelt reaction; to be so near, to have got so close only for him to pull back, was more than she could take.

'Don't you dare hold back on me now, Rico. Don't you dare give with one hand and then take with the other. How can you say you love me, you need me, and then just shut me out?'

'Because as you said before, Catherine, you should be loved as you deserve to be loved, and I cannot promise you that. My mother died young, my brother also. Dr Sellers wants me to have tests; he says it may be hereditary, that there is a chance it could happen to me also. I cannot put Lily through another loss, and I will not put you through it either. How can I stay when I don't know if I can promise you a future? How can I be the husband you deserve when I don't know how many tomorrows there will be?'

'And how can you not?'

There was a simplicity to her question, clarity that cleared the littered way for him.

'Rico, there are no guarantees in life; we've both learnt that the hard way. But if you love me as much as I love you then there can be no question of you walking away, no question of you dealing with this alone. I'd rather face the rest of my life without you, knowing I had one tiny slice when you were truly mine, than face a world without you ever having loved me at all.'

'I've always loved you, Catherine…' She heard his pause, knew there was more to come, but she shook her head and this time it was her finger hushing him with the softest of touches.

There was nothing left to qualify.

No words were needed now.

Love would see them through.

EPILOGUE

'I REALLY don't think you have anything to worry about. I know the books say that at this age toddlers can be very jealous of a new baby, but you must remember that Lily's very advanced.'

Antonia's voice carried across the veranda table and Catherine smothered a smile as Rico caught her eye.

'She is,' Antonia insisted. 'Anyway, we'll make sure she doesn't have a moment alone to feel jealous. Your father and I can hardly wait to have her stay with us.' She shot a rather impatient look across the table and this time Catherine didn't try to smother her smile; in fact, she threw her head back and laughed.

'I'm not due for another two weeks yet, Antonia. And, given the fact that first babies often come late, you might be in for a wait before Lily comes and stays with you.'

Selecting a strawberry from the fruit platter, Catherine bit into it, enjoying the sweet ripe taste, enjoying this lazy Saturday afternoon with her family by her side and a glimpse of the exciting times that lay ahead, and trying not to spoil this precious time with the pensive mood that had taken her today.

'Maybe Lily should have a trial run?' Rico's voice was so casual, his stance so nonchalant anyone else would have missed the meaning behind his words, and Catherine's eyes darted nervously to Antonia, watching the older woman's reaction as Rico's words hit home. 'Maybe she should go home with you both tonight?'

'You mean it?' Antonia didn't wait for an answer, scooping Lily up in her arms, ordering Carlos to load the car and showering her beloved granddaughter with kisses as Catherine packed an overnight bag. She slipped in a couple of bedtime stories for Carlos to read to her, albeit slowly. But *Three Little Ducks* was somehow so much more romantic with a Sicilian accent, and Lily was eternally patient, delighting in her doting grandfather's efforts, the perfect audience as he falteringly discovered the joy of reading.

'You've made their day.' Catherine sighed as they waved them off, leaning back on Rico, resting her head against his chest as his hands cupped her swollen stomach.

'It's the right thing to do,' Rico murmured, more to himself than to Catherine. 'Anyway, I had an ulterior motive. Do you realise this is probably our last night alone for a very, very long time?'

'Night feeds, dirty nappies.' Catherine sighed again. 'Are you sure you're ready to do it all again?'

'More than ready,' Rico affirmed. 'Aren't you?'

She was! Oh, for a while she'd been scared to glimpse the future. Rico's multitude of tests had consumed them, brave words no barrier against fear, but they had faced it together. Dark times were so much easier shared, and the blessed relief of a clean bill of health was so much sweeter with a family beside you.

'I'm ready, Rico.' She nestled against him, forcing herself to continue, forcing herself to share what was in her mind, as they had promised each other they would—only Rico got there first.

'Just not today, huh?'

'Just not today,' Catherine whispered back, grateful for his insight, and glad, so glad, she didn't have to hide her feelings any more.

'I've got something for you,' Rico said solemnly, turning her around to face him, pulling a piece of paper out of his pocket and handing it to her with trembling hands. 'I know it's going to make you cry, but it's something I think you should have—something I think *we* should have.'

She stared at the paper for an age and Rico was right, it did make her cry—but then every thing made her cry at the moment. Since Rico had switched on her emotions the world seemed to be a vivid contrast of delicious highs and lows, and she relished the rollercoaster she rode alongside him.

Somehow she even managed to relish standing in their courtyard on a Saturday afternoon, remembering the child they had lost one year ago on this day.

'I named a star.' Rico's voice wavered as he spoke and she waited patiently for him to continue. 'It *was* meant to be, Catherine. Our baby brought us together, made us the family we are today, and though I couldn't see it at the time I can see it so very clearly now. Our baby had a purpose.'

It was the most beautiful thing he could have said, the most beautiful thing anyone could have said, and as he took her hand and led her back to the house—a house that was now a home, filled with love, blessed with their beautiful Lily and a new baby soon to follow—Catherine knew the future was there for the taking, and that she was the luckiest woman in the world.

Tonight, though, was for them.

THE MORETTI MARRIAGE

BY
CATHERINE SPENCER

Catherine Spencer, once an English teacher, fell into writing through eavesdropping on a conversation about romances. Within two months she changed careers and sold her first book to Mills & Boon in 1984. She moved to Canada from England thirty years ago and lives in Vancouver. She is married to a Canadian and has four grown children—two daughters and two sons (and now eight grandchildren)—plus three dogs. In her spare time she plays the piano, collects antiques and grows tropical shrubs.

CHAPTER ONE

Friday, August 21

SUNLIGHT bounced off the swimming pool and patterned the bedroom ceiling with shifting reflections of the water. Another brilliant day in an endless summer that had left the grass scorched yellow except here, in her mother's garden, where in-ground sprinklers worked under cover of night to preserve the velvet-smooth emerald lawns.

It was after nine o'clock, a good two hours later than she usually awoke. But that tended to happen when a person had tossed restlessly throughout most of the night, unable to sleep. Now, lying flat on her back, with only a sheet to cover her, Chloe Matheson mentally reviewed the day ahead. The morning spent at the office, taking care of business, and a quick visit with Baron. Lunch with Monica, her best friend and matron of honor, followed by final dress fittings for both of them. One last meeting with the caterer, and a late afternoon consultation with her hair stylist. Then, as a grand finale, the cocktail party here at the house, to meet the groom's parents, newly arrived from Ottawa.

How had it happened that the small, intimate ceremony she and Baron had envisaged had turned into the social event of the season? How had a select guest list of twenty blossomed into something closer to a hundred and twenty?

They should have eloped, except that was something only the very young and impetuous did. She and Baron were too sensible, too mature, to act like Romeo and Juliet....

No! A door in her mind clanged firmly shut. *Not like Romeo and Juliet.* Chloe wanted no part of *anything* to do with them.

On the terrace below, her mother, Jacqueline, and grandmother, Charlotte, were taking breakfast. The low buzz of their conversation and the faint chink of china drifted through the open window, mingled with the aroma of coffee. Although she couldn't discern their actual words, Chloe knew they'd be discussing the wedding. It was all anyone talked about these days.

"You're making too much fuss about this," she'd objected, when the event had started to gather the speed of a runaway train. "It's not as if it's a first marriage for either Baron or me."

"If you care enough for one another to want to make it legal, then it's worth getting excited about," her mother had overruled. "And no daughter of mine is going to settle for some tacky little hole-and-corner wedding when I can afford to give her the best."

It hadn't seemed worth fighting about, back in April when Baron had proposed. Now though, Chloe wished she'd stood firm. But with the invitations sent out six weeks ago, all spare bedrooms in the house prepared for out-of-town guests, and every room at the nearby Trillium Inn reserved for the overflow, it was too late to apply the brakes.

Tucking a pillow behind her head, she glanced down at the silhouette of her body under the sheet. Her hip bones projected like clothespins anchored to her body by the concave dip of her abdomen. Her breasts lay so flat, they were barely discernible.

"Poached egg boobs are what we've got—the legacy of having nursed our babies," Monica had laughed, the day they'd gone shopping for wedding outfits. Then, realizing she'd stepped on tender ground, she'd sobered and said, "Sorry, Chloe, I forgot. I didn't mean to be insensitive."

Chloe, though, never forgot, and turning now to look at the silver-framed photograph on the nightstand, she met the solemn, dark-eyed gaze of her son, captured forever on film at two months. "Hey, angel," she whispered, her throat thick and aching.

Downstairs, the phone rang. With a tremendous effort, Chloe pulled herself back from the abyss of grief and regret forever waiting to swallow her up. Kissing her fingertip, she pressed it to her son's tiny mouth, curved in the beginnings of a gummy smile, then flung aside the sheet and headed for the shower.

Neither Jacqueline nor Charlotte heard her step out to the terrace, some twenty minutes later. They were too busy with their heads together, cooking up something so furtive that when Chloe said, calmly enough, "Good morning!" they sprang apart as if they'd been caught shoplifting.

"Darling!" her mother exclaimed, almost knocking over her coffee cup. "You're up! How...lovely!"

"I don't know what's so lovely about it, Mother," she replied, observing both women mistrustfully. "It's something we all do, every morning."

"But you look so *rested,*" her grandmother chirped, which was an outright lie because Chloe knew very well that no amount of concealer had been able to disguise the smudged shadows under her eyes.

They were doing their very best to appear guileless, but something about their expressions—"smug" was the word that sprang to Chloe's mind—made a mockery of their pathetic attempts to behave as if this were just another morning in the long week leading up to the wedding.

"All right," she said, plunking herself down at the breakfast table. "Out with it. What's going on?"

They exchanged a shifty glance, then hurriedly broke eye contact. "Well," her mother practically twittered, "you have a dress fitting this afternoon, a meeting with the caterer—"

"I'm perfectly well aware of what's on *my* calendar," Chloe informed her testily. "It's *your* agenda that worries me."

Her grandmother bathed her in a sunny smile. "Have you forgotten? We're entertaining Baron's parents tonight, and we want everything to be quite...perfect." She spooned fresh blueberries into a small crystal bowl and passed it to Chloe. "After all, you never get a second chance to make a good first impression."

"Exactly." Her mother poured her a cup of coffee. "Don't look so suspicious, darling. What do you think is going on?"

"That you're both stonewalling me." Ignoring the blueberries, Chloe added a little cream to her coffee and stirred. "Who was that on the phone earlier?"

"Nobody," Jacqueline said, just a fraction of a second before Charlotte chipped in with, "The florist."

Chloe eyed them severely. "Would you like me to

leave you alone for a few minutes, so that the pair of you can get your stories straight?''

''Oh, stop being such a lawyer!'' her mother said, in that pooh-pooh voice Chloe well knew was designed to throw her off track. ''We haven't committed any crimes that we're aware of. Eat your blueberries. I read somewhere that they're very good for you.''

But her grandmother's next remark left Chloe feeling too sick to the stomach for her to eat so much as a mouthful. ''Just remember, precious, that things don't always turn out the way you expect them to. Life sometimes throws you a curve.''

''You think I don't know that, Gran?'' she said quietly. ''You think I didn't learn that lesson in the most cruel way possible?''

''Of course you did, my sweetheart, and it's not my intention to open up old wounds. All I'm trying to say is that, no matter what might come about, your happiness, your...*choices*...are the most important things in the world to us. We only ever want the very best for you.''

Choices? That was an odd word, surely, especially at a time like this? ''Then you must be thrilled that I chose Baron, because he's the best thing that's happened to me in a very long time.''

''If you say so, Chloe.''

''I do, Gran. So why, I wonder, don't you believe me?''

''Perhaps,'' her mother cut in, ''because you don't seem able to whip up any great enthusiasm for this wedding. To put it bluntly, Chloe, no one would believe you're the bride, the way you're distancing yourself from it all. Why, when you married Nico—!''

"I was twenty-two, and foolishly idealistic."

"You were so eager to become *Signora* Nico Moretti that you practically galloped down the aisle to meet him at the altar." Jacqueline closed her eyes and let out a sentimental sigh. "I remember your veil flying out behind you like a parachute, and the crinoline on your dress swinging like a pendulum. Your joy was so infectious, everyone in the church was smiling by the time you reached his side. They all commented on how radiant you were."

"Nerves will do that to a person."

"You were deeply in love—and so was Nico."

"Not quite deeply enough, as it turned out. Our marriage didn't last."

"It could have," Charlotte said. "It *should* have."

Annoyed, Chloe pushed aside the blueberries. "Is there a reason you're both raking up the past like this? Is it, by chance, your way of telling me you think I'm making a mistake in marrying Baron?"

"Do *you* think you are?" Jacqueline asked.

"No!" she said, a shade too emphatically. "And if you two do, you've left it a bit late in the day to mention it." Beset by her own niggling uncertainty, she glared at the women she loved most in the world. "You're the ones, after all, who insisted on turning a small, quiet wedding into a three-ring circus!"

Jacqueline's face almost crumpled, but at the last minute she regained control of herself. "Because we wanted to show you how much we love you, Chloe. We want so badly for you to move forward with your life and find real happiness again."

"I know," Chloe murmured, ashamed. It wasn't their fault she couldn't let go of the past.

"We hoped marrying Baron would be the key, but you seem so…*indifferent,* somehow—as if marrying him is just another case to deal with. You weren't even going to buy a proper wedding dress until we bullied you into it. As for the gifts people are sending, why, you haven't bothered to open half of them!"

"Because I'm preoccupied with my workload at the moment," she hedged. "Taking all next week off is bad enough, but tack on the month we'll be in the Bahamas after that, and it's asking a lot to expect others in the firm to cover both for me *and* Baron. As for buying a wedding dress, well, it seemed a bit over the top for the second time around, especially given the closet full of clothes I already own."

"Even a quiet second wedding deserves some fanfare," her grandmother observed. "It *is* a special day, after all."

"You're right, of course." Tired of the subject, she directed her next question at Jacqueline. "How many people are we expecting tonight, Mother?"

"About a dozen, only—just family, those in the wedding party, and a few friends. We didn't want to swamp the Prescotts with too many new faces all at once. What time are they flying in from down east?"

"Eleven-twenty, I believe. Baron's going to pick them up and take them to lunch, then leave them to settle in at their hotel and catch an afternoon nap before the party." She pushed back her chair. "Which reminds me, I'd better get going. I promised him we'd sneak away for coffee before he heads out to the airport. We've both been so busy this last few days, we've only seen one another in passing, and it doesn't look as if the coming week's going to be much better.''

"You'll have the rest of your lives together after next Saturday," Jacqueline pointed out. "In the meantime, with all the social engagements we've got planned, you'll be seeing each other pretty much every day, even though you won't be going in to the office."

This was true, but the fact was, Chloe needed some private time with her fiancé, away from all the pre-wedding hoopla. She needed his steadying influence to soothe her frazzled nerves; his calm, quiet voice to drown out the diabolical whispers of doubt which persisted in creeping up on her. She needed to feel his arms around her, to bask in the warmth of his slow, sweet smile.

That's all it would take for her doubts to evaporate, and bring home the realization of how lucky she was to have found him. How could it be otherwise when he was everything a woman could want in a husband—patient, kind and loyal? And so in tune with her own wishes that it was little short of miraculous.

"Before you give me your answer," he'd cautioned, the night he'd proposed, "I have to reiterate what I've mentioned before. I really do *not* want children, or a house in the suburbs, with a big garden and neighbors who like to get together around the barbecue every Friday evening. I'll be forty in November, and I don't see myself spending weekends mowing lawns or coaching soccer for small boys. You and I are dedicated professionals, Chloe, with both of us putting in long hours Monday through Friday. When we're not working, I want us to be free to concentrate on each other, to be able to lock the front door and take off, without the attendant stress of babies who'll eventually grow up to be…'' He'd shuddered. ''…teenagers. Am I asking for too much?''

''Absolutely not!'' she'd told him, closing the door on memories of how it had been the last time a man had proposed to her. ''We're exactly in tune on the kind of life we want. So yes, I'll marry you, and be proud to call myself Mrs. Baron Prescott—socially, at least.''

''Of course.'' He'd stroked the hair back from her face and regarded her fondly. ''I'd never ask you to give up everything you've worked so hard to achieve. It goes without saying that, professionally, you'll always be Ms. Chloe Matheson, attorney-at-law.''

And that, she'd thought at the time, was more than enough to make her happy. Because Baron was right. The steady stream of desperate women coming to her for help in escaping an unbearable marriage, haunted her. As for the innocent children caught up in such messes, they broke her heart. And Baron, dealing mostly with wills and estates, witnessed sufficient family in-fighting to persuade him that nothing brought out the ugliness in siblings more than the division of a parent's worldly goods. Cocooning their lives around just the two of them made perfect sense.

Only now, with her second wedding day just little more than a week away, did it occur to her that accepting his terms so readily might have had a lot less to do with love than it had with safety—from hurt, disillusionment, loneliness…and always, always, from grief.

*   *   *

She might have wished for a more scaled-down wedding, but Chloe had to admit that, if a grander affair was in the scheme of things, no one could beat her mother at doing it in style. As a prelude of even greater things to come, the cocktail party was a triumph of understated elegance.

Of course, it didn't hurt any that the balmy evening meant the French doors could stand open, allowing guests to drift from the drawing room to the patio, to admire the sunset gilding the Strait and etching the distant islands in flaming gold. Add an endless supply of the very finest caviar, accompanied by enough excellent champagne to float a battleship, and by the time daylight dwindled to dusk, it was small wonder most people had loosened up a little.

But despite the surface conviviality, Chloe found the party a strain. Baron's parents moved in an elite social circle. His late grandfather had been a member of parliament, his father was a renowned archaeologist, and his mother the retired headmistress of a prestigious private school for girls. Although pleasant enough, there was no hiding the fact that Mrs. Prescott was sizing up not just Chloe, but Jacqueline and Charlotte, as well as the house, to determine if the bride's upbringing had equipped her sufficiently well that she'd fit in as a Prescott wife and daughter-in-law.

"So how did you find the Prescotts?" Jacqueline inquired, closing the front door as the last car drove away.

"Not all warm and fuzzy, if that's what you're asking," Chloe said bluntly. "Frankly, I'm glad they live at the other end of the country. From the way Baron's mother quizzed me about the fact that I'd been married before, I got the impression she considered me soiled goods.''

"I noticed that, too,'' her grandmother remarked. "She was really rather snooty at first, although she did warm up to us a little, toward the end.''

"It was the Waterford chandelier that did it.'' Jacqueline choked back a laugh. "Myrna Prescott almost swallowed her teeth when she saw it. I think both she and her husband went away quite favorably impressed with our standard of living.''

"As they should have!'' Charlotte said, still the protective parent even at seventy-six. "They might have an illustrious family tree, but you didn't exactly grow up on the wrong side of the tracks yourself, my love. Tonight's little get-together was a triumph. You really outdid yourself, and you must be exhausted.''

"I am a little tired.''

"Then I'm taking you to the Inn for dinner. It's been a long time since just the two of us went out.'' She paused delicately. "Of course, you're welcome to join us, Chloe, if you wish....''

"Oh, absolutely not!'' Chloe was quick to answer. "I want nothing more than to kick off my shoes and relax. Go ahead and have a good time. Heaven knows you're both working hard enough putting this wedding together that you deserve a bit of a break.''

They didn't bother to put up an argument. In fact, they seemed almost eager to leave her behind. Not that they said as much, of course. Instead, they agreed that she was quite right to take it easy, then the pair of them hurried out to the car and drove off before she could change her mind.

By then, it was well after eight but although dark-

ness had fallen, the heat of the day lingered, leaving
the air so soft and warm that, instead of taking a long,
luxurious bath, she pulled on an old bathing suit and
went down to the pool for a swim.

"Just eight more days to get through, then all this
craziness will be over. A week from Sunday, we'll be
on our way to the Bahamas," Baron had whispered,
when he kissed her good-night. "I can hardly wait,
Chloe...."

Slipping into the limpid water, Chloe floated on her
back and gazed up at the heavens, willing herself to
share his eager anticipation. Next Saturday at this time,
they'd have been married nearly five hours. They'd be
in the honeymoon suite of the hotel where they
planned to spend the night. Chances were, they'd already have made love for the first time.

Would it be wonderful, the way it had been with—?

Her mind snapped shut on the thought, as suddenly
and mercilessly as a leg-hold trap. She would not allow
Nico to creep in; he had no place in her life anymore.

Just then, a meteor streaked across the velvet sky in
a shower of sparks. A lucky sign, according to some.
Make a wish, they'd say—and she would, if she didn't
already have everything any woman could wish for.

Everything, except one thing, that is. And there was
no use wishing for that, because it was asking for the
impossible. Neither prayers nor superstition could
breathe life back into her little son.

Instead, "I wish I could forget," she whispered,
tears blurring her vision and turning the blanket of
stars into a shimmering arc of rainbows. "I wish it
really was possible to start afresh and leave the past
behind."

*   *   *

He picked up his phone on the second ring. *"Sì?"*

"The coast's clear, Nico. Make your move."

"Does she suspect?"

"Not a thing."

He smiled, switched off the phone, and headed out the door.

She hadn't known he'd been watching her all evening as she moved about the garden with her fiancé and his family, the mother fat as a pigeon, the father tall and thin. She'd had no idea that he'd stood at the dormer window in the gardener's lodge and seen how his replacement had slung his arm around her shoulder and nuzzled her hair. How he'd kissed her when he thought no one else was looking—full on the mouth, with the sort of hungry need Nico understood only too well.

Treading stealthily, he followed the brick walk from the lodge to the main house, shrouded in darkness now except for the light shining from her bedroom. Of course, she'd be shocked to see him. Shocked and furious, probably. But his business interests gave him a perfectly valid reason to be in town the same week that she happened to be marrying someone else, and although he could have changed his dates and avoided seeing her again, wild horses hadn't been able to keep him away—especially not after he'd heard her mother's reservations.

"I'm not saying she isn't fond of Baron," Jacqueline had told him. "But there's no real spark there, Nico. She's going through the motions, that's all."

It had been all the encouragement he'd needed to stick with his original plan. "I'll be there by Friday."

"That'll leave you only a week to make her reconsider."

"*Dio,* Jacqueline!" he'd said with a laugh. "It didn't take me more than a day, the first time!"

"But she's different now. She's...wounded."

"We all are," he'd reminded her. "But that's no reason to use another marriage as a refuge from the pain."

"Exactly! Baron's a good man, Nico. He deserves the best, and much though I love her, I'm not sure he'll be getting the best if he marries my daughter. I'm not sure she's able to give him her whole heart."

"I understand."

"Do you? Even though *you* might be the one who ends up being hurt? I'm going only on a mother's instinct here, Nico—a sense that my child is taking the line of least resistance because it's easier to give in than to fight. But I could be wrong. It could be that Chloe really does want this marriage for all the right reasons."

"I've never been afraid of taking risks, you know that. And it seems to me, Jacqueline, that the risk to you is even greater. She might never forgive you for interfering like this."

"It's a chance I have to take."

"There you have it, then. We do what we have to do, and pay whatever price is asked of us. She is worth it, *sì?*"

"Yes."

Which brought him to where he was now, making his way through the shadowed garden, with the advantage of surprise on his side. By catching her with her guard down, he hoped to shock her into revealing a glimpse of that part of her she kept so well hidden from everyone else.

Except that, in the end, he was the one caught off guard, when he stepped out from behind a tall calla lily and activated the motion-detector security lights. Which would have been fine, if she'd been inside the house where he expected her to be. But she wasn't. She was floating on her back in the pool, instead, and before he could dart back behind the concealing foliage, she'd let out a startled squeak and, raising her head, stared straight at him.

Her hair hung around her shoulders in a riot of water-soaked waves, and her legs—those long, glorious legs that used to wrap around him as if they never wanted to let him go...oh, they were a beautiful sight, slicing through the water as she struggled to stay afloat!

There wasn't much point in trying to hide then. So he did the next best thing. He stood there and unashamedly drank in the sight of her.

CHAPTER TWO

CHLOE'S first response at seeing him was one of such utter shock that she swallowed a mouthful of water which went down the wrong way; her second, that either the mixture of light and shadow was playing tricks on her, or she was seeing a ghost. "Tell me you're not real!" she choked, floundering to the side of the pool.

But the figure at the edge of the pool deck looked and sounded frighteningly real. "*Ciao,* Chloe," he said, in that velvet-smooth, sexy Italian voice, and moving forward with his easy, long-legged grace, neither of which appeared to have diminished with time. "Did I startle you?"

"Yes!" she spat, and slapped his hand away when he leaned down and tried to help her out of the water. "Don't you dare touch me!"

He broke into his old, devilishly charming grin, and something turned over inside her in a slow-rolling somersault of awareness. She hadn't felt anything like that in more than four years, and it terrified her. Climbing onto the pool deck, she pushed the wet hair away from her face, flung her towel around her shoulders, and planted her fists on her hips.

"I don't know what you think you're doing here, Nico," she said, with as much controlled dignity as she could manage, given the total upheaval taking place inside her, "but I can assure you, you're not welcome. So unless you wish to spend the night in jail, I suggest you remove yourself from my mother's property immediately.''

''I—'' he began.

''Because,'' she continued, riding roughshod over his attempt to get a word in edgewise, ''if you don't, I'll call the police and have you carted away from here in the paddy wagon.''

He tried to look wounded, but the laughter in his eyes betrayed him. ''You'd do that to me, *cara?*''

''In a heartbeat,'' she informed him stonily. ''And don't call me *cara.*''

''What should I call you, then? *Signora* Moretti?''

''I dropped that name, the day we divorced.''

''You might have dropped the name, but that doesn't change the fact that we were once husband and wife. But I don't suppose you want to be reminded of that, with another man waiting to step into my shoes, in little more than a week's time. What will you call yourself then, my dear?''

''Mrs. Baron Prescott—not that it's any of your business.''

She might as well have saved her breath. Undeterred, he continued his inquisition. ''And you love this Baron person?''

''Why else do you think I'm marrying him?''

He hooked his thumbs in his belt loops and stepped closer. ''What I think isn't the issue here, my lovely Chloe. It's what you think that matters.''

Right at that moment, with him standing close enough that she could detect his faint, alluringly familiar scent, she could barely think at all. *Picture Baron!* she ordered herself. *Concentrate on him!*

But Baron had receded to the farthest reaches of her

mind, dwarfed by the vastly more compelling flesh-
and-blood presence of Nico. Helpless to tear her eyes
away, Chloe gazed at him.

On the surface, he'd changed little since she'd seen
him last. He was still outrageously handsome. Still un-
mistakably European in the way he wore his clothes,
with such sinuous grace that even the unremarkable
blue jeans and white polo shirt he had on now assumed
the elegance of an Armani suit.

His black hair was as thick as ever, and bore not a
trace of gray. His mouth, his teeth, his smile, continued
to invite intimacy. As for his darkly beautiful
eyes…oh, she couldn't look into his eyes. They reminded her too much of her son's.

"Why do you care what I think or how I feel?" she
said bleakly. "I'm not part of your life any longer."

"We had a child together. For that reason alone,
there'll always be a connection between us. Nothing
and no one will ever break it. You can take a dozen
new husbands, *cara mia,* but they'll never succeed in
wiping out the memory of the life and the love we
once shared."

She pressed her lips together and looked away, des-
olation sweeping over her in relentless waves. No,
she'd never forget, because to do so would mean wiping out the too brief time Luciano had been part of her
life, and that she could never do. Memories of him
were all she had left. "Do you still miss him, Nico?"

"All the time," he said, knowing without having to
ask that she was referring to their baby. "Not a day
goes by that I don't think about him, and wish things
had turned out differently. He would be four, if he'd
lived, and you would not now be contemplating mar-

rying another man, because you'd still be married to me.''

''But he didn't live!'' she cried, all the grief she tried so hard to contain tearing loose inside her like a river bursting its banks. ''And it's your fault that I lost my little boy!''

He jerked his head aside as if she'd slapped him hard across the face, but not so quickly that she didn't see the devastation written there. After a second or two, he turned to look at her again, the suspicion of tears gleaming in his eyes. ''He was my child, too, Chloe.''

Mortified, she clapped a hand to her mouth and whispered, ''Oh, I'm so sorry, Nico! I shouldn't have said that. I know it's not true. But the hurt never really goes away, and seeing you again brings it all back as if it happened just yesterday.'' She huddled more closely into the towel, shivering suddenly despite the mild air. ''What are you really doing here?''

''I always stay here when I come to Canada.'' He shrugged, as if making himself at home in his ex-mother-in-law's house was the most natural thing in the world. ''You might have divorced me, but Jacqueline never did. She has always made me welcome.''

''But why now?'' she pursued, hiding her dismay at his revelation. ''If you knew I was remarrying next week, you must have realized this was not the time for you to show up unannounced.''

''It could not be avoided. When business calls....'' He shrugged and to her shame, she found she couldn't quite drag her gaze away from the easy shift of his broad shoulders under his shirt. ''I must answer, yes?

And since I will be here for at least ten days, Jacqueline invited me to attend your wedding. Such a lovely, gracious lady, your mother!''

With each shocking disclosure, he moved toward her. And every time he did so, Chloe took a step back, desperate to maintain distance from him because she didn't dare think of what might happen if she let him come too close. Bad enough that her body ached with vague yearning, as if it recognized that there'd been a time when he'd brought it to vibrant, thrilling life. *''She did not!''*

''She most certainly did,'' he said, lunging forward without warning and grabbing her around the middle.

His hands almost spanned her waist, his fingers so strong and sure that she hadn't a hope of escaping him. ''One more step and you'd have toppled backward into the pool,'' he murmured, drawing her away from one kind of danger and toward another, far more perilous.

At once panic-stricken and hypnotized, she stammered, ''I don't believe you! Why would she do such a thing?''

''Because ours was the most civilized divorce in the world, so where is the harm in wishing you and this new man well, and showing him he has nothing to fear from me?''

''He already knows that.''

''Then my being here won't disturb him, will it?''

''Not a bit!''

''And what about you, Chloe? Will knowing I'm close by make you less sure of yourself and the plans you've made?''

''Absolutely...not...'' The denial emerged on a sigh, defeated almost before it was uttered, because he was stroking his hands up her ribs, over her shoulders, down her arms, and robbing her of every last ounce of strength. Her legs grew weak as water, her vision clouded, and she felt herself swaying toward him.

He put her from him very firmly. "Then there's no problem. Consider me nothing more than another guest, here to witness your marriage and toast your future happiness. It'd be a shame for me to have come all this way and miss such a grand event. You know how much we blue-collar Italians love a good party."

Throwing cold water in her face would have been less shocking than what he proposed. The strength flowed back into her body, fortified by a dose of righteous indignation. "You are not coming to my wedding, and that's final! I'll see you in hell, first!"

"Darling," he said lazily, "I've already spent enough time there. I doubt anything you can devise to punish me now will ever equal that."

How easily he could seduce her with a touch wasn't the only thing she remembered. He was beyond stubborn, too, once he'd made up his mind about something. "Be reasonable, Nico," she begged, trying to keep the frantic edge out of her voice. "You'll feel awkward…a man alone at a wedding is out of place. People will talk and wonder why you're here. And even if they don't, I can't imagine why you'd want to see me marry someone else."

"Because your happiness is important to me."

"But why do you care? You're not responsible for me anymore."

"I'll always feel responsible, *cara*. You suffered more sorrow with me than any woman should have to bear. If I couldn't be the one to heal you, I want to shake the hand of the man who can.''

She saw the obstinate set to his jaw, the way he planted his feet apart, as though to say, *If you want rid of me, you're going to have to pick me up and remove me by force.*

Trying to disguise the desperation creeping up on her, she said, ''I won't allow this, Nico. You're not going to bully me into letting you stay. I don't want you here, it's as simple as that. Consider yourself un-invited.''

''Can't do that, it wouldn't be polite,'' he replied, all sweet reason. ''Your mother's the one who issued the invitation, and this is her house. Until *she* tells me I'm not welcome, I stay.''

I will kill her! Chloe vowed furiously. *So help me, I will wring my mother's scheming neck, the very first chance I get!*

''We'll see about that,'' she told him. ''Unlike you, my mother can be persuaded to change her mind.''

''Why does my being here make you so nervous, *cara?* Are you afraid I'll embarrass you?'' He indi-cated his snug-fitting jeans, his blindingly white shirt. ''Do you think I'll show up dressed like this on your big day? That I'm still scratching to make ends meet, and can't afford a decent suit and tie? Because if so, rest easy. I'm respectably rich now.''

''If how much you're worth was that important to me, I'd never have married you in the first place,'' she said scornfully. ''I didn't fall in love with your money.''

He laughed. ''How could you? I didn't have any!'' Then he sobered, and when he spoke next, his voice had grown gentle with nostalgia. "I remember so well the day we met. Do you?"

"Not really."

He looked up at the stars and smiled, as if he and they shared a secret. "It was a Tuesday."

"Thursday," she corrected.

"At a jewelry booth."

"In an antique shop which happened to sell estate jewelry, which isn't quite the same thing."

"*Sì!*" He nodded and adopted the smiling pose of a professor faced with an unusually bright student. The only thing missing was a beard—and so help her, if he'd had one, she'd have pulled it out by the roots! "It was just as you say. I had found a cameo brooch which I planned to give to my sister, Abree, for her birthday."

"I found it first, but you tried to outbid me on it."

"So I did." His smile shifted to her face and bathed it in unsettling warmth. "But in the end, I let you win because why quibble over such a trifling piece, when already you had stolen my heart?"

"Your heart had nothing to do with it! You couldn't meet my offer, and pulled your jeans' pockets inside out to prove it."

But it was the way he'd laughed as he relinquished his claim that had won her over. In the blink of an eye, he made her forget that she'd come to Italy to visit fabled art galleries, to walk the ancient streets and experience history firsthand, in still-living color. Meeting him that day in Verona instantly became the most memorable event in the tour she and Monica embarked on, to celebrate their having graduated *summa cum laude* from university.

"I will concede defeat," he'd said, with irresistible Latin charm, "only if you will let me take you to lunch. I have just enough lire in my pocket to buy us a carafe of wine and a bowl of pasta. Do we have a deal?"

She'd agreed without a moment's hesitation, and was in love with him before they arrived at the *trattoria* he chose, tucked away in a tiny sunlit square which she'd never have discovered on her own. To say he typified an Italian matinee idol would have been to sell him so far short of reality that it was an insult. Nico was the most beautiful, the most gallant, the most beguiling man she'd ever met. It hadn't mattered one iota that he was virtually penniless.

"I recently invested my limited assets in a business on the brink of bankruptcy," he told her cheerfully, over ravioli and a jug of rough red wine.

"Everything?" The future lawyer in her had been appalled. "What if you end up with nothing?"

He'd laughed. "I grew up with nothing, *la mia bella,* and if I die with nothing, it will matter not at all, as long as I squeeze from life every last drop of joy it has to offer. A man must make the most of his time on earth, *sì?"*

She'd realized then how different they were in outlook. He was the kind of man who dared to imagine; to take risks; to act on impulse and live with the consequences. She was nothing like that, and although she admired those qualities in him, they were also what made him dangerous. But that was something she didn't discover until it was much too late.

"Do you still have it?" he asked her now. "That brooch which brought us together?"

''No,'' she said. ''I gave it away at about the same time that I left you. I couldn't bear the reminder of what it represented.''

''Did getting rid of it help you to forget?''

''No.''

''I'm glad. There was too much that was good between us for it all to be cast into oblivion.'' He touched her hair. ''We were happy for a little while, weren't we, Chloe?''

Oh, yes! Blissfully so, almost from the second she first set eyes on him...until that terrible, terrible night. Perhaps that was why the grief that followed was so hard to bear.

Monica had continued touring the country, but Chloe stayed in Verona, any thought of discovering more of Italy abandoned. In fact, ''abandoned'' was a very good word to describe the way she'd behaved over the next month.

Within a week, she and Nico were lovers. By the end of the summer, he asked her to marry him and just as well, or she'd have proposed to him.

With a tiny diamond on her finger, she flew home at the beginning of September and flung herself into preparations for a wedding to take place in early October, even though her mother and grandmother voiced reservations at the suddenness of it all.

''What about your career?'' they'd wanted to know, and she'd told them, ''Nico is my career now.''

''How can you be sure?'' they'd said. ''At least wait until next summer before you marry him, to give yourself time to find out if this really is love, or just a holiday infatuation.''

But she was not to be dissuaded, and when Nico

arrived in Vancouver at the end of the month, both her mother and grandmother fell under his spell as swiftly and easily as she had.

"When the right man comes along," Jacqueline had decreed within twenty-four hours of meeting him, "the timing isn't important. You're meant for one another, my darling daughter. I can't think of any other man I'd sooner call son-in-law."

Clearly, nothing that had happened since that day had changed her mother's mind. She still considered Nico family; still thought the sun rose and set on him. Why else would she have jeopardized her only child's future by allowing him to come back on the scene now?

"You don't answer me, Chloe," Nico said, sliding his hand around the back of her neck. "Were we not happy for a little while? Our wedding day, was it not perfect?"

She had to force herself to answer truthfully. It would have been so much easier to dismiss both him and the question, if she could have said "no."

Instead, "Yes," she admitted grudgingly, "though if I'd been in your shoes, I wouldn't have found it so special. None of your family came to see you get married."

"The distance and cost involved made it impossible for them to attend, and in truth, I hardly noticed their absence. *You* were there, beyond beautiful in white satin and lace, and that was enough for me. Indeed, you could have worn sackcloth for all I cared. That you were about to become my wife was the only thing that mattered. I might not have had the means to fly my family here from Italy but, that day, I felt like the richest man on earth. What was money, compared to your promise to remain by my side, through good times and bad, for as long as we both should live?''

The passion in his voice, the drugging seduction of his fingers strumming a love song over the nape of her neck, were making deadly inroads on her self-possession, and she had to put a stop to them before she fell so far under their spell that she ended up in his arms.

''I think your memory is deceiving you,'' she said, trying to wriggle out of his reach. ''Being poor bothered you a very great deal—to the point that making money eventually became your obsession.''

''I needed to provide well for you and our son, Chloe. Do not fault me for that. Before I met you, I'd made myself a promise that I wouldn't marry until I could support a wife and family in some sort of style. But you bewitched me into forgetting all that. I knew the day I met you that you were the woman for me. But I never regretted making that decision. I still do not, even now, even though we ended up so far apart.''

''Perhaps we both wanted too much, too soon. Perhaps what we had was too good to last.''

''Or perhaps we didn't fight hard enough to hold on to it.''

''How do you hold on to a three-and-a-half-month-old baby lying in a casket, in a church graveyard?'' she cried. ''How do you *ever* recover from that?''

''By sharing your grief with the one person in the world who really understands it. But we couldn't do that, could we, Chloe? Instead of turning toward each other, we turned away, and in doing so, lost so much more than our son. We threw away everything else that was good and beautiful between us.''

''Don't you see, we had nothing left? Everything we were, or hoped to be, died with him.''

''If you truly believe that, then you're doing the right thing in marrying your Baron.''

''I do believe it, Nico,'' she said with hushed vehemence. ''I believe it with my whole heart. I can make a fresh start with him because he doesn't threaten my peace of mind. He is…my safe harbor. He won't hurt me.''

''Then no wonder you are finally ready to trade me in for this older model.''

''*Mature* is how I'd describe my fiancé!''

''Ah!'' He rolled his eyes. ''If only I could have been such a paragon of manly virtues!''

She wrenched herself free of his touch and raced toward the house, stopping at the far end of the pool deck just long enough to hurl a final bit of advice over her shoulder. ''Do yourself and everyone else a favor and go home, Nico, because if you have any idea of upsetting my wedding plans, you're wasting your time here. I'm going to marry Baron next Saturday, and nothing you can say or do is going to change my mind.''

Nothing? ''We'll see about that, *tesoro*,'' he murmured softly, remaining in the garden long after she'd disappeared inside the house. ''I have seven days in which to prove to you that, whatever you might want to believe, all the passion you think died with our son is still very much alive. And it will be my very great pleasure to reawaken it. I think then that you will be unwilling to settle for *a safe harbor* with this Baron Prescott. I think you'll find he will not be enough for you, after all.''

CHAPTER THREE

Saturday, August 22

ANOTHER perfect summer's day, another breakfast on the sunny patio, and the only storm on the horizon the one brewing between mother and daughter.

"How *could* you?" Chloe exploded, glaring at Jacqueline across the table. "And spare me the injured innocence act. You know perfectly well what I'm talking about. What in heaven's name possessed you to invite Nico to stay here?"

"He always stays here whenever he's in town. I thought you knew that."

"But why *now?*" She shook her head, so baffled she could scarcely string two words together without exploding. "You've spent weeks orchestrating this wedding, Mother. So why, at the last minute, would you go out of your way to turn it into a shambles?"

"Because, in the final analysis, a mother has to do what she thinks best for her child, especially if that child is determined to hide her head in the sand and pretend everything's perfectly lovely, when it would be apparent to a blind man that it's not."

"Are you saying you deliberately encouraged Nico to come here at this time in the hope that he'd ruin things for me?"

"No. I had no idea he'd planned a visit to coincide with your wedding. But when I found out, I couldn't help but think that destiny was stepping in and taking a hand in your future.''

Stunned, Chloe said, ''In other words, you might not have planned it, but you're hoping it will happen anyway?''

''He can't spoil anything unless you allow him to. If you're absolutely sure you're doing the right thing in marrying Baron, you won't let anyone stand in your way. But if, simply by his being here, Nico changes your mind, he'll have saved you and Baron both from making a terrible mistake.''

''He won't change my mind! I know what I'm doing.''

''So you keep saying. But it's not the impression I've been getting lately.''

''Then take another look! I'm twenty-eight years old, Mother, and capable of making my own decisions. I haven't needed you to wipe my nose since my first day in kindergarten, and I don't need you interfering now in something that's absolutely none of your business!''

Unruffled, her mother said, ''You'll always be my business, Chloe, just as you'll always be my daughter, no matter how old you are. And I could not, in all conscience, stand idly by and do nothing when, the closer you get to your wedding day, the more unsettled you become.''

''I am *not* unsettled!''

''Certainly you are. I'd even go so far as to say you're depressed. Now sit down and have a peach.''

She'd sooner eat worms! Clutching the back of her chair in a white-knuckled grip, she asked mournfully,

"Have you considered how Baron will feel when he finds out what you've been up to?"

"One way or the other, I suspect that, in the end, he'll thank me."

Bewildered, Chloe stared at her. "I thought you and Gran liked him."

"We do, darling—enough not to want to see him hurt."

"You've got a funny way of showing it! Inviting my ex-husband to stay here is bad enough, but to suggest he's welcome at the wedding...how am I supposed to explain that to Baron in a way that makes any sort of sense?"

"You're not," her mother said, unperturbed. "If there's any explaining to be done, I'll take care of it."

"Over my dead body!" Chloe dropped down on her chair, exhausted before the day had properly begun. "You've caused enough trouble, Mother! *I'll* speak to Baron. If you really want to do something worthwhile, get rid of Nico, and spare us all a lot of grief."

As if he'd been lurking in the bushes waiting for the right moment to make an entrance, Nico suddenly strolled around the corner of the house. "Did I hear someone mention my name?"

Chloe scowled at him, but her mother and grandmother, their faces wreathed in welcoming smiles, chorused, "Good *morning,* Nico!"

"Did you sleep well?" Charlotte inquired solicitously.

"Like a baby, *Nonna!*" he replied, bending to kiss her cheek. "You're looking wonderful, as usual, and younger than ever."

Jacqueline, meanwhile, poured him a cup of coffee.

"Here you are, dear. Strong and black, just the way you like it."

He dropped a kiss on her cheek, too. "*Grazie,* Jacqueline! As always, you know exactly how to make me feel at home."

Chloe, though, refused to acknowledge him, and stared instead at the coffee cooling in her own cup. Totally unfazed by her chilly reception, he took a seat next to her. "*Buon giorno, bella! Come sta?*"

"No happier to see you today than I was last night," she informed him bluntly. "Don't make yourself too comfortable in the lodge, Nico. You won't be staying there, after all."

"No?" She didn't need to look at him to sense his smile. She could feel its warmth stealing over her face like a second sun. "I am to take over my usual room here, in the main house?"

"We don't have space for you there, either. If you're determined to hang around, you'll have to move to a hotel, and it won't be the Trillium Inn, because it's booked up with people whom Baron and I *want* to have at our wedding. So you'll be forced to look at something downtown."

"Chloe," her mother interposed gently, "why do you care where Nico sleeps, as long as it isn't in your bed, with you?"

The mere suggestion of such a possibility sent such a stab of forbidden pleasure coursing through her body that Chloe was left blushing and breathless. And of course, *he* noticed! Leaning so close that his shoulder brushed hers, he murmured, "Don't worry, *cara.* It will happen only when you give the word."

"Dream on!" she choked indignantly.

Trying to avert another storm, Jacqueline quickly changed the subject. "So sorry we couldn't welcome you properly last night, Nico, but as I mentioned when you phoned during your layover in Toronto, we were entertaining Baron's parents whom we met for the first time. I'm sure you understand how awkward it would have been to explain your presence to them, had we included you in the party."

"Do not be concerned," he practically crooned, so full of beaming good cheer that Chloe came perilously close to smacking him. "I found the key to the lodge exactly where you said it would be, and was comfortably settled in by what…?" He lifted his shoulders in one of his supremely careless shrugs. "Six o'clock? Half past?"

"And you have everything you need?"

"But yes! More than enough. The bed…." Another shrug, this time accompanied by an expansive forefinger-to-thumb gesture of approval. "*Molto comodo!* Very comfortable!" He angled a sly glance at Chloe. "But much too big for just one person."

"Don't give me that look," she informed him tartly. "It'll be a cold day in hell before I jump into any bed with you again!"

"Did I ask that you do so, *cara?*"

"No, but it's what you're thinking!"

"And since when am I not allowed to dream?"

"Since you found out I'm engaged to another man." She drew in an irate breath. "I won't tolerate your causing trouble for Baron and me, Nico. Contrary to the impression my mother might have given you, we thought long and hard before we decided to get married, and we're not about to let you or anyone else put an eleventh-hour dent in our plans.''

"But, darling, how could I if, as you claim, you're meant for one another?"

Dar-ling, he said, endowing both syllables with such husky, continental emphasis that her spine tingled. She tossed down her napkin and abruptly rose from her seat. "You can't, and you won't get a chance to try. If it were up to me, I'd have you tossed out of here on your ear, but since it's not, I'll make sure we cross paths as little as possible. And on those occasions when our being in the same place at the same time is unavoidable, I shall ignore you. And now, if you'll excuse me, I have things to do." Sparing her mother but a passing glance, she dropped a kiss on Charlotte's head. "I'll see you later, Gran."

"You're going out?" Jacqueline sounded surprised, and more than a little disappointed.

"Yes. Baron and I are doing the tourist bit with his family today."

"So early? It's only just after nine. What's the big rush?"

"He's picking me up at half past, and I'm not quite finished getting ready."

"Oh, sit down and finish your breakfast!" her mother declared impatiently. "You look perfectly fine as you are.''

Nico glanced up from the brioche he was dissecting and swept a critical eye over Chloe's gray linen dress. "No, she doesn't. She needs to wear something more attractive.''

"Oh, really?" Chloe fixed him in an affronted glare. "And exactly what's wrong with what I have on?"

"It is dull and does not suit you." He waved his butter spreader dismissively. "It has no style, no pizzazz. It makes you look like a prison matron. I do not like it."

"How odd!" she cooed, masking her outrage with a heavy dose of sarcasm. "You must have mistaken me for someone who *cares* about your likes or dislikes!"

She swept away then, chased by his taunting laughter and the echo of his words. They followed her inside the house and up the stairs to her bedroom. ...*No style, no pizzazz... I do not like it...like it...like it....*

"Much he knows!" she muttered scornfully. "He wouldn't recognize style if it jumped up and bit him in the face!"

But when she crossed to the full-length mirror in the corner, what she saw staring back at her was not a sleekly elegant woman wearing a designer creation the color of sea mist, but a drab, featureless individual in a drab, featureless dress. Her hair, newly styled just the day before, hung around her face in a limp brown mass, looking as defeated as she felt at that moment. Her eyes, which Nico once had compared to sparkling sapphires, reflected the emptiness in her soul, their dark blue irises lifeless. Even her skin appeared faded.

When had it happened? Since yesterday? Or had the change been more subtle, and crept up a little at a time, as her wedding day grew closer?

"Ah!" Furious with Nico for making her doubt herself, and with herself for letting him get away with it, she rushed into the bathroom. Smoothed blusher on her cheeks, and a trace of lilac shadow over her eyelids. Brushed a mascara wand over her lashes, and applied rosy lip gloss to her mouth. Dabbed a little perfume behind her knees and in the crook of her elbows. Then, snatching up a brush, she raked it through her hair until her scalp burned.

"There!" she muttered, watching as her hair bounced gently into place. "Now tell me I look like a prison matron!"

But how she looked wasn't the issue. It was that Nico's opinion could carry such weight after all this time. What kind of fool was she, that she'd let him derail her so easily?

Taking a deep, calming breath, she returned to the bedroom and, refusing to listen to the little voice telling her to change into something else, she hunted through her jewelry case for an item to accessorize her dress.

Not the plain gold locket and chain, she decided: it had no *style!* And definitely not the dignified pearls; they lacked *pizzazz!* But the long string of turquoise baroque beads, with matching dangling earrings? Now there was drama and color enough to turn a prison uniform into haute couture, and let anyone try to tell her differently!

When she came back downstairs, the front door stood open. "So you travel over here fairly frequently, then?" she heard Baron say as she reached the bottom step, and realized with utter horror that he'd arrived already and was speaking to Nico.

"*Sì.* At least three or four times a year."

That often? She'd had no idea! Had thought, from her mother's passing references, that he'd visited only once or twice since the divorce.

"Business must be good, then."

"I do not complain. And with you, business is also good?"

"No complaints here, either. I keep busy, but always find time to put in a round or two of golf each week. Do you play?"

"Not as often as I'd like, but I enjoy it when I have the chance."

"Maybe we can work in a game while you're here."

Time to step in and effect a little damage control, Chloe decided, and practically flew the last several yards from the foot of the stairs to the front door. "I can't see that happening, with everything else going on," she said breezily, sweeping past Nico as if he were just another planter of petunias, and pressing a kiss on Baron. "Hi, sweetheart. I didn't hear the car arrive, or I'd have been down sooner."

"I got here only a couple of minutes ago. Just long enough to say hello to your mother and meet Nico." He caught her hand. "You look beautiful, Chloe. But then, you always do."

"Thanks." She squeezed his fingers, so grateful for the understanding she read in his smile that she could have wept. He knew her so well; better than anyone else ever had. She didn't need to tell him how distraught she was. His calm blue eyes saw it all. "We should be on our way, don't you think? Your family will be waiting."

"Yes." He paused with his hand on her elbow and nodded amiably at Nico. "Nice meeting you. We'll see each other again, I'm sure."

"But certainly," Nico returned, his gaze resting fleetingly on Chloe before focusing on Baron. "*Ciao!* Enjoy your day."

She waited just long enough for the car doors to slam closed before starting to explain. ''I didn't invite him,'' she began. ''Honestly, Baron, I had no idea he was coming, or I'd have put a stop to it. I don't know what my mother was thinking about.''

Baron reached over and briefly covered her hand. ''Honey, it's okay. I don't mind that he's here.''

''You don't?'' Thunderstruck, she stared at him. ''He's my ex-husband, for heaven's sake!''

''He's also a family friend, and strikes me as a decent enough guy. His timing might be a bit off, but I can handle it, if you can.''

That was the trouble in a nutshell; she wasn't sure she could. Wasn't sure of anything anymore, if truth be told. ''What will your parents think?''

''That he's just another guest, unless you choose to tell them differently. They don't have to know you were once married to him. It's none of their business.''

''He thinks he's coming to the wedding, Baron!''

''Where's the harm in that? I hardly expect he's going to fling himself down on the ground and throw a tantrum in the middle of the ceremony. He doesn't strike me as the type. In fact, if he still harbors any romantic affection for you, seeing you marry me might be the one thing to give him closure.''

More confounded by the second, Chloe shook her head. ''You amaze me! If it were your ex-wife we'd just left standing on the doorstep, I can tell you I wouldn't be taking it nearly this well.''

''Why not? Don't you trust me to know who it is I want to be with?''

''You know that I do.''

''Well, the same goes for me. Unless you tell me

differently, I'm assuming nothing's changed between us." He patted her hand again. "I know you well enough to recognize that you don't have a dishonest bone in your body, Chloe. You'd never lie about your feelings."

He was trying very hard to make her feel better, she realized. What he couldn't begin to guess was that, with his every word, she felt worse.

Nico spent the day in business meetings in the city, returning to the house just as dusk fell.

"Come join us for dinner," Jacqueline said, intercepting him as he left his rental car and was about to head down the brick path to the lodge. "It'll be just the three of us. Chloe phoned to say she was dining downtown with Baron's family, and won't be home until later."

Not sure if he was disappointed or relieved by the news, he allowed himself to be persuaded. Seeing Chloe again had unraveled him more than he cared to admit. They'd been divorced for more than four years; time enough for both of them to move forward along separate paths. But just as she couldn't come to terms with the death of their son, so he, Nico realized, couldn't accept the idea of some other man replacing him in her life.

Coming upon her in the pool last night had shaken him to the core. He hadn't been prepared to find her so scantily clad that it required no imagination at all to picture her naked.

Ludicrous though it sounded, loss and grief had made her lovelier, stripping her down to a finely sculpted version of the sweetly rounded girl he'd married. Her skin was stretched more tightly over her bones, lending her face an almost ethereal beauty. No one looking at her would guess she'd given birth to a three-kilo baby boy. Her waist and hips were trim, her belly flat, her breasts small and firm, her long, luscious legs unblemished.

"You left so quickly this morning that I didn't get the chance to ask you then," Jacqueline said, the very second they sat down at the table, "but there's nothing stopping us from talking now. So, how do you find her?"

He laughed. His former mother-in-law had always been one to get straight to the point. "Is it possible we're talking about Chloe?" he teased.

"Well, of course! Who else?"

Aware that both mother and grandmother were eyeing him expectantly, he chose his reply with care. "I sense it would not take much to break her."

"So you see it, too!" Jacqueline leaned back in her chair and nodded with satisfaction. "Oh, we're so glad you're here, Nico! You're the one person who might be able to talk some sense into her."

"Or I could be the one to push her into this marriage you feel will be such a mistake. You saw how she was with me this morning. As far as she is concerned, I'm very much a part of her past, and have no place in her present. What makes you think she will listen to anything I say? And perhaps more to the point, do I have the right to say anything at all?"

"I believe you do," Charlotte said in her quiet, thoughtful way, "because I also believe that in her heart, Chloe still loves you. But she can't get past the hurt, and it blinds her to her true feelings. Instead, she's hiding from them, and using Baron to do it.''

''What about you, Nico?'' Jacqueline asked, observing him closely. ''Do you still love Chloe?''

Did he? Was it love that had sent his heart slamming against his ribs, and left his groin aching painfully, when he'd seen her last night? Or just the normal reaction of any red-blooded man to the sight of a beautiful woman? ''We've been apart a long time, Jacqueline. We don't know each other anymore. We've both changed.''

''But you care about her?''

''She was the mother of my child. I'll always care.''

''Sufficiently to see if there's enough left of what you once had, to build something new?''

Unwilling to let them see the doubt in his eyes, he pushed away from the table and paced to the long windows overlooking the Strait. Had he and Chloe *ever* had enough to make marriage work, if they came apart at the seams the first time something went wrong?

Until that dreadful night, they'd thought they were immune to the woes that afflicted other couples. Had laughed at the idea that anything could ever tarnish their love. Yet in the space of a few minutes, their entire world had crumbled, and only after the dust settled had he realized their marriage lay in ruins because of it....

He'd come home late in the afternoon, to the house they'd rented just before Luciano was born because it had a little alcove off the only bedroom that would serve as a nursery, and a sunny garden where the baby could take his afternoon naps.

He'd burst through the front door, full of excitement. At last, one of his investments had paid off. For the first time, he'd seen a light at the end of the long tunnel of poverty which had marked his childhood and dogged him as a man.

"Put on that dress I like so much, the yellow one, with the daisies all over it," he'd told Chloe, swinging her off her feet in a dizzying circle. "I'm taking you out to dinner, to somewhere fancy, for a change! Tonight, we have something to celebrate!"

"We can't go out," she'd said, laughing down at him. "We're parents now. We have a baby to think about."

"We'll get a sitter—Erstilia, from next door. She's said often enough that she'd be happy to look after Luciano."

Chloe had been aghast. "But we've never left him with anyone else, not even your mother! He's only fourteen weeks old, Nico. What if he needs me?"

"We'll have our phone with us. If there's a problem, we'll come home right away. And Erstilia's twenty—a responsible young woman, who could use a few extra lire to help with her university education."

He'd lowered Chloe to the ground, holding her so close that he felt every inch of her lithe and lovely body sliding against his on the way down. By the time her toes touched the floor, he was hard and wanting, and she...she'd looked up at him, her eyes clouding in that way they did when the passion began to run riot through her veins.

"Come with me," he'd whispered, talking about the restaurant, but meaning the other thing, too; the wild, unfettered loving that they did so well.

She'd sighed, her protest dying, and moved her legs apart so that he could run his hands up under her skirt, pull down her panties, and touch her in exactly the right place to make her whimper and shudder and beg. Then there, against the whitewashed wall just inside the front door, he'd taken her. Swiftly, urgently, with all the raging hunger of a man bewitched by his woman. Felt her contract around him, felt himself surge and explode.

"I love you, Nico," she'd sobbed, burying her face against his neck. She often cried when she came.

"And I adore you, *tesoro*," he'd replied, holding her close. "You are my life."

Luciano had started to wail then, as though he knew he was being left out. They'd drawn apart, smiling, and gone together to soothe him.

"I wouldn't feel right, leaving him," she'd said, leaning over the crib. "He's still so young."

But Nico had coaxed and wheedled until at last, reluctantly, she'd agreed they'd go out to dinner—but *only if* he'd let her wait until Luciano was asleep. *Only if* Erstilia was comfortable about being left with him. *Only if* they didn't stay out too long.

"What is this?" he'd asked, scowling in mock anger. "Am I now number two in your life, that my time with you is rationed to a few short hours?"

"You're my husband," she'd replied softly, "but he is my son and he depends on me to take care of him. Don't make me feel guilty about that."

"Don't make me feel selfish for wanting you to myself, for a change." He brushed his hand down her face and cupped her jaw. "Do you realize we haven't gone out together once in the last three and a half months, unless Luciano's been with us?''

She'd looked at him searchingly, nibbling the corner of her lip the whole time. ''All right, you win,'' she'd said at last. ''We'll go to dinner, just you and me.''

And they had, to one of Verona's finest *ristorante,* in the picturesque Ancient town neighborhood. Overriding her protests, he'd ordered an expensive bottle of wine, a meal fit for a queen and her consort, and laughed when she insisted on keeping the phone beside her on the table so that she'd be sure to hear it, if it rang.

''There's no rush, *cara mia,*'' he'd insisted, when she'd suggested they skip dessert and head home. ''You know Luciano will sleep a good eight hours. We'll be back long before he needs to be fed again.''

''It doesn't feel right to be away from him,'' she'd said.

''He doesn't even know we're gone,'' he'd replied, unable to curb the impatience creeping through his voice. ''*Per carita,* Chloe, I begin to think you don't even know I exist!''

The call that changed their lives forever came at precisely twenty-one minutes after eleven. She'd snatched up the phone on the first ring, and he'd known at once that something had gone terribly wrong. The blood had drained from her face, leaving her white as chalk. And her eyes…dear God, they were the eyes of a woman staring straight into the jaws of hell.

''No!'' she had said, quietly at first. And then over and over again, more loudly, until at last she was screaming the word, and people had come running from all over the restaurant to find out what had happened.

He'd tried to take the phone from her, but she clutched it so tightly that, in the end, he'd had to wrench it from her by force. "I can't wake him up," he heard Erstilia saying, her voice high and terrified. "Please, *Signora* Moretti, come home quickly. He will not open his eyes."

"Call for an ambulance," he barked, suddenly so short of breath that he could barely get out the words. "We'll be home in fifteen minutes."

They were too late. No sooner had they got to say "hello" to their son, than it was time to say "goodbye."

Sudden Infant Death Syndrome, the doctors told them; something no one could have foreseen. It was just one of those things, one of those cruel tricks of fate. No one knew why. No one was to blame.

But Chloe didn't believe them. She blamed him.

He hadn't been able to comfort her. *Dio,* he hadn't known how to comfort himself! The darkness had grown blacker, thicker, until he couldn't move away from it. Couldn't find his way back to the light. It took months...years, before he could look life in the eye again.

By then, he wasn't the same man he'd once been. He lost more than his son, that night. He lost his wife, too, and the best part of himself with her....

He turned away from the windows to confront the two women watching him with such hope in their eyes...such trust. "You're asking the wrong person," he said. "You're looking for a miracle, and that's something only God can grant."

Charlotte sank back in her chair, disappointed acceptance written on her face. But Jacqueline left the table and came to where he stood. "And God helps those who help themselves, Nico!" she said forcefully. "So I ask you again. Do you at least care enough for my daughter to make her stop and look clearly into her own heart, before she walks down the aisle a second time and marries a good man who, through no fault of his own, happens also to be the wrong man?"

Torn between his own selfish needs, and the common decency one man extends to another when a woman is involved, he drew in a breath so deep, he thought his ribs would crack.

Seeing his indecision, Jacqueline struck without mercy at his most vulnerable point. "If you won't do it for yourself or Chloe, Nico, do it for your son. Make Luciano's short time with us amount to more than a memorial to misery and grief. Make it a monument to the healing power of the love he brought into all our lives. He deserves better than to be remembered only for the tears."

CHAPTER FOUR

Sunday, August 23

GIVING up her west-end apartment at the end of July had been a big mistake, Chloe decided. It left her with no place in which to seek refuge; no place to escape the curiosity and gossip Nico's presence aroused. Because keeping his connection to her secret was impossible, something which became glaringly apparent that morning, when her godparents, Phyllis and Steve Stonehouse, who weren't expected until the Monday, showed up a day early.

At Jacqueline's request, Nico was on the patio, busy taking apart the barbecue, when they arrived, "Because," as her mother explained, "the left burner isn't working and I want to cook a salmon on it tonight."

"Well, I never!" Phyllis exclaimed, immediately recognizing him, and hugging him even though his hands were grimy and he had soot smears all down the front of his T-shirt. "Imagine seeing you, of all people! Are you here for the wedding?"

"Only by accident," he replied, favoring her with a grin that would have put a floodlight to shame. "It's coincidence that I happen to be here the same week that Chloe's getting married again."

Practically swooning with pleasure, Phyllis said, "Well, it's lovely to see you, whatever the reason!

52

And it's *wonderful* that you and Chloe have remained such good friends, even though you're divorced.''

Taking immediate advantage of her godmother's misconception, he'd slipped his arm around Chloe's shoulders and squeezed her fondly. ''I'll always want what's best for Chloe,'' he'd announced magnanimously.

What a liar! If he really had her best interests at heart, he'd have made himself scarce. Taken off for New Guinea, or some other far-flung port of call. But no, he was in her face every time she turned around, watching her every move, and smiling an enigmatic little smile the whole time, as if he nursed some hilarious secret.

After lunch—to which Nico was invited, though why he couldn't make his own meals in the lodge kitchen, was beyond her understanding—Chloe shut herself in the library, on the pretext of sorting through the wedding gifts still waiting to be opened, and writing notes of thanks. But concentrating was difficult, with the low murmur of Nico's voice drifting through the open French doors every other minute.

''Don't be ridiculous!'' her mother had scoffed, when he'd made diffident noises about spending the afternoon in his quarters because he didn't want to intrude on family time. ''It's too nice a day to be indoors. Get your swimming trunks, and join us by the pool. And if you really feel you have to earn your keep, you can man the barbecue later on. Whenever I use it, I more often than not end up setting fire to whatever I'm cooking.''

So there he was, sprawled out on a chaise, basking in sun and approval, and charming the socks off everyone. Meanwhile, Chloe, who had a *right* to be outside, hid in the library and tried not to give in to the urge to sneak a peek at him from between the slats of the blinds on the door.

Why bother? She knew what he looked like, wearing next to nothing. Too darn sexy for his own good—or hers! Which no doubt explained why she couldn't keep her mind on the task at hand.

"What am I trying to prove here anyway?" she muttered, tearing up another ruined envelope in disgust, and adding it to the pile of crumpled paper in the waste basket. "And why in the world am I ostracizing myself from relatives whose company I seldom get the chance to enjoy, and acting as if I don't belong, when *he's* the interloper?"

Because you're afraid of how he makes you feel, Chloe, the brutal, go-for-the-jugular lawyer in her replied. *If, as you claim, you're sure Baron's the man you want, you'd be out there enjoying the afternoon with the rest of your family, regardless of who else happened to be there, not hiding from temptation in here.*

"I'm not afraid," she informed the rows of crystal and sterling and bone china gifts, lined up accusingly on the big library table. "And I'm not tempted!"

No? her alter ego snorted. *You could have fooled me!*

Outside, a chair scraped over the patio paving stones, and Nico's voice, so loaded with the flavor of Italy that she could practically smell the medieval streets of Verona, floated on the air. "*Scusi, per favor, signore e signor.* Much though I'm enjoying your company, there's a business call I must make."

''Use the phone in the library,'' her mother was quick to offer. ''Chloe's in there, but I'm sure she won't mind being disturbed.''

Go ahead and do your worst, Mom! Chloe thought sourly, making tracks for the door to the hall before he could act on the suggestion.

But he had other ideas. ''*Grazie,* Jacqueline,'' she heard him reply, ''but I need my notes which are in my briefcase. Better, I think, that I phone from the lodge.''

''Well, all right. Just don't forget we're counting on you to take charge of the barbecue, later on.''

''It will be my pleasure.''

And mine, Chloe decided, scuttling upstairs to change into the sleek black one-piece bathing suit she'd been saving for her honeymoon, *to establish my rightful place in this cozy little family gathering, while you're gone.*

When he came back some thirty minutes later, she was ensconced in the chaise he'd previously occupied, with a towel draped ever so casually over her lap, sipping iced tea and giving a very good impression of utter indifference to his return.

''So,'' he murmured, dropping down beside her, ''you were waiting for me to leave before you came out to enjoy the afternoon?''

She lowered her glass, and swung her head toward him, eyes wide with feigned astonishment. ''*You* had nothing to do with it.''

''But you hoped I would stay away.'' There it was, the know-it-all smile.

''Believe it or not, Nico,'' she retorted scathingly,

''you play no part in any decision I make. I was busy earlier. Now I'm not. It's as simple as that.''

''Ah, yes.'' He shrugged off her lie with the same disregard that he rid himself of his short-sleeved white shirt, leaned back on one hand, and stretched his long, powerful legs out in front of him. ''Weddings can consume a person to the exclusion of all else, can they not?''

Unfortunately, in her case, *not.* At that moment, all her attention was fastened on him, despite her best efforts to keep her eyes averted. But the sight of Nico Moretti in navy swimming trunks, lazing like some great tawny cat sunning itself on the warm paving stones, was not a sight any woman in her right mind could ignore easily.

He'd said he had money now, and judging by the expensive rental car he was driving, the very classy gold watch he'd left lying on the patio table, the sunglasses he toyed with in his free hand, and the fine quality cotton shirt he so carelessly cast aside, she supposed it must be true. Yet his body retained the toughness of a man used to hard physical labor. No soft middle or overhanging waistline for him; he was all lean, iron-hard muscle, with arms as strong as ropes and shoulders wide enough to fill the average doorway.

I'm afraid I'll crush you, he'd sometimes say when they were making love, and he'd lift her on top of him, and settle her astride his hips, fitting himself so deeply inside her that she could almost taste him. *That's better,* he'd murmur huskily, cupping her breasts. *I can touch you...watch you...cosi bella....*

He had wonderful eyes; lover's eyes, dark and long lashed. With one meaningful glance, he could make her stomach turn over, her heart take flight, and leave her damp and aching for him.

Aware that his gaze was fixed on her now, that memory had left her nipples hard as pebbles and her skin flushed, she swallowed to relieve her parched throat, and said, ''Please excuse me. The sun's a bit more than I can take.''

Then, schooling herself not to scuttle away like a frightened mouse, she threw off her towel, and strolled as nonchalantly as she could manage along the deck to the deep end of the pool.

Leaping to his feet, he joined her, and making hardly a ripple, dived cleanly into the water. ''Come join me,'' he invited, surfacing with his hair plastered to his skull and his lashes clumped together in glistening black triangles.

''No, thanks!''

She shied away from the edge, but not soon enough. His hand shot out and fastened around her ankle.

''But if, as you already admitted, the sun is too much for you, why such reluctance? Surely there is no sin in two people sharing such a big pool, as long as they remain in sight of their three chaperones?'' His voice, already low and hypnotic, fell to a near whisper. ''So what is it that you're really afraid of, *tesoro?*''

''That I might not be able to resist the urge to drown you.''

The way he laughed tore at her heartstrings. There'd been a time when they laughed together so often. In public, sometimes, over silly things, but so infectiously that people hearing and seeing them would shake their heads and smile. And sometimes in private, in the quiet intimate way of a couple so deeply in love that all it took to make them happy was being with each other.

"I'll take my chances," he said now, and jerked at her ankle so suddenly that she toppled into the water almost on top of him.

They went under together in a tangle of arms and legs. Of tough masculine muscle and soft feminine curves colliding, then floating apart again. Of hands sliding and clutching at body parts they hadn't touched in years. Of such primal physical contact that Chloe's eyes flew open in shock, and she saw that he had his eyes open, too, and the fire in their depths was such that no amount of water could have quenched it.

Deliberately, he pulled her toward him again, his movements slow and graceful. She drifted close, flotsam caught in a tide too powerful to withstand. Felt herself bump gently against him a second time, limb to limb, hip to hip, shoulder to shoulder. Felt his leg slide between hers, his hands skim past her ribs to cushion her bottom and pull her intimately against him. Against the erection he made no effort to disguise.

Her lungs were burning, her heart thudding. She shook her head, pointed up to where the blue sky shimmered high beyond the water, and pushed against his chest. He nodded understanding, touched his mouth briefly to hers and, with a powerful kick, sent them both shooting to the surface.

"Were *you* trying to drown *me*?" she gasped, when she could draw breath enough to speak.

"No," he murmured ambiguously, his hands circling her waist, his thighs nudging at hers, and his gaze never wavering. "I was trying to save you."

"I don't know what that's supposed to mean!"

"Don't you?" he purred, his eyes stripping her to the soul.

"Chloe? Are you all right?" Another man's voice, horrifyingly familiar, cut through the moment, and Baron, his dear, dear face creased with concern, came running along the deck to where she and Nico bobbed like corks near the diving board. Worse yet, his parents, their expressions variously painted in shades of perplexity and disapproval, observed the entire scene from the patio.

Wishing she *had* drowned, Chloe kicked herself free of Nico's hold and grasped the hand Baron extended to haul her onto the deck. "I'm fine," she said, praying he'd attribute her flush to a coughing fit, and not the guilt which was the real cause. "I just...tripped into the pool and..."

"Swallowed too much water?" He smiled, and tucked a strand of wet hair behind her ear.

"Um...yes."

"Good thing you didn't hit your head on the diving board when you took a tumble."

Pity she didn't! At least if she'd knocked herself out cold, there'd have been some excuse for being found languishing in Nico's arms, and her future mother-in-law might now be regarding her with a smidgen of sympathy, instead of outright suspicion.

"What are you doing here, Baron?" Chloe asked, turning her back on the pool and its lone occupant. "I thought we weren't supposed to get together until Tuesday, at the town house."

"Well, that's the reason we stopped by, honey. I'm hoping you'll let me beg off going with you to meet the landscape architect. You've got a much better eye for design than I have, anyway, and I thought, since we're booked pretty solid from Wednesday on, that I'd take my folks up to Whistler tomorrow, for a couple of days. It's the only chance they'll get to see the area. They're flying home again right after the wedding.''

"Oh…well, of course. Do that."

"You're sure you don't mind being left behind?"

What, two days when she didn't have to deal with his overbearing mother, whose expression grew blacker by the second? "Not in the least! Go, and have a good time," Chloe said, almost as dismayed by her relief as she was to notice that Nico had swum the length of the pool, toweled himself off, and was in the process of being introduced to Baron's family by her godmother.

Phyllis, bless her heart, didn't subscribe to the theory that less was more; in her view, you could never have too much "more." And given the astounded disbelief with which Mother Prescott was regarding Nico, it was pretty obvious that she was being regaled with a whole lot "more" than she cared to hear.

"Yes, Chloe's *first* husband," Phyllis confirmed, as Chloe and Baron joined the group. "He lives in Italy, but he comes over on business once in a while, and always stays here, I'm told. Even though they're divorced, he's still part of the family. Quite an unusual arrangement, wouldn't you say?"

"Quite!" Mrs. Prescott replied frostily. "Baron's ex-wife is certainly not welcome in my home. I wouldn't dream of entertaining her." She turned a glacial eye Chloe's way. "Hello, Chloe. I gather we should have phoned before we dropped in. We obviously caught you unprepared.''

"Not at all, Mrs. Prescott,'' Chloe replied, meeting her glance head-on. "You're welcome anytime, as I'm sure my mother's already told you.''

"Exactly,'' Jacqueline said. "In fact, why don't the three of you stay and have dinner with us? Nico's going to barbecue a salmon, and there's plenty to go around.''

"He *cooks?*'' Mrs. Prescott regarded Nico with the kind of acute disfavor anyone else might have reserved for a serial killer. "I hope you aren't expecting *my* son to don an apron, once he becomes your husband, Chloe? I've always considered it the woman's job to prepare the meals.''

Clearly aiming to keep the peace at any price, Baron jumped in before Chloe could dish up an answer to that one. "Times are different now, Mother,'' he pointed out. "I daresay Chloe and I will share the household chores. Don't forget she plans to continue working at the law firm after we're married.''

"When I became a wife, I managed to pursue a career *and* cater to your father's needs,'' Myrna Prescott declared loftily. "I've no doubt that's one reason our marriage has lasted.''

Charlotte, who until that moment had been content to listen without comment, said mildly, "I rather think there's more to making a marriage work than who wears the apron. Chloe's grandfather served me coffee in bed every morning until the day he died—and we were very happy together for over forty-five years.''

"Which just goes to prove there's no right or wrong way to go about things,'' Jacqueline said, and gestured to the comfortable chairs scattered around the patio. "Have a seat, everyone, and I'll bring out a little refreshment. Chloe, will you come and help?"

"Of course." She nodded at the Prescotts. "Excuse me, please. I'll be right back."

"Well!" her mother exclaimed, the moment they were safely out of earshot in the kitchen. "If you didn't know before what's expected of a Prescott wife, I guess you do now!"

Beleaguered on every front, Chloe wilted in despair against the counter. "This whole wedding week's turning into a nightmare that never ends, Mom! First, Nico and now Baron's mother! What's next, I wonder?"

"Marriage, and spending the rest of your life with Baron," Jacqueline said somberly, removing plastic wrap from a tray of appetizers she took from the refrigerator, and turning on the oven. "And you do keep insisting how much you're looking forward to that. Or are you ready to admit you're having second thoughts on the matter?"

Chloe buried her face in her hands, caught in the sense of time running out, of impending doom, much like the opening scenes of a movie in which the camera switches from a car racing along a darkened road to a train speeding along the tracks. Without a word being said, people watching know instinctively that, sooner or later, disaster will hit, and all they can do is sit there helplessly, with the tension tightening like an unforgiving screw, until their nerves are ready to snap.

"Don't keep asking me that," she said brokenly. "I feel as if I don't know anything, anymore! My head tells me I'm doing the right thing, but…"

"Your heart tells you differently?" Her mother's

arms came around her. "Maybe you should listen to it, darling."

She wiped a hand across her eyes and broke away. "The last time I did that, it ended up getting broken. I swore then that I'd never let anyone put me through that kind of agony again."

"You can't control everything life throws at you, Chloe. Part of being adult means coming to terms with what fate hands out, and another part means having the guts to admit when you've made a mistake. If you're not ready to get married, just say so. It's not too late to call off the wedding, or even just postpone it. It won't *be* too late until you've said 'I do.'"

"Have you any idea what you're suggesting? Half the guests who live across country are already on their way here. There's enough stuff in the library to open a gift store. Baron and I have bought a town house. We've ordered furniture and rugs and window blinds." She stopped just long enough to draw an overwrought breath, then rushed on, "There's a five-tier cake being decorated, even as we speak, and over a hundred Cornish game hens had their necks wrung and their feathers plucked, to provide the main course at the reception!"

"So?" Jacqueline calmly popped the tray in the oven and began setting out wineglasses and napkins.

"So it's not just about me, Mom!" she almost screeched.

Her mother stopped what she was doing and fixed her in a very direct look. "Is it about Nico?"

Chloe turned to the window, unable to meet Jacqueline's gaze. Outside, her godparents were doing their best to keep Baron's mother and father entertained, which was surely a lost cause. Baron, meanwhile, stood to one side, chatting with Nico.

Both men were tall, well over six feet, but there the similarity ended. Baron was slender, and very handsome in a subdued, refined sort of way. With his wide, intelligent forehead, mild blue-gray eyes, and slow, sweet smile, he looked exactly like what he was: a fortyish, rather shy lawyer of indisputable moral integrity.

Nico, on the other hand, stood larger than life; a man who took it in his bare hands and bent it to suit his ambitions. Black-haired, dark-eyed, strongly built and tanned, he exuded raw animal magnetism at its most alluring. He had the face of a Roman centurion, all high, angular cheekbones and hard, determined jaw—and the driving will of a gladiator bound to succeed, or die trying.

By comparison, Baron was but a pale imitation of his predecessor. Not as searingly sensual. Not as wickedly humorous. And never as irresistible. But oh, so much less dangerous to love!

She relied on his steadying influence, his calm reason. He never made her feel as if she were teetering on a ledge, thousands of feet above a raging river. With him, she felt safe.

And not so very long ago, she'd thought that would be enough. She'd believed the days of wild, unfettered passion, like the turbulent teenage years, were something she'd outgrown; that she was ready for a more serene affair of the heart.

"Well, Chloe?" her mother persisted. "Just how much does Nico have to do with the way you're feeling?"

She took a last look at Baron. A late afternoon breeze blowing in from the sea played tag with his thinning hair and crept under his shirt to make a sail out of it. He tucked the shirt neatly into the waist of his trousers, and passed his hand over his hair, restoring both to order.

But Nico remained impervious, untouched. If Baron was the harbor which offered shelter from life's passing storms, Nico was the lighthouse, squarely facing whatever the elements chose to fling at him; daring them to defeat him, and relishing the challenge of the battles that might entail.

"He's got everything to do with it, Mom," she said, "which is exactly what you were hoping would happen when you invited him to stay here. But I'm not falling for it—or him. Not again. He's an adventurer, an irrepressible optimist who always comes back fighting, no matter how slender the odds of his winning. And that's not how I want to live my life anymore."

"Then everything's running according to plan?" The Prescott mother paused between sips of wine, and surveyed the company seated around the large patio table. The remains of the salmon Nico had cooked lay on a platter on a serving trolley, along with what was left of a tossed salad and a bowl of small *patate,* which he'd steamed and smothered in butter and oregano. "The wedding's taking place as scheduled?"

"Why wouldn't it be?" the groom inquired, reaching for Chloe's hand—a move which had Nico gnashing his teeth in envy.

"Oh, there's always the possibility of a slip-up

somewhere between saying 'yes' to a proposal, and 'I do' to a marriage, Baron.''

"Not for us," Baron informed his mother. "Next week at this time, Chloe and I will be in the Bahamas at the Atlantis Resort, dining on fresh Caribbean lobster, after a day of snorkeling with schools of tropical fish in the Paradise Lagoon."

"So that's where you're going." She sniffed delicately. "Since it's to be a summer wedding, I'd hoped you might choose to spend your honeymoon at the lake. You know how lovely it is there, at this time of year, how warm the water is, and how much you always enjoy swimming in it. What does the Paradise Lagoon have that's so very different from that?"

"Spend our honeymoon at the lake with you and Dad? You're not serious!"

"Well, not *with* us exactly. There are, after all, two cottages on the property, so you'd be quite alone, most of the time."

"Newlyweds usually like to be alone *all* the time, Myrna," the meekly mannered husband pointed out.

She set down her knife and fork, and regarded him sourly. "I might agree, if this were their first trip down the aisle, but spending a small fortune on a splashy honeymoon for a second marriage strikes me as being almost as tasteless as the bride wearing white."

"It just so happens that Chloe's dress *is* white," Charlotte said. "And I'm sure she'll look perfectly lovely."

"Actually, it's closer to off-white, Gran," Chloe murmured.

"As it should be," *la madre* ruled. "Under the circumstances."

Up to that point, he'd been content to sit back and observe. At this last remark, though, Nico decided Chloe's future mother-in-law had aired enough opinions on matters that were none of her business, and appointed himself to put an end to them. "I introduced Chloe to Venice on our honeymoon, but we didn't spend any time swimming in the canals, did we, *cara?*"

"Hardly," she replied, sending him a killing glare. "They were filthy."

"What else did you expect?" Myrna Prescott served up another disparaging sniff. "Venice always did carry its own distinctive...odor. The place has become such a cliché with tourists that they've completely ruined it."

"I don't consider myself a tourist, *Signora*," he said evenly. "I have lived all my life in Verona, *La Città degli Romeo e Giulietta.* You might not be aware that it forms part of the Venetian arc. Although there exists friendly rivalry between the two cities, they are close neighbors and I have spent many satisfying hours exploring the treasures of Venice."

"And is that where you learned to cook salmon like this?" She very pointedly pushed aside the food she'd barely touched.

"*That* I learned from my mother. Veronese traditional cuisine relies heavily on seafood."

"Far too much garlic for me, I'm afraid. I find it quite overpowering."

"Perhaps you'll find dessert more to your taste," Chloe said, rushing to keep the peace. "We're having *tiramisu.*"

"More Italian cuisine? Good gracious, my dear, if

you're so fond of the country, I can't imagine why you want to marry a North American and settle down here. You'd be much happier over there.'' She mopped her mouth with her napkin. ''I'll pass on the dessert, thank you. All other considerations apart, I'm watching my weight.''

As you should! Nico told her silently. *Dio,* but the woman was a viper! And her son, was he as much under her thumb as the husband, who merely sat there looking *imbarazzato,* instead of being man enough to speak up and silence her?

Jacqueline, catching his eye and giving a barely perceptible shake of her head before quickly looking away again, spoke up then. ''In my opinion, both countries have a great deal to offer.''

''And Jacqueline should know,'' the well-meaning but bird-brained godmother, Phyllis, piped up. ''She stayed for weeks when Chloe had her little boy.''

''You have a son?'' Scandalized, the virago turned on Chloe, who sat frozen in pale-faced misery.

''Er...Mother...'' Baron began. ''This isn't something—''

But she silenced him with a peremptory flap of her hand. ''You're surely aware, Chloe, that Baron has absolutely no interest in bringing up a child of his own, let alone someone else's?''

A pity she was a woman, Nico thought, containing himself with difficulty. Had she been a man, he'd have lunged across the table, grabbed her by the throat, and shaken her like a rat.

To his credit, Baron looked thoroughly outraged. ''Drop the subject right now, Mother,'' he ordered, a surprisingly steely edge to his voice.

''I will not! You can't expect me to stand back and

watch you enter another marriage doomed before it starts, not after—''

''Do not concern yourself, *Signora*,'' Nico interrupted harshly, cut to the quick by Chloe's whimper of distress, and the way she appealed to him for rescue, her eyes so wide and wounded that his own heart clenched in pain for her. ''Your son will not be inconvenienced by mine.''

''Oh.'' The Prescott woman blinked. ''You mean, the boy lives with you, in Italy?''

''You could say so. He is buried in the graveyard of a church close by my home in Verona.''

A moment's silence spun out before Jacqueline spoke. ''We can take our coffee inside, if you prefer. I'm finding it rather chilly out here.''

At that, at last, the husband spoke up. ''Thank you, but we won't impose on your hospitality any longer, Mrs. Matheson. I'm afraid we've already overstayed our welcome. Come along, Myrna. Let's leave these people to enjoy what's left of the evening if, in fact, that's still possible. Baron, we can take a taxi if you'd like to stay.''

''No,'' he said. ''I'll drive you. Chloe looks ready to collapse. I think she's had enough for one day.''

The gaze he cast on Chloe, full of tenderness, caused a stab of regret to spike through Nico. This Baron was a good man at heart; a likable man. And he loved Chloe. He wasn't to blame for things going wrong between them, and he deserved better than to be left standing at the altar.

But Nico knew better than anyone that it wasn't always possible to control fate. Sometimes, bad things happened to good people.

*   *   *

"Well?" Jacqueline regarded him anxiously when, having seen the visitors off, they escaped to the kitchen on the pretext of clearing up the remains of the meal. "What did you think of that performance?"

"That the not-so-good *Signora* Prescott has made up my mind for me," Nico said, the anger still simmering. "She does not want her son to marry your daughter, *cara,* and after tonight's episode, I will do my best to see that she gets her wish."

"I hope you succeed!" Jacqueline pressed the tips of her fingers to her forehead, as if to block out the worries besetting her. "That awful business about Luciano just about put Chloe over the edge."

"So I saw." He seized her hands and gave them an encouraging squeeze. "Don't despair, *mia suocera cara.* There is hope yet that we can avert disaster."

"Oh, I hope so." She worried her bottom lip. "But we have only five days, Nico. What if it's not long enough?"

"We can't control the passage of time. We must work with what we have."

"But Chloe's pride's on the line, and she's so torn she doesn't know which way to jump. What do we do if she digs in her heels?"

"That's no reason for us to give up. What is it you say in English—the large lady has yet to join the opera?"

She smiled for the first time in hours. *"It's not over until the fat lady sings!"*

"Then how fortunate," he said, drawing her into a hug, "that all the women in your household are so slender!"

CHAPTER FIVE

Monday, August 24

SHE awoke early, almost before the sun rose. Not that she'd slept much. Who could have, after yesterday's disastrous evening?

Quietly, so as not to disturb her mother and grandmother, she dressed in a pair of old shorts and a top, slipped through the side door behind the garage, and followed the trail through the woods, to the little clearing at the edge of the bluff where she'd played as a child. The tree house of her girlhood had long since disappeared, but the stone bench she'd loved as a teenager was still there, stained in places with a fine coating of moss, and covered with the remains of last year's fallen leaves.

She swept them aside and, hugging her elbows, sat down facing the water. For long minutes, she remained utterly motionless, letting the peace and tranquility soak into her bones, in the hope that it might clear her head. Her mind was cluttered with such chaos, her emotional resources so exhausted, that she couldn't think straight.

A squirrel, traversing a low-hanging branch, squatted on its haunches and regarded her from bright, inquisitive eyes. A nose-twitching rabbit popped out of the underbrush to snack on the sweet grass edging the path. To the southwest, the San Juans floated on a bank of morning mist; islands lifted straight from the pages of a fairy tale and set down on the shimmering blue sea. And all of it coming together to create the perfect setting for a happy-ever-after ending.

Was such a thing still possible for her and Baron? she wondered. Could she emerge from the maze of memories and confusion in which she was lost, and find her way back to him?

Suddenly, the squirrel chattered indignantly and scooted up the tree trunk, alerting her to the fact that someone else had approached. The rabbit froze momentarily, then hopped away to safety. A second later, Nico dropped down on the bench next to her.

Chloe wasn't really surprised to see him. Somehow, no matter how far apart they might be in miles or mood, they'd never quite severed that special intuitive connection of two people who'd once known one another so intimately that they anticipated each other's every thought. That he was there beside her now was strangely comforting; the one constant in a world gone suddenly haywire.

He didn't speak and nor, for a while, did she. They simply sat side by side, and stared across the curve of Semiahmoo Bay to Mount Baker's snowy peak, rising majestically south of the border, in Washington. Finally, without looking at him, she said, "How did you know where to find me?"

"I was walking in the garden, and saw you leave the house. I would have followed you immediately, but you seemed very pensive, and I sensed you needed some time alone."

"I did."

"Has it helped?"

She lifted one shoulder. "No."

"You're brooding about dinner, yesterday?" He made a noise deep in his throat; a growl of disgust. "The *infernale* mother of the groom, she needs to keep her mouth shut."

"It's not about her, Nico. She lives over three thousand miles away. We'll seldom see each other."

"No, it is not about her," he said, his gaze still focused on the view. "It is about you, *sì?*"

"Yes." A sigh shook her. "I have to learn to let go, to wipe out the past and concentrate on the future. I know that, up here." She tapped her forehead, then let her hand slide to her breast. "But I can't accept it *here.*"

"It is not easy to erase a portion of one's life."

"Yet you've managed it."

"You think so, *la mia bella?*" She felt, rather than saw his glance shift to encompass her. "You are mistaken. I have merely come to terms with those things I cannot change."

"How did you do that?"

"By remembering the good times," he said. "I was surprised at how many there were."

She turned to look at him then, as if, by doing so, she could draw on his strength. It was a mistake. His gaze locked with hers and wouldn't let go. It lured her very soul and, against her will, she found herself inclining toward him until his breath feathered over her face.

"And by refusing to concede defeat until the war is won," he whispered, just a nanosecond before his mouth ghosted over hers in gentle persuasion.

She knew it was madness to let her lips cling; to

close her eyes and submit without protest. Knew she should have turned aside at the last moment, and denied herself the illicit comfort of his kiss. It wasn't as if he held her and refused to let her go. He didn't touch her at all, except with his mouth. And then only barely.

But that was enough. Enough to remind her of how it used to be, before. Before it all went wrong.

When at last he pulled away, the terrible emptiness he left behind undid her. The floodgates opened, letting loose all the pent-up misery she'd suppressed for so long, and she burst into tears.

"Why are you crying?" he asked her gently.

"You know why," she said, around the sobs turning her voice harsh and ugly.

"You're thinking of Luciano?"

He remained so calm in the face of her distress, so completely in command of himself, that she flung the question back at him in anger. "Aren't you?"

"Always," he said. "But not in the way that you are. For me, the memories of our son, they shine, Chloe. I see him in the cool fresh air of morning, in the bursting open of flowers in the spring, the ripening of the grapes on the vine in early autumn. Everywhere I look, everything that touches me with its innocence and purity, reminds me of the great gift with which we were blessed. And I cannot believe such a gift doesn't still live, somewhere, somehow, and that one day I'll find him again."

"I wish I had your faith," she said bitterly, lifting the front of his T-shirt to wipe the tears from her face.

"I wish you had, too. I wish that you could heal." His voice hardened. "Perhaps then you wouldn't be racing headlong into a marriage for which you have no heart, with a man who cannot make you happy.''

She pulled away and glared at him. ''What gives you the right to make such an assumption?'' she cried, the sting of his rebuke more than she could bear just then. ''You don't even know Baron.''

''But I know you—well enough to recognize how little you're able to bring to this union. You have no raging hunger, no insatiable desire. None of the drive that makes you prepared to do whatever is necessary to hold on to him at all costs. You are in limbo, *la mia inamorata.*''

He was wrong. She was in hell, and had been ever since he'd walked back into her life! ''That's your male pride talking. You just can't stand the idea that I've found someone new.''

''Not so! What I can't stand is your self-deception. You used to be so honest, Chloe. When did you decide settling for second best was preferable to facing up to the truth?''

''I've never lied to Baron, or he to me. We've approached our marriage like mature adults, and are in complete agreement as to what we expect from each other.''

''And what is that, exactly?''

''For a start, neither of us wants children.''

''What if they happen anyway?''

''They won't. Baron took steps to make sure of that.''

''Ah,'' he said, that infuriating smile playing over his mouth again. ''He agreed to a little surgical snip-snip, did he?''

''You don't have to be so vulgar,'' she snapped.

"And you can wipe that smirk off your face, as well. Just because you're bursting at the seams with agile little swimmers doesn't mean a thing to me."

"It did once, *cara mia*. As I remember, you were rather thrilled about it."

"I've changed. The measure of a man has nothing to do with his sperm count."

"Did Baron undergo the procedure to please you?"

"No. He made the decision before we met. He's *never* wanted children."

"He might not want them," Nico declared, his tone taking on a brutal edge, "but if he marries you, he'll end up being a father anyway, because that's all you really want from him, isn't it, Chloe? Someone to lean on, someone to take care of you and shield you. Does he know there'll never be any grand passion between you, or are you doing such a good job of faking it that he hasn't yet figured out you're just going through the motions?"

"Our sex life will be just fine, thank you!"

"*Will* be?" He reared back and stared at her, his eyes dancing with evil amusement. "You mean to say, you don't already *know?*"

She sniffed scornfully, as if he'd asked the most absurd question yet to be uttered by modern man. At least, that's what she aimed to do. But the blush scorching her face put paid to her effort in a hurry.

Of course, he saw right through her pathetic attempt to bamboozle him. "You haven't made love with him, have you?" he said, feigning astonishment. "He has to settle for a chaste kiss. Or do you let him put his tongue in your mouth and touch your breasts, once in a while, just to keep him hooked?"

"It's none of your business," she replied, investing her answer with a healthy dose of haughty disdain, "and I can't believe we're having this conversation."

Unimpressed, he said, "I can't believe he's prepared to go through with this charade of a marriage. Wake up, Chloe! I might not know Baron well, but I know what a man expects of his woman. How long do you think he'll put up with a wife who's merely going through the motions, who brings no real commitment to the relationship?"

"My goodness," she scoffed. "I had no idea you were such an expert on what makes a marriage work!"

"I learned firsthand that, as long as there is love, the rest at least stands a fighting chance of falling into place." He caught her hands, turned them over, and before she could guess his intent, bent his head and pressed his mouth first to one palm, then to the other. "I learned, too, that love doesn't die just because you want it to. If it's the real thing, it endures regardless."

Shockingly, a streak of pure sexual pleasure sizzled the length of her, and settled with stunning impact between her legs. "Stop that!" she whimpered, making a feeble effort to tug herself free.

He wouldn't release her. Instead, he slid his mouth to her inner wrist, to where her pulse ran so hard and fast that it was a wonder it didn't leap out of her skin. "We had all the love in the world, Chloe," he murmured, looking up at her from beneath the dense sweep of his lashes. "It was what made the magic between us."

"But it didn't last, Nico," she said sadly. "Our son's death killed whatever we once felt for one another."

"Did it? Then why do I find myself aching to hold you again? To kiss away the shadows lurking in your lovely eyes? To feel you, warm and alive and eager, beneath me?"

Another surge of sensation bolted through her, leaving her underwear damp with yet another flush of melting heat. "You have no right to be saying such things to me now."

"Why not?" Lifting his head, he exerted just the slightest pressure on her wrists. Pulled her just close enough for his chest to brush tantalizingly against her nipples. "What I'm saying doesn't strike a chord with you?"

She sighed, capitulation sweeping over her so fiercely that she couldn't find the wherewithal to lie. "More than you know!"

"Then stop fighting it." His voice flowed around her, casting a low, hypnotic net. "Let yourself feel again, *tesoro*. Set yourself free."

Suppressing an inner shudder, she said, "I can't, Nico. I'm afraid."

"Don't be afraid. Trust yourself. Trust me."

Trust me, Baron had said. *Know that I will never hurt you.*

"Chloe...*preziosa*...!" Nico's arms went around her. His lips roamed over hers, drawing her ever closer to the edge of destruction.

"I can't do this," she sobbed, wanting to so badly that she ached with the pain of it. "It's not right!"

"It feels very right to me."

She slapped out wildly, at his chest, his shoulders, his upper arms. Anger was so much easier to deal with than fear. ''Because you're selfish and don't care about anyone but yourself!''

He let go of her so suddenly that she almost tipped backward off the bench. ''You are the selfish one, *cara mia*,'' he declared flatly. ''You would shackle a man to you for no other purpose than to use him as a shield between you and anything you perceive to be hurtful. You would condemn him to a living death, just as you've condemned yourself.''

''If that's what you think of me, then you should be grateful I had the good sense to put a stop to your seduction before it went any farther, because God forbid I should end up choosing *you* over Baron! But then, that's not exactly what you want to have happen, is it? Your only aim is to make me doubt myself, and spoil what I have with him.''

''Why would I bother, when you're doing such a good job of that all on your own? Why *is* that, do you suppose? Because you think you don't deserve to be happy again? Is this your way of punishing yourself for Luciano's death?''

''I'm not the one who insisted on leaving him with a sitter, that night. If anyone needs punishing, it's you!''

''But of course it is,'' he said, his words dripping with sarcasm, and smacked his forehead with the flat of his hand. ''Nico, *stupido,* how is it that you weren't blessed with divine foresight enough to realize the tragedy about to befall you? How come you're but a man, instead of God?''

''If you hadn't been so hell-bent on going out, if you'd let me stay home with him, the way I wanted to—''

"You could have done nothing. Do you hear me, Chloe? *Nothing!*" He started out softly, and ended roaring like thunder, so filled with fury and frustration that she almost cowered.

"You don't know that for sure!" she retorted shrilly. "If I'd been there, I might have realized the moment he stopped breathing, and been able to help him. But no, you had to have things your way. You had to show off by taking me to a restaurant we couldn't afford, and spending money we didn't have, and for what? Who did you think you were impressing, while our son lay dying?"

"You," he bellowed, his eyes shooting sparks, his jaw thrust forward belligerently. "*You!* But you were too wrapped up in our baby to notice. Sometimes, I think it was a blessing that he was taken from us because, had he lived, you would have smothered him with your coddling and turned him into a *mammono*— a mother's boy tied to her side by her apron strings!"

"At least he'd have known he had one parent who cared about him!"

They were hurling words at each other; using them as missiles to wound and destroy. And as the realization struck home, they sank into an appalled silence punctuated only by their ragged breathing. By mutual consent, they drew apart and stared out to sea again, because they couldn't look one another in the eye.

Seconds ticked by; became a minute, then two. Chloe knew she should leave, that she was courting disaster by exposing herself to the gravitational pull existing between them despite everything. Yet she remained motionless, too drained to move.

At length, he said quietly, "Do you remember the

last time we sat side by side on a hard stone bench in August?''

''In Verona, in the Roman amphitheater. You took me to the opera there. We forgot to bring cushions.''

''But we didn't notice. We were too wrapped up in the music and each other.''

''I'd found out that morning that I was pregnant.''

''And you told me just as Act 3 started. I missed the rest of the performance after that. You were all I could see or think about.''

''Not exactly,'' she said. ''You stood up and announced to the entire arena that we were expecting a *bambino*. You made such a fuss that people around us started complaining and told you to sit down and be quiet, or else take me home. But you said I deserved better than to spend the night in such a poor, cramped apartment.''

''So I did,'' he said, something of a smile in his voice. ''Instead, we drove into the country, to a place by the river that I'd known as a boy.''

''On our neighbor's Vespa which you 'borrowed' without asking.''

''*Sì*, and it was wonderful! You sat behind me, with your arms wrapped around my waist, and your body pressed close to mine.''

''And you sang at the top of your voice, the whole way. It's a wonder we weren't arrested for disturbing the peace.''

''I was serenading my pregnant wife. The *polizia* would have understood.'' His tone grew husky with nostalgia. ''What a magical night we had, there on the banks of the Adige. The grass and trees, the shadows deep enough to hide a couple hungry to possess one another…do you remember, Chloe?''

Remember? She could almost smell the sweet green scent of summer, the musky scent of love! If she closed her eyes, she'd see the pale glimmer of moonlight on naked limbs, hear again his impassioned murmurs and her own sighing responses. ''Vaguely. As I recall, we slept there until sunrise.''

''We made love, *cara mia,* all night long. We celebrated your pregnancy in the same way that we promoted it. With passion and tenderness. We lay naked in each other's arms beneath the stars. You cannot have forgotten that.''

Oh no, she hadn't forgotten!

''I laid my head against your belly and whispered to our child.''

He'd done a lot more than that! He'd sunk his head lower, eased her legs apart, and with an unerring instinct for knowing exactly how to arouse her, settled his mouth *there.*

''For you, little one, from your papa,'' he'd murmured, and blown gently against her flesh, to send his kiss fluttering inside her.

Already aroused to fever pitch, she had shattered into orgasm. Clamped her thighs together and held him captive at her core. And he, intimately acquainted with every nuance of her sensuality, had played his tongue over her, prolonging the ecstasy.

After, when he'd found release also, they remained locked together and watched the sunrise. ''This child will never know want, Chloe,'' he'd promised. ''I will provide handsomely for him and for you. Before long, we'll live in a mansion, with servants. You'll drive an expensive car, and shop in all the best places.''

"I don't need servants or a fancy car," she'd told him. "All I'll ever need is you."

"You have me, for now and forever."

But in the end, it hadn't been enough. When push came to shove, they'd hadn't been able to help one another. Instead, they'd isolated themselves in their separate grief, and *forever* had translated into a lifetime without the son they'd loved so dearly.

"Now it all seems so long ago," he said, with palpable regret.

She nodded. "In some ways, yes."

So long since she'd held her baby in her arms and felt his sweet breath winnowing against her neck. So long since he'd tugged at her breast, and splayed his tiny fingers over her skin. And yet, not long enough. It would never be long enough for her to accept the unkind stroke of fate which had affected her so profoundly. Even all this time later, her nipples ached and tingled, as if preparing to release her milk. She still cried herself to sleep, sometimes. A sudden reminder of what she'd lost could still leave her eyes stinging with tears in the middle of a busy day.

It didn't take much: watching a mother chase her toddler through the fallen leaves in the park; a little boy, the same age as Luciano would have been, sitting on Santa's lap in the mall, certain that life really was full of miracles.

Stirring, Nico said, "A great deal has changed in the interim."

"Has it?"

"*Senz'altro!* For a start, you're engaged to another man."

"And what about you, Nico?" she asked, glad to shift the conversation to another topic. Luciano's death was never something she could discuss with equanimity. "Is there a new woman in your life?"

"At present?" He shook his head. "No."

"But there have been others, since me?"

"*Naturalmente.* You surely didn't expect me to live like a priest?"

"Of course not."

"Yet you disapprove?"

"I have no right either to approve or disapprove," she replied, with just the right note of indifference. "You're single, and free to associate with whomever you please."

Yet the truth of her answer stung, which she hadn't expected. Somehow, whenever she'd thought about him in the years since they'd divorced, he'd always been alone. But she had only to look at him to realize the arrogance of such an assumption. He was a man in his prime; handsome, successful, confident and sophisticated. If she'd found him irresistible when he had nothing, inevitably other women would be even more attracted to him now.

"Do you think you'll marry again?"

"Of course, when the right woman is ready to say 'I do.'" He shrugged. "I am, after all, only thirty-four. I do not see myself living without the comfort and companionship of a wife for another fifty years. It is not in my nature."

Shaken, Chloe realized that *she* did not see him with anyone but herself. That he could so calmly discuss

the idea of sharing his life with another woman...!
"What about your family?" she said, hastily turning
to another subject. "Your sisters, how are they?"

"Doing very well. Carmina and Rogero had another
baby last year, a daughter at last, bringing them up to
four children. Just as well, otherwise Rogero would
have been in trouble. Abree and Chiaro have three
girls."

"What about Belva? She was pregnant when I left
Verona."

"She had a boy, Sabatino. He's four now. And since
then, there've been two more boys, Augusto, two, and
Vincenz who just turned one."

"And Delia? She has children?"

"Three. Blanche, who'll be four in December, eigh-
teen-month Milinda, and the latest, a boy, Riccardo,
just two months old."

"How lovely!" she said, working her tongue around
the bitter taste of envy nipping at her words. So many
babies, and not one of them lost!

Not that she'd wish such tragedy on anyone, least
of all a family who'd embraced her with so much
warmth and kindness. Indeed, their sorrow had almost
matched hers when Luciano had died, and they'd come
together *en masse* to try to comfort her. But she'd
barely been able to acknowledge them, surrounded as
they were by children of their own.

"*Sì.*" Nico laughed ruefully. "And how noisy,
when they all get together!"

"You must be a very devoted uncle, that you remember how old each one is, and keep tabs on their
birthdays."

"I love them," he said simply. "They are part of my family."

"I guess your mother's kept busy when they all come over for Sunday dinner."

A shadow passed over his face. "My mother died last year."

"Oh, Nico, I'm sorry! I didn't know. I remember her with such fondness. She was always wonderful to me."

He cleared his throat. "I don't know if you'll want to hear this, but her last words to me were that she would look after Luciano for you, and that he wouldn't be alone anymore."

The damnable tears, always so ready to betray her, flooded Chloe's eyes.

Dashing them away, she choked, "How like your mother to be thinking of others at such a time."

"She loved you, *cara*. We all did."

"I loved you, too."

And could again, if I let myself!

The thought rose unbidden to her mind, shocking her. It was too late to be second-guessing her feelings, she reminded herself sternly, overwhelmed yet again by the inexorable sequence of wedding preparations marching through her mind.

Ice sculptures, beluga caviar, pagoda tents, red carpets, string quartets, dance bands; the corsages and bouquets and table arrangements and rented linens and chairs; her wedding dress, hemmed and ready to be collected from the bridal boutique, her going-away outfit, her suitcases still needing to be packed...dear heaven, was there no end to it all?

"Are you happy, Chloe?" The question, gently uttered, washed over her like a shroud.

She could not look at him. Dared not. "What do you think, Nico?" she said, staring off into the distance.

"That you are the saddest bride I ever saw. That your heart is empty, and you find yourself backed into a corner from which you see no escape."

He was wrong. Her heart was full to overflowing—with regret for what, in her horrifying fall into despair, she'd left behind. For what she'd thrown away, out of fear and hopelessness. And most of all, for the fact that she'd left it too late to rectify her mistakes.

"Supposing you're right, Nico," she said, worrying the diamond solitaire on her ring finger, "what do you suggest I do about it?"

CHAPTER SIX

Tuesday, August 25

JACQUELINE phoned him just as he was heading back to his office after a lengthy business lunch. "I know you've got enough on your mind today, and can probably do without me asking for favors, Nico—"

"But you have a problem and would like my help," he finished, recognizing an uncommonly frantic edge in her voice. "What's the trouble, Jacqueline? Don't tell me Chloe and Baron have eloped?"

"Not that, thank heaven! To the best of my knowledge, he's still at Whistler with his parents. But because I had to bring my car in for servicing this afternoon, and Chloe wanted to stop by her office before she met with the landscaper at her new house, we came in together, in theory to save us bringing two vehicles across town."

"But that wasn't the real reason?"

"No. She's so hung up on all the wedding arrangements, Nico—the expense, the *material* things—that she's lost all sense of proportion. And that, I'm afraid, is my fault. She never wanted an elaborate affair, but I went ahead and turned it into a huge production anyway. I hoped, if I had some time alone with her, I might persuade her to look past all that and consider the untold cost, to herself and Baron, if she insists on ignoring the very real doubts she has that she's making a mistake in marrying him.''

''And were you successful?''

''No. She still insists it's just stress that's making her so antsy, and that she'll be fine once all the fuss and folderol is over. But you and I both know that's not the case.''

''Indeed not. She is in turmoil.'' And frighteningly close to breaking point, as he'd realized yesterday morning when he'd drawn her into his arms. Her body had been racked by fine tremors, not easily detected by the naked eye, perhaps, but impossible to miss upon close physical contact. She was as fragile as thistle-down in a breeze, likely to fall apart without notice. And he wasn't helping matters. ''Unfortunately, Jacqueline, I don't think she'll be any more forthcoming with me.''

''But that's not why I'm calling. No, the problem is, my car's still being serviced and won't be ready until closer to five-thirty—something to do with the air-conditioner not working. But Chloe's stranded at the town house and expecting me to pick her up around four. I can't call her, because she accidentally left her cell phone in my car, and the telephone isn't hooked up at the new place yet.''

''So you would like me to pick her up and take her home, is that it?''

''Oh, if you could, it would really help. I've got a hairdressing appointment in ten minutes, followed by a list a mile long of other things I still need to get done, and time's slipping away at an alarming rate. But I've borrowed a courtesy car, and could run most of my errands if I didn't have to worry about meeting her on time.''

''Consider it done.'' He fished a pen from his inside pocket. ''What's the address?''

She rattled off directions, which he scribbled on the back of the restaurant bill, told him he'd saved the day, and hung up.

''But who will save the bride?'' he wondered aloud, dodging the traffic as he crossed the street to the tall office building on the other side.

Making his way through the crowd in the lobby, he rode the elevator to the fifteenth floor and strode down the hall to where a heavy glass door bore the *NM-Internazionale* logo. Even after two years, seeing it still gave Nico a thrill. Success and money were things he never took for granted.

Donna Melino, his Vancouver-based shipping broker, met him in the reception area. ''Nico, we've got big trouble,'' she greeted him, something he'd already figured out from the look on her face. Normally unflappable, she was clearly agitated.

''Come into the office,'' he said sharply in Italian, conscious that the receptionist and junior assistant were all ears and wide, curious eyes. ''Whatever it is, there's no need to advertise it to the whole world.''

''I'm sorry,'' she said, once the door was closed and they had complete privacy. ''I didn't mean to be indiscreet, but I'm afraid I'm in a bit of panic.''

''I'd never have guessed!'' He filled a glass with ice water from a carafe on the credenza and handed it to her. ''What happened? Another foul-up on the docks? A shipment not coming in on schedule?''

''Worse.'' She held the side of the glass against her

flushed cheek and closed her eyes. "That container ship you purchased—"

"What about it?"

"The sale's fallen through. I just heard from Bob Holmes, the vendor's agent. They can't deliver, after all."

"What the devil do you mean, *they can't deliver, after all?* They damned well *have to!* They signed a contract!"

She flinched at his subdued roar, and looked at him wearily. "Try telling that to Mr. Holmes, Nico. He'll be here momentarily. I warned him up front that he'd be dealing with you on this one."

He paced the floor, struggling to keep his anger under control. But the ramifications of the situation went far beyond a sale gone sour. He stood to lose money—a lot of money—and perhaps more important, a reputation he'd worked hard to earn.

The prospect brought out the street fighter in him. On the surface, he might look like an executive in his tailored Italian suit; a man of moderation and reason, who never got his hands dirty. But inside, something of the boy he'd once been still remained. He remembered how it felt to be cheated.

He'd been fifteen, the first time it happened. For months, he'd saved his earnings from delivering groceries and running errands for the neighborhood merchants, all so that he could afford a Polaroid camera. His plan had been to photograph tourists and sell them instant pictures of their time in Verona. Even then, he'd been an entrepreneur.

For two weeks, he'd tasted success beyond his wildest expectations. And then, in the space of time it took for him to hand over a print of an elderly couple standing on the *Ponte Pietra,* a youth raced past and snatched the camera. Nico had given chase and caught the thief, a boy of about seventeen, both taller and heavier than he'd been at the time, but he hadn't let that deter him.

The scuffle had been brief but furious. He'd retrieved his prized possession and left his adversary bleeding in the gutter. What he hadn't known was that the kid belonged to a gang of four whose specialty was petty crime. The other three had come after him that evening, and this time the fight was longer and more vicious. He went home with a black eye, a bloody nose, and a cracked rib. But he left the others with three missing teeth, and two split lips among them, as well as enough scrapes and bruises to keep them howling for a week.

After that, word had spread: *don't mess with Nico Moretti.* It was a lesson *Signor* Holmes was about to learn.

"Make sure, when he arrives, that we're not interrupted," he instructed Donna grimly. "In fact, why don't you and the office staff leave early for once? Go to Stanley Park and enjoy the sunshine."

"Nico, you're not a juvenile, sorting out your grievances in the back streets of Verona, and let off with a slap on the wrist if you play rough," she warned.

"You're absolutely right, Donna, *la mia amica.* I've learned a thing or two since those days. Don't worry. *Signor* Holmes will walk out of here unaided—but he'll be sweating when he does so."

* * *

Although heat still hung heavy in the air, the afternoon had turned overcast, with ominously dark clouds scudding in from the west and banking steeply against the Coastal Range. A summer storm, Chloe thought, surveying the small, enclosed garden behind the town house. The landscape architect had proposed elaborate plans for creating the illusion of space there, with clever plantings around the patio, and a miniature waterfall trickling down the back wall into a raised pond.

Poor man! He'd become somewhat irritated by her lack of enthusiasm for the project. She should have explained that nothing much held her interest anymore—nothing, that was, except the forbidden subject of Nico Moretti.

The first fat raindrops, forerunners of the deluge shortly to follow, left black spots the size of dimes on the pale stone of the patio. Lightning flickered over the distant mountains.

Going back into the house, Chloe rinsed out her water glass at the kitchen sink, and glanced again at her watch. Almost five-fifteen. Her mother was over an hour late, probably caught up in traffic, with commuters trying to beat the storm as they headed home, but it was unlike her not to phone.

Restlessly, Chloe wandered from room to room, squaring a cushion here, straightening a painting there, but bypassing the master suite with its connotations of married intimacy. Baron had been gone two days, and she had not missed him once. She didn't want to think of sharing a bed with him. Couldn't afford the time. There was too much to do between now and Saturday.

A quarter to six, and still no sign of her mother. What could be keeping her?

Giving the towels in the guest bathroom one last twitch, Chloe returned to the second floor sitting room where she'd left her purse. Jacqueline hated talking on the phone when she was driving; said she found it too distracting. But the storm was right overhead now, turning the evening prematurely dark, and Chloe was beginning to worry.

From the window, she could see past the courtyard complex to the road. Cars swished by, their headlights throwing a bright arc ahead of them, water spraying fountain-like from beneath their tires. The wail of sirens a block or so away competed with the intermittent crack of thunder. Like it or not, Jacqueline was about to take a call.

Chloe was still rooting around in her bag for her phone when the doorbell finally rang. "Thank God!" she muttered, and ran down to the main floor foyer to let her mother in.

Instead, she found Nico on the doorstep, his expression as dark as the weather. The rain dripping from his hair joined that already staining the shoulders of his pale gray suit. The knife-sharp pleat down the front of his pants had softened to a gentle curve. *"Merda!"* he grumbled, unceremoniously pushing his way past her. "How do you live in such a climate?"

"Nice to see you, too," she retorted, furious at the way her entire body leaped with sensual awareness at the sight of him. The tumult in her stomach alone was enough to leave her feeling faint, and never mind other, less decorous parts that fairly throbbed with delight. "And just for the record, no one asked you to stop by, so don't bother taking off your jacket."

Ignoring her, he hung it on the brass coatrack and

surveyed his shoes grimly. "Save your sweet welcome for someone else, Chloe. I'm not here to make myself at home. Jacqueline sent me."

"Why isn't she here herself? What's happened to her?"

"Nothing but a slight inconvenience, which is more than I can say for my shoes. They'll never be the same again. Remind me to wear hip waders, the next time I visit Vancouver."

"Stay away from Vancouver, and you won't have to bother," she said, barring his way when he went to climb the stairs. "And what do you mean by *a slight inconvenience?*"

"She had problems with her car, and was delayed. I had expected to be here much earlier, but I, too, had other matters requiring my attention. I'm sorry if you were alarmed."

"She should have phoned and let me know. I could have taken a taxi home."

"I wish that had been possible. I have better things to do than chauffeur such an ungrateful passenger more than fifty kilometers past the city limits. But if you'd tried using your phone, you'd have realized why it was impossible for her to do as you suggest, since you don't have it with you. Jacqueline found it in her car, after she'd dropped you off at your office. So, instead of throwing up obstacles at my every word, why don't you behave like the gracious hostess you were brought up to be, and offer me something to dry off my hair? Your mother would be scandalized if she saw how you're treating your guest and savior."

Some savior! He threatened everything Chloe held dear: peace of mind, stability, security...all the things she'd fought so long and hard to achieve and thought were so vital to her happiness, but which, since he'd barged back into her life, didn't seem so important, after all.

"I'll go get you a towel," she said, being anything *but* gracious because that was the only way she could arm herself against him. "And you wait here."

Once again though, he ignored her, as she discovered when, towel in hand, she turned to leave the powder room on the second floor, and found him blocking the doorway. "Very *elegante*," he decreed, eyeing the black toilet and washbasin, gold faucets and towel rail, and deep burgundy walls appraisingly. But the mockery in his tone suggested he found the overall effect amusing, rather than chic.

"*We* like it."

"Do you?"

She flung the towel at him. "Yes!"

"*Buono.*" He cast around another wry glance. "At least someone appreciates it."

Seething, she watched as he took his sweet time mopping his hair and finger-combing it into some sort of order. The sooner they were on the road, the safer she'd be.

But he quickly dashed that hope. "*Grazie,*" he said, handing back the towel, then stood there regarding her expectantly.

"Now what?" she snapped, just about at the end of her rope.

"Aren't you going to give me the grand tour of this place you claim to like so much?"

"Certainly not," she said, wishing he'd move. The powder room was never meant to accommodate two people, especially not when one of them was his size. He was stealing so much air, she could hardly breathe. "You're going to drive me home. Now!"

"Not as long as this rain lasts. I had to park over two blocks away, and you'll get soaked running to the car."

"So what? I won't melt."

"But I might, especially if you keep shooting sparks at me from those beautiful blue eyes."

"Stop it, Nico," she said, her voice quivering almost as badly as her insides. "We aren't going to do this again."

"Do what, *tesoro?* All I'm suggesting is you show me your new home while we wait for the rain to pass. What did *you* have in mind?"

"Absolutely nothing," she replied, exhausted with his taunting. It was easier to give in than try to match wits with him. And agreeing to show him the rest of the unit at least meant they wouldn't both be crammed in the smallest room in the house. "If a tour's that important to you, a tour is what you'll get. Follow me."

He did, more closely than he needed to, so that the scent of him—wet hair faintly spiced with whatever shampoo he'd used that morning, a lingering trace of aftershave, and summer-fresh rain—wafted around her in tantalizing invitation. Deciding the only way to resist falling under its spell was to keep three steps ahead of it, she fairly raced him through the various rooms and levels.

"That's it," she told him, winding up in the kitchen, five minutes later. "Everything there is to see. Satisfied?"

"*I* don't have to be," he replied, trapping her in his molten gaze. "I'm not the one who has to live here. But if I were faced with such a choice, I tell you plainly that I'd rather live in a tent than find myself cooped up in this tall, sterile chimney of a home, with so many stairs, and rooms so small."

"Considering where you grew up, I'm surprised you can afford to be so critical," she shot back, miffed. "As I recall, you and your sisters lived above a shop, in only four rooms, all of them tiny. You showed me where you slept as a boy, in an alcove off the kitchen."

"Because my parents were poor and after my father died, that was the best my mother could provide for us. But the windows on one side looked out on a street alive with color, and on the other to the Adige river. And there was such love and laughter under that roof that we never missed the luxuries so important to those born with a silver spoon in their mouths. But what do you have here, Chloe, apart from a high-rent address?"

He shamed her with his answer; made her feel shallow and pretentious. Looking at the house through his eyes, she saw that "sterile" suited it very well. Everything was too pristine, too perfect, and the total effect completely devoid of soul.

"It's different for us," she explained, trying to justify the sleek Art Deco furniture, the efficient stainless-steel appliances. "Baron and I are out at work all day. We'll spend only the evenings and weekends here—and even then, not always. We didn't want a place that required a lot of upkeep. Our whole aim was to be able to lock the door and go away, without having to worry about hiring a house-sitter to water plants or feed a dog.''

''Just as well.'' He shot a disparaging glance at the three feet of floor between kitchen counter and breakfast nook. ''Even a small dog could not be happy here.''

''It's an adult-oriented unit, not intended for dogs or young families.''

''Adult-oriented, hmm?'' He studied her, his gaze sweeping her from head to toe. ''Is that why you're choosing to leap into middle age?''

''Middle age?'' she choked. ''What the hell do you mean by that?''

He shrugged insolently. ''Well, how else would you describe yourself, all neatly repressed in your lawyer's stark black power suit, with your hair scraped back into a breakfast bun, and your eyes so empty that you might as well be dead?''

Another brilliant flash of lightning struck, occurring almost simultaneously with a deafening crack of thunder, and a second later the lights went out, throwing the area into gloomy relief. Rain pelted the skylight at the top of the stairs.

''I don't know what's put you in such a sour mood today, Nico,'' she told him, raising her voice above the din, and choosing to rise above the urge to stab him with a kitchen knife. ''If it's having to go out of your way to pick me up, I apologize. But if you can't find something positive to say about my new home— or me, for that matter!—I'd just as soon you didn't say anything at all.''

He wiped his hand down his face and sighed. ''You are right, *cara.* I am not being kind. The truth is, I had an unpleasant afternoon, but that is no reason to behave badly toward you."

Hearing the weariness in his tone, she softened. "Something to do with business?"

"Everything to do with business." He shook his head and stared out at the dismal afternoon. "Sometimes, I think I was happier when I was poor and thought I had nothing. I seldom lost sleep over that." His shoulders lifted in another shrug, this one laden with self-deprecation. "Of course, when it was too late, I learned that I had more than any other man on earth, and realized the true depth of loss—but that's another story, one with which you're already familiar."

"What happened this afternoon?" she said, steering him away from the personal and back into the much safer waters of the professional.

"A sale I had thought was final didn't come to pass."

"Something big?"

"A ship, Chloe. Your once-impoverished ex-husband already owns six, and had fancied himself about to acquire a seventh."

"Ships?" No amount of self-discipline could hide her astonishment or stop the gauche reply falling out of her mouth. "Good grief, Nico, you must be filthy rich if you can afford to buy ships!"

He almost smiled. "I suppose I am."

"Ships…!" Try as she might, she couldn't shake the astonishment from her voice—or quite wrap her mind around the fact that he'd managed to parlay risky, small-time ventures into a successful world-wide enterprise.

"Don't let your imagination run wild, Chloe," he advised, accurately reading her mind. "I'm not talking about Mediterranean cruise ships with swimming pools and casinos. Mine are ocean-going container ships carrying cargo from all over the world."

"So that's the reason you have business here?"

"Certainly. As you must be aware, Vancouver is the largest foreign tonnage port on the west coast of North America. My ships arrive here regularly, carrying goods from Asia, Europe and South America."

She swallowed and tried not to gape. "You must be very proud of having accomplished so much in such a short time."

"You'd think so, yes? Yet today, I am not so proud. I am ashamed. I fancy myself a gentleman of means, but this afternoon I behaved like a thug, losing my temper and threatening a man who was nothing but the unfortunate go-between for someone every bit as unscrupulous as I can be when things don't go my way."

"Why, Nico?" She sank down on the window seat in the breakfast nook, disturbed by his admission. "During our marriage, you craved success. Pursued it with a determination bordering on obsession. Why, now that you've found it, isn't it enough? Why does it matter that you weren't able to buy another ship?"

"It matters," he informed her flatly, "because it amounts to more than a sale falling through and Nico Moretti having one less toy to play with. A domino effect is taking place. My Vancouver agent has sold container space contingent upon my having that extra vessel in operation. I am unable to honor those commitments. My company's reputation is at stake. I have to subcontract the work out to another shipping line, at substantial cost to my company.''

''And money is important to you.''

It was a statement of fact, not a question, and he recognized it as such. ''I have made it important,'' he said, joining her on the window seat. ''It has driven me to where I am today. It is why I ignored the advice the experts gave me, and staked everything I had on a fleet of ugly, seaworthy vessels with plenty of cargo space. Not the kind of thing you'd choose for a honeymoon cruise, certainly, but then, I'm dealing with freight, not romance.''

''And you prefer that?''

''It suffices,'' he said, staring down some dark, invisible tunnel of regret. ''Marriage, love, they can turn on a man and squeeze every last drop of blood from his heart. Can take the things he prizes above all else in the world and turn them to dust. But if he acquires worldly possessions, he retains control of his life. They keep his bank account healthy without robbing his soul.''

''Oh, Nico, I'm so sorry!'' she whispered brokenly, grabbing his hand in both of hers. How, when Luciano died, could she have been so caught up in her own pain that she never fully understood Nico's? Why couldn't they have turned toward one another, instead of away?

''Don't be.'' Misunderstanding, he swung his empty gaze on her. ''I shall overcome this latest setback, because it has to do *only* with money. And that is something a man can hold in his hand and bend to suit his will. And if, by chance, he loses it through some unkind turn of fate, there is always more where it came from.''

''But is it enough to make you happy?''

''Does anyone ever have enough of anything, for that?'' His hand tightened over hers, crushing her engagement ring against her finger. ''Are *you* happy with all you have? With this sleek, expensive town house, with your work?'' He glanced down as she winced and tried to withdraw her hand. ''With this big diamond ring, and the man who gave it to you?''

''What if I were to say I'm not?'' she said, bringing them back full circle to the question she'd put to him yesterday. ''What would you have me do about it?''

And just as he had yesterday, he threw the question back in her lap. ''Why ask me, Chloe, when you're the only one who knows that?''

''Because I'm afraid of the answer,'' she quavered, all her carefully constructed defenses crumbling under his scrutiny. ''Because, despite everything, I'm very much afraid that I'm still in love with—''

Something slapped wetly against the window just then and remained plastered there, cutting short her confession. ''The landscape blueprints!'' she wailed, leaping up and running to the sliding door to rescue them.

They came away from the glass in soggy strips, their neat blue lines blurred beyond any sort of recognition, and clung to her fingers when she tried to spread them over the kitchen counter. ''I was supposed to keep these for Baron to see, and now look at them!'' she cried, silly, pointless tears rolling down her face. ''Now they're ruined, just like everything else to do with this marriage!''

"Perhaps destiny is trying to tell you something," Nico said, watching her. "What is it they say, about the best laid plans going astray? Maybe this is a sign. What were you about to tell me, before you allowed yourself to be interrupted?"

"I don't remember," she lied.

"I do. It had something to do with your still being in love with something." He came closer, unpeeled the paper from her hands, and pulled her around to face him. "Or was it someone, Chloe?"

Beside herself, she said, "You know it was. And you know *who* it was."

"I want to hear you say it again, and I want you to look me in the eye when you do so."

She couldn't keep up the charade. Never mind pride or decency; right or wrong. The truth would not be silenced. *"I'm still in love with you! I'm afraid I always will be! There! Are you satisfied?"*

Her words emerged on a howl of pain, and she braced herself for whatever, and however, he might reply. With amusement? Distaste?

But he did nothing, and instead let the silence spin out until she wanted to die from the shame of her outburst. "Say something," she muttered. "Tell me I'm hysterical, a fool. Just don't leave me drowning in nothingness."

"I do not have the words, *tesoro*. All I have to offer you is this."

He took her in his arms then, as if he had every right to do so. And she went willingly, because it *felt* so right to do so. For the first time since he'd stormed back into her life, she offered no resistance. Instead, she lifted her face for his kiss.

His lips were gentle. Warm, tender, life-restoring. They blotted out time, silenced conscience. They gave her courage.

Outside, the rain continued to batter against the window. Inside, her heart beat an echoing tattoo. The blood pounded in her veins. A bone-deep, aching need to feel alive again consumed her.

Yesterday faded. Tomorrow didn't exist. Nothing mattered but this moment.

CHAPTER SEVEN

Wednesday, August 26

IF CHLOE had known ahead of time that her matron of
honor had planned a bridal breakfast, she'd have
locked herself in her room and refused to come out.
As it was, she had no idea a celebration was in the
offing until she shuffled into the morning room and
found her grandmother, godmother and Monica lined
up, ready to squeal, *"Surprise!"*

She didn't need any more surprises. After last night,
all she wanted was to be left alone—in a room with
no mirrors, so she wouldn't have to look at herself and
see the shame and guilt stamped all over her face.

Numbly, she allowed Monica to steer her to the seat
of honor at the round table. A huge balloon bouquet
floated above her chair. "I'm not dressed for a party,"
she mumbled, painfully aware that she was the only
Cinderella in the room. Barefoot and wearing an old
denim skirt and white blouse, she needed only an
apron and floor mop to complete her ensemble.

"You look absolutely perfect!" Misty-eyed,
Charlotte surveyed her fondly. "Doesn't she,
Phyllis?"

Chloe's godmother beamed. "Of course she does!"

But Jacqueline, coming from the kitchen to pour
champagne and orange juice into her best crystal
flutes, looked as if her smile had been glued into place,

and her penetrating gaze left Chloe squirming in her seat. "She looks exhausted, if you ask me! What time did you get in last night, Chloe?"

Had it been ten o'clock, or half past? "I'm not sure."

"You waited out the storm, I assume?"

"Yes. By then, it was well past the dinner hour, so we stopped for a bite to eat on the way home."

"I need a drink," Nico had declared, when they'd finally ventured from the town house and made a run for his car. "And from the looks of you, you could use one, too."

Her mother's glance didn't waver. "Everything went well yesterday afternoon?"

Chloe lowered her eyes, afraid of what they might betray. "Not quite the way I expected."

"But you're pleased with the outcome?"

Pleased? Hardly! What woman about to become one man's wife could approve how she'd behaved with another? Yet despite her guilt, the memory of what she and Nico had said and done last night, left her insides fluttering with forbidden pleasure.

"This is not a good idea," he'd murmured against her mouth, when that first, comforting kiss had strayed beyond the boundaries of decency into much more compromising territory.

"I know."

"We should stop now, while we still can."

"Yes."

But he continued to kiss her, and she made sure he didn't stop. She ran her fingers over the polished cotton of his shirtfront and renewed acquaintance with

*the lovely, sculpted planes of his chest. She felt his
heart thudding in time with hers.*

*Lured past all caution, she undid the buttons and
slid her hands inside his shirt. Oh, the tactile bliss of
rediscovery! Crisp dark hair and smooth tanned skin.
Muscle and bone; sinew and strength.*

"Here, girlfriend." Monica reached over, tucked a
linen napkin on Chloe's lap, and raised her glass.
"Happy breakfast, happy wedding, happy life!"

Chloe did her best to smile and project the image
of radiant bride everyone but her mother seemed to
expect. Lifting her own glass, she stared blindly at the
beads of moisture on its delicate surface.

*He'd lifted his head. "La mia inamorata," he'd
whispered thickly, his eyes devouring her, "do you
know what you're doing? Where this will end?"*

"I don't care," she'd told him.

*"But you will care, once you've had time to reflect.
You aren't one who likes to live dangerously. You've
said so yourself, many times in the last few days."*

*She'd pressed her fingers to his lips. Shaken her
head in reproof, shushing his well-intentioned warning. The intensity of his gaze had seared her. Rendered
her weak and oh, so willing!*

*Without volition, her head had fallen back, leaving
her neck exposed and vulnerable. Eyes heavy with desire, she'd watched the rain slip-sliding down the window in long, diagonal streams.*

*Then his mouth was doing the same, but tracing a
path from the corner of her mouth to her jaw, and
from there down her throat, leaving behind a chill,
damp trail that made her skin pucker.*

He ducked his head lower…lower. Nudged aside the

*collar of her blouse, worried its buttons with his teeth
until, frantic with impatience, she pushed him aside
and with her own two hands ripped the damned things
open and unsnapped the front clasp of her bra.*

*His mouth danced over her naked flesh, evoking lost
sensation, invoking newer, greedier desire. She whimpered a soft plea. He answered with another deft touch
of his tongue. Lit a fire in her that sent warmth shooting from her toes to the distant, befuddled area of her
brain that cared not a whit for what was decent or
proper, but craved only him.*

"What happened to your appetite, dear?" Her godmother shook a reproving finger at the minute amount
of food on Chloe's plate. "You need to keep up your
strength. Getting married takes a lot out of a woman."

"I'm just so…overwhelmed. I had no idea you'd
planned all…*this.*" Chloe eyed the tray of fresh fruit,
the Belgian waffles heaped with raspberries and snowy
mounds of whipped cream, the Canadian back bacon,
the hot chocolate, poured from her grandmother's
prized antique china mocha pot, and drunk from
matching cups so delicate they were almost transparent.

She nearly gagged. Repressing a shudder, she said,
"You shouldn't have gone to so much trouble, especially not with everything else that's going on this
week."

"You didn't leave us much choice," Monica
pointed out. "You wouldn't let me host a bridal
shower, but I'm your best friend as well as your matron of honor. I wanted to give you something special
to remember."

"*I've tried to forget you, Nico,*" she'd whispered,

holding the back of his head close, to imprison his mouth at her breast.

"Some things are meant to be remembered, tesoro. You and I, together as a couple, are among them," he said, *before closing his lips over her nipple.*

He swirled his tongue around its beaded tip. Nipped gently at it with his teeth, then drew it deep into his mouth. The ensuing electrical charge short-circuited the last of her control. She let out a startled squeak and arched convulsively as a spasm shook her.

Growling low in his throat, he straightened to tower over her. Fleetingly, his palms cupped her breasts, shaped her ribs, smoothed over the slight curve of her abdomen, the flare of her hips.

He caught at her skirt and gathered it up, a handful at a time, until it lay bunched around her waist. Then cushioning her bottom, he brought her up snug against him; against his erection, thrusting powerfully despite being confined by his clothing.

From behind, his hand stole between her legs. They fell slackly apart, giving him freedom to wreak whatever havoc he chose. His finger caressed the strip of smooth bare skin above her stockings, and eased under the elasticized edge of her panties. Found the slick seam of her femininity. Stroked over it lazily. Once, twice.

The second spasm shook her to the core. She staggered, dug her fingers into the firm muscle of his shoulders, and clutched at him for support. He raised the pressure a notch, trespassed more deeply between the folds of her flesh. Sank his fingers deep inside her.

And all the time, from the front, he rocked against her, the rhythm of his movements measured and delib-

erate, awakening a clawing, desperate need in her. She wanted to touch him; to hold him in both her hands and return in full measure the same exquisite torment he inflicted on her.

She wanted to prolong the moment, to make it last all night and for the rest of her life. But he was making her come, and nothing she could effect could prevent the climax from gathering strength. It rolled closer; threatened to destroy her. But she wanted him to die with her. Wanted to hear again his stifled groan of defeat. Feel the hot, urgent spurt of his seed. Taste life again in its most elemental form.

Catching him by surprise, she wrestled down the zipper at his fly, and found the opening in his shorts. Already he was seeping with the prelude to full ejaculation.

Beholding his awesome strength again, feeling the heavy, silken weight of him in her hand, tipped her over the edge. Burying him between the soft inner curve of her thighs, she rode the lavish tide of orgasm. Let it wash over her in undulating waves, each more ferocious than the one before. And realized, from the sudden hot stream scalding her skin, that she had not traveled alone to that sublime and distant place. Nico had succumbed as helplessly as she.

''More hot chocolate, dear?'' Charlotte held the mocha pot poised over her cup. ''Or would you prefer something cooler—juice, perhaps? You're looking a little flushed.''

''Water would be nice,'' Chloe managed, using her napkin to fan her face. ''With lots of ice.''

''If you're all done eating, we can get started on the fun part.'' Monica rolled forward the brass tea trolley loaded, Chloe noticed belatedly, with ribbon-tied boutique gift boxes.

"Now you're really going overboard," she protested. "The breakfast was more than enough."

"The breakfast was merely the introduction. This is the main event."

This turned out to be elegant trousseau items nestled among layers of tissue paper. A silky peach peignoir trimmed with creamy marabou feathers; a very brief, very sexy nightie; sheer cream stockings to match her wedding shoes; high-cut panties paneled in embossed satin and embroidered with dainty blue forget-me-nots. And perhaps the most extravagantly ridiculous of all, a Merry Widow strapless bridal corset threaded with ribbons and overlaid with cobweb-fine lace.

"You'll need nimble fingers to help you get into this," Phyllis predicted, counting the long row of hooks and eyes down the back.

"That's where I come in," Monica said. "We'll have a dress rehearsal, just to make sure we don't run into any snags on the big day. But it'll have to wait awhile because we've got something else to take care of, first."

Unable to contain her dismay, Chloe said, "Oh, please! Not another surprise!"

"Try to act like the blushing, ecstatic bride you're supposed to be, instead of a prisoner about to be given a lethal injection," Monica admonished. "Although now that I come to think about it, you're not having too much trouble blushing this morning. If I didn't know better, I'd think you had a guilty conscience."

"I do," Chloe said, grasping at the first plausible excuse to present itself. "You've got a husband and two children who need looking after. You shouldn't be here, spoiling me.''

"Your mother and grandmother did most of the work. I just gave directions.'' Monica squeezed her arm affectionately. "Don't look so worried, girlfriend. Nothing terrible's about to happen. We just decided we'd do the 'something old, something new' thing today, instead of waiting until Saturday, that's all. By then, you'll have a houseful of guests and likely be pressed for time.'' She produced a shiny, tiny gift bag patterned with daisies. "So here's your 'something new' from me.''

Chloe's heart flopped around inside her chest like a wounded bird when she saw the gold locket, engraved with her new initials. They'd been *C.A.M.* all her life, including the years she'd been married to Nico. There was something disturbingly final about the curlicued *C.A.P.;* it marked a definite break with the past.

"I expect you know what the 'borrowed' is,'' Jacqueline said matter-of-factly, dropping a jeweler's box into her lap. "Grandmother Matheson's pearl and diamond necklace and earrings. They'll look quite lovely with your wedding dress.''

"And here's a blue garter,'' Phyllis tittered, swinging the ruffled item around on one finger until it twirled like a demented merry-go-round about to take flight. "Wear it below the knee, dear, in case Baron wants to remove it with his teeth.''

God forbid! Chloe thought miserably, awash with memories of the clever things Nico could do with *his* teeth. The thought of *any* other man taking such liberties made her flesh crawl.

"I didn't wrap mine because we've been using it,''

Charlotte said, coming to sit beside her. "I'm the 'old' part, Chloe—in more ways than one, as I'm sure you're aware!—and I'm giving you my mocha set because I know how much you've always loved it. I had planned to give it to you when you and Nico…" She stopped and pressed her lips together a moment, the way a woman might, to control the onset of tears. "Well, that's another story altogether, and I've learned it doesn't do to put things off, or the chance to give pleasure to someone you love might not come around again. So enjoy this in good health and happiness, my darling, and think of me when you use it."

Chloe opened her mouth to thank her grandmother, and burst out crying instead.

"Oh, nice going!" Monica teased. "You really know how to turn a party into a howling success!"

"I'm so sorry," she choked. "Please forgive me. It's just that everything's suddenly…too much…." *Because the person whose forgiveness she should really be seeking was Baron.*

"Pre-wedding jitters," Phyllis pronounced sagely. "I've seen it often. You'll be all right, dear, once you start down the aisle. One look at Baron, and you'll forget you ever heard the words 'nervous bride.'"

"Exactly," Jacqueline said, with dismaying good cheer, as if all the doubts she'd formerly expressed had disappeared overnight. "Dry your tears, and I'll open another bottle of champagne. I think we could all use it."

Blotting her face with her napkin, Chloe pushed herself away from the table. "Let me. It'll give me something to do besides make an idiot of myself."

But her mother had already disappeared and was in

the butler's pantry before Chloe caught up with her.
"Go back to the party, Chloe," she instructed, stoop-
ing to retrieve another bottle of Bollinger from the
wine cooler. "I can manage this perfectly well on my
own."

But, "I'm not leaving," Chloe said flatly, "until
you clear up something which has me totally confused."

"Sure, if I can." Jacqueline spared her a passing
glance before concentrating on stripping the foil from
the neck of the champagne bottle. "What's on your
mind?"

"Why are you going along with all this celebrating
when, more than anyone, you've been trying to dis-
suade me from marrying Baron?"

"Well, there's not much point in beating a dead
horse, is there, dear?" her mother replied airily. "You
insist you know what you're doing, so I'm taking you
at your word. If you'll forgive the mixed metaphors,
it's your bed and you're the one who'll be lying on
it." She set about untwisting the wire restraint securing
the champagne cork, her face the very picture of innocence. "You do *know* what you're doing, right?"

"What have I done?" she'd moaned, after it was
*all over and they'd made themselves presentable
again.*

*Nico, stationed at the window with his hands
jammed in his pockets, had turned and fixed her in a
disturbingly blunt stare. "Do I have to spell it out for
you, cara? We just made love. I know that, for you,
it's been a while since the last time, but you surely
can't have forgotten how it feels?"*

*"No, we didn't go quite that far," she'd protested,
making a hopeless bid to acquit herself.*

"Because I wasn't inside you when I came?" Self-loathing colored his reply. *"That's a questionable technicality at best, and I refuse to hide behind it."*

"But we didn't actually... I wasn't totally unfaithful to Baron."

But Nico wouldn't let her get away with that specious line of reasoning. *"In your mind you were,"* he said implacably. *"In your heart, too, if you were telling the truth when you said you're still in love with me. Any woman who admits that to a man other than her fiancé is guilty of infidelity, no matter how she tries to rationalize it."*

Limp with despair, she'd sagged against the kitchen counter. *"So now what do I do?"*

"That's not my decision to make, Chloe."

"Is that all you have to say?" she'd cried, desperation lending a shrill edge to her reply. *"It's not your decision to make? I didn't notice you backing off so discreetly a few minutes ago, so why the sudden reticence? Are you saying that you're washing your hands of me, now that you've had your daily fix?"*

Utter disgust transformed his face. His mouth—the same mouth which had seduced her so expertly minutes before—tightened in anger, and his eyes, recently smoldering with passion, glowed with unbridled contempt. *"If that's all I wanted, there are women who would gladly accommodate me, for a price—one considerably less than you're going to exact, I suspect."*

He'd never before spoken to her so harshly; never adopted so cold and cruel a tone. But then, much about him was changed from when they'd been married. He'd become harder, tougher, in every respect. More brutal, less compassionate.

This was how he'd achieved success in business ne-gotiations, she'd realized, standing her ground with difficulty: unwilling to compromise; uncaring that he might leave his opponents crushed. "If, by that, you're suggesting I'm going to cite you as co-respondent in what just took place between us, you can relax, Nico," she said, drawing on what few scraps of pride she still retained. "Our dirty little secret is safe with me simply because I'm too ashamed to speak about it to anyone, even a priest!"

"You think keeping quiet about it will absolve you?" He made a sound midway between a sneer and a jeer. "Then I pity the poor unfortunate marrying you on Saturday! And I pity you, Chloe. I thought you were possessed of more backbone and decency than that."

His disdain lacerated her. "It's easy to despise something you don't understand, Nico, and you've never understood me. Never understood that I don't have your strength or your bold courage."

"And you think admitting to weakness exonerates you from honesty, and justifies deceiving a man like Baron?"

She looked away, unable to meet the absolute lack of respect she saw in his eyes. "You seem willing enough to deceive him. I don't hear you offering to come clean with him about the way you behaved, the minute his back was turned."

"I'm not the one marrying him. Nor do I have a fiancée waiting for me at home. I am free to do as I please, with whoever chooses to be with me at the time. And you came to me of your own free will, cara mia."

He turned the endearment into an insult. Shame-faced, she whispered, "I know that."

"And do you also know how you're going to act like the willing wife, on your wedding night? Have you thought about how you'll feel when your husband climbs into bed beside you and exercises his conjugal rights, and you cringe from his touch because he's not the man you really want?"

"Baron would never force himself on me!"

"Perhaps not, but he'd be less than human if he didn't expect you to cooperate when he finally gets you between the sheets."

"You're a pig, Nico Moretti, do you know that? You reduce everything to the level of...of..."

"What?" he'd snarled. *"A common Italian laborer, who grew up in a four-room apartment over a bakery, and should have known better than to think he could lay his dirty hands on a rich American princess?"*

She clamped down hard on her lower lip, to the point that her teeth drew blood. But even that punishment wasn't enough to still her trembling chin. *"Don't you dare label me a snob, on top of everything else! I loved you for yourself, not for what you did or didn't have. And I'm sorry I made that remark about your home. You know I didn't mean it. I'd have lived in a cave, if that's the best you could have given me, and counted myself fortunate to call myself your wife."*

"Until I made the cardinal mistake of proving myself fallible and no more capable of sparing you tragedy than any other man," he raged, *"and then you couldn't wait to boot me out of your life! So much for your protestations of love, Chloe!"*

"That wasn't why I left you," she flung back.

"Don't tell me it was for another man—for Baron.

I'm not sure I can survive the irony, given this afternoon's events.''

''How dare you even suggest such a thing! I invested everything of myself in you, my marriage, my son. Everything! But losing him ripped a hole in me that never healed. It left me with nothing to fall back on. I couldn't help you or myself. I was of no use to anyone.'' The anger fueling her words dwindled into quiet despair. *''Divorcing you had nothing to do with not loving you. It had to do with my own emptiness. I had nothing left to give you, Nico.''*

''You have nothing to give Baron, either,'' he said mercilessly. *''I feel sorry for him, always trying so hard to please you. He will end up 'dominato dalla moglie' just like his father.''*

''Dominated?'' she exclaimed, latching onto the one word that had some meaning. *''By me?''*

''Exactly by you. He will be chicken-bitten.''

For a moment, she'd stared at him, bewildered. Then, understanding dawned. *''Henpecked, you mean?''* she said, so outraged she could barely enunciate. *''You're actually accusing me of being just like Mrs. Prescott?''*

He gave a careless shrug. *''They do say men marry women who remind them of their mothers. I suspect you'll prove the truth of such a legend.''*

''You bastard!'' She flew at him, hell-bent on wiping the smug expression off his face.

But his reflexes were quicker, and he fended her off easily enough with one hand by planting it squarely in the middle of her chest. This time, there was nothing seductive in the way his fingers splayed between her breasts, nor anything the least bit pleasurable. Instead, *the two of them remained caught in a tableau defined by disillusionment and ugly recrimination.*

At length, as the fight seeped out of her, he lowered his hand and said, "Enough of this. It serves no useful purpose."

"No," she agreed, turning away from him, embarrassed. "None at all."

Only in the exhausted aftermath of their own fury did they realize that the storm outside also had subsided. The rain had stopped and the shredded clouds thinned sufficiently to allow a pale suggestion of moonlight to touch the windows.

"Dio!" Nico said softly, staring out at the dark, sodden garden. "Is this what we've come to, that we lash out at each other and utter hurtful words that can never be taken back? How do two people who once were so closely attuned, find themselves so far apart that they cannot leap the distance between them?"

"I don't know," she'd wept, the ache of all they'd lost gnawing at her and laying bare her frailty. "I just wish things had ended differently. Then we wouldn't be in this place now. You wouldn't feel such disgust for me, and I wouldn't be carrying a burden of guilt that nearly kills me."

"It wasn't all bad. We knew some good times, didn't we, before everything fell apart?"

"Yes," she said, aching for those lost, enchanted years. Remember it all, she'd chided herself. Remember the pain, as well as the pleasure, or how else will you ever go on?

But memory was selective and chose to settle on the whispered words of endearment they'd shared, the tight interlocking of bodies, the deep, intense silence of completion. Of love. Of absolute faith in the future.

She let out a painful sigh. *"I wish we could turn back time, that we could find our way back to what we once had."*

"But we can't. We can only go forward." He shot back his shirt cuff to look at his watch. *"And speaking of time, it's almost eight and we should head back to your mother's. Shall we stop somewhere for dinner, first?"*

"If you like," she said, snatching at any chance to delay the inevitable. To experience another stolen hour with him, because that was the most he was prepared to offer.

Soon enough, she'd have to face the fact that, the second she confessed she was still in love with him, her already jeopardized future had spun completely out of control. Any hope she'd entertained that she could make a life with Baron had gone up in flames.

And what had been Nico's reply to her admission of love? *"I do not have the words!"*

But although she'd listened, she hadn't heard. Hadn't wanted to. Because what he'd really said was that he couldn't return her sentiments. He might still have found her desirable enough that he'd lost control of himself sexually, but not enough to say he still loved her, too.

He'd stripped away the intervening years, all the healing she thought she'd accomplished since their divorce, and left her with nothing. Having convinced her that marrying Baron would be her biggest mistake yet, he considered his work done, and was willing to walk away, and leave her to live with the consequences.

"It's taking you a long time to answer," her mother said, wrapping the champagne bottle in a clean white towel. "Are you quite sure you know what you're doing?"

Chloe lifted her shoulders in a hopeless, defeated shrug, ready to spill out the entire truth in all its ugliness and beg her mother's help, when the door to the butler's pantry swung open and Baron came in.

"Charlotte told me I'd find you in here," he said, pulling her back to lean against him and nuzzling her neck. "How are you, Chloe?"

"Surprised," she said, chill with horror at what he might have overheard, had he arrived a moment later. "I wasn't expecting you until later this afternoon."

"We came back early. Last night, as a matter of fact." He dropped a kiss behind her ear. "The weather changed at Whistler, making it pointless to hang around, so we headed back to town."

"You should have let me know."

"I would have, but by the time I'd stopped by the new house to show my parents where we'd be living, then taken them to dinner, it was getting pretty late."

She went cold all over. "You stopped by the town house?"

"Yes."

Totally unaware of the potential fall-out from his revelation, Jacqueline hoisted the wine bottle. "And you got *here* just in time to join the party, Baron. Care for a glass of champagne?"

"Sure," he said, after a momentary hesitation. "It's not every week that a man gets married. By all means let's celebrate."

But Chloe, still reeling from his alarming disclosure,

couldn't let it drop. "What time? What time was it when you got to the town house?"

"I can't say precisely. Eight, maybe? Half past?" He shrugged unconcernedly. "Somewhere around then."

"Seems no one was aware of time passing last night," Jacqueline remarked slyly. "Strange how that happens sometimes, isn't it?"

Chloe shot her a quelling glare. Not noticing, Baron said, "What was even stranger is that when we arrived, half the lights in the place were on. How come, Chloe?"

"I forgot I hadn't turned them off," she said, guilt at what had *really* distracted her causing unpleasant pinpricks of perspiration to speckle her skin. "The storm caused a power failure."

"So they told us, when we got to the hotel." His brow furrowed in surprise. "But that happened around seven. What were you doing, still hanging around at that hour?"

Her mouth ran dry and her lungs contracted. "We—um, that is, *I*..." She coughed lightly to cover her embarrassment, and tried again. "Well, I was..."

"I drove her into town, since I was going in myself anyway," her mother said, finally coming to her rescue, "but I ran into car trouble and wasn't able to pick her up on time."

A completely truthful answer riddled with lies, Chloe thought despairingly. Where would it all end?

"Oh." Baron nodded sympathetically. "I'm sorry I wasn't here to help out."

Not nearly as sorry as I am, she told him silently. *If you'd been here, I might still be able to look you in the eye without flinching!*

CHAPTER EIGHT

Thursday, August 27

JACQUELINE came to see him early that morning, banging on the door just after seven o'clock. "Do you know what day it is, Nico?" she demanded, when he answered.

"*Sì*. I am well aware." He retraced his steps to the kitchen, leaving her to accompany him or not, as she wished.

She wished, following so close on his heels that she almost tripped him. "Then you realize we're running out of time? That if *something* doesn't happen in the next forty-eight hours, we'll have left it too late to avert a disaster?"

When he didn't reply, but simply continued preparing his morning meal, she planted herself squarely in front of him. "Listen to me! I've tried everything with Chloe—reason, sarcasm, persuasion. As a last resort, I've even changed tactics and started acting as if this marriage is the best thing to come along since the invention of the wheel. But none of it's working, and I'm fresh out of ideas, Nico. It's up to you, now."

He heaved a sigh and swung away from her accusing gaze. "I have done enough, Jacqueline," he told her, pouring boiling water over the coffee he'd measured into the press-pot and lowering the plunger. "In all conscience, I cannot continue to make Chloe's life a living hell. I have endeavored to open her eyes to the truth of what she is doing. I believe she knows that marrying Baron Prescott is no longer feasible, and that canceling the wedding is her only option. But I cannot make the choice for her.''

''You could, if you offered her an alternative.''

''Then let me rephrase my reply. I *will not* make the choice for her. I will not be the reason she does not go through with this wedding. That is a decision she must arrive at on her own.''

''But she is *miserable!* Anyone who knows her can see that.''

''She is not miserable enough. If she were, she'd do something about it.''

''What if she doesn't have the strength?''

He poured the coffee. ''Then she must live with the consequences.''

''Perhaps you can abide by that, but I'm her mother, and I can't,'' Jacqueline said, accepting the mug he passed to her. ''She's my only child, Nico, and she's suffered enough in her twenty-eight years. I can't stand by and watch her stumble into more unhappiness because she thinks it's all she really deserves.''

Seeing the distress on her face, he touched her arm in sympathy. ''Yes, you are her mother, Jacqueline, but you are also wise enough to know that you cannot always protect your child from hurt. Chloe is a grown woman. An intelligent, educated woman. She understands better than most what heartache a marriage gone wrong can cause, and not just from her own experience. She deals with such cases every day in her work. If, despite knowing this, she persists in going forward with her plans, there isn't a thing you or I can do about it. We have interfered enough. More, some would say, than we had any right to do in the first place.''

A sheen of tears filmed her eyes. ''I really thought all that time the two of you spent alone on Tuesday evening would do the trick. When nine o'clock came, and you still hadn't brought her home, I hoped it was because you were keeping her out all night. That would have been enough, Nico. She'd have canceled the wedding by now, if the two of you had made love. But of course, you'd never have let things go that far without declaring yourself.''

He could not look at her, this woman who'd welcomed him into her home and her heart, and who continued to treat him like a beloved son. *Your faith is misplaced,* he should have told her. *I do not deserve your trust or your affection.*

In truth, he could barely look himself in the eye. He'd snatched at the excuse to be with Chloe, to make one last bid for *them.* He'd done it because he couldn't let her go, because he loved her still—or so he'd told himself. But what kind of love brought a woman nothing but pain and heartache? By what right did he march back into her world and turn it on its ear?

Was it really for love, or because he wanted to punish her? Because she'd been *his* trophy, and he couldn't stand the idea of her belonging to another man? Was that why he'd refused to say the words he knew she'd longed to hear, the *I love you* which would have set her free to be with him again?

Or had it more to do with his being afraid? He didn't like to think of himself as a coward, but was there not the very real fear, buried deep inside him, that the only reason she was turning to him was to have him bail her out of her current predicament?

His doing so offered no guarantee that she'd still want him afterward. Sure, she'd said she loved him, but so what? She'd loved him before, but it hadn't stopped her from leaving him.

Jacqueline sipped her coffee, her face the very picture of distress. "I honestly don't know how I'm going to get through the wedding, Nico," she confessed. "Thank goodness a marriage commissioner's conducting the ceremony and there won't be any of that 'does anyone know just cause why this couple should not be joined in holy matrimony' stuff, because I really don't think I could keep my mouth shut."

"There's still a chance she'll come to her senses before then," he said, wishing he believed the tripe he was handing out. But he hadn't walked the floor all night because he needed the exercise. His mother-in-law wasn't the only one in agony. He was grappling with his own set of demons. He just managed to hide them better, was all.

"You think?" A sliver of hope lightened Jacqueline's expression.

"I know she is a woman of conscience, and too morally upright to enter into a binding contract under false pretenses. She will not go through the motions of marriage unless she is willing to embrace it fully, with her whole heart."

"I pray that you're right."

She wasn't the only one! He'd spent much of the last twenty-four hours making bargains with God. "There is still time, Jacqueline. What is it you told me, just the other day?"

"It's not over till the fat lady sings?"

"*Sì.*" He kissed her cheek. "And we do indeed have a fat lady, in the person of Baron's mother. Truly, Jacqueline, I cannot imagine such a harridan bursting into song. There is hope yet that all is not lost."

"I suppose," she said, returning his hug. "But I'd feel a lot better if you hadn't retired from the field."

"Let me put it this way," he said. "If Chloe decides I'm the one she wants, she knows where to find me. My door is always open, *cara.* But I cannot force her to cross its threshold."

An influx of out-of-town relatives, beginning late Wednesday morning and continuing well into the afternoon of the next day, turned the house into one long party. Chloe, caught like a piece of driftwood drawn ever closer to the eye of a vicious whirlpool, was helpless to fight the unrelenting current.

She was the bride, the center of all attention; the *reason* for all the fuss. But gripped by an emotional paralysis, she relinquished her role as guest of honor and became merely an observer, one whose fixed smile never wavered, and whose spirit was so devoid of life that she might as well have been a portrait hanging on the wall.

When everyone went upstairs to dress before dinner on the Thursday, she hadn't resolved a single one of the dilemmas facing her. Baron still believed they were getting married two days later. Mrs. Prescott, caught between sour, albeit justified disapproval of the bride, and the overweening need to show everyone she was *au courant* with her duties as mother of the groom, was still of the opinion that she was hosting the rehearsal dinner the next night.

And Jacqueline continued to behave as if she'd never once questioned the wisdom of Chloe's decision to marry Baron, and greeted every new arrival on her doorstep with a smile that stretched from one ear to the other.

Only Charlotte seemed aware that all was not well with her granddaughter, but she was too discreet to say so openly. Of course, she might have been more forthcoming if Nico had been around to encourage her, but there'd been no sign of him since Tuesday night. Once he'd succeeded in destroying any hope Chloe had of making a go of things with Baron, he'd made himself scarce, although the lights shining in the lodge at night showed he was still in residence there.

"We'll be so many for dinner tonight that I've reserved a private dining room at the Inn," Jacqueline announced to the house guests gathered on the patio for the cocktail hour. "It's only a ten-minute walk away."

"And will the groom and his family be joining us?" a second cousin, twice removed, inquired.

"Of course." Her mother shot Chloe another in her seemingly endless supply of fond and brilliant smiles. "Baron and Chloe can hardly bear to be apart. The wedding day can't get here soon enough, can it, darling?"

Chloe feared her answering smile more closely resembled the rictus of a woman suffering death throes.

The Trillium Inn, renowned for its fine dining room as well as its old-world hospitality, sat among several acres of beautifully landscaped gardens. The Dogwood Room enjoyed a particularly spectacular view of the large man-made lake where black swans floated majestically among the lily pads. Even the hard-to-please mother of the groom was impressed.

"I can't imagine why you wouldn't have held the wedding here," she fluted, over her duck à l'orange. "It's quite charming, and much more suited to a large affair such as you have planned."

"My bride wanted to be married at home," Baron said, inching his chair closer to Chloe's.

"And how about your wishes, Baron? Don't they count for something?"

"Whatever Chloe wants is fine with me, Mother," he said easily. "All I really care about is that we're getting married."

Oh, Baron! Chloe mourned inwardly, her stomach tied in such knots that she was afraid she might throw up. *You deserve so much better than what you think you're getting.*

Her face must have given away something of her inner distress, because he bathed her in a glance filled with loving concern. "Sweetheart, is something wrong?"

He was handing her the perfect opportunity to come clean, but his timing was completely off. "I need to be alone with you for a while," she hedged, excruciatingly aware that his mother sat close enough to hear every word. "We haven't had a moment to ourselves in what seems like days and there are…things that we need to talk about."

"Next week," he promised, stroking his hand up her back and massaging the nape of her neck. "We'll have all the time in the world, then. It'll be just us, the moonlight and the tropical breezes.''

''No,'' she said urgently. ''I can't wait that long, Baron.''

Mrs. Prescott didn't quite snort with contempt; she was above such things. Instead, she wagged a reproving finger and proclaimed, ''If that's not typical of young people nowadays! You don't know the meaning of self-denial. You want instant gratification—preferably yesterday.''

It was all Chloe could do not to bite that fat, ringladen finger clean through to the bone. ''Don't presume to tell me what it is I want, Mrs. Prescott,'' she said, more beside herself by the second. ''You haven't known me long enough to have the first idea.''

Although the general level of talk and laughter at the table was loud enough that most people weren't aware that the bride and her prospective mother-in-law had taken off the gloves and were ready to go ten rounds, the sudden lull in the conversation of those sitting closest made it glaringly apparent that Baron wasn't the only one taken aback.

Charlotte stared fixedly at her plate, Phyllis sputtered into her wineglass, and even Jacqueline's mouth fell open in shock. The only person unaffected by Chloe's outburst was Mr. Prescott, who continued to chew his way stolidly through the steak he'd ordered.

''Perhaps not,'' his wife said, dropping her reply, syllable by crystal-clear syllable, into the small well of silence surrounding her. ''But I do know my son, and he is not given to the rather bizarre impulses which seem to be part and parcel of *your* makeup, Chloe. I refer not just to the here and now, but more specifically to the afternoon we found you cavorting in the pool with your ex-husband. I can't help but think that, although Baron might presently consider such odd behavior charming, he will find it tiresome, once the novelty wears off.''

''That's enough!'' Baron, normally so mildly spoken, issued the order with the crisp authority of a sergeant major. ''You will apologize to Chloe for that remark, Mother.''

''No.'' More embarrassed than she'd ever been in her life before, Chloe laid a hand on his arm and turned to his mother. ''I'm the one who should apologize, and I do, Mrs. Prescott, most sincerely.'' Her mouth trembled and she made a monumental effort to control it, before continuing, ''I'm afraid I'm not myself tonight. I haven't *been* myself for quite some time. Please forgive me.''

Mrs. Prescott hesitated fractionally, then inclined her head. ''Certainly. I'm sorry, too, if I spoke out of turn. I'm afraid weddings are emotionally taxing, not just for the bride, but for the mothers whose children are about to take such a life-altering step.''

''It doesn't have to be like that, Myrna,'' Baron's father stopped chewing long enough to remark. ''It's all a matter of how you look at it.''

Ignoring him, she turned again to Chloe, an unexpectedly compassionate gleam in her cool gray eyes. ''Men just don't understand, do they?'' she said quietly, as if she and Chloe were the only two people in the room. ''They just take everything at face value, and never bother to scratch below the surface to find out what's really going on. But we know better, my dear. We might fool ourselves for a little while, but eventually we have to confront the truth, regardless of how painful it might be.''

Chloe met her gaze head-on. ''Yes, we do.''

''Then I apologize again for my previous comment.'' She held Chloe's gaze a moment longer, then gave a tiny, conspiratorial nod. ''If you and Baron have matters to discuss once dinner is over, his father and I will take a taxi back to our hotel.''

''Thank you.'' Chloe turned pleading eyes on Baron. ''May we please do that?''

''No,'' he said flatly, even though his calm smile never faltered.

Stunned by his refusal, she said, ''But it's important, Baron.''

''I'm sure you think so, but it's going to have to wait a few more hours.''

''It can't!'' she insisted. ''You don't understand—''

''But I do, Chloe, much better than you seem to realize. All these weeks of wedding preparations have left you worn to a shadow. More than anything else, you need rest, my love. Whatever it is that has you looking so wretched won't seem nearly so bad after a good night's sleep.''

He spoke with such kindness, looked at her so sorrowfully, as if, deep down, he already knew his hopes of a happy ending with her grew slimmer by the second, that her heart almost broke. How could she let him down at this late date and live with herself afterward? Surely, if she tried very hard, she could make *him* the one to haunt her dreams, the one she wanted with desperate, driving hunger?

His gaze roamed over her face as if he were committing every last feature to memory. ''Please don't look so anxious," he murmured. "I promise you, everything will be all right. One way or another, we'll sort out whatever's troubling you."

She wanted to believe him. Had never wanted anything as much in her entire life...except for Nico. Dear God, what kind of monster did that make her?

Still in a festive mood when they returned from the Inn, the house guests weren't at all interested in making an early night of it. More wine flowed, music filled the downstairs rooms, someone started a conga line. And suddenly she was the only one not taking part.

"Come on, Chloe!" they urged, laughing, and dragged her into the middle of the floor. "Live it up while you can!"

They all wanted so badly for her to be happy, that it pained her to look at them. Trying to match their smiles was as impossible as staring into bright, oncoming headlights and trying not to squint.

Perhaps Baron had been right in refusing to let her talk to him tonight. Although outwardly serene, inside she was like a wild animal, trapped and running blindly in all directions, seeking escape. But no matter which way she turned, she ended up banging into the bars of the cage containing her—except that, in her case, they were bars of her own making, and until she broke them down, she had no right inflicting pain on anyone else. One way or another, she *had* to resolve her fluctuating ambivalence, and put an end to the maelstrom of emotion tearing her apart inside.

Unwilling to give rise to unwelcome speculation and injured feelings by openly shunning the party, she chose her moment when everyone was admiring the wedding gifts, muttered the excuse that she needed a breath of air, and slipped through the French doors to the garden.

Once there, she simply opened her consciousness and let the tumult of her thoughts run wild in whatever order they chose. One strand overlapped another, untangled again, and eventually came together in a certain logical sequence that hinged entirely on one thing: love.

She'd learned years ago that it wasn't simple or easy. It didn't die on command. Despite her best efforts not to do so, she still loved Nico. She'd always love him. How could she not, when he was her son's father?

Yet that didn't preclude her loving Baron, too. Not quite the way she loved Nico, perhaps—nothing would ever equal that blind, youthful intensity—but sincerely nonetheless, and deeply enough that the thought of hurting him made her physically ill.

He was such a good man; such ideal husband material. They'd started out as colleagues, become good friends, and on that solid foundation of mutual respect gradually made the transition to romance.

She'd loved his integrity, his sense of fair play, his dry humor and unfailing good temper. Wearing his ring had made her proud, and if fireworks didn't explode around her when he kissed her, that was all right, too. He was, after all, a man of contained passions. It was what made him such a good lawyer.

But sex would be good between them. Not earth-shattering, the way it had been with Nico, but good just the same. Baron would be a tender and considerate lover. If there weren't any soaring highs with him such as she'd shared with Nico, she knew for certain that there'd be none of the despair-filled lows, either.

She'd thought it was all she ever wanted: to know that she'd never again have to visit that dark and dreadful place of grief; to live with the sure knowledge that she wouldn't be blindsided by a vicious stab of sorrow because she happened to look at her husband's face, and see there a living resemblance to the child she'd lost.

All those reasons remained valid. None of the fine qualities which had drawn her to Baron in the first place had lessened since Nico had come back on the scene. If anything, she esteemed him even more for the generous way he'd accepted the presence of a man few other people would have tolerated.

She tried to imagine not having him by her side, and could not. Could not begin to comprehend the gaping hole his absence would leave in her life. Yet she was tormented beyond endurance by longing for another man.

If only Nico would disappear and never come back! If only she could scour away the memory of that scene in the town house, on Tuesday, and the residual guilt that went with it!

If only she could stop loving him!

Music filtered from the open windows of the house, a number from the soundtrack of *Mamma Mia,* so haunting and unbearably beautiful that she wanted to weep.

Clapping her hands to her ears, she ran down the brick path, to the gate beyond the rose garden. A lilac hedge rose up on the other side, its blooms long since withered, but its leaves offering concealing sanctuary from anyone who might be watching at the house.

Pushing the gate open, she went through and huddled at the far edge of the lawn fronting the lodge, at the place where it sloped down to the edge of the cliff overlooking the Strait.

How long she stood there, her chest heaving, the tears rolling down her face, she couldn't have said. Gradually, though, she became aware of footsteps approaching and coming to a stop directly behind her.

She knew without looking that it was Nico because every pore in her skin responded to his nearness. Every pale and tiny hair on the nape of her neck quivered to attention. The very air crackled with silent electricity.

Do not turn around, she commanded herself.

Strong masculine hands closed over her upper arms. A voice uttered her name. Nico's hands, Nico's voice, resurrecting near-forgotten memories of the warm, sweet night breeze of Verona sweeping softly over her naked body, and moonlight throwing dusky blue shadows over her skin. And Nico, limned in the pale light like some ancient, beautiful god come to steal a mortal's soul, hovering above her, murmuring words of love that fell from his lips like music...*tesoro...angelo...la mia moglie adorata...te amo...*.

She squeezed her eyes shut, so tightly they stung.

Do not acknowledge him...!

His lips settled quietly at the spot just below her ear. Slid in a smooth arpeggio down the side of her neck, and from there to the curve of her shoulder. His lashes fluttered against her skin, a charming, alluring afterthought that left a trail of goose bumps in its wake.

Do not let him in…!

Even though her flesh burned where he touched it, even though every nerve in her body jumped in shimmering anticipation of a pleasure she'd only ever found with him, she could not let him know.

Baron was the better choice, the man who offered her the constancy she craved. *He* was the one who should be seducing her softly.

But it was Nico who ran his palms down her night-chilled arms and laced his fingers in hers. Nico who whispered sweet Italian nothings in her ear.

Do not listen! Do not turn around!

But her body didn't hear. Didn't care. Instead, it took on a life of its own, swiveling in response to the persuasion of his hands, and bringing her face to face, breast to chest, hip to hip, with the one man in the whole wide world to whom she'd never been able to say "No."

"What are you doing out here, all by yourself at such a late hour?" he asked, the question whispering over her mouth like a breeze.

"I have nowhere else to go," she replied brokenly.

Without another word, he swung her off her feet, cradled her against his shoulder and covered the distance to the lodge in long, swift strides. The magnolia trees and lilac hedge blocked out the sight of the main house. The sleepy swish of the waves rolling ashore drowned out all the music except for the anthem beginning in her heart.

Reason couldn't dictate the right or wrong of it, because there was nothing reasonable about the wild anticipation thrumming through her veins. The one true voice she heard was that which told her she was where she belonged.

He didn't pretend to bother with social foreplay. No offer of a glass of sherry to warm her shivering body, of conversation to ease her afflicted mind. Instead, he kicked the front door closed behind him and marched straight up the stairs to the bedroom.

The windows stood open, letting in the sweet, heavy perfume of night-scented stocks and nicotiana. Only a smattering of stars winked between the branches of the copper beech outside, and the moon, just rising, offered next to no light at all. But a lamp on the dresser cast enough of a glow to penetrate the shadows of the room. Enough that she could see the passionate curve of his mouth as he lowered her to the floor, his heavy-lidded gaze as it traveled the length of her, the slow rise and fall of his chest.

His hands circled her waist. Inched her toward him until she stood close enough for his breath to winnow over her face. The slow torment it inflicted left her whimpering helplessly. She lifted her mouth to his, mutely begging to be kissed. But he continued to toy with her, hovering but never quite touching.

Then, after what seemed like forever, he brushed his lips across hers—one way, the other, like a bird unable to decide where it wished to settle. A fleeting taste of heaven here; a brief, burning promise there. A swift, openmouthed sweep, warm and wet across her parched lips, followed by tormenting withdrawal, and another long, silent scrutiny from eyes so dark and shadowed she hadn't a hope of reading what lay in their depths.

"I hope you know what you're doing, Chloe," he said at last, his voice coated in sugared gravel. "I hope that, this time, you're quite sure I'm the one you want and there aren't going to be any recriminations flying, afterward.''

Her breath caught on a splintered sigh. She framed his face between her hands so that he had to look at her, had to see the truth she knew he'd find written on hers. "I'm sure.''

If permission was what he'd been waiting for, he heard it in her answer. Felt it in the urgency with which she pressed herself against him. The time was past for leisurely explorations; for *almost* touching, *almost* kissing.

With a low growl of satisfaction, he ripped down the zipper of her dress, tugged at the bodice until it fell around her waist, then walked her backward until she fell across the bed with him on top of her.

In the throes of her own wild need, she tore open the buttons on his shirt, pressed her eager mouth against the smooth curve of his shoulder, slid her hands inside the waist of his pants, and over his taut, slim buttocks.

"I want you naked,'' he muttered between fevered breaths. "I want to feel all of you underneath me.''

And so it was. Clothing tossed aside haphazardly. A brief, breathless suspension of time while they devoured each other with their eyes, renewing acquaintance with physical features they'd once known so intimately that they'd have recognized each other by touch alone in a crowd of thousands.

How could she have forgotten the slight bump along his collar bone, broken in a game of street soccer when he was nine? The tiny raised scar just above his ribs, the legacy of a fight when he was in his teens? The imposing width of shoulder, the narrow waist, the way the crisp haze of dark hair on his chest softened to silk as it narrowed down his flat belly, then flared again to nest around his manhood?

How could she have thought for a second that *any* other man could ever raise her to painful, quivering expectation just by the sight of his powerful, vibrant arousal? Nico was strong, in mind and body; a force to be reckoned with regardless of most circumstances. Yet when it came to mastering his sexual response to her, *she* was the one in control.

Barely had the thought taken root, though, before he reminded her of the other half of the sexual equation between them. His fingertip, running in a straight line from her throat to her navel with a feather-light touch that barely grazed her skin, made her gasp aloud. A rush of heat pulsed through her body, leaving her thighs shaking and the folds of flesh between them puddled with excitement.

''You are still beautiful,'' he allowed, knowing she had learned her lesson, and that there were never any winners when it came to making love.

Wanting to punish him with similar pleasure, she let her finger skate from the indentation separating the muscled planes of his chest, and all the way down his torso until she found the sleek, vulnerable tip of his penis. ''And you, Nico.''

The breath hissing between his teeth marked the end of the preliminary skirmish. No more holding back after that. No more questions, no more *thinking*. Just him and her, skin to skin, the way it was meant to be. Mouths seeking, tongues playing, unhindered, wherever they chose to go.

The taste and texture of him, pure male, pure sex, drove her wild. His fractured gasp of pleasure when she took him in her mouth, his steely determination not to submit to her torture...oh, they made her feel victorious, invincible—until, again, he exercised his own exquisite form of mastery and brought her tumbling into submission.

Effortlessly, he flipped her onto her back so that she lay spread-eagled beneath him. He knelt astride her. Probed gently with his hard, heated flesh at the juncture of her thighs. Slid easily between their welcoming inner curves, then withdrew again, a nanosecond before penetrating farther. Flirted with her repeatedly, each time tossing her closer to heaven.

She thrashed beneath him, inarticulate sounds issuing helplessly from her throat as the encroaching waves of orgasm threatened to engulf her. She could not hold them back, and yet, by themselves, they were not enough to satisfy her. She wanted him—*all* of him—deep inside her. Wanted to welcome him with her own flesh convulsing around his.

She flung out her arm, as if by doing so, she might tame that part of her body refusing to submit to patience. She succeeded in a way she could never have anticipated.

Her fist cracked against glass. Shocked, she turned her head and saw she'd struck a brass picture frame on the bedside table, hinged down the middle and containing two photographs. The first was of her, silhouetted by sunshine and hugely pregnant; the other of Luciano, taken shortly before he died.

Never again, she'd vowed, when Nico, desperate to avoid the divorce and somehow put right a world forever gone wrong, had suggested that, in time, another baby might help ease her pain. *Never again!*

Yet here she was, so bent on finding escape from today that she hadn't given a thought to tomorrow's possible consequences. She'd ignored logic for instinct, and it had led her straight to the brink of disaster again. Good God, would she never learn?

CHAPTER NINE

Friday, August 28

HE MADE a note of the flight information he needed, and replaced the phone in its cradle. It was over. Done.

Once the anger subsided—and it had been directed at himself, more than at her—he'd known exactly what his next move had to be. Now that he'd taken it, he felt better. Less morally reprehensible, although not entirely guilt-free. But that was the price a man paid for putting his integrity on the line, and acting against his better judgment for a woman he'd once loved with an all-consuming passion.

Well, no more. She wasn't the only one who'd changed. This time, he wouldn't beg, and he wouldn't sacrifice his own needs in order to satisfy hers. If she was bound and determined to screw up her life…well, hell! It was hers to do with as she pleased, and all he could do at this point was let her get on with it.

"Sorry, Chloe," he'd said the night before, not even bothering to go downstairs and see her out. "You're the one who showed up outside my door, this time, certain you were where you wanted to be. I did my best to give you what you said you wanted, and once again, at the last minute, you backed off."

"You know why," she cried. "And it had nothing to do with my not knowing what I want."

"Perhaps not. Perhaps, this time, it's a matter of my

knowing what I *don't* want. It's over between us, Chloe. I'm finished with this whole mess.''

''Just like that? You give me an ultimatum and there's no room for negotiation?''

''None at all,'' he told her, unable to look at her tear-stained face for fear he'd cave in. ''I'm all talked out.''

She'd left without another word. He'd watched her go, knowing that, this time, she was walking away for good, and he would do nothing to try to bring her back.

It was better this way.

''So…!'' The next morning, Baron slid into the empty chair across from Chloe's in the restaurant, and shook out his napkin. ''Getting together for breakfast was a great idea. I'm glad you thought of it. Did you order for me?''

''Yes,'' she said. ''Unsweetened grapefruit juice, two poached eggs, dry toast and black coffee.''

He smiled. ''You know me so well, Chloe. We're going to do very well together.''

''Baron—''

''Are you all set for the rehearsal dinner tonight?''

''No. I'm—''

''Not that we're having a rehearsal, as such.'' Another smile, slow and sweet and heartbreaking. ''We've both done this before, after all. We know the ropes. I suppose, to be accurate, we should be calling tonight's affair the groom's dinner, and leave it at that.''

''Baron, I can't go through with it.''

''The dinner? Of course you can, Chloe. My mother's promised to behave herself.'' He made a big production of perusing the menu. "You know, I think I might change my mind and have the eggs Benedict."

"Not the dinner, the wedding." The words fell out of her mouth as bald and clumsy and cruel as bricks smashing through crystal. "I have to call it off, Baron. I'm so sorry. And so ashamed."

He buried a sigh and put the menu to one side. "I was afraid this might happen."

Too engulfed in misery for the resignation in his answer to register fully, she spread her hands in a hopeless gesture, as if they might convey the regret no words could adequately express, and said again, stammering this time, "I truly am so very sorry! I wish I didn't have to do this to you."

"Are you quite sure that you must, Chloe?"

"Yes. It's the only honorable thing I *can* do. If I weren't such an abysmal coward, I'd have spoken sooner. But I kept hoping…" She tried to swallow the humiliation threatening to choke her. Wished she could offer a reason that would exonerate her from culpability, and knew there was none. "I kept hoping things would work out for us, and if they couldn't, then that some*one,* or some*thing* else would make it impossible for us to go through with our plans, so that I wouldn't have to be responsible. I'm not proud of myself for that, Baron."

"When did you reach your decision?"

"I knew for sure last night." She ventured a glance at him, the import of his earlier response finally hitting home. "And you don't seem too surprised."

"I might not be the most brilliant man in the world, Chloe, but I'm not completely lacking in perception. I knew the moment Nico came on the scene that it was only a matter of time before you realized you couldn't marry me.'' He shot her a look of such utter sympathy that she flinched. ''If anyone should apologize, I should, for not having let you off the hook sooner.''

''Oh, please, Baron!'' she said, struggling for composure. ''Please don't make me feel any more ashamed than I already do. This was my responsibility to shoulder, not yours. And to be fair to Nico, I can't lay all the blame on him. I was having doubts before he showed up. He just made me face up to them.''

Baron laid a consoling hand on her arm. ''Listen to me. You've had a great deal to contend with in the last month, buried as you've been in a steady stream of wedding details that left you no time to stand back and gain any sort of perspective. But I have no such excuse. I saw the chemistry between you and Nico— I'd have had to be blind not to!—and I did nothing. Instead, I stuck my head in the sand and chalked it all up to wedding nerves. So you see, I'm an even bigger coward than you, Chloe.''

''I think you're saying all this just to be kind and make me feel better.''

''No, I'm telling you the truth. This wedding took on a life of its own and steamrolled over anything that got in its path. You didn't know how to stop it, and I didn't care to try.'' He patted her arm one last time, then withdrew his hand. ''I won't pretend my pride isn't taking a bit of a beating, but I promise you I'm not about to drive my car off a cliff or overdose on antacids. You and Nico can go ahead and start over with my blessing.''

''No, we can't.'' She hung her head, hating what

she knew she must add. But Baron deserved to know the full truth. "He...doesn't want me."

"Not like this," Nico had raged, when their lovemaking came to a sudden and premature end because she'd undergone another last-minute attack of scruples. "Damn you, Chloe! Come to me because you can't stay away, not because you need an excuse to leave Baron!"

"Why does it have to be all or nothing with you?" she'd cried.

"Because that's the kind of man I am. I'm not interested in being your temporary savior, someone you need for just a little while. I worked too hard to come to terms with your walking out on me once before, and I'm not about to go down that road again."

"What if we could make a real go of things, this time?"

The scorn in his laugh had flayed her to the bone. "With your screwed-up approach to coping? Not a chance!"

"Why not? Because I wouldn't have sex with you tonight unless you used a condom?"

He'd laughed again, more bitterly than ever. "If this was just about tonight, I'd insist on using one. But it's about tomorrow and next month and next year. It's why you're all set to marry Baron—because he's willing to settle for half a life with half a wife. Well, not me, sweet face! I want a woman who's brave enough to face the future without having it sugar-coated in a guarantee that it'll always be safe and perfect and free from pain. A woman who stares destiny in the face and defies it to strike against her a second time."

"Are you saying you want more children?" she'd asked, her voice hushed with trepidation.

"You bet I want more children! I won't let one unkind stroke of fate reduce me to a whimpering coward. What the devil does a man work for, if not for a wife and children? What the hell else is there that amounts to a damn thing worth having?"

He'd seen the doubt on her face, and his own had contorted with disdain. *"Your trouble is you've been spoiled your whole life, Chloe. Coddled to the point that you take each and every setback as a personal affront, and I'm as much to blame for that as anybody. But, guess what? You're not the only mother to have lost a child. It happens all the time to other women. The difference is, they don't let it cripple them. They grieve, and you can bet they never forget, but eventually they get up and go on living. But you...you might as well have died with our son because you're right. You don't have a damned thing left to give to anyone else."*

She'd known he was capable of rage, had seen him grapple with it when Luciano died, but never had she expected him to direct it at her with such unbridled contempt.

"If this is how you really feel, I don't know why you bothered to open your door to me tonight."

"Because I feel sorry for you," he'd said, wiping a weary hand down his face and sounding as drained as she felt. *"Almost as sorry as I do for the man you're about to marry. Thank God it's Baron and not me!"*

"I wouldn't have you if you were the last man on earth!"

"Good, because I'm not offering! You want a pain-

*less life, and I know better than to think I can give you
one, because there is no life without pain. How does
anyone learn to savor the good times, if they never
learn to cope with the bad?''*

She'd started to cry then, hopeless, helpless tears
that just wouldn't stop. He might not have come right
out and said so, but he despised her, and who could
blame him? Good grief, she despised herself—for her
weakness and timidity and dishonesty. He was right.
She was afraid—of him, of herself, of living life to the
fullest—and quite willing to hide behind someone else
so that she never had to face up to her fears.

He'd watched her dispassionately for a while, then
handed her a tissue from the box beside the bed, and
said, ''Go home, Chloe, and do yourself a favor.
Unless you want to wind up in the divorce court a
second time, take a long, hard look at what you're
asking of yourself and Baron, by going ahead with this
marriage.''

''What do you care,'' she'd sobbed, ''as long as you
don't have to clean up the mess?''

''I don't care,'' he said flatly. ''But only because I
won't let myself.''

''And if Nico did want you, would you go with
him?'' Baron asked now.

''No,'' she said, the endless tears of the previous
sleepless night having at last washed away all the clut-
ter from her mind and left it receptive to the kind of
brutal soul-searching so long overdue. ''I've been running away from myself for a long time now, and it has
to stop. I don't much like the person I've become,
Baron. I've never thought of myself as a user, but I'm
afraid I've taken unconscionable advantage of you *and*

Nico. The difference is, he won't let me get away with it, whereas you always make allowances, always show yourself ready to settle for what I'm willing to give, without once asking for more.''

''You don't hear me complaining, Chloe. And in all honesty, neither of us has ever pretended ours was the love match of the century. I think we both know that's something that rarely happens in real life.''

''But it *did* happen to me, that's the trouble. I know how it feels to love a man so madly that he fills my dreams and occupies my every waking thought to the exclusion of everything else.''

Baron beat his fingertips in a soft tattoo on the linen tablecloth. ''Perhaps that's where we differ the most, then, because I'm not sure I'm capable of that kind of passion. I'm not sure I ever want to be,'' he said thoughtfully. ''That's why we made such a good couple—or at least, I thought we did. But I've seen another side of you this last week, Chloe, and I realize I was wrong. The real you has been undercover all this time, and it took Nico to bring you out of hiding.''

''It's not that I don't love you, Baron, because I do,'' she said, hating that she sounded so trite and condescending.

''I love you, as well. You will always be very dear to me. But you know, I've been divorced for over thirteen years and I have to confess that there've been times when I've questioned my ability to give up the rather solitary life I've enjoyed for so long.''

''You say that now, because you want to make me feel better about jilting you at the last minute, but if I hadn't called off the wedding, you'd have gone through with it.''

"Yes, I would have. As I said before, you're not the only coward in the mix, Chloe. I'd have gone ahead and made the best of things, and I don't suppose it would have been too difficult. We are, after all, very good friends." He smiled again. "Perhaps that's all we were ever meant to be."

"You're one of the finest men I've ever known, and your friendship means more to me than you'll ever know." She shook her head, her relief at having at last done the right thing diluted by a terrible feeling of regret for all the hurt she'd caused. "So where do we go from here?"

"I suppose the first thing is to cancel as many arrangements as possible. Have you told anyone else what you've decided?"

"No. The least I could do was let you be the first to know."

"Then I suggest you tell your mother and grandmother next. Let them help you. I'm sure they won't—"

"There are bigger issues at stake than canceling the wedding arrangements, Baron! What about the town house, and our working together?"

"The real estate market's very hot right now. We'll have no trouble selling the house. As for working together, there's no reason we can't go on as before. It's not as if we see that much of each other in the office, anyway." He regarded her over the rim of his coffee cup, a glimmer of amusement in his eyes. "In any case, I rather think you'll be leaving the country eventually. It's a very long commute from here to Italy."

She started crying again at that, overwhelmed by a generosity she didn't begin to deserve. "If that ever happens," she said, dabbing at her eyes with her napkin, "I'm going to miss you very much."

By noon, the most urgent phone calls had been made, and word that the wedding was officially off had gone the rounds. There was a host of details still needing attention, of course, perhaps the most time-consuming being to return wedding gifts with an appropriate note of thanks and explanation. But the most onerous task in Chloe's opinion, once she'd spoken to Baron, was facing Nico again.

She didn't expect him to fall all over himself just because she'd finally had the guts to do what she should have done at least a week ago, if not before. But she hoped she could at least regain a little of his respect.

Any such notion died as she pushed open the gate at the bottom of the garden. Such an air of quiet solitude enveloped the lodge that she knew what she'd find, even before the front door swung open to confirm there was nothing behind it but empty rooms. He was gone, not just to walk on the beach, or attend another business meeting downtown, but *gone*—as in *left completely, never to return.*

The kitchen was spotless, the cushions on the sofa in the sitting room tidily in place, the clothes closet empty. Nothing remained to remind her that he'd been there, except for the sheets and towels dropped in the laundry hamper in the bathroom—and the photograph of her, which he'd removed from the double picture frame and left torn in half on the nightstand as a telling finale before he'd rung down the curtain on their relationship.

If there was to be a sequel, she'd have to be the one to enact it, and for both their sakes, it couldn't be soon. Aware of the risk invited by delay, because there surely were legions of women who'd be happy to fill the shoes she'd left empty, it was nevertheless a chance she'd have to take. Nico wanted a partner able and willing to share the load, and until she could offer him total commitment, she had no right to importune his love.

I don't care, he'd said last night, shortly before he'd booted her out of his life, *but only because I won't let myself.*

It wasn't much on which to pin her hopes for a happy ending to their love affair, but it was all she had, and she clung to it as she faced the long road of recovery ahead.

The wedding didn't happen, after all, Jacqueline wrote, at the beginning of October. *Just as we hoped, Chloe came to her senses at the last minute, and it didn't seem to come as much of a surprise to anyone, least of all Baron. They remain good friends and colleagues, and though it was all a bit frantic for a while, everything's settled down now. She moved into her own place last week, a condominium on the west side, and plans to spend Christmas in Mexico. She never mentions you, Nico, and I don't ask, but Charlotte and I both so hoped the two of you would kiss and make up. Perhaps, the next time you come over here, you'll find a way....*

It wasn't going to happen. He'd appointed Donna Melino CEO of his North American operation, leaving him free to concentrate on his other business holdings and his nonexistent private life. He'd suffered punishment enough at Chloe's hands, and only a fool would keep going back for more. It was time he shed the emotional baggage he'd carried around for so long, and made a fresh start with someone whose wounded, reproachful eyes weren't a constant reminder of all he'd lost.

While she was sunning herself on the Mexican Riviera, he'd be actively shopping for a new wife. The next time a wedding was in the offing, it would be his.

Trouble was, although women were easily come by, finding one who held his attention for more than a week or two proved next to impossible. Either they were too much like Chloe, or not like her enough. When the new year rolled in, he celebrated with his sisters and their families, and was the only man at the party who didn't have a woman in his arms at midnight.

"Your problem," his brother-in-law Hector told him, in a hung-over bout of confidence the next morning, "is that you want to turn back time. You want Chloe the way she used to be, before your little son died. But you know, *l'amico,* losing a child changes a person forever. You're not the same man she married, either."

"It doesn't take a genius to figure that out," he'd replied shortly. "You've only got to look at me to see I've changed."

"I'm not talking about the fact that you appear more successful on the surface. It's what's going on underneath that counts. Even though you've achieved so much, can you honestly say you're ever able to forget you were once a father? Can owning a fleet of cargo ships deflect the grief that sneaks up when you're not expecting it, and leaves you feeling as if you've been punched in the kidneys? If you were to take another wife, would that be enough to make you put away your memories and never think of Luciano again, or to forget that Chloe is the only woman you'll ever really love?"

Depressingly probing questions that would accept nothing but the truth for answers! He'd never forget his son, and Chloe…? Damn her, she was in his blood still, and no number of fresh transfusions seemed able to get rid of her.

So he stopped searching, stopped the interminable round of dating, and devoted himself to the one thing that never failed to bring him satisfaction: he made more money, with a series of daring investments that left his broker on the verge of a heart attack. Ironically, because it didn't much matter whether or not they paid off, they brought in handsome returns.

He bought himself a new Ferrari and a classic Bugatti.

"What's wrong with the Lamborghini?" his sister Delia wanted to know. "You can only drive one car at a time. Why own three?"

Annoyed, he said, "Because I can afford them."

He bought a place on the shores of Lake Garda, a mansion just outside Sirmione, formerly owned by an American movie star, and large enough that all four of his sisters and their families could stay there at one time.

"You already gave us that chalet in the Alps," Abree reminded him. "Why this house, too, when we spend most of our time in Verona?"

"Does there have to be a reason?" he snapped. "Isn't it enough that I enjoy spending money on my family?"

It sounded all very fine in theory, but the fact remained that he gained no pleasure from any of it. Once upon a time, his ultimate dream had been to have more money than he could spend. Now that he'd got it, he found it was as empty as any other dream based on ignorance of what really counted in life.

CHAPTER TEN

April 14, the following year

SHE'D come to Verona as a young woman, been entranced by its history, and fallen in love in the summer shade of its medieval buildings. In the end, though, she'd endured some of her darkest hours there, and left it, vowing she'd never return. Yet the second she set foot on the ancient streets of *La Città degli Romeo e Giulietta* again, she felt she'd come home at last.

Nico hadn't the first idea of what lay in store. Indeed, she hardly knew herself. There'd been no contact between them since the previous August, when he'd unceremoniously turfed her out of the gardener's lodge, and out of his life. For all she knew, he might well be in love with someone else by now, and that would be a hard thing to accept. But Chloe was willing to deal with the possibility, if only to prove to herself and him that she was in control of her life and ready to confront whatever shape it might assume.

He was in town, she knew. Her mother had agreed to release that much information, along with his address. But Chloe didn't expect him to be home until the end of the business day, which was just as well. There was another place she needed to visit first, one she'd left too long neglected.

The churchyard lay bathed in sunshine. Making her way unerringly to her son's burial site, she crouched on the grass, a bouquet of spring flowers in her arms. She was not the first to stop by that day. Another arrangement, as freshly cut as hers, lay at the base of the simple marble plaque marking his place.

She traced her finger over his name, let it linger on her lips, then knelt, spread her hands palms down on the warm sod covering him and, for a little while, she cried. But not as she'd expected she might. There were no great, convulsive sobs, no feeling that her heart was being torn from her body. Rather, they were quiet, cleansing tears that ran down her face, and when they were done, she was left with a sense of peace she had not known in years.

She stayed there for nearly an hour, then walked back to where the taxi driver patiently waited, and directed him to take her into the center of town. Once there, she wandered the familiar streets and revisited some of the places to which Nico had introduced her, that passion-filled summer they met.

The *trattoria* in the sun-splashed square where they'd shared their first meal was there still, also the bakery above which he and his sisters had lived as children. The red geraniums his mother had loved bloomed in profusion from the window boxes, just as they had when she was alive.

The market in the *Piazza delle Erbe* bustled with its usual lively activity. He'd stolen two tangerines from a fruit stall, she remembered, and had laughed at her horrified gasp at his lawlessness.

After that, she strolled to the simple gray house at 23, *Via Cappello*—the famous House of Capulet, as it was still called, with its delicate balcony still hanging on the wall outside Juliet's window.

"You are my Giulietta," Nico had told her, the night they became lovers, "but our story will have a happier ending than hers. We'll live and love to a ripe old age together."

She'd believed him, and why not? Who could have foretold that it was their son who'd meet an early death, and not either of them, or that losing him would rob them of each other? But, God willing, it wasn't too late for them to make good on that early promise.

Dusk was falling when she finally found herself on the street where he lived, in an area of town clearly too high-rent for the average man. His front door was painted shiny black, with brass numbers marching vertically down its center panel. The white interior shutters at his windows were angled so that he could observe passers by without their being aware of his surveillance.

For a moment, the courage which had carried her this far evaporated. What if he happened to be looking out now, and saw her standing on the sidewalk? Would he be happy, angry, amused?

There was but one way to find out. Composing herself, she marched up the short walkway fronting the house and pressed the brass bell on the wall beside the door.

He took his time answering and looked none too pleased at being disturbed. When he saw who his visitor was, he wiped his face clean of all emotion and didn't betray by so much as the flicker of an eyelash his inner response to her presence. He merely stood there and waited for her to speak first.

Her own reaction was much more difficult to hide. Even though *she'd* been prepared to see *him,* her insides rolled over in one long, dizzying somersault. Her blood churned, her lungs froze, the *calzone* she'd eaten for lunch, nearly six hours before, rose up in her throat. As for her poor, beleaguered heart, it beat so hard and fast that the front of her blouse fluttered.

How long the silence lasted, she couldn't have said. All she knew was that she couldn't drag her eyes away from the sight of him. Even with a five o'clock shadow darkening his jaw, and his hair slightly mussed, he looked so handsome...so wary...so remote. And oh, so unmoved by his uninvited caller! Clearly, it would be up to her to break the ice—a metaphor, she thought dazedly, that all too well fit the occasion. His reception couldn't have been colder.

"Ciao!" she said, pasting what she hoped was a poised and relaxed smile on her face, but suspecting she looked as rattled as she surely sounded. "I guess I'm the last person you expected to see."

He inclined his head slightly, said, *"Sì,"* and continued to regard her without a trace of expression.

More discomfited by the second, she shifted from one foot to the other. "I...um, I arrived this morning."

No reaction, no curiosity, no interest. She might as well have been speaking in foreign tongues for all the acknowledgment she received.

Hating the desperation surely evident in her tone, she said, "I went to see Luciano today. Took some flowers to his grave, but there were others already there."

At last, a sign that he had heard, that he was listening. "I visited him myself, just this morning."

"You did?"

"I go every week, except when I'm away on business, and so do his aunts. We have not abandoned him.''

Though his tone remained neutral, the rebuke was unmistakable and it stung. ''And you think I have?''

''I try not to think of you at all,'' he replied cuttingly.

Oh, he was not going to make this easy on her! But then, why should he, when, in the past, she'd rebuffed his every attempt to help her? ''You're frequently in my thoughts, Nico.''

He shrugged, as if to say *And I should care?* ''What brings you to my door, Chloe?''

''I hoped we could talk. There's a lot I'd like to say to you.'' She glanced around at the darkening street, at the couple loitering a few houses away. ''But not out here where strangers might overhear. May I please come in?''

He lifted his shoulders in a faint shrug and stood back to allow her entry.

''Thank you.''

Stepping by him, so close that his dear, familiar scent pierced her senses, almost brought her to her knees. Clenching her hands around her purse, she stumbled into a wide entrance hall and waited, uncertain where he wished her to go next.

''I am in the middle of making myself something to eat. We will talk in the kitchen,'' he announced, and led the way past a formal dining room and long, elegant drawing room, to the rear of the house.

Hurrying to keep up with his impatient stride, she caught only a fleeting impression of the decor, but the compilation of polished floors, thick, pale rugs, and silk-paneled walls suggested discreet expense combined with flawless taste.

The kitchen might have been lifted straight from the pages of a glossy magazine. Sleek built-in appliances, lacquered cabinets and granite counters swept around three sides of one half of the vast room stretching the full width of the house. The fourth, containing a free-standing breakfast bar and two stools, separated the working area from a family room furnished with deep, comfortable sofas and an entertainment unit. A brick-faced fireplace filled the far wall.

Gesturing to the open bottle of Bardolino on the bar, he said with chilly, perfect courtesy, "I was about to pour myself a glass of wine. Do you care to join me?"

"Oh, yes. *Please!*" Although she didn't normally resort to alcohol to steady her nerves, at that precise moment, she'd have been happy to take a straw, stick it in the neck of the bottle, and drain the entire contents in one go. She hadn't expected he'd burst into song and dance in unabashed pleasure at the sight of her, but nor had she been prepared for such a stony, indifferent reception.

Unaware—or more likely uncaring of the anxiety ravaging her, he reached up and removed two long-stemmed glasses from a brass rack suspended above the bar. "What is it you came to say, Chloe?" he inquired politely, pouring the Bardolino.

"I hardly know where to begin." She climbed on one of the stools and cradled the bowl of her glass between her hands. Very fine crystal for everyday use, she noted absently. "After our last meeting, I'm not even sure *how* to begin."

"Try speaking plainly. I assume something more

pressing than visiting our son's grave compelled you to travel halfway around the world.''

''You're not making this easy for me, Nico.''

''I'm under no obligation to do so. You're the one paying the unexpected visit, not I. The ball, as they say, lies in your court.''

She took a deep breath, followed it with a fortifying mouthful of wine, and plunged in. ''I wanted to tell you, to your face, that you were right. My marrying Baron would have been a monumental mistake. I canceled the wedding the day before it was supposed to take place—the same day that you left the country without a word. I came to see you afterward, but I was too late. If you'd waited just a few hours more—''

''There was no point,'' he interrupted. ''We'd reached a dead end.''

''Yes. At that point, we had. But I've done a lot of soul-searching since then, Nico, and I thought...I hoped we might try to find a way out of that dead end, and start afresh.''

''It took you eight months to decide that?'' he scoffed. ''What happened, Chloe? Did you run out of other options and decide that making do with me was preferable to having no one at all?''

''No!'' she gasped, recoiling from such a low blow. ''You made it clear enough that you had no use for an emotional cripple, so what would have been the point in my showing up sooner?''

''No point at all,'' he said flatly. ''I meant what I said.''

''As did I, a moment ago,'' she returned, with a flash of anger. ''But I'm beginning to wonder why I bothered. If I've left it too late and you've moved on, just say so. I'm not going to slit my wrists in your bathroom and leave you to clean up the mess. I'll be hurt and disappointed, but I've survived worse, and I'll survive this.''

He leaned against the other side of the bar, hands lying flat on the tiled surface, arms braced. The knot in his silk tie hung loose, the top button of his shirt was undone, yet his pose was anything but casual. Although his dark glance never wavered, the air around him fairly crackled with tension. Finally, sounding almost ashamed, he said, ''Did I really call you an emotional cripple?''

''Not in so many words, perhaps, but that was the message I received.''

He chewed that over for a minute or so, then said, ''If being with me was really so important, why take a chance on waiting this long to say so? It's been almost a year, Chloe. How do you know I'm not involved with someone else?''

''I don't,'' she admitted, ''and the thought that you might be, has haunted me for months. But if I'd acted on impulse and come to you right after I ended things with Baron, would you have believed I was sincere?''

''Probably not. I'd have thought you were running *away* from the situation you'd left behind, rather than running *to* me.''

''Exactly. Which is why I took as long as I needed to heal myself first, even though that meant taking the chance that a third party might lay claim to your affections.'' She stared at the dark red wine in her glass, unable to meet his gaze and painfully aware that she sounded more as if she were presenting a case in court, than speaking from the heart to the man she loved. ''Is that what's happened, Nico? Is there another woman in your life?''

''There have been others in the months since I saw you last,'' he said.

Pain clutched at her heart and her palms went clammy with sweat. Worse, she knew a sudden dire need to use the toilet. Her bladder had always been her barometer for measuring mental stress, and at that moment it felt ready to burst. ''And now?''

He swung away and went to the stove where a pot simmered. ''I'm making fish soup,'' he said. ''If you'd like to stay, there's enough for two.''

If it wasn't the answer she'd been hoping for, it wasn't an outright rejection, either, and at that point she was prepared to take whatever he was willing to offer. ''Is it your mother's recipe?''

''*Sì.*''

''Then I'd love to.''

He flung her a glance which seemed not quite as chilly as its predecessors. There was even the faintest trace of amusement in his voice when he said, ''I can't help noticing that you're squirming around on that stool, Chloe. Will it help relieve your discomfort if I tell you the powder room is just to the left of the front door?''

She slithered off the stool with more speed than grace. ''You know me too well,'' she said, and made a beeline down the hall.

She wasn't the only one who needed a few moments alone. He was in pretty rough shape himself. Finding her on his doorstep had rocked him badly. He'd had the devil of a time subduing the burst of hope which had flared through him. Maintaining an impassive front had stretched his control past human limits, but he'd played similar scenes with her too often in the past, not to be cautious now.

His experience last summer had taught him that she might turn to him when she was uncertain, when she was in a bind, when she needed to be rescued. Otherwise, she stayed away. That was enough for him to remain on his guard until he had solid reason to think this time would be any different.

There was a fine distinction, though, between holding something of himself in reserve, and being churlish. Whatever her real motive for seeking him out now, she didn't deserve the ugly treatment he'd meted out. But the sad truth was, she terrified the wits out of him.

He could deal with thugs if he had to, wasn't the least bit afraid to use his fists or whatever else came to hand, if he must. But her big, anxious eyes and soft trembling mouth unmanned him in a way that was downright embarrassing.

She could fell him with a glance, a word, a sigh. One touch of her hand, a single faint whiff of her perfume, and he turned to putty, any memory of other women blasted to kingdom come so completely that, on pain of death, he couldn't name one of them.

He drained his glass and debated pouring himself something stronger. He wanted to believe what she'd told him just a few minutes earlier. *Dio,* he'd never wanted anything as badly in his life! But he'd learned too much about his own frailty simply to take her at her word. He had to be sure; had to drive her to her own limits before he could be certain she wouldn't push him past his.

"Let me do that," she said, coming back to the kitchen as he was tossing dressing over mixed salad greens.

"No," he said, the jutting angle of his shoulder denying her the right to invade his space. "You're a guest here."

"Well, at least let me set the table."

"We'll eat at the bar."

Her sigh penetrated his shirt and rippled warmly up his spine. *Dio!*

"I thought we were making progress, Nico."

"Perhaps so," he acknowledged, steeling himself to remain distant, "but one small step at a time, yes? Where are you staying?"

"At the *Due Torri Baglioni*."

"I used to wait on the street outside that hotel in the summer, and offer to act as a guide to tourists—one of my more enterprising adolescent get-rich-quick schemes."

"Was it successful?"

"No. The people who could afford to stay there weren't interested in having a fourteen-year-old tow them around town in a homemade cart attached to his old bike." He shook his head and laughed bitterly. "Now, I could buy the entire place for pocket change, yet in some ways I'm no better off than I was twenty years ago."

"I guess we've both learned that happiness isn't something that can be acquired."

"Have we?" He pinned her in a searching gaze. "Have *you*, Chloe?"

"Yes," she said, on another sigh. "No one else can

give it to us. It comes from within ourselves, or not at all.''

He placed the salad on the bar, and turned to give the fish soup one last stir.

She was saying all the right things, but how deeply did she believe them? ''Are you happy?''

She gave the question a moment's thought. ''I'm content,'' she finally said. ''I'm at peace with myself, and with the past, and that's worth a lot to me. If what I have now is the best I'm ever going to get, I can live with it. But I'd be happier if...'' She drifted into thoughtful silence and stared at the darkening window.

''Yes?'' he prompted. ''If what?''

''I've tried to undo most of my mistakes...all except one, really. I have to try to put that right before I can say I'm truly satisfied.'' She stopped again and bit her lip. ''You know why I'm here, Nico. I've already spelled it out once. But if you need to hear me say it again, I will. I'll say it as many times as it takes for you to believe me. *I want you to give us another chance. I want us to be happy together.*''

''On what terms?''

''No terms,'' she said. ''I'm offering unconditional surrender.''

''And if I tell you that I cannot be quite so generous? That I would exact a price?''

''You want more children.'' She inclined her head. ''I know.''

''I want the possibility of such. A fresh start to me means giving everything a second chance, and if that should mean more children, well—''

''I know, and I agree.''

''Just like that?'' He tilted his head and regarded

her askance. "You must forgive me, Chloe, if I'm somewhat cynical of such a complete turnaround. Is it perhaps that you're so eager for us to be a couple again that you will agree to anything now, only to change your mind once you are assured that my heart is yours to trample on as you see fit?"

"No, it isn't," she replied, her eyes fixed on him unblinkingly. "But I don't expect you to take my word on that, just because I say so. I'm not asking to move in here and pick up where we left off. I'm not asking you to marry me. But I *am* hoping that, in time, you'll come to trust me enough to allow for both to become a possibility."

"How do I do that, with you living thousands of kilometers away? A long-distance relationship isn't my style, *cara*. Or have you forgotten the last time we tried such an arrangement?"

"Hardly," she said, with the first inkling of a smile she'd shown all evening. "The phone bills were astronomical!"

"So how, then, do we enter into this experiment?"

"By my living here."

"Here?"

"Not *here* here," she amended. "Here in Verona. I'm back to stay, Nico, whether or not you want me."

"You know that I want you, *mia strega piccola!* That is one thing that has never changed. But what you're proposing is not practical. You have a career."

"Had," she said. "I *had* a career until I realized that I'd be better off solving my own marital problems, instead of other people's. I resigned from the law firm, terminated the lease on my condominium, packed up the things most important to me—family photographs,

a few heirlooms, my clothes, that kind of thing—and had them shipped over. They should be here by the end of next week. Meanwhile, I'll stay at the hotel until I find an apartment. I've already been to the police station and applied for my temporary Resident's Permit. That's good for three months. If, at the end of that time, you're still undecided about us, I'll apply for a permanent certificate of residence and a work permit.''

''You cannot practice law in Italy.''

''Certainly I can, as long as I meet national standards and pass the bar exam. But I'm hoping that won't be necessary.''

She sounded so sure of herself, so full of confidence, but he saw the uncertainty in her eyes and didn't have the heart to leave her dangling a moment longer. ''No wife of mine will work to support herself,'' he informed her severely. ''She will devote herself to her husband and children.''

A flush rose up her face. Tears filmed her eyes. ''Exactly what are you saying, Nico?''

''That if you still choose to do so, you have come home, Chloe. At long last, we will become a couple again, and we will make it official with all due speed.''

''Are you saying that we'll be married?''

He threw up his hands in frustration. ''*Sì,* we will be married, if not tomorrow, then the day after! How much more plainly must I put it, woman?''

''Well, you could show me, instead of shouting at me.''

''And how would you like me to do that?''

She shrugged. ''At the very least, you could kiss me.''

He came around the breakfast bar, to where she sat perched on the high stool. "And at the very most?" he said, daring at last to touch her.

"Oh well," she murmured, batting her lashes provocatively, "that's really up to you. You're the boss, after all."

"Will you give that to me in writing, *Signorina L'Avvocato,* to make a legally binding agreement of it?"

"Why not? I'm giving you everything else that I am."

He gripped her shoulders and looked deep into her eyes, more beautiful and blue than the Adriatic in high summer. He saw truth there, and trust, and belief in the future. "That is good," he murmured, "because without you, *la mia inamorata,* I am nothing."

"I've been running for such a long time, for years away from sadness and loss, and, in the last few months, toward hope and happiness," she confessed, leaning into his strength and letting him bear her weight, just as she used to, before they'd allowed tragedy to tear them apart. "To feel your arms around me again and know I've finally come back to the place where I belong…" She bowed her head and pressed her face against his shirtfront a moment. "Nico, you can't begin to guess how good it feels to leave the shadows behind and step into the sunlight again."

"I understand better than you might think, my angel," he said, the slow burn of desire simmering through his veins growing fiercer by the second. "I let perfection slip through my fingers when I lost you, and came close to losing my mind also. Now that you're back where you belong, I'll never let you go again."

CHAPTER ELEVEN

THEY forgot the fish soup was still simmering on the stove, that the salad, left sitting far too long at room temperature, grew warm and limp and inedible.

"Didn't you say we should take small steps?" she asked, as he carried her up the stairs.

"Impossible," he laughed. "A man my size doesn't know how."

"But I didn't come prepared for seduction, Nico."

He stopped at the threshold to his bedroom, a slight frown casting a cloud over his smile. "If you're worried you'll get pregnant, don't be. I will protect you. There'll be no baby conceived tonight, and you may be assured I do not intend to pressure you on this, Chloe. We will know when the time is right."

"You don't understand," she said. "I'm not talking about contraception. If I conceive tonight, it will be because it was meant to be. But..." She touched her blouse, the wrinkled cotton of her skirt. "I would have liked to be prettier for you. After all the mistakes and near misses of last summer, I'd have liked our first time together in our new life to be romantic and perfect."

"*Cara,*" he said, "in my eyes you have never been more beautiful and nothing can mar the perfection of this night. But if more romance is what you need, then more you shall have. What will it take? Tell me, and I'll make it happen."

"Oh, nothing too elaborate," she said softly, winding her arms more tightly around his neck and pressing a kiss to his mouth. "A hot bath would do it very nicely."

He set her on her feet and steered her toward a door on the other side of the room. "My home, such as it is, and everything in it, is yours to share, Chloe. Help yourself. I'll be here waiting when you're ready."

She was in no hurry to rejoin him, not because she needed to be sure the next step she'd take was the right one. She'd never been more certain of anything in her life. It was that she wanted to make each minute last; preserve forever in her memory each perfect second.

While the bath filled, she shampooed her hair in the glass-enclosed shower stall, and took deep delight in the implied intimacy of using *his* shampoo, *his* towels. In lieu of perfumed bath crystals, she added a dollop of his Alfred Sung aftershave to the bathwater, soaped the sponge which knew every long muscle, every hard plane of his body, and let it caress her own body until not an inch of her skin was left untouched.

Finally, she slid down in the tub deeply enough for tiny waves to ripple at her throat and fragrant steam to curl around her face, and allowed herself the pleasure of contemplating the night ahead.

Pure bliss and simmering expectation made for a potent cocktail, and when he rapped on the door several minutes later to inquire, "Did you drown, my angel?" she was more than ready for the next stage in the ritual of their renewed courtship.

Swathed in a velvety bath sheet, she returned to the bedroom, but stopped short at the sight awaiting her. He hadn't been twiddling his thumbs during her absence. Pinpoints of soft light glimmered from more than a dozen tealights floating in crystal brandy snifters stationed on every flat surface about the room. Creamy pink rose petals, their scent so sweet that they must have been plucked from their stems only minutes before, lay scattered in a path from her feet to the turned-back covers on the bed.

He stood by the window, stripped naked except for the towel slung around his waist. His hair was damp and even though the candles cast only a muted glow, she could see that he'd shaved. "If you'd told me you were going to bathe, too," she said, resorting to the mundane because the fact that he was there, in the flesh and not just in her dreams, rendered her almost mindless, "we could have done it together."

His low laugh floated through the night and wrapped itself around her. "A cold shower for my ladylove? I think not! But we *will* make love together."

Everything was so utterly idyllic, so beyond even her most optimistic hopes, that she wanted to pinch herself. "We really are here together, aren't we, Nico? This isn't a figment of my imagination?"

"We are indeed here, *mia moglie,* starting over as I've so often prayed we might. I thought of putting champagne on ice, to celebrate the occasion," he said huskily, his eyes devouring her, "but I want you to come to me with every sense alive, with every beat of your heart aware of the step we're about to take. I don't want you to wake up tomorrow filled with any regrets."

She'd wondered if she'd feel shy; if time and their painful history might make it awkward for her to relax with him. She had not expected he might be the one needing reassurance. He was so confident always, so positive he could turn every situation in his favor. That he harbored even the smallest doubt of his ability to do so tonight melted her already willing heart.

"There'll be no regrets, my love," she said, going to him without hesitation, aware of the towel unraveling as she moved until, just as she reached him, it fell away entirely. "No second thoughts, no changing my mind at the last second."

His smile undid her. For once it was not brash and beguiling, but slow and so tender that it left her weak at the knees. He loosened the knot anchoring his own towel and let it fall to join hers on the floor. "How can I be sure?" he said.

She placed her hands on his chest. Splayed her fingers to discover his flat, dark nipples. Bent her head and kissed the swell of muscle underlying his smooth olive skin. Grazed her cheek against the dusting of black hair shadowing his breastbone. "By this?" she whispered.

He might have been carved from marble for all the response he made. Only his magnificently aroused flesh betrayed his tortured pleasure.

Spurred to a daring beyond anything she'd attempted before, she slid her arms around him and traced her fingers down his spine to his buttocks, all the while following a path to his waist with her tongue. "Or this?"

Encouraged by his barely suppressed moan, she pressed a wet, openmouthed kiss at his navel, then continued lower to string feather-light kisses in the narrow triangle formed by his hips.

The breath hissed between his lips. His fingers knotted in her hair.

Slipping her hand between his thighs, she cradled the vulnerable cluster hidden there, then took the silken tip of him in her mouth.

"Enough!" he groaned, shuddering as violently as if an earthquake had struck. "I am convinced!"

She was trembling herself, by then; aching and eager all over, and so weak with longing that she'd have collapsed at his feet had he not drawn her up until she was imprinted against him, inch for inch.

How joyfully her body remembered his; how easily the two melded together, soft feminine warmth and unyielding male strength in perfect harmony. His arms enfolded her, tight and possessive, and when at last he kissed her, as if he could never get enough of the taste and texture of her mouth, the hell of their long separation faded away, and left heaven hovering so close, she could almost touch it.

She had no clear recollection of how they came to be lying together on the petal-strewn bed. All she knew was that the erotic play of his hands at her breasts, her waist, her hips, sent sensation pooling low in her body. An undulating rhythm, the forerunner of complete surrender, pulsed so insistently within her that all he had to do was touch his mouth to her core, flick once with his tongue, and the world as she knew it fell away.

Grasping and clutching at him, she submitted as wave upon wave of sheer ecstasy washed over her. She heard her own moans echo inside her head. Heard Nico calling her name.... "Chloe, Chloe...*tesoro!*" followed by a string of other words, erotic words uttered in Italian, but so full of unrestrained passion that there was no mistaking their meaning.

When at last, he slid inside her, he did so with the reverence of a man entering a sacred temple, and with each slow penetration, he soothed away the last rough, hurting edges of her soul.

Opening her eyes, she stared up at him. The candlelight painted shifting shadows of bronze and umber and gold over his skin, and filled his eyes with dark fire. "I love you, Nico," she breathed, locking her gaze in his.

Buried thick inside her, he increased the tempo of his loving, his thrusts deep and urgent, slick and fast. And she, caught up in his fierce possession of everything she was, felt herself lured a second time, ever closer to the merciless whirlpool of capitulation.

Defying her every attempt to subdue it, the pleasure swept her in ever diminishing circles, then sucked her without mercy into its bottomless depths. She screamed softly, blinded by its power, deaf to all but the blood drumming in her ears, and aware only of the hot spurt of Nico's seed running free inside her.

He filled not just the yearning in her body, but all the empty spaces in her heart. For the first time in over four years, she felt whole again.

Devastated by the emotional catharsis, she clung to him and burst into tears. He understood the reason, held her safe in his arms as the storm raged, and smothered her cries with kisses until she grew calm again.

Later, lying sated and sleepy with her head on his shoulder and the moon beaming full through the window, she murmured dreamily, "It feels as if we were never apart."

"Darling," he said, holding her closer, "in my heart we never were divorced. It just took me a while to convince you of it."

CHAPTER TWELVE

THEY decided on a summer wedding. "But something small," Nico insisted, afraid Chloe would overtax herself. "Just family and a few very close friends."

The problem lay in the fact that he had such a large family and so many friends, all of whom had missed seeing him get married the first time around. But in the end, they pared the guest list down to forty adults and thirteen children.

"Thirteen and a third, if truth be told," Nico whispered the week before the wedding, placing his hand possessively over Chloe's womb, as they lay in bed in the Verona house, with the moon beaming full through the window on their naked bodies. "But that will remain our little secret for a few more weeks."

She had never known such tranquil happiness.

"Do not concern yourself, *Signora*," the obstetrician had told her, just that morning. "The odds of your suffering another tragedy such as you knew with your first child are so small as to be negligible. There is every reason to believe this child will grow up to be as strong and healthy as his father."

"And if it's a girl?" she'd asked, smiling.

His eyes had twinkled. "She will be beautiful like her mother, and before she is out of the cradle, her father will be gray-haired and exhausted from fighting off the boys."

Of course, Jacqueline and Charlotte flew over for the wedding, arriving just two days ahead of time.

"Long enough for us to recover from jet lag, but not long enough for us to do any damage," Charlotte explained mischievously. "We didn't think it wise to come any sooner, not after the way we meddled before and ended up making such a mess of everything."

But nothing and no one could dim Chloe's radiance, or spoil things for her. Nico's sisters had welcomed her back into the family with more warmth than she felt she deserved, and showered her with love, throwing themselves wholeheartedly into the wedding preparations, and providing unconditional support of the marriage.

"I don't need to ask if you're sure you know what you're doing this time," Jacqueline said fondly when Chloe came to help her settle in and unpack her suitcase. "Your smile's enough to blind a person! But I don't mind admitting, your grandmother and I had more than a few sleepless nights after you left Vancouver and came here without so much as a hint of how Nico would receive you. We're so delighted it all worked out for you, darling. You and Nico are meant to be together, and we know you'll both be very happy."

Although she and her husband came for the wedding, Monica begged off acting as matron of honor because she was nearly eight months pregnant with her third child, "and I'd need a tent to cover this," she said wryly, stroking her swollen abdomen.

But there was no shortage of flower girls offering to take her place: Nico's six nieces, ranging from two to five-and-a-half, couldn't wait to dress up like princesses and steal the show.

Disappointed, the nephews complained that everyone liked girls best, and gave them all the special favors. "Not this time," their uncle told them. "You boys will be my groomsmen—at least, those of you who aren't still in diapers—and it'll be your job to keep the girls in line."

He and Chloe chose the mansion on Lake Garda as the place to hold the wedding. "Outdoors, if possible," she suggested. "Down by the water on the lower terrace, for the ceremony, and on the upper one, right outside the main salon, for the reception. It'll be more convenient there for the caterers."

"Whatever you want, my angel," Nico said, seducing her with his smile in full view of anyone who happened to be watching. "And we can host the entire occasion indoors if it rains. The house is certainly big enough."

"You couldn't have chosen a more beautiful setting," her mother sighed, leaning against the fat stone balusters forming the wall between land and lake, on the wedding eve, and gazing out at the mountains beyond the old town. "Just look at that view! It's like something out of a fairy tale. Oh, I hope the weather cooperates tomorrow."

It did. Not a breath of wind marred the surface of the water, or disturbed the path of rose petals—creamy pink to match Chloe's ankle-length dress, though why she chose that particular color scheme was something known only to her and Nico!—strewn from the French doors of the house by the flower girls.

Adorable in white organdy with coronets of pink

rosebuds, they meandered along the flagstone path to Franck's *Fantasie,* played by Nico's brother-in-law, Hector. The concert grand had been rolled out to the upper terrace earlier by the crew who'd also erected a flower-draped arch on the terrace, where the couple would exchange their vows.

The groomsmen, meanwhile, stood at attention beside Nico, taking their roles very seriously. Their mission earlier had been to make sure bride and groom didn't see each other before the ceremony, and the boys had adhered to the task religiously.

Chloe chose the *Theme* from Tchaikovsky's *Fifth Symphony* to herald her own entrance. Although the women grew a little misty-eyed when she stepped out of the house, her face shaded by a wide-brimmed cream hat trimmed with pink roses, their tears turned to laughter when the youngest flower girl, Lisabetta, already bored with the proceedings, wandered away from the wedding party and plunked herself down on the lawn to pick daisies.

Chloe knew there was speculation among the immediate family that perhaps she was in the early stages of pregnancy. She'd lost her breakfast, seven mornings running, and looked, according to her future sisters-in-law, as if a stiff breeze might blow her away, "the way a woman often does during her first trimester."

They'd find out soon enough that they were right. Today, though, was not about a baby, but about Nico and her. Indeed, there might just as well have been no guests there to witness the marriage, for all the attention she spared them. She had eyes only for her groom, and he for her. The priest had to cough twice before they tore their gazes away from one another and turned to hear what he had to say.

Fifteen minutes later, they were again man and wife in the eyes of God, and the State. Just as well. Neither Nico's family nor hers would have looked kindly on her giving birth to an illegitimate baby. As for keeping her pregnancy secret, given her new husband's protective concern for his bride and the way he hovered over her, he might just as well have announced the news to the entire congregation.

But then, she was just as solicitous of him, reaching up to secure his rose boutonniere more firmly to the lapel of his cream jacket, and smooth her hand down his cheek as she whispered, "I love you," before they exchanged their first married kiss in nearly half a decade.

And what a kiss it was, long and sweet enough to make up for the arid years they'd been apart. Tender enough to make the men smile and the women dab their eyes again.

The wedding supper, held on the upper terrace, began as the sun started to sink behind the mountains. Kerosene torches illuminated the scene for the waiters serving a feast of seafood chicchetti, grilled swordfish, black lobster ravioli with a cognac basil cream sauce, crab gnocchi and other delicious pastas, all accompanied by a selection of the finest regional wines.

The dessert buffet which followed rivaled anything the world's most renowned restaurants might offer. Tiramisu, of course, and zabaglione; delicate Venetian pastries, and assorted fresh fruits and cheeses. And for the children, six different flavors of gelato.

"Our arteries aren't thanking us for this," Jacqueline

told Charlotte, as they sampled the decadent confections, "but we'll worry about that tomorrow."

Throughout the lengthy banquet, a pair of musicians wandered among the candlelit tables and provided dreamy background music on a mandolin and accordion. There was much laughter and singing, champagne toasts and many long speeches, and a handful of telegrams conveying good wishes and congratulations from distant friends, including one from Baron. He wasn't able to attend because he was in the midst of moving across country, to take up the position of senior partner in his grandfather's old law firm. Mrs. Prescott, Chloe thought, amused, would surely approve.

Later, with the moon carving a silver swath over the lake, and the children put to bed, Nico took Chloe in his arms for the first dance. The mandolin plucked at the heartstrings of all who watched, the accordion sighed; *Non Dimenticar…Mala Femana…Arrivederci Roma…Volare….*

His ring warm on her finger, his arms firm around her still-slender waist, Chloe gazed into her husband's eyes and saw a future full of promise. She knew with absolute conviction that although most times would be "for better," if "for worse" happened anyway, she and Nico would face it together.

This time *was* forever.

WEB/M&B/RTL3

Discover Pure Reading Pleasure with

MILLS &
BOON®

**Visit the Mills & Boon website for all
the latest in romance**

🌹 **Buy** all the latest
releases, backlist
and eBooks

🌹 **Find out** more
about our authors
and their books

🌹 **Join** our community
and chat to authors
and other readers

🌹 **Free** online reads
from your favourite
authors

🌹 **Win** with our
fantastic online
competitions

🌹 **Sign** up for our
free monthly
eNewsletter

🌹 **Tell us** what you
think by signing up to
our reader panel

🌹 **Rate** and review
books with our star
system

www.millsandboon.co.uk

 Follow us at twitter.com/millsandboonuk

 Become a fan at facebook.com/romancehq